P9-EMK-675

Praise for
Annette Broadrick

"I can think of a dozen adjectives that would apply
equally to Annette Broadrick's books, such as
exciting, passionate and irresistible. But I can
wrap it all up by saying simply that her books
make you feel good when you read them.
She's one terrific writer."
—International bestselling author **Diana Palmer**

"Annette Broadrick's glorious love stories always
sparkle with irresistible joy and grace."
—Melinda Helfer, *Romantic Times Magazine*

Critical Acclaim for
Justine Davis

"One of the most outstanding talents in the genre."
"...an extraordinary storyteller."
"An author of uncommon brilliance."
—*Romantic Times Magazine*

"Ms. Davis's ability...will leave you in awe."
—GEnie On-line Reviews

ANNETTE BROADRICK

believes in romance and the magic of life. Since 1984, when her first book was published, Annette has shared her view of life and love with readers all over the world. In addition to being nominated by Romantic Times Magazine as one of the Best New Authors of that year, she has also won the Romantic Times Magazine Reviewers' Choice Award for Best in its Series for Heat of the Night, Mystery Lover and Irresistible; the Romantic Times Magazine W.I.S.H. award for her heroes in Strange Enchantment, Marriage Texas Style! and Impromptu Bride; and the Romantic Times Magazine Lifetime Achievement Awards for Series Romance and Series Romantic Fantasy.

JUSTINE DAVIS

is the author of more than thirty novels. She also writes single-title romances under the name Justine Dare. Her books have won several Romantic Times Magazine awards, and she has been given their Career Achievement award twice. She is a four-time winner of the coveted RWA RITA Award, and in 1998 was inducted into the RWA Hall of Fame.

Long involved in law enforcement, Justine says that years ago a young man she worked with encouraged her to try for a promotion to a police position that was, at that time, occupied only by men. "I succeeded, became wrapped up in my new job, and that man moved away, never, I thought, to be heard from again. Ten years later he appeared out of the woods of Washington State, saying he'd never forgotten me and would I please marry him. With that history, how could I write anything but romance?"

ANNETTE BROADRICK
JUSTINE DAVIS

LOVE
CHILD

Silhouette Books

Published by Silhouette Books

America's Publisher of Contemporary Romance

If you purchased this book without a cover you should be aware that this book is stolen property. It was reported as "unsold and destroyed" to the publisher, and neither the author nor the publisher has received any payment for this "stripped book."

SILHOUETTE BOOKS

ISBN 0-373-21704-8

by Request

LOVE CHILD

Copyright © 2000 by Harlequin Books S.A.

The publisher acknowledges the copyright holders of the individual works as follows:

WHERE THERE IS LOVE
Copyright © 1992 by Annette Broadrick

UPON THE STORM
Copyright © 1992 by Janice Davis Smith

All rights reserved. Except for use in any review, the reproduction or utilization of this work in whole or in part in any form by any electronic, mechanical or other means, now known or hereafter invented, including xerography, photocopying and recording, or in any information storage or retrieval system, is forbidden without the written permission of the editorial office, Silhouette Books, 300 East 42nd Street, New York, NY 10017 U.S.A.

All characters in this book have no existence outside the imagination of the author and have no relation whatsoever to anyone bearing the same name or names. They are not even distantly inspired by any individual known or unknown to the author, and all incidents are pure invention.

This edition published by arrangement with Harlequin Books S.A.

® and TM are trademarks of Harlequin Books S.A., used under license. Trademarks indicated with ® are registered in the United States Patent and Trademark Office, the Canadian Trade Marks Office and in other countries.

Visit us at www.romance.net

Printed in U.S.A.

CONTENTS

Dear Reader,

Over the years I've enjoyed writing stories about men who live, work and survive with danger as a daily companion. I came up with an obscure (and fictional) government agency dealing with covert operations, and wrote several books where my heroes worked for an enigmatic and cigar-chomping man referred to as Max.

Imagine my surprise when my editor, Tara Gavin, suggested that I might want to tell Max's story. How could she possibly think that Max was hero material? I wondered.

Of course, once the thought had been planted in my head, it would not go away and eventually I discovered who Max was and why he was such a tough, terse and tenacious man. Where There Is Love became Max's story, one that would never have been told without Tara's unexpected suggestion.

I blame this book on Tara—she made me do it.

Can't remember if I ever thanked her for the idea. If not, I need to, because Max turned out to be one of my favorite characters, after all. All I needed to do was take the time to get to know him better.

I hope you will feel the same way about him.

Sincerely,

Annette Broadrick

WHERE THERE IS LOVE
Annette Broadrick

This book is dedicated to Ann Matthews Stroud,
a dear and close friend for forty-six years!
Here's to the next forty-six!

Prologue

Her blood pounded so loudly in her ears that she wasn't sure at first whether the noise she heard was her rapidly beating heart or footsteps striking a steady rhythm from somewhere behind her. She paused in her flight, holding her breath for a moment. Into the silence came the sound she had been dreading: heavy footsteps echoing on the cobbled street of the ancient city. She could no longer count on having eluded her pursuers.

She'd been out of the business for too long; her skills had grown rusty. She'd almost gotten herself killed earlier, and the danger was far from over. She was afraid to return to her hotel room because they might be waiting for her there.

Frantically she glanced around the darkened street, looking for a place to hide. She tried to reassure herself. Perhaps the person she heard approaching was only taking a shortcut home. *Please let it be so,* she whispered fervently. Please let him be a late-night reveler innocently wending his way home before dawn.

Even if the man approaching was not looking for her, she couldn't afford to be seen by anyone—not the way she was dressed. She glanced down at her frothy evening gown and frivolous dancing slippers. They made her much too conspicuous. She could be easily remembered and described. There was no safety for her at the moment other than to remain hidden.

She edged closer to a nearby building and pressed herself against the stuccoed wall where the darkest shadows offered hope for concealment. Her lungs ached from restraining the impulse to gasp for air. Instead, she forced herself to take small, shallow and soundless breaths while she waited to see who was approaching.

The footsteps never hesitated as he drew nearer to her. Still hidden, she began to relax. If he was following her, surely he would have approached the dark area with more caution.

Now he was just a few feet away from her, an indistinct form in the deep shadows. He passed her without breaking stride, continuing on his way as though familiar with his surroundings.

She waited until the streets were silent once more, then took a deep breath. So far, so good. There was no reason to panic, she reminded herself.

She was a professional, after all, even if she hadn't worked in the field for six years.

She waited for her pulse to slow to a more normal rate before she ventured down the street once more.

All right. She was safe enough at the moment. What she needed to do now was to decide on a new plan of action. All of her previous plans would have to be discarded.

After considering her options she finally faced what she had to do, but she didn't like it. She would have to turn for help to the man she had spent the past six years avoiding.

Once again she studied the deserted street, looked down at her dress and gritted her teeth.

She really had no choice. The only thing left for her to do was to find a public telephone on a quiet street somewhere.

She could only pray that he wouldn't hang up on her!

One

Shrill ringing shattered the late-night silence. Max groped blindly for the telephone.

"H'lo." Sleep caused his normally gruff voice to sound more intimidating than usual.

"Max?"

The voice on the phone was too faint to identify, but he recognized the gender and the urgency. One of his agents must be in trouble.

He leaned over and flipped on the light beside his bed. It was close to midnight in Washington, D.C. Not late by some standards, but Max had had a rough day. He'd lost another operative, something that was happening with alarming frequency. He'd spent the day investigating the loss and had been in bed less than two hours, just long enough to have been deeply asleep.

"Who is this?"

A wave of static swept over the line as she answered. He had a sinking feeling that he was about to get some more bad news about one of his people.

He swung his legs over the side of the bed and sat up. As soon as the static wave receded, he spoke.

"I didn't catch your name. Will you please repeat it and tell me where you're calling from." He grabbed a pen and paper.

The next time she spoke, her voice was as clear as though she were standing in front of him.

"This is Marisa Stevens, Max. I'm in Barcelona. I know we didn't part on the best of terms, but I stumbled onto something tonight that's over my head. I could use your help."

When he realized who was calling, he felt as though he had been hit in the solar plexus. Memories immediately swirled through his mind. Emotions of all kinds were evoked by the mere sound of her voice. As though he'd seen her only yesterday, he pictured her face—wide-spaced green eyes, slightly tilted; a provocative smile that had always had the ability to curl his toes; and a mass of flaming red curls that gave mute evidence to a fiery and fiercely independent nature. A call for help was the last thing he ever expected to receive from Marisa Stevens.

"Tell me what you need."

"A change of clothes and a place to hide. I inadvertently overheard a conversation between two men who should not have been seen together.

They're going to do whatever is necessary to make sure I don't live to repeat what I heard.''

There was silence on the line for a moment before she continued. ''I'm wearing an evening dress, and I'll look very conspicuous once people begin to stir in a couple of hours. I don't dare go back to my hotel room in case they're waiting for me there.'' There was a longer pause. ''I need to get out of Spain, but I don't have a clue how to leave without being spotted.''

He rubbed his forehead, forcing the last sleep from his brain. ''Barcelona,'' he murmured, trying to think of a safe place for her to go. A face flashed in his mind. Santiago had originally come from a small fishing village on the coast not far from Barcelona. Max had been there on more than one occasion to meet with Santiago.

''Marisa? There's a woman I know in that area who will help you.'' He gave her instructions and directions to the fishing village. ''I haven't heard from Teresa in a couple of years, not since her son, Santiago, died, but I'm sure she'll help you. Since she doesn't have a phone, I can't call her and alert her to your situation. When you get there explain that I sent you and told you to wait until someone contacts you.''

''Thank you, Max. I really appreciate this.''

''What are you doing in Spain?''

''It's a long story.''

''You haven't worked in our business for years and Spain is a long way from Seattle. What's happened to put you in danger?''

There was a small pause. "I wasn't aware you knew where I was or what I was doing."

"I've always known, Marisa."

There was another pause. Then Max spoke again. "You haven't answered my question. I need to know what's going on if I'm going to help."

"I was trying to contact a man from Seattle. I'd followed him to Barcelona. Before I could approach him directly I inadvertently overheard a conversation between him and a man I used to know years ago. Their conversation was rather incriminating. When I attempted to get away from them they heard me, and I'm afraid they recognized me."

"Can you name names?"

"The man I'm following is Troy Chasen. It's a personal matter. The other one is a former agent. We worked together on a couple of assignments."

"His name?"

"Harry O'Donnell."

"Harry is still with the Agency, Marisa."

"Oh, Lord, then it's worse than I thought!"

"What do you mean?"

"They were planning a shipment of goods. From their reaction when they discovered I was there, I assume the stuff is contraband."

"Thanks for the information, Marisa. It could be invaluable on a matter I've been dealing with for some time. I'll follow up to see what more I can find out."

"I still have to find Troy."

"Even if he sees you as a threat now?"

She sighed. "I can't just give up. This is too important."

"Maybe I can help you."

"No! I really think I can handle this one on my own."

"Then why did you call me?"

"What I mean is, if you can get me out of Spain, I can contact Troy. They were talking about another meeting in Nice. Once I've spoken to him and gotten the necessary information from him, I'll promise to stay out of his life."

"If he's smuggling, I have a hunch he won't shake your hand and wave you a cordial goodbye, Marisa. You know better than that."

He caught the hint of a sob in her voice. "I have to try, Max. I can't give up on this one. Thanks for your help." She hung up before he could say anything more.

Max stared frustratedly at the phone he continued to hold in his hand. She could be the most aggravating, irritating, bullheaded agent he'd ever worked with, and that was saying something! He should have been glad she quit the Agency, glad she moved across the continent from him.

He slammed down the phone and reached for a cigar. In the course of one rather short conversation he had just learned the name of at least one of the possible traitors in the group as well as the name of a man who might be part of the smuggling ring his unit had been tracking for years. Marisa could very well have stumbled onto the key that would open several doors to apprehending the perpetrators.

Troy Chasen. Marisa had said her business with him was personal. What in the hell was she mixed up in?

And why did he care?

He turned away from that last thought. Whatever had been between them had ended abruptly six years ago. He wasn't very proud of the way he'd handled the situation. It was the only time in his career when he had lost his objectivity and his professionalism, both necessary for an agent's survival.

The irony of his subsequent promotion had not escaped him. By then the damage had been done— he'd already become emotionally involved with her. The damage could not be undone.

After six years she was back in his life, if only temporarily. He hoped he'd gained some perspective during those years.

He glanced at his watch. It was almost one o'clock in the morning, but he needed some answers. If Harry had turned, then the work they'd been doing had been compromised. A slow rage began to build within him. There was nothing more lethal than an agent gone bad.

And it looked as though Marisa was right in the middle of a deadly situation.

Several hours later Max sat across the desk from his superior. This was the man who had peremptorily recalled Max from the field six years before and put him in charge of their special unit. Max thought of him by the nickname of "Obi-wan," a character in a famous science-fiction movie series who had a habit of appearing in spirit form to characters in the movie during a time of great danger, offering advice and building their morale.

At the moment Max could definitely use some advice. The information he'd gathered during the past several hours had been daunting.

After twenty years in the business, he wondered if he was losing his grip. How could he have missed what now seemed so obvious, once some of the missing pieces had been supplied?

He had begun by reviewing Harry's reports to the Agency over the past three years. Now that he knew what he was looking for, a pattern began to emerge. Harry had given him bogus information that kept his operatives away during times when shipments were made. Every time an agent came too close, he was eliminated.

Max had tapped into classified government files to find out everything he could about Troy Chasen. He had learned a great deal about this man's financial situation. Chasen was a very successful businessman whose import-export headquarters were located in Seattle, Washington, but all his business operations looked legal.

He still hadn't found the connection between Chasen and Marisa, and he didn't like the direction his thoughts were taking. Would she have given him the potentially incriminating evidence about Chasen if she was having an affair with the man?

She could have changed a great deal these past few years. He didn't know, but he was damned well going to find out.

"You requested this meeting, Max," Obi-wan stated, making it clear that he didn't want his time wasted.

"Yes, sir. I received information late last night that sheds some light on what's been happening to some of my agents."

"Is your source reliable?"

"I'd say so. It was Marisa Stevens. She used to be with the Agency."

"Marisa. Hmm. Your last assignment in the field was with Marisa, wasn't it?"

Since the man had a photographic memory, Max considered the question to be rhetorical, but answered anyway. "Yes, sir."

"She left soon after your promotion."

"Yes."

"Why?"

"Because I wouldn't give her any more field assignments."

"Why?"

"Because I felt she could better serve the Agency as an analyst in her field of expertise."

"Which is?"

"Southeast Asian culture."

"She disagreed?"

"Yes. She insisted that she preferred to work in the field. I refused to send her. She resigned." Max forced himself to remain perfectly still.

"What has she been doing since that time?"

"According to our file, she moved to Seattle, went back to school for her doctorate and has been teaching at the university there."

"How would Marisa stumble across information that would implicate one of our agents?"

"She's in Spain and accidentally ran into Harry O'Donnell there, where he had no business being. She overheard a conversation that was incriminating."

"Why do you suppose Marisa called you, her former recalcitrant boss, to report a traitor in the ranks? Is she feeling more charitable toward you these days?"

"Not so you'd notice," Max replied wryly. "I'm not fully apprised of her situation. But I intend to be before long."

"O'Donnell, is it? Well, well." Obi-wan's brows arched. "No wonder you've had trouble pinning our phantom down." He placed his fingers in a precise steeple and studied them. "I'm sorry to hear your news, Max. He's one of the best."

"Yes."

"So what do you intend to do about it?"

"Go after him."

"How?"

"At the present time, Marisa is safely hidden away in a small fishing village on the Spanish coast. I want to get her out of there and back to the States. Then I intend to go to Nice and confront Harry."

"Alone?"

"If necessary."

"As laudable as your plan is—my God! I can see you now, galloping in to save the day—I need you here, Max. Send someone else."

"I thought of that, sir. At the moment, I don't know who I can trust. Harry might not be working alone."

"Hmm." The man sat there for a few moments, studying Max. "I suppose I can spare you for a few days."

"Then you agree that I should go?"

"Let's just say that I don't disagree with your assessment of the situation. You're good at what you do. If anyone can outsmart Harry, you can. This is a very touchy situation. A breach of national security is always a nasty business. Whoever got to Harry has a great deal of clout. We can't underestimate these people."

"I never have."

"I know. That's why I have you in your present position. Be sure you make it safely back to continue."

"Yes, sir." Max came to his feet, relieved that he'd accomplished his goal.

"Oh, and Max. Give my regards to Marisa."

Two

Max waited until almost midnight before he had two of the fishing trawler's crew lower one of its small boats and row him to shore. He was thankful there was no moon. He was also thankful that he was still familiar enough with the shoreline along this part of Spain to recall the seldom-used cove where they were heading.

Long after the two crew members had left him on the deserted shore, Max waited, watching to see if he had been observed disembarking from the small craft. Once he was certain that no one had seen him, he searched for and found the path that led to the roadway above.

He glanced at the glowing dial of his watch, now set for local time. He should reach Teresa's small cottage a couple of hours after sunrise.

The sun had been above the horizon almost three hours by the time Max reached the outskirts of the small fishing village where Teresa lived.

Teresa's cottage hadn't changed much, but her garden was growing wild, uncared for. That wasn't like Teresa. He let himself into the back gate and moved quietly up to the door that he knew opened directly into the kitchen. Teresa should be there by now preparing breakfast. He hoped everything was all right.

He tapped lightly on the wooden door. When there was no answer after a moment or two, he tapped a little harder. A whisper in Spanish asked who was there. In equally soft Spanish, he replied,

"It's Max, Teresa. May I come in?"

The long silence after his announcement worried him. He reached for the revolver at the small of his back.

The door swung open and a figure stepped into the morning sunlight. Max relaxed.

"What in the world are *you* doing here?"

"Hello, Marisa."

She stood before him in an unadorned white cotton blouse and black skirt. Her red hair seemed to catch fire in the sunlight.

He'd been prepared to see her and still it was a shock to him, so he could imagine how she must feel. He stood there staring at her, looking for any differences in her appearance.

She was still beautiful. All of the familiar responses swept over him and he mentally cursed.

Marisa couldn't seem to adjust to the sudden

shock of Max's appearance. He'd told her that someone would contact her. Never in her wildest imaginings had she thought it would be Max himself.

He wore a black T-shirt that snugly fitted across his broad shoulders and muscular arms. Black jeans molded his trim waist, taut buttocks and muscular thighs. He still wore his brown hair short, almost military in style, and his sherry-colored eyes had not lost their mesmerizing quality. Those eyes had haunted her through the years.

She had hoped that time had changed him, that sitting behind a desk had softened his body, made him less dangerous looking. The only change she could see was a hint of silver around his temples. He continued to radiate a raw sexuality that seemed to reach into a part of her that she had kept determinedly locked away. In the six years since she'd seen him, no man had gotten close to her. One look at Max and she could feel a tight coil deep inside her beginning to unwind, leaving her prey to her deepest emotions.

Max stepped inside with a lithe movement and closed the door behind him. His quick glance encompassed the kitchen before he asked, ''Where's Teresa?''

''She isn't here.''

He returned his gaze to the woman who stood so stiffly before him. With a slightly lifted brow, he asked, ''Then how did you get in?''

Marisa realized that she felt defensive and forced herself to say calmly, ''She was here when I arrived yesterday morning. She'd come to check on the place before returning to her sister's home in the hills. Her sister has been quite ill and Teresa's been looking after her family. When I explained my situation, she invited me to stay as long as necessary. I assured her that I could look after myself. She plans to return at the end of the week.''

''We'll be leaving tomorrow night.''

That meant that she would be there alone with Max, a situation Marisa wanted to avoid at all costs. ''Why can't we leave tonight?''

Max could see that very little had changed between them. She was going to challenge everything he said. Well, he would have to make the best of the situation that he'd helped to create. He turned away and walked over to the stove where he found a pot of coffee. He poured himself a cup before he answered, hoping the delay would give him a stronger grip on his impatience with her fractious attitude.

''I wasn't sure of the situation here or how long it would take to get to and from the point of rendezvous. To be on the safe side, I gave us an extra day.'' He took a sip of his coffee, then went over to the small table and sat down. ''In the meantime, you can brief me on exactly what happened to you and why.''

''Why isn't important. I was—''

His control wavered. ''The hell it isn't. I don't give a damn about your personal life, sweetheart, but you *will* tell me exactly what is going on. I'll decide what's important.'' She stood in the middle of the floor, watching him warily. With poorly concealed irritation, he pointed to the chair across from him. "Sit down."

Marisa could feel her temper flaring at his peremptory order. After a slow count to ten, she said, "I no longer work for you, Max." Despite her words, Marisa walked over and sat where he had indicated.

"Oh, I'm very aware of that, Marisa. You moved clear across the continent to get away from me." He caught the tinge of bitterness in his voice and was irritated with himself.

"Not you, Max."

"That isn't the way I saw it."

"I just knew that the situation wasn't going to work. It was one thing for us to work together on equal terms. It was another matter when you were given authority over me."

Max leaned back in his chair and studied the woman across from him. "Was it me personally, or do you resent taking orders from any man?" he drawled.

She gave him a level look. "That's a rather low blow, isn't it, Max?"

He shrugged, feeling slightly ashamed of himself. "Maybe."

"I never resented being given orders. I followed them implicitly. I was a good agent, but that didn't seem to matter to you. You refused to let me go back out in the field."

He glanced down at the cup he held in his hands.

Without meeting her eyes, he muttered, "I had my reasons."

"What were they?"

"They no longer matter, if they ever did." He glanced up and said, "Chasen's married, you know," watching to see if he would get a reaction.

Her amused grin caught him off guard.

"As a matter of fact, Max, I was there when he got married."

She'd turned the tables on him. He was caught totally unprepared. He stared at her, unable to comment.

After a moment, she relented, saying, "He's married to my sister Eileen."

"Your sister!"

"That's right."

Why hadn't he known that? She'd gone to Seattle after she resigned and stayed with her sister. Her sister had been single at the time. He mulled the information over in his mind for several minutes before he asked,

"Do you think Chasen is using his import-export business as a front?"

She was quiet, obviously thinking as she gazed out the window beside the table. "I never thought so before," she eventually admitted in a slow voice. Turning to look at Max, she said, "Now, I don't know what to think."

He leaned forward, staring at her intently. "Tell me exactly what happened to you the other night."

Feeling suddenly restless, she got up from her chair and began to pace.

"Eileen and Troy have not been getting along for several months. He's been gone a great deal lately. Whenever he came home they fought about his schedule. After one of their fights he stormed out of the house, saying he wasn't coming back. She was upset and crying, of course. She went on to bed and waited for him. He never showed up again.

"The next morning she went in to check on Timmy and discovered he was gone."

"Timmy?"

She turned away from him and walked over to the window. Gazing at the flowers, she muttered, "Her son."

"Chasen's records don't show that he has a son."

"No. Because Timmy isn't his."

"I see. But you think that Chasen took him, anyway?"

She turned away from the window and looked at him. "I don't know. He and Timmy have a good relationship, but it makes no sense to me. That's why I came after Troy. I think he's playing games with Eileen. I don't know. Nobody seemed to have heard anything from either of them. I couldn't sit around and wait for answers, so I decided to go after him."

"Does Chasen know your background?"

"No. He knows I worked in Washington after I finished college, but he's never shown any interest in what I did there."

"Obviously he didn't expect you to follow him."

"No. It took some effort to find out that he'd come to Spain. When I did, I flew here immediately, hoping either to locate Troy or find someone who knew him. I have some friends whose relatives live here. They've often suggested that I look them up, so I did. When they invited me to attend a rather grand reception, I agreed to go because I thought I might meet someone there who knew Troy."

"So what happened?"

"I was at the party and was returning from the ladies' room when I rounded a corner and recognized Troy's voice. He was talking with someone and heading toward me. I decided to wait until he was alone to confront him, so I darted through the first door I saw, thinking I'd wait until after they passed. Instead of continuing down the hallway, they came into the room where I was. I barely managed to hide behind the draperies before they turned on a lamp and continued their conversation.

"It was while I was waiting for them to leave that I realized I recognized the second man, as well. It was Harry. They were discussing a shipment and how difficult it was becoming not to get caught. Troy said something like, 'What about Jameson?' and Harry replied, 'Don't worry about him. I'll take care of him just like I did the others.'"

"A chill went through me at his tone of voice. At first when I recognized Harry I assumed that Troy was helping the government apprehend the smugglers. After Harry's remarks, I knew better. I also knew that I had to get out of there before either of them spotted me. I eased the window open and crawled outside. My shoe must have scraped against the stucco, because they stopped talking. Harry jerked the drapes aside just as I let go of the windowsill and dropped to the hedge below. I got only a quick look at his face, but I saw anger, recognition and determination. Believe me, I didn't hang around after that. I ran until I was far enough away to feel safe. Then I called you.''

''As soon as I get you out of here, I'm going to Nice. As far as Harry will know, I'm on vacation. While I'm there I'll see what I can find out about Troy and your nephew.''

''I want to go with you.''

''No.''

''Max!''

''You're no longer a part of the Agency, Marisa.''

''Fine. Then you can't tell me what to do.''

''I sure as hell can. You're a private citizen who had no business getting involved in this matter.''

''That's nonsense, and you know it. I'm already involved. Why, you wouldn't even know about Harry if I hadn't contacted you.''

''And you were in over your head or you wouldn't have called me.''

''So? All that means is that together we can deal with this situation. We've worked together before, Max. We can do it again.''

''Absolutely not!''

"Oh! You are the most infuriating, obstinate, arrogant man I've ever had the misfortune to be around."

"I seem to recall hearing similar sentiments the last time I saw you."

"I hoped you had changed over the years, mellowed a little. Hah!"

"If anything, you're more beautiful than I remembered," he said in a husky voice.

She'd been pacing, obviously trying to get a grip on her temper. When he spoke she came to an abrupt halt and stared at him suspiciously. "Why did you say that?"

He looked at her in surprise. "I don't know. I guess I was thinking out loud."

She came toward him and leaned her palms on the table. "Max, you've got to let me do this. What if Troy has Timmy with him? You don't want any harm to come to an innocent child, do you?"

"Of course not! I'm not a monster, Marisa. How old is the boy?"

She straightened. "Why do you ask?"

Impatiently, he said, "Because his age has a great deal to do with how I handle the matter."

"He's five," she stated in a flat voice.

"Are you close to him?"

"Yes."

"Then you wouldn't have any trouble getting him to go with you if we did find him."

"None whatsoever."

"I'll think about it."

She started to say something, then closed her mouth and spun away from the table.

Max knew that he needed to get away from Marisa for a while. Being around her once again was taking its toll on his ability to control his feelings and his reactions to her. "I think I'm going outside for a while to work on Teresa's garden. She could use some help around here."

"That sounds like a spectacular idea. I'm tired of pacing in here, waiting. That's all I've done for the past day and night."

So much for getting away from her. At least outside he could distance himself from her. He started toward the door. "You were never very patient."

"I can be, when there's a need for it. Waiting to be spirited out of the country has been nerve-racking, I'll admit. I guess I've lost my edge."

She followed him outside and watched as he gathered the shears and flower clippers. He handed her the clippers, then walked away, moving over to the front gate.

"This really feels strange," she said after they had worked for more than an hour without saying anything.

Max paused in his trimming and removed his shirt, then wiped the perspiration from his face with the large handkerchief he pulled from his back pocket. Only then did he look around at Marisa and ask, "What are you talking about?"

"We've known each other a long time. We worked together; we've been in some really dangerous places together; and yet we've never done anything quite so domestic as working together in a garden.''

"That's not surprising. In my line of work, I don't get much of a chance to be domestic.''

"Have you ever thought about giving it up?'' she asked, pulling weeds about three feet from where he worked on the hedge.

"No,'' he said immediately, not having to think about his answer. "It's what I do. Why? Do you miss it?''

She took her time in replying. "Not really, and that does surprise me. What I came to realize was that I'd become addicted to the adrenaline rush that comes when you know your life is on the line. By the time I decided to go back to school I knew that I no longer needed that kind of excitement in my life.''

"So why didn't you come back and work in the Agency again?''

"You mean, in the job you offered?''

"Yes.''

"I didn't figure you'd want me. I felt that was the reason you offered it to me in the first place, so that I would quit.''

He stopped what he was doing and turned to face her. "You really believed that?''

"What other reason could you have had? I was good at what I did. I knew that. So did you. But for some reason you no longer wanted me around.''

"No! That wasn't true at all! Dammit, you know the training. You can't afford to get close to anyone in this business. You can't afford to make friends.

It can get you killed. After our last assignment, I'd lost my objectivity where you were concerned. I explained all of that to you during that night we spent together. I thought you understood. I knew that I would never be able to be assigned a job with you again. Then I was called back to Washington and promoted.'' He turned away from her, forcing himself to concentrate on trimming the bushes around the front gate instead of the woman kneeling so gracefully in the flowerbed. ''I could no longer send you out in the field,'' he admitted in a low voice. ''I could no longer risk your life or take a chance on losing you.'' With bitter irony he added, ''As it turned out, I lost you, anyway, but at least you were safe.''

When she didn't say anything after several minutes, Max risked a glance over his shoulder. She was still kneeling, with her head bent. While he watched, she made a swipe across her cheek with her grimy hand. ''Why didn't you tell me this six years ago, Max?'' she muttered in an angry tone.

''I didn't think I had to, not after the night we'd spent together.''

She glanced up at him and he saw the pain on her dirt-smeared face. ''How was I supposed to know how you felt about that night? You never made reference to it again.''

He rested his hands on his hips. ''Just when would I have had an opportunity? If you will recall, we were immediately flown back to the States where I was informed that I would take over another position. I had a crash course in learning a new job. You certainly didn't make things any easier at the time, insisting that I send you out again.''

"Well, I got bored sitting around with nothing to do but to wait for an assignment.''

"I told you that we would talk about it, remember?''

"Your idea of 'talking about it' was to tell me that you wanted to put me behind a desk.''

"You never gave me a chance to explain further. You blew up and ended up walking out of the office. I got your resignation in the mail two days later.''

Their voices continued to rise until they were practically shouting at each other.

Max didn't want to remember the pain and intense loss he'd felt when he received her notice of resignation, to become effective immediately.

The sudden silence between them seemed to ring with suppressed emotions. Max could hear the buzzing of an insect in one of the flowers, the sound of distant voices down the roadway.

When she spoke, he barely heard her words. "I wish I'd known.''

Her voice sounded so wistful that he could only look at her in surprise. "You mean it would have made a difference to you?''

"Oh, yes,'' she whispered, her eyes filled with painful memories of decisions made and losses suffered. "All the difference in the world.''

Three

Marisa lay on a narrow bed in one of Teresa's upstairs bedrooms, unable to sleep. She had pounded and reshaped her pillow until it threatened to burst its seams. She had kicked off her covers, pulled them back up to her chin and now lay with them wrapped around one leg, leaving the other exposed beneath a short cotton nightgown.

All she could think about was her desperate need for sleep. Well, that's what she *wanted* to think about—going to sleep. What she *didn't* want to think about was Max lying across the hall in the other bedroom, in the other narrow bed, sound asleep.

She had spent the better part of the day making certain that she didn't look directly at him, particularly while he worked outside without his shirt.

Without his shirt, what had only been hinted at before had been blatantly revealed. She hadn't needed the reminder, hadn't needed to know how she still reacted to the man, regardless of the years that had elapsed since she had last seen him.

Marisa sighed. Max had always reminded her of a caged panther. Although he looked tame enough, and he acted tame enough, there was always something about him that made her feel he might spring at any moment—a coiled restlessness just beneath the surface.

Now as she lay twisted in her bedclothes, she recalled her strong reaction when he had arrived so unexpectedly at Teresa's door that morning. Nothing had changed for her. She had a hunch that nothing ever would.

She remembered the very first time she'd seen him. She had worked for the Agency for only a few weeks when there had been a briefing to announce that a small, very special unit was being formed to gather information on several activities that were strongly affecting the United States: the taking of hostages, illegal trading in guns and drugs, and the smuggling of artifacts into the United States.

Max had walked into the room that morning in conversation with another agent. She had noticed him right away, which surprised her when she thought about him later that night. The room had been filled with many men. He looked too rugged to be considered handsome, too tough to be gentle, too hard to admit to human emotions. And yet...and yet there was something about him that continually drew her eye to him. He appeared tall, even though he was little more than average height. He had the build of a runner or a swimmer and moved with a natural athlete's grace.

She never forgot him, even though it was months later when Marisa was formally introduced to Max.

The head of the division had introduced them, adding, "Marisa will keep you on your toes, Max. She graduated head of her class at our special training school. There are a great many diverse talents packed away in that petite body."

Max had nodded but ignored the hand she had offered him. "How long have you been with the Agency?"

"Almost six months now," she said, smiling.

He didn't return her smile. "And you're going to be part of this unit?" He glanced at the other man in surprise. When the division head didn't say anything, Max returned his attention to Marisa. "Don't you think you'd like a little more experience under your belt before you join a special unit?"

She shrugged, a little nettled by his attitude. "Obviously someone must have believed that I was qualified, or I wouldn't have been offered the job." She was doing her best to hold on to her temper.

Max either didn't notice her anger or ignored it. His next question was more in the nature of an interrogation than social conversation. "Are you aware that we may be working together from time to time?"

Why did he have to make it sound as though she'd only recently been hatched from an egg? Determined to keep her cool and retain the semblance of a polite facade, Marisa limited her response.

"Yes."

"I won't be in a position to train a rookie," he warned brusquely.

That did it! Marisa gave him her loveliest smile and said, "Neither will I."

The division head laughed. "That will be the least of your worries, Marisa. Max has been with the Agency for years."

She glanced back at Max, deliberately widening her eyes in awe. "Really? And how's your reaction time? I don't want to be slowed down, you know."

What amazed her was that Max laughed, really laughed. His sherry-colored eyes, which had been studying her with a glacial glint just moments before, now filled with warm and wicked light. They gleamed with amusement.

"All right," he admitted with a grin, "so maybe I *was* coming on a little strong."

"A little? I was expecting you to send me back to the nursery and forbid me to associate with the adults."

They parted with a truce of sorts. During the next few years she worked with several agents, Max included. She learned a great deal during those years, about herself as well as about her chosen profession.

She *had* been green and much too naive when

she'd first started, but she had managed to survive while she was learning.

By the time she and Max were assigned to follow up reports of drug running in Southeast Asia, she knew her strengths and her limitations. More than eighteen months had passed since their last assignment together. Max had taken the lead—not because he was male but because he was the senior agent. Max had always made it clear that he wouldn't make any allowances for her, and she respected him for that.

As usual for Max, he had kept his distance from her, dealing with her on a professional basis only. She didn't mind. He was one of the best agents they had. She had considered it a privilege to work with him.

Marisa had wondered if his excellence as an agent was one of the reasons they were placed together on this particular assignment. Had his concern for her as a woman been reflected in a similar way by their superior? Did the boss think Max could compensate for any lack she might show on an assignment?

She never knew because she never had the courage to confront her superior with her suspicions. She wanted the job too badly to risk such a confrontation.

For a moment her mind leaped to the last heated discussion between her and Max after he'd been promoted. She'd really blown it that day. She'd lost control over her temper and said to him all the things she'd harbored since she had taken the job.

It was no wonder that he thought she was holding him responsible for everything that had happened to her since she'd joined the Agency. She'd certainly made it sound that way!

She still cringed with embarrassment at the way she'd left his office, storming out of there like some beleaguered Brunhilde. By the time she calmed down she had faced what she had done. Because of what happened between them during that last assignment, Max was certain to feel that she was using their intimacy as leverage to throw her weight around. Just thinking about it made her squirm with embarrassment.

She'd done the only thing possible. She'd mailed her resignation and run, going into hiding like some burrowing animal into the safety of its earth home.

Well, now Max was back in her life, at least temporarily. Would she have called him for help if she had known that he would come after her himself? There was no way to know, of course. She now had to play out this particular hand and see what happened.

Once again Marisa kicked off the sheet across her lower body and flopped over onto her stomach. She prayed for sleep, chanted brief phrases to convince herself that she was truly sleepy and attempted to make her mind blank. Her traitorous mind responded by recalling in exquisite detail the one night she most wanted to forget—the night everything went wrong on their assignment…:

Marisa stayed on the cliffs overlooking the cove in accordance with Max's instructions. For a week they had been playing tourist along the coast of east Malaysia, scouting the area where, according to their sources, a large drug shipment was to be brought from the interior for distribution to various parts of the world.

Their job was to find out exactly where and when the drugs were to arrive and how and by whom they were to be shipped out. They were to share this information with local authorities and help to map out a strategy to capture the leaders of the operation.

Max had positioned himself close to the water, in one of the many outcroppings along the rugged beach. It was a precarious spot at best because of the tide.

Marisa waited and watched through binoculars. When the firing began she realized that someone knew exactly where Max was and that he was the victim of an ambush.

She never remembered later going down the steep cliffs. All she ever recalled was firing on the three men, catching *them* off guard and giving Max a chance to slip out of his hiding place and run toward the bluffs. She joined him and they raced along the sand in the shadow of the cliffs.

Unfortunately they were being followed, which was an easy enough task since they were leaving footprints in the dampened sand.

As it turned out, the tide that they had been so concerned about ended up saving their lives. As it came ever higher they were forced to search along the bluffs for an escape route. What they found was a well-concealed cave whose entrance was totally covered by water during high tide.

Max pointed out that just inside the entrance the cave began to climb higher. They had run out of time. The water prevented them from going any farther on the beach. They had to take their chances in the cave.

"I feel fresh air coming from somewhere up ahead," Max said. "So there's got to be a way out of here. C'mon." With a small flashlight, he led the way. She scrambled to keep up.

The passage continued to narrow until Marisa was convinced they could go no farther, but Max kept moving. Eventually they were rewarded when the pathway widened and they found themselves in a glowing underground room. The glow came from the phosphorescent rock that made up the walls of the cathedrallike area.

"Look!" Max pointed upward.

Marisa's gaze followed his gesture. The ceiling of the area was, in her estimate, at least thirty feet above them. In the middle of it was a ragged opening, at least three feet wide. From where they stood, they were able to see the night sky and the twinkling stars.

"Where are we? Do you know?" she whispered.

Max shook his head. "Not really."

"Will someone be able to look down and see us?"

"If they know about the opening and where it leads, I suppose they can." He looked around the area. "But they'd have a tough time getting to us from there." He touched some rubble nearby with his toe. "I would guess that more than one unsuspecting animal has fallen to its death."

She shivered.

"With any luck, those guys will think we drowned."

"Either that, or they'll be waiting for us at the entrance of the cave when we emerge at low tide."

He had been walking the perimeter of the airy rock room. He came to an abrupt halt at her words. "Well, aren't you a shining tower of optimism tonight."

She stiffened. "I'm just being realistic, Max. You were almost killed out there."

He strolled back to where she stood. "That's quite true. I didn't have a chance until you showed up, guns ablazing."

"One gun, Max. That's all."

"One was enough. Thanks for saving my butt."

"That's what I was there for."

He grinned. "Well, you certainly performed your duties well." Now that he was standing so much closer she realized that his calm voice had deceived her about his mood. He was still keyed up, adrenaline still coursing through his body.

In a totally unexpected and uncharacteristic gesture, Max pulled her into his arms and hugged her to him.

If Marisa had learned nothing else about Max since she'd known him, she had learned that he didn't like to be touched. Not by anybody. She was shocked to her toes.

This was Max, the aloof and hard-to-know agent who did his job and went his own way.

Max, who was all business and whose personal life remained a mystery, even to those closest to him.

Max, the man she had secretly desired since the first day she'd met him.

Max held her in his arms. The heat of him wrapped around her chilled and shivering body, warming her, began a blaze that went straight to the core of her.

The ensuing moments were a blur. She recalled scattered moments: his lips scalding hers with passion; her arms tightening around him in a convulsive grasp; fumbling with his jacket and shirt in an effort to find his bare skin so that she could rub her hands over his back and chest in a frenzy of exploration.

He felt wonderful to the sensitive tips of her fingers and her palms...firm and muscled...smooth skin covering a well-honed body.

She didn't remember how they had ended up on the floor of the cave, their clothes forming a crude pallet of sorts. All she knew was how much she had dreamed about such a moment. She was living out all of her most erotic and sensuous fantasies with the man of her dreams.

He wasted no time claiming her. She clutched him in a frantic embrace, urging him on, until the fire that he had begun had grown from a tiny flame deep within her to a conflagration that consumed her entirely.

Long after the fire began to ebb with only an occasional spark as a reminder of what they had shared, he continued to hold her in his arms, his chin resting on the top of her head, which lay on his chest.

Never in her life had Marisa felt so at peace. She was drifting off to sleep when Max spoke.

"This has to be one of the most stupidly unprofessional things I have ever done," he said in a disgusted voice.

Marisa was glad he couldn't see her amusement at his tone of voice, which was a far cry from the gentle way he held her.

When she didn't answer, he went on. "Don't get me wrong, honey. I've wanted to jump your bones since the first time I saw you, but I knew better than to entertain the idea then, and I thought I'd tamped down all those erotic thoughts since."

Although his words sounded harsh, his voice was mellow. Hearing him admit to feelings much like those she had experienced over the years was at once reassuring and revealing. Perhaps not all the tension between them had been due to his reluctance to have her as his partner.

Marisa raised her head from its very comfortable pillow and brushed her lips across his.

"What was that for?"

"For letting me know how you feel," she whispered.

"I'm irritated as hell, and you're pleased about it?" he demanded to know.

"Max, you are a human being. Why are you working so diligently to be perfect?"

"Hah. I'm far from perfect. Anyone who knows me is aware of that."

"But who is that, Max?"

"What do you mean?"

"Who knows you? You keep yourself so aloof from everyone." Her hand continued to rest on his chest so that she felt his heart rate increase. She waited—almost holding her breath—for him to say something—to say anything—that would allow her to get to know him better.

"There's a suburb in Southern California with several foster families who know more than they want to know about me."

"Tell me, Max. Tell me about that time in your life."

He was quiet for so long that she was certain he had no intention of saying another word. He had begun moving his hand up and down her spine in a slow, lazy fashion. When he started speaking his voice was very soft, softer than she had ever heard it, so soft that she could almost see the young boy he described. She could hear the child as he described his pain.

"I had just finished the first grade that summer. I'd been let out to summer pasture and I was making the most of it. We had a typical tract home on a street lined with large shade trees. The area was a paradise for young boys who loved to climb trees and play in tree houses. Our next-door neighbors had two boys, one a year older, the other almost a year younger than I was. They had a tree house that my dad had helped their dad build for us. It was something else. We loved it. We spent all the time we could up there, spying on the world from our leaf-hidden eyrie.

"I was up there one morning when my mom called me to come home and clean up. They were going to town to do some shopping. I climbed down and went running to convince her to let me stay home and play with the neighbors.

"I remember her looking at my dad and communicating in that nonverbal way they had. As hard as I tried I couldn't tell how they did it. I never could read anything in their expressions, but she could ask and he could answer without a word being said. She said she'd check with our neighbor to make sure she didn't mind keeping an eye on me while they were gone. I knew she'd do it. She and Mom always traded off like that.

"Mom was getting Amanda dressed. My sister was fourteen months old, and reminded me of an animated doll. She had great big blue eyes...so blue they looked like they were painted on...and golden-white curls that bobbed on her head because she was never still for a minute, unless she was sound asleep. God! I loved to play with her. She thought I was so funny. As soon as I walked into the room she'd laugh out loud at me. Of course that encouraged me to clown around a lot, just to hear her laughter echoing in the house.

"I remember that she grabbed for my hand while Mom was trying to hold her still and Mom said, 'Don't play with her now, son. I'm trying to get her changed and dressed.'

"My dad tousled my hair and asked me if I wanted to go fishing with him the next morning. I loved going anywhere with my dad. I said 'Sure.' He reminded me that we had to get up really early. He always reminded me of that, as though I'd change my mind. It was kind of a game with us.

"So I waved goodbye, standing there in the driveway, watching them back out into the street. Everyone waved back, including Amanda, bouncing in her car seat between them."

He stopped speaking. Marisa had felt his muscles tensing during the telling of the story. Because she was once again lying with her head on his chest, she was aware when he swallowed, then swallowed a second time before saying in a monotone, "I never saw them again. They left that morning planning their day, expecting their lives to continue on indefinitely, but it didn't work out that way." He choked on the last word and just lay there in silence.

"What happened, Max?" The words were little more than a wisp of sound in the echoing cavern, but she knew that he heard them.

"It was one of those freak things you hear about. They had driven onto the main artery that fed traffic onto the freeway. They had just entered the freeway when a car changed three lanes at a high speed in an effort to elude a police car. They just happened to be in the wrong place at the wrong time, that's all. They were hit from behind and went into a roll. Before the car had stopped, it burst into flames. They never had a chance.''

"Oh, Max, no! How horrible!''

"The neighbors had me stay with them awhile. They said I was too young to understand what had happened, too young to attend the funeral. So I never had the chance to say goodbye to my family.

"Of course they couldn't keep me indefinitely. They turned me over to the authorities and I was placed in a series of homes. I'm the first to admit that I was impossible. No one would have wanted to be around a kid acting the way I did.''

"What did you do?''

"Anything I could to show my anger at the world, at the people around me, at myself for not having gone with my family that day. I was a destructive little beast, no denying that. I knew that I should have been with them. If I hadn't wanted to stay and play with my friends, I would have been there, too.''

"But, Max! You would have been killed!''

"But I would have been with them.'' Once again she heard the small boy's lament as he said softly, "They went off and left me all alone. They abandoned me. So I did everything I could to make those around me understand that nobody would ever hurt me like that again.''

"Oh, Max.'' She wrapped her arms around him and hugged him, holding him even closer than before.

After a long silence he said, "By the time I was thirteen I was on the streets, tougher than the tough." She could feel him beginning to relax. "I look back now and wonder how I managed to survive. I ran with a gang that would give any mother nightmares."

"So how did the Max of the streets become the Max I know, fighting for truth and justice and the American way of life?"

He chuckled. "It wasn't an easy transition, let me tell you. I happened to pick the wrong guy to mess with one night. I thought he was an idiot to be out in our neighborhood alone past midnight, but I was cocky enough to figure that I could take him. He had me on my back in less than a minute with a raging headache and a broken wrist. That's how I met Johnny Davenport. He was a detective with the police department. After he half killed me he took me home with him, cleaned me up, took me to Emergency to have my wrist put in a cast, then demanded to know where my folks lived. Rather than book me, he was determined to take me home and make me face whatever I was running from. When he found out I didn't have anything to run from, he ended up taking me in to live with him and his wife. God, was he tough! I thought I was such a hard case. This man was something else. Of course he made up a bunch of rules that made me furious. I had to go back to school; I'd dropped out two years before. I had a curfew. I had to report everything I did. I thought I was in jail. But the thing was, I respected this guy. He was everything I was trying to be. So I stayed; I listened; I watched; and I learned. He sent me off to college. I couldn't believe it. He was willing to put his money into my education. Me, some punk kid who tried to steal from him.''

"Where is Johnny now?"

"He died during my senior year at college. I found out from Sarah, his wife, that he had discovered two months before he died that he had cancer. He didn't tell me, of course. That wasn't his way. He'd insisted that I live on campus, so I wasn't seeing much of him, although we talked on the phone fairly often. He left me a letter, telling me all the things he had never been able to say about his feelings for me. About how much I had contributed to the fulfillment of his life. How he expected me to go on and make something of myself, that I had to do it for me and that I had to do it for him, too. That he never backed losers and that he'd recognized a winner, even if I'd worn a powerful disguise.''

"He sounds like a wonderful man.''

"Yeah. He was.''

"What happened after college?''

"I was recruited by the government to work for them. I was ideal for the purpose. No family to worry, no problems with the law. As much of the punk stuff as I pulled, I'd managed to keep my record clean. Of course they had investigated me and knew about everything I'd ever done. Hell, they must have interviewed every person that had even a speaking acquaintance with me. I've never understood why they decided to hire me."

"Somehow that doesn't surprise me, Max. You don't seem to have a clue why anyone would want to get closer to you."

Once again he ran his hand up and down her spine. "Well, I have to admit that you're pretty damned close to me right now."

"And enjoying every minute of it!"

"You've gotta be kidding. I've bored you with the story of my life...." His voice trailed off with his words. "You know, I don't recall ever telling anyone about my life before. Johnny never asked; the Agency already knew. I've spent so many years putting it behind me that I haven't even thought about it."

"I'm glad you did. It helps me understand you better."

He kissed her...a slow, leisurely and very thorough kiss. And for the next few hours their conversation was the whispered murmurings of new lovers—exploring, sharing, expanding their knowledge of each other.

Lying now in Teresa's bedroom, Marisa stretched and turned one last time before falling asleep, a smile of contentment on her face.

Four

Max lay on the narrow bed in one of Teresa's upstairs bedrooms, unable to sleep. He had pounded and reshaped his pillow until the stuffing was in danger of falling out. He had kicked off his covers hours ago, allowing the slight breeze to brush over his overheated nude body.

All he could think about was his need for sleep. Hell, he hadn't had more than a couple of hours' sleep at a stretch since Marisa had called him... how many nights ago was that? Two? Three? It seemed more like a hundred nights. He needed some sleep, dammit. He didn't need to be lying there thinking about Marisa in the other bedroom across the hall. She sure as hell wasn't having any trouble sleeping.

He thought about their conversation in the garden. He didn't believe that she would have done anything different, regardless of what he had told her about his feelings for her.

Given what he'd learned about her the night they were almost killed, he understood why she had trouble accepting the idea that he would be the one giving her orders. He had managed to suppress the memories of that night for years—until Marisa's call. Now he couldn't get them out of his mind. With eyes closed, he began to live through the sequence of events once more....

Everything seemed to be going according to plan when suddenly he'd found himself surrounded. Three men were moving rapidly toward him. There was no way he could have handled three of them. The shot she had fired from somewhere near the bottom of the cliffs had caught them by surprise, and within minutes he had sprinted to her, breaking through the ambush that should have killed him.

By then the tide was coming in, effectively trapping them at the bottom of the cliffs. He'd been searching for a way up the sheer bluffs when he'd stumbled across the hidden entrance to the cave. He had hoped it would lead to an opening in the bluffs that would put them above the water mark that clearly showed along the top of the entrance. They didn't have much of a choice but to explore the cave and hope they'd find an escape route.

What he remembered most vividly was Marisa's willingness to follow him wherever he led. He'd never known a woman with so much courage.

He'd followed the narrow passageway, encouraged by the fresh air that swept through it. When they stepped out into the fairyland glow of the large cave, he felt as though he'd stepped onto the set of a Spielberg movie. Any minute a lake would appear with a pirate ship floating upon it.

The relief of recognizing that they had beat the odds, that they were safe, hit him so solidly he could scarcely stand. They'd made it, thanks to Marisa's quick thinking.

He remembered grabbing her, wanting her to know what he was feeling, but those feelings were all mixed up—fear, sexual desire, joy, a sense of deliverance. The overwhelming rush of emotions that he'd always been so careful to control swept over him.

By the time a bit of sanity had returned to him, it was too late. He'd blown his professionalism all to hell. He'd made love to her.

Even now he winced at the memories. What a stupid, stupid thing to do. He could rationalize all he wanted to, but the fact remained that he'd made a mess of things.

As if that weren't enough, he'd compounded his stupidity by pouring out all that garbage about his childhood. Why had he told her all of that?

As polite as she'd been, he knew she must have been bored.

But she had listened...and he'd felt a release that was as intense as any sexual release he'd ever experienced. He would never forget the hours afterward as long as he lived, when he had turned to her with conscious deliberation and showed her how much he loved her.

Once again he relived the sensations as though they were happening to him all over again.

Still curled beside him, she responded as though she knew just what he wanted and needed from her. Her skin felt like satin beneath his callused palms. He cupped her breast and slowly lowered his mouth until he could flick his tongue across an exquisite peak.

She moaned slightly, moving so that his mouth more fully covered her breast. Her restless hands explored and stroked his body until a fiery need engorged him. His need had been so great the first time that he had rushed their lovemaking. Despite the increasing urgency now, he continued to take his time, leisurely exploring her body with his mouth until she was quivering in his arms.

By the time he finally took her they were both past their limits of control. This time he set a strong, not frantic, pace...exhorting her to grab a handful of those stars they could see shining in the nighttime sky. He kept a tight rein on himself, determined to pleasure this woman as long as his endurance held.

When he finally reached his limit, he gave one final lunge and buried himself deep within her, holding her to him in a convulsive and primitive possession.

They had fallen asleep for a while. He didn't know what awakened him later...perhaps a shifting of the rocks around them, perhaps a trickle of pebbles and dirt from somewhere high above. He'd opened his eyes and looked around. The cavern still glowed like a fairyland. He glanced down at Marisa, curled in his arms.

He lay there watching her, thinking that she was the loveliest person he'd ever seen...knowing that he would love her until the day he died.

So what in the hell was he going to do about it? After all that maudlin talk of his past she was probably bored with him, although she certainly hadn't acted as though she were bored when he'd made love to her. He'd never made such tender love with anyone, or been treated so tenderly in return. It almost brought tears to his eyes, thinking about what had just happened between them. He felt whole... and renewed...as though he could have it all: a profession and a personal life. What kind of personal life would be up to Marisa, of course.

She stirred, her eyes fluttering open. When she saw that he was awake, she glanced around them with a quick scrutiny. "What's wrong?"

God, he felt good! "Nothing's wrong. Everything's right from where I'm looking." His gaze lovingly surveyed the diminutive length of her.

Her smile looked sleepy and very content.

"You know," he said in a tender voice, "I don't know much about you at all. Here I've been spilling my guts. What about you?"

She ran her hand across his chest. "What about me?"

"What made you get into this profession?"

"I suppose I wanted to learn how to protect myself, how to provide for myself, how to fulfill a vow I'd made when I was a little girl—never to have to rely on anyone but myself."

"Were you an only child?"

She shook her head. "I was the oldest of three girls."

"Where are your sisters now?"

She was quiet for a moment. "Julie lives in California. Eileen is in Seattle."

"What was your childhood like?"

She sighed. "Learning to be as unobtrusive as possible. Whenever my father drank, which was almost every day, he came home in an unpredictable mood. He had a terrible temper, and my sisters and I were scared to death of him. We never had a clue what would set him off, what we had done...or not done. As soon as we heard his pickup truck drive up, we'd run and hide.

"I remember one time when he was upset about something...I never did know what...and he hit my mother. She fell against the table and hit her head on the corner. Looking back now, I realize that he thought he'd killed her. I've never seen him so scared. I can't remember how old I was at the time...I was still in grade school...but I remember being so upset over my mother and embarrassed because the ambulance came and took them away, and everybody came running over to see what had happened. I didn't want anyone to know that he'd hurt her. So I made up a story about my mother being up on a chair trying to get something off a kitchen shelf. I said that she had fallen...and wasn't it wonderful that my dad had been there to take care of her." She shook her head. "I was always making up stories about my dad. I wrote glowing papers for school about what a great father he was and how he took us places and bought us things. I completely invented a mythical father."

"Did he behave differently toward everyone after your mom was hurt?"

"For a while. He used to come home much earlier, right after he got off work, rather than stop off at the bar for a few drinks. But he was just as irritable. Julie used to say that he was very even-tempered: he was mean all the time."

"Did your mother ever consider leaving him?"

She sighed. "The subject came up once as I was growing up. I had gotten a job working after school as soon as anyone would hire me. I saved and saved my money until I thought I had enough. Then I went home and gave it all to her and told her that now we could leave him and start over somewhere else. I'll never forget the look on her face. She was shocked at the suggestion. Absolutely stunned. She said that she loved him. That she would always love him. That she couldn't imagine life without him. I guess she was right. He was killed in a one-car accident when I was seventeen. He didn't make a curve, ran off the road and hit a tree. Mother died six months later. I always felt that she stopped living the day he died. It just took six months for her body to give up."

They were both quiet for several moments before

Max asked, "What happened to you and your sisters after that?"

"Mom's oldest sister took us home with her. She lived about five hundred miles from our home, so we had to relocate. I didn't really care where we lived. I just wanted to get away from that town where everybody knew us, and everybody knew that my dad was drunk when he died."

"But you went on to college."

"Yes. My aunt and her husband offered to send us all to college. I refused their offer. From that point on, I was determined to do everything for myself. I never wanted to be dependent on anyone the way my mother was. Between working two jobs and a couple of scholarships, I managed to put myself through school."

"You'd just gotten out when you came to work for the Agency."

"That's right."

"You were carrying a pretty big chip on your shoulder, as I recall."

"At least with you, I was!"

"Why me?"

"Because I felt that you didn't think I could do my job, that someone else would have to cover for me."

"Instead, you covered for me tonight. I wouldn't be here, holding you in my arms, if you hadn't jumped into danger to save my neck."

She ran her hand along his thigh. "Not to mention other parts of your anatomy."

"You're a wanton woman, I must say...and I

just want you to know how much I appreciate that aspect of your personality.''

They both laughed and during the ensuing playfulness they managed to turn the fun to sheer sensual pleasure. The pleasure once again became fulfillment.

Reliving six-year-old memories wasn't helping him get to sleep, that was certain. Max got off the bed and walked to the window of Teresa's small bedroom. How the hell did he expect to sleep if he was going to dwell on memories like that! He reached for one of his cigars, which were lying on the small table near the bed, and put it to his mouth. After striking a match and touching the flame to the tip of the cigar, he drew on it until it glowed hotly in the dark.

They'd had one night together, not knowing what would greet them the following morning.

As soon as it was light enough to see if someone was waiting for them, they had carefully made their way back to the entrance of the cave. There was a broad expanse of sand awaiting them and no sign of their would-be assassins.

Eventually they had made their way to their hidden car and returned to their base. When Max had called the man whose position he had later assumed, he'd been told to abort the assignment and come home.

He wondered if she regretted telling him about her father. He had heard the pain in her voice and her determination not to be like her mother. She was certainly nothing like her mother. He couldn't imagine the Marisa he knew allowing anyone, male or female, to treat her harshly.

But he had realized that she was afraid of commitment and that he could scare her off very easily if he told her how serious he was about her. He was surprised himself. He would have to use caution and diplomacy and tact with her if he hoped to keep her in his life. She had left before he'd been able to talk to her.

The heat of the cigar against his fingertips brought Max to the present once more. Quickly he stubbed out the cigar and turned back to the bed.

He had to get some sleep. He was so tired that he could scarcely stand, and yet his mind refused to shut off.

What he needed was— Never mind what he needed. Never mind that she was a few feet away, just across the hall. Never mind that his body ached for her.

Never mind...never mind...never mind.

Five

They approached the small cove in silence, as the night spread its cloak of concealment around them. They had fallen into their working relationship with an ease that surprised Max, considering the length of time that had passed since they'd last worked together, as well as the tension that seemed to spring up between them at the least provocation.

He scanned the area for long minutes before signaling to Marisa to begin their descent to the water's edge. He had arranged to meet one of the small boats from the fishing trawler at midnight. They were only a few minutes early. He edged closer to the water and looked out to sea.

There was no sign of anything on the water. He motioned to Marisa to head for the deeper shadows that clung to the base of the steep incline. As they silently moved to that side of the cove, he saw what he'd been looking for.

A small boat waited in the shadows made by a clump of rocks near the water's edge. Max felt relief surge through him that they would be able to leave tonight.

After the previous night of restless sleep, then another day spent in Marisa's company, he was hanging on to his hard-won composure by a very thin thread.

They had bought her another change of clothing—black slacks with a black knit sweater. They'd covered her bright hair with a scarf.

He watched Marisa now as she acknowledged the two men waiting beside the boat. Following their mimed instructions, she scrambled inside as they pushed off from shore. Max waded out with the men until the water was deep enough for the three of them to get in without dragging the bottom of the boat against the shallow shoreline.

They kept their voices low in order not to attract any attention. He and Marisa had arrived at the rendezvous by taking a very roundabout route to make sure they weren't followed. They had seen no one on the way. He planned to keep it that way, if possible.

As soon as he was settled next to Marisa, she leaned over and whispered into his ear, "This really brings back memories of the times you and I worked together, doesn't it?"

He made a guttural sound in his throat and hoped she would accept it as his response. He didn't want to think about the fact that she was so close to him, not in his present mood and condition. He was a professional, dammit, and a good one. He'd spent the past six years reminding himself how fortunate he was that things had worked out as they had between them. He must have been temporarily insane to have considered the possibility of the two of them having a future together. He'd been caught up in all those fantasies of the moment, that's all. He should have left them behind in the fantasy cavern.

But he *was* human and he still found her extraordinarily attractive. Having her pressed tightly against his side at the moment did nothing to relieve the problem.

The two crewmen picked up their oars and began negotiating the waves back to the trawler while Max did his best to ignore the heat of her body against him.

He glanced around when he felt her move and watched as she leaned forward slightly so that her arm was free, then retied the large black scarf she wore over her hair. He found it irritating that he noticed every move she made, but he didn't seem to be able to ignore her.

As soon as they boarded the trawler the captain weighed anchor and started the engines. One of the men took them below, pointed to bunk beds, and then left them.

"Shall we flip a coin?" Marisa asked with a teasing smile.

He could have done without her cheerful acceptance of the primitive surroundings. He felt like the Grinch to her Mary Poppins. He turned away as he said, "Take whichever one you want. I don't care. I'll be on deck for a while."

"Max?"

He turned and looked at her. "Yes?"

"We make a good team. We'll get O'Donnell, and we'll find Timmy. Somehow I know we will."

Their eyes met and held. In this close area the tension between them was almost palpable.

He turned away once again. "Get some sleep. I'll be back down later."

Marisa watched him go before she turned to the bunk. She decided to sleep on top so that he could slip into bed later more easily. She sat down on the edge of the bunk and removed her shoes, then climbed up on the top bunk and stretched out.

She was tired but too keyed up to sleep. She lay there thinking about the past few days, thinking about Timmy. Had she guessed right? Did Troy have the boy with him? If so, why would he use an innocent child in such a way? Was Timmy frightened? She couldn't allow herself to think that way, or she'd go mad.

She closed her eyes, determined to fall asleep.

It was several hours later when a sudden blast of thunderous sound and a wild rocking threw Marisa out of the bunk. She landed on the deck with a thump. She felt as though she were in a nightmare, but this was real. The rough surfaces around her scraped her arms and legs, and pulled at her hair.

Gasping, she felt around in the dark, trying to

come to grips with what had just happened. There must have been an explosion on board the trawler. She could smell smoke but could see nothing in the murky darkness.

Before she could fully draw breath she heard Max's voice from somewhere nearby. "Marisa! Are you all right? Where are you?"

"Here!" she managed to say, still without much breath. The small space had a rakish tilt that she found ominous. She felt his hand brush against her face. She grabbed it and said, "We've got to get out of here!"

She heard his chuckle, a sound she had never expected to hear from him again. And why now, for God's sake!

"I always said you were quick in an emergency."

He was teasing her! Maybe she *was* dreaming, after all.

The trawler gave a shuddering groan just as Max tugged her toward what she presumed was the only escape.

"Watch the steps."

She used her other hand to reach out and try to identify her surroundings. Her toe hit the rung of the first step of the stairway. Max grabbed her waist and shoved her upward. She wasted no time scrambling to the top and glancing around. Controlled chaos was the best description of the scene. All the members of the crew were busy working on several small fires.

Max was beside her in seconds. "We've got to

get off this thing before it blows sky high. C'mon."
He knelt beside a metal bin and began to throw out
life preservers and jackets. "Put on one of these,"
he ordered, following his own instructions.

One of the crewmen came up. "The captain sug-
gests you take one of the boats, sir."

"What about the rest of you?"

"He hasn't given orders to abandon yet, sir."

Max shook his head, then gave the crewman a
hand lowering the boat over the side.

The flames cast an orange-red glow on every surface. *This is what I always imagined hell would
look like,* Marisa thought.

With the crew member's help they started to
climb down to the boat. The waves were choppy,
causing the boat to bounce around. Marisa gazed
down at it in dread. It was bad enough trying to
transfer to a smaller boat...a moving target was
even scarier.

"Hurry!" Max ordered.

She closed her eyes and lowered herself down
the short ladder, then opened them in time to spring
into the boat, grabbing the gunwales and inching
toward the bow, out of Max's way.

Later she was never sure what happened. One
moment Max was balancing, ready to leap into the
smaller boat, the next moment a large swell lifted
the boat away so that when he jumped, Max was
thrown against the gunwale, hitting his head.

"Max? Are you all right?"

She scrambled over to him, ignoring the fact that

they were now drifting away from the damaged ship. "Max?"

He lay where he'd fallen. There was so little light. He was just a shadowy figure slumped in the middle of the small boat. She reached him and touched his face. He didn't stir.

"Oh, Max!" She felt along his cheek and discovered a large bump on his temple. Frantically, she looked around her, seeking help. They were continuing to drift farther and farther away from the burning ship.

The water looked black and oily in contrast to the bright flames emanating from the ship. She looked to see if there were other boats being lowered, but she could see nothing.

She felt around until her fingers touched a locker. Praying that she could find help, she lifted the lid. The first thing she touched was a flashlight, thank God! She turned the beam toward Max. He didn't respond to the light at all. She checked his pulse and was relieved to discover a steady beat, although too rapid to be normal.

The side of his face showed bruising and was beginning to swell.

She attempted to get in a more comfortable position, then pulled a blanket from the locker and covered him. She didn't know what else to do. The trawler had disappeared from view except for an occasional sighting when they topped a swell.

Why would a fishing boat suddenly go up like that, for no reason? Or were they, perhaps, the reason? She shivered. They could have been killed.

Even now, drifting as they were, they could still die. What if Max didn't regain consciousness? She wouldn't allow herself to think about it. She had been in tough situations before; she'd been trained to keep her head in emergencies. Without his guidance, she would have to make the decisions on her own.

She heard an explosion and glanced back the way they had come. Flames shot into the sky and she knew the trawler was gone. She watched in silence until the sky was dark once more and prayed that the others had managed to escape.

She wondered what time it was. She had no way of knowing whether she had been asleep for hours or mere minutes before the explosion. There was no way to guess how long it would be before dawn.

She dug into the locker, examining their supplies. There was a canvas that could be used to shelter them from the sun, as well as packaged food and bottled water. There were also some flares.

Marisa lost track of time as she set off the flares, praying that someone would find them. Periodically, she checked on Max. He didn't stir.

Eventually her energy flagged and she fell asleep, Max's head cradled in her lap.

When the hail came, Marisa opened her eyes in confusion and glanced around. Early-morning sunlight surrounded them. But more important, there was a large yacht not far away with a smaller boat nearing them.

She glanced down at Max. Oh, dear God, but he

looked bad. His coloring was gray, except for the brilliant hues on the side of his face.

"Max? Can you hear me? We've been spotted, Max. Help is on its way." She leaned down and laid her cheek against his. "Hang on, will you?"

She glanced up at the approaching cruiser. Whatever possible danger they might be in as a result of their rescue, it would be up to her to protect them. If the explosion had not been an accident, if someone was actively seeking survivors, then they were far from being out of danger.

But Max needed medical attention. It was up to her to do what had to be done.

Six

"Ahoy there, are you all right?" a voice hailed from across the water.

"Oh, Max," she whispered. "Here's hoping I handle this well enough to keep us both alive." Then she turned and waved to their rescuers. She leaned over Max, attempting to shield him from the bright sunlight while she checked his pulse. It had slowed to a more regular beat, which eased her fear.

The runabout came alongside of them. One of its occupants leaped to their smaller boat and attached it to the larger one, then waved for the other boat to head back to the yacht.

Marisa knew she had to come up with a story, right now, that would be plausible and still protect their identity. She remembered their last assignment and knew that their cover story then would have to do now.

She didn't have to fake her relief when she turned to the man in the boat with them and said, "I don't know how you spotted us, but I'm certainly thankful you did. My husband and I had to abandon our sailboat. He was knocked out just before we managed to get away." She turned back to Max and placed her hand on the undamaged side of his face. "I hope he's all right."

"Don't worry, ma'am. We'll be at the yacht in just a few minutes. There's a doctor on board."

That was certainly good news.

"I'm Marisa Chapman...and this is my husband, Max," she lied with a smile. "We've been vacationing here in the Mediterranean and having a wonderful time until last evening, when the boat we rented developed a mammoth leak and we had to abandon her." She rubbed her forehead. "It's going to be such a mess, trying to work out the damages and rental fees and all."

She hoped she sounded like a befuddled woman who couldn't function well without her mate. "Max always handles those things, you know," she added for good measure. Glancing down at him, she said, "I don't know what I'd do without him."

As soon as the words left her mouth she felt a flash of insight. She knew the truth of her words. She didn't know what she would do if she didn't know that Max was somewhere in the world, doing what he needed to do, being who he was.

She had run from that strength and sense of purpose. She'd felt threatened by it. And yet...now that he was helpless, she realized that she much preferred him the other way. She wanted to see him strong again, wanted to hear his brusque voice giving orders and impatiently waiting to see them carried out.

Somehow she had changed over the years. She wasn't as easily threatened by the men she met. She looked down at Max, seeing his vulnerability, and she wanted to protect him from all harm until he could regain consciousness and protect himself.

"Where are you people from?"

"Kansas City, Missouri. That's the Midwest, you know."

The man nodded. The Chapmans from Missouri, she reminded herself. She'd need to tell Max as soon as he came to.

By the time they reached the yacht Marisa realized she was shaking with nerves. She prayed that Max's injury wasn't too severe and that he'd regain consciousness before much longer.

As soon as they were on board, a distinguished-looking man wearing a swimsuit and shirt greeted them.

"Welcome aboard the *Tempest*. I'm George Olson, originally from San Diego, California," he offered with a grin, "but since retiring I haven't spent much time there."

He took her hand and shook it as the crew member who had been with her in the boat introduced them before helping the others to move Max.

Marisa watched them carry Max's limp body inside and turned to follow them.

George smiled and said, "I know how worried you must be. Let me show you to the guest room where you and your husband will stay until we can return you to shore." Obviously trying to allay some of her fears, he continued to talk as he held open a door for her. "Because of some medical problems I've been having, I have a highly skilled doctor on board. He's waiting below to examine both of you."

"Oh, I'm all right," she hastened to assure him. "Thirsty, perhaps."

Marisa glanced around the interior of the yacht. She had never seen such elegance. She followed their host through a magnificent stateroom and down a hallway. He paused beside an open doorway and motioned Marisa to precede him.

If this was a guest room, she wondered what the master suite looked like! She couldn't seem to take all of it in. What her mind and eyes focused on was the bed where Max lay. A man in a white shirt and shorts, who Marisa assumed was the doctor, examined him. He looked up when he heard Marisa.

"He's definitely suffering from a concussion. Do you have any idea how long he's been unconscious?"

"Since sometime last night. I don't know exactly when the accident happened." It didn't take much effort to sound worried and ineffectual. "I didn't know what to do. It was just awful." She stared at Max. "Is he going to be all right?"

"Head injuries are unpredictable. At this point all I can do is monitor him. We'll have to see how it goes. Has he regained consciousness at all?"

"No."

She turned away from the man, ashamed of the spurt of tears that suddenly filled her eyes.

George spoke in a kind voice. "I'll have the steward bring you something to eat, Mrs. Chapman. I know this has been difficult for you." She nodded without speaking. "Why don't you shower while I find some fresh clothes for you? My daughter has several things on board, although she's away at college at the moment. I'm sure she won't mind if you use some of her clothing and other items."

Marisa glanced down at her clothes and made a face. There was a tear in the knee of her pants, and a ragged patch on her shoulder where something must have snagged her sweater.

"Thank you. I really appreciate your help."

"No problem, no problem. I'm just glad we spotted you."

He turned and left the room. The doctor walked over to her. "I'd like to check you, as well," he said. She sat down docilely and allowed him to check her vital signs. When he was through, he nodded. "Nothing a little food and rest won't cure. You were both quite lucky, you know."

She remembered the sky lit up with flames and shuddered. "Yes, I know."

He patted her on the shoulder. "You'll feel better after a shower and some sleep."

She watched him leave the room, quietly closing the door behind him. She went over to the bed and sat down on its edge. "Oh, Max." She took his hand in hers. "Please be all right."

She sat there with him until the steward appeared with a tray and a small stack of clothing.

"Thank you," Marisa said, taking the clothing and watching him set the tray on a small table nearby.

She went into the bathroom and for the first time got a glimpse of herself. No wonder they thought she was in bad shape! Her hair stood out from her head as though she'd just been electrocuted. Her forehead, nose and cheeks were fiery red. The rest of her skin was so pale it looked almost green!

Turning away from the unsavory reflection, she stripped out of her clothes and crawled under the shower, feeling its warmth soothe and ease her tense muscles.

By the time she dried off, she felt much better. She looked through the clothing she'd been given and found underwear that was stretchy enough to fit. A pair of shorts and a sleeveless blouse completed her attire. She returned to the bedroom and ate the salad that had been left for her. By the time she finished, she could scarcely keep her eyes open. Stretching out beside Max, she fell asleep.

Where was he? Max blinked his eyes, trying to focus them. He had one hell of a headache—a world-class hangover—and he was having trouble with his vision. Finally, he realized that it was night. No wonder he couldn't see. He shifted slightly, trying to ease the ache in his head. A groan escaped him.

"Max?"

He heard the gentle whisper and turned his head.

"Oh, Max, you're awake. How are you feeling?"

He started to speak, and for the first time became aware that his mouth and throat were so dry that he could scarcely swallow. Anticipating his need, she reached for a glass nearby and handed it to him. He wet his lips and allowed the water to trickle down his throat.

"The doctor left some tablets for you, in case you needed them for pain."

"Doctor?"

"Oh, of course you don't realize where we are now."

"No," he admitted, accepting the tablets and swallowing them. He handed her the glass.

"Oh, Max, I was so worried. You hit your head when we were leaving the fishing trawler. Everything happened so fast. I wasn't able to signal to anyone that you were injured and we ended up drifting away from it. Thank God we were able to leave before that last explosion. I hope the others got away all right."

He thought about what she said for several moments, trying to assimilate it.

"The doctor said you must be quiet for the next few days. As it turns out, the man who owns this yacht was heading toward Monaco, so we won't be far from our original destination.'' When he didn't respond, she said, ''I told them here on the yacht that we're on vacation and were on our way to Nice. I just hope this doesn't delay my catching up with Troy to see if he knows where Timmy is. Do you think you're going to be in good enough shape by the time we get there to face Harry O'Donnell? Should I send a coded message to your office requesting assistance?''

Max closed his eyes, too confused to follow her remarks. He would rest. Perhaps by morning he would be able to make some sense out of what she had said.

Marisa watched him for a long time. The tablets must have worked. He didn't stir for the rest of the night.

The next time Max awakened, the room was bright with sunlight. He was alone. With careful movements he climbed out of bed and made his way into the bathroom. When he washed his face he gazed into the mirror in perplexity. He obviously hadn't shaved in a few days. One side of his face looked puffy and was multicolored. He stared in silence at the image that looked back at him with a steady gaze.

His name was Max.

All the rest of the information the woman had given him the night before was jumbled in his mind. They were headed toward Monaco. They were trying to find someone by the name of Timmy. He was expecting to have a confrontation of sorts with a Harry O'Donnell. He was on vacation.

There had been something about a coded message. What had that meant?

Who was the woman who'd shared his bed last night?

The pounding in his head increased. He needed to lie down.

By the time he reached the bed, he felt exhausted. He lay down, closing his eyes. As he drifted off to sleep, he heard voices just outside the door.

''I'll check your husband, Marisa, just to confirm what you've already told us. I agree with you, though. Now that he's awake we can rest a little easier. I'm certainly glad to hear your news.''

Too tired to attempt conversation, Max allowed his eyes to remain closed as he drifted toward oblivion once more.

Her name was Marisa. She was his wife.

The next day Max felt well enough to sit out on the deck with the others. He sat and watched and listened and waited.

He watched to see how each person in the party interacted with one another. Who felt what about whom.

He listened for information about the people, about their plans, about their lives.

He waited for his memory to return.

He didn't question that he had no intention of telling anyone that he couldn't remember anything.

He merely followed his instincts. He was not going to give anyone the advantage of knowing how vulnerable he felt.

Not even Marisa. Not even his wife.

He watched her the most, trying to remember. Surely he would remember her, the woman he had chosen to marry.

His mind remained blank.

So he waited, he listened and he watched.

He also attempted to learn about himself. He had a very suspicious nature, he'd noticed. He didn't trust too many people. Of course he trusted Marisa, or at least he assumed he did. He just didn't want to give away any advantages that he might have.

He'd awakened from a dream in the middle of the night. He'd been making love to her.

Marisa.

His wife.

The dream didn't surprise him that much. He seemed aware of her no matter where they were, what they said, or what they did.

He noticed that she didn't touch him, which made him wonder about his constant need to touch her. Was it his present sense of isolation that made him want to reach out to her? Or was it the fact that they probably hadn't made love in a few days?

He had a hunch they had a very active love life. He'd certainly shown good taste in choosing her for a wife. Not only was she a dynamite-looking woman, she showed a high degree of intelligence and a very keen sense of humor.

He stood, uncomfortable with the strong bodily

reaction he had every time his thoughts dwelled upon Marisa. "I think I'll go inside. The sun's a little too bright for me."

"Are you feeling all right?" Marisa asked.

"Just tired. I may take a nap."

The doctor, who'd insisted they call him Henry, said, "Good idea. Give that head of yours a chance to heal."

Max wished to hell it would hurry. And by the way, how about returning his memory at the same time?

Once again his sleep was filled with dreams, or were they? Scenes appeared, then swirled away into the mist, only to be replaced by more and different scenes.

When he opened his eyes later, he felt more rested and more at peace. Things were coming back to him in fragmented pieces. He'd been in a classroom; later walking some cliffs with Marisa.

Invariably he was making love to her.

He got up and headed toward the bathroom. He had already stepped inside the small room when he discovered that Marisa was there. She'd obviously just turned off the water for the shower because she stood in the miniscule stall reaching for a towel.

"Oh!"

She was as exciting to see in the flesh as she'd been in his dreams. Why did he need to dream about her when she was there?

He picked up the towel and smiled at her. "Need some help?"

He was amused at her confusion. Why should she look so astonished at his suggestion? Surely it wasn't the first time he'd been with her in such an intimate situation. He took her hand and gently pulled her toward him, then carefully...and very thoroughly...dried her body.

Neither of them made a sound.

By the time he had completed his self-appointed task she was quivering, her eyes filled with the same need he was experiencing.

When their mouths touched at last, it felt like spontaneous combustion. He couldn't wait any longer. He needed her right now...at this moment. Without releasing her he slid his shorts off, the only item of apparel he wore at the moment, then lifted her, urging her legs around his waist.

She felt so damned good against his heated body. When she rubbed her breasts against his chest he wasn't certain he could hang on to his control and he groaned.

He'd intended to carry her to the bed, but he couldn't wait. Leaning her against the countertop, he eased himself inside her waiting warmth, grateful that she was obviously ready for him. Her response spoke volumes. She had needed him as much as he'd needed her.

It was over much too soon. He didn't want to release her. Not just yet. Placing her limp arms around his neck, he picked her up and carried her to the bed that he had left such a short time before.

He stretched out beside her, running his hands over her, reenacting all of his dreams about her.

"You're obviously feeling better," she managed to whisper, her breath coming in quick pants.

He grinned, feeling quite pleased with himself. "It would seem so." He leaned down and licked the pointed tip of her breast. Her body reacted as though she had received a sudden jolt of electricity. He settled against her to enjoy her response.

Eventually he began to explore, stringing a line of kisses downward, over her stomach, down her thigh to her knee, then returning along a path on her inner thigh until he paused, intimately touching her lightly with his tongue.

Once again her body jerked in response, her hands kneading his scalp and shoulders much like a kitten flexing its paws. He shifted and began to kiss her more fervently, holding her as she reacted to his intimate touch. He drove them both to a place of mindless overload of the senses before he relented and took her once more.

They shared touches and quick kisses while their bodies settled into a matched rhythm of offering, then releasing, giving, then withdrawing.

Max framed her face with his hands, holding her still so that he could enjoy each feature, each expression that flitted across her face. He whispered, "It's been so long." He felt safe in offering the comment. Even two days and nights was too long to wait for this.

He watched the myriad of expressions on her face at his words. Was he behaving differently than he usually did? Was it his fault that she hadn't been showing much affection toward him since he'd awakened to find himself without a memory?

Perhaps it *was* his fault that they had been so distant from each other. But he would make it up to her. He would show her how much he loved and desired her.

Such a task wouldn't create a hardship for him, regardless of his lack of memory of the past.

He could feel his body rejecting his conscious restraints, until he was forced to let go and allow his body its release. He felt her tightening around him, squeezing like a gentle vise until he cried out with the pleasure she was giving him. At his cry her body gave a convulsive surge, then began to pulse around him, drawing him closer and closer until they were no longer two distinct people, but one whole and perfect unit, complete in itself.

Max felt drained, the muscles in his body quivering at the release of tension. He turned so that he was stretched out beside her, both of his arms still around her.

She snuggled to him, drifting into sleep. He smiled to himself as he joined her.

Sometime later he awoke instantly when she began to stir.

"Where are you going?" he murmured, holding her against him.

"I think it's getting close to dinnertime. I thought I'd go shower and get dressed."

He heard a slight hesitancy in her voice and wondered at it. "Marisa, what's wrong?"

She pulled far enough away from him to see his

face. After searching his expression, she shook her head a little, as though puzzled. "I'm just confused, that's all."

"About what?"

"You...me...us."

"What's so confusing about you...me...us?" he asked, deliberately mimicking her words.

"You've been so distant these past few days. And now—I guess I don't know what to think or how to act or—"

Knowing that they were on vacation, he was a little taken back by the fact that he had been distant.

"Oh, honey, I guess I've had so much on my mind that I didn't show you how I felt."

She eyed him uncertainly. "Max? Are you certain you're feeling all right?"

"I'm feeling better by the hour. Obviously, I was more than ready for a vacation."

"A vacation," she repeated carefully.

"So maybe this isn't like the one we planned, but we certainly can't complain about the luxuriousness of our surroundings. And George makes an admirable host. Once we get to Monaco we can—"

"Max?"

"What?"

"Do you know who I am?"

He smiled. "Of course I know who you are. You're Marisa."

Her relief was evident. "Do you remember why we're here on this yacht?"

"They rescued us. Why all these questions?"

"I don't know. I guess I'm just trying to figure out if that blow to the head created more of a problem than I first thought."

"Why? Because I wanted to make love to you?"

"Well, you have to admit your behavior is out of the ordinary."

He stroked over her sloping rib cage down to her narrow waist, then up over her hips, pausing at her thigh. It felt very natural, very normal to be lying here with her, touching her whenever and wherever he felt the urge. How could that possibly be out of the ordinary?

"You're acting as though we've never made love before."

"Well, it's been so long...I mean, we never really talked about what my leaving did to our relationship. I didn't know until I saw you again why you behaved the way you did. I got the impression that you no longer cared."

Ah, so that was it. The vacation was more in the form of a reconciliation. That explained a great deal to him. No doubt he was a proud man. As much as he might love her, having his wife walk out because of a fight wouldn't sit well.

"Well, I was hurt, of course. I mean, we belong together, and for you just to walk out like that, without giving us a chance to work things out, made me angry."

She was quiet, obviously considering what he had said. "You're right, of course. I was a coward to leave the way I did. But your promotion seemed to have changed so much for us. It was one thing to work as equals, but when you became my boss I was afraid that you would use your new power over me, not only as a boss, but as the man I loved."

She had admitted it! he thought with obvious relief. She loved him. Well, of course he had known that on some level by the way she had responded so wholeheartedly to his lovemaking. But for her to come right out and say so made a tremendous difference to him.

Knowing that she had left him had hit a nerve inside of him. He didn't like being left. He wasn't sure how he knew that, he just knew that it was true.

"Well, at least we're together now."

She sighed. "Oh, yes, we're together now. And we're safe...at least until we get to shore."

Safe? An alarm went off in his head. Hadn't they been safe before? Well, obviously there had been some sort of mishap at sea. Perhaps that was all she was referring to. But just in case, he would need to stay vigilant to the nuances around him.

She leaned over and gave him a quick kiss. "Let's go shower together. We'll save some time so we won't be late for dinner."

On the contrary—because they decided to shower together, they were very late for dinner!

Seven

"**D**o you like to fish, Max?" George asked at dinner that night.

Without hesitation, Max replied, "No, George, I don't." Then he wondered how he was so certain. He glanced at Marisa who was staring at him in surprise, her fork halfway to her mouth. *Oh hell, don't tell me I've been spending every weekend of our marriage fishing!*

"I don't suppose there's too many places to fish around Kansas City," George offered with a smile.

Max had a sudden flash of another place and time, of going out in a boat along the seashore. Kansas City? But hadn't he come from California? How did he know that? Even so, maybe he'd moved as a kid. But Kansas City? He drew a blank.

When Max didn't say anything, George said, "If

you two aren't in any hurry, I thought we might spend tomorrow in an area where I like to do some fishing. Of course if you need to get to shore right away…'' He allowed his words to trail away.

Once again Max glanced at Marisa. She was watching him intently. Perhaps she was wondering if he would insist that they leave the yacht as soon as possible.

But a vacation was a vacation, wasn't it? George was a hospitable host. At the moment he didn't care what he did for a living. No doubt there were people covering for him while he was on vacation.

He smiled at George. ''We're in no hurry,'' he said, and reached for Marisa's hand. ''Are we, darling?''

He noted that she quickly masked her surprise at his response but could not control the quiver of her hand in his. So she wasn't as sure of him and their relationship as she'd pretended. It was going to take some time to convince her, that was for sure, but he had to admit he was looking forward to it.

Later, while he stretched out on the bed and watched her getting ready to join him, Marisa said, ''I was surprised to hear you say you didn't like to fish.''

''Were you?''

''But then, maybe it isn't so surprising. You always went fishing with your dad. Your feelings about that time of your life must be all mixed up with the activities you shared with him.''

He shrugged. ''I guess I never gave it much thought.''

"I also thought you considered our getting to Nice urgent."

He smiled. "Nothing seems as urgent to me as being with you. I feel as though I woke up to a whole new life the other morning. I want to savor it."

She rose from the small dressing table and came to him. "Oh, Max, do you feel that way, too? I feel as though we've been given a second chance to work things out between us."

He pulled her down beside him. "I feel the same way," he said with a grin, sliding the borrowed robe off her shoulders and revealing her fully to his view.

"Do you think you should contact your office? It wouldn't hurt to let someone know what's happened to you."

Call his office on his vacation? What sort of workaholic tendencies had he developed?

He kissed her below her ear and along her jawline. "If you really think I should call, I will… tomorrow."

Maybe by tomorrow he'd remember a little more about his life. In the meantime, he was going to enjoy each and every moment of today.

After breakfast the next morning, Marisa drew Max aside and said, "I decided to call your office for you this morning since you had slept in. I thought your boss would accept my explanation that you were fine, but after I told him you'd been hurt, he insisted that you call him. He even gave me a more direct number to call than the one I knew.'' She handed him the slip of paper and Max frowned at it.

His memory was improving, just as he'd hoped. Unfortunately, not so he could make any sense out of what he remembered. He kept seeing things as though he were a child. There were many scenes where he felt desolation and despair. He wondered why. What had gone wrong in his early life that the few memories surfacing would make him feel so much pain?

He was seriously thinking about telling Marisa about his memory loss, but he hesitated to do so. Would she be upset that he hadn't told her from the very beginning? How would she react to the fact that he had no memory of her before they boarded the ship? Would she feel that he had taken advantage of the present situation? As far as he knew, they had just met. He didn't remember a thing about their marriage. Nothing at all.

He wouldn't blame her if she were to be upset. And what purpose would it serve, anyway, for him to tell her? And yet it would be a relief to be able to discuss the matter with someone.

He glanced down at the piece of paper he was holding. Maybe he had found the answer for the moment.

Using George's state-of-the-art phone system, Max soon heard the ringing of the phone on the other end of the line.

''H'lo?''

"This is Max. Marisa said you wanted to speak to me."

"Yes. She said that you received a blow to the head and were suffering from a concussion, but that you seemed to be fine now. I wanted to make certain you were capable of handling Harry on your own. Otherwise I can have assistance waiting for you when you arrive in Nice."

Obviously he wasn't going to be able to handle Harry if he didn't know who the hell he was. Why jeopardize his job for the sake of secrecy?

"Actually, I do have something of a problem. I believe it will take care of itself as I grow stronger, but at this point I'm a little hampered."

"What's wrong?"

"It's a little complicated. The thing is, I, uh, don't remember anything."

"You what?"

"I've got some form of amnesia. I mean, it's not so severe that I don't know how to function or anything. It's as though everything prior to waking up with a god-awful headache was wiped from my mind."

"Max, this isn't something to be taken lightly. Why didn't Marisa mention it when she called?"

"She doesn't know. I haven't told anyone, including the doctor."

"How is that possible? If you don't remember anything how did you know to call me?"

"Marisa mentioned it. She was obliging enough to give me a new number, as well."

"So in your own inimitable fashion, you've been

feeling your way along without any help and without giving anything away.''

"Are you saying my behavior is typical, then?''

"Unfortunately, yes, it is. You never give away an advantage, no matter how small. I don't suppose she told you who I am?''

"No. Just that I work for you.''

"That's true. Now listen to me. I don't want you attempting to play hero. As soon as you get to shore, take the next plane back to the States. We'll have you see a specialist. Forget O'Donnell for now. He can wait. Now that we know the truth about him, we can take care of him soon enough.''

"Would you just answer one question? Exactly what sort of business are we in?''

There was a long silence. "I'm afraid I'm not at liberty to discuss the matter at the moment.''

"Does our business have anything to do with my being in Europe on a yacht owned by George Olson?''

"Not directly, no. But you're safe enough there. I had him checked out thoroughly. He's who he says he is.''

"What's all this business about being safe? Marisa mentioned it last night. I didn't want to question her too much.''

"Marisa can answer your questions, Max. I'm curious why you've chosen not to tell her about your problem.''

"I'm not certain. I just don't feel right about doing so.''

"I've always trusted your instincts, Max, and I

will continue to do so, regardless of the fact that you don't remember anything. Get back to the States as soon as possible. Perhaps your memory will start coming back by then. If not, we'll be able to get you the help you need.''

"You're probably right. I keep getting flashes of scenes, but at the moment they don't mean anything to me. By the way, where are you?''

"Washington, D.C.''

"Then why does everyone on board think we're from Kansas City?''

"Maybe that's one of the covers you and Marisa used in the past.''

Covers? What was he talking about? "I'm afraid I don't follow you.''

"Sorry. I can't go into any details at the moment. We'll talk again when you return.''

Max hung up the phone and left George's office, his head pounding. He would go lie down for a while and see if that helped. Otherwise he'd get some pain tablets from Henry.

The pain was almost blinding. He felt his way down the corridors to their room, then let himself inside with a sense of relief.

He stretched out on the bed and took several deep breaths, trying to make his mind blank. Just as he began to drift away he remembered a question he'd meant to ask.

How long had he been married?

A slight noise at the door brought him abruptly awake sometime later. He was reaching under the pillow for his pistol when he realized that it was Marisa coming in.

His pistol? Why would he keep a pistol under his pillow?

"Oh, did I wake you?" she asked. "I'm sorry. I thought you were going to join me on deck when you got through with your call."

He allowed himself to relax back on the pillow. His head had eased somewhat, for which he was thankful. He wanted to avoid taking the pain tablets, if possible. They dulled his senses too much. He needed to stay alert.

Where had *that* thought come from?

"Marisa, we need to talk." He sat up on the side of the bed.

She sank down into a chair nearby. "What's happened? Has he heard from O'Donnell?"

"O'Donnell?"

She frowned. "Isn't that what we need to talk about? My trying to locate Troy and your neutralizing O'Donnell?"

He shook his head as though trying to break something loose that had become stuck. "I've got a slight problem, and you might as well know about it."

She leaned forward. "Okay."

"That blow to the head has left me a little confused. There are some memory lapses and I'm having trouble putting things together."

"Why haven't you mentioned it before?"

"I thought everything would come back to me without my having to say anything. I mean, it isn't as though I've forgotten *everything.*'' He attempted a laugh that sounded a little ragged. "I mean, I didn't forget how I feel about you."

She studied him for a moment. "Are you certain? A memory loss would explain some of your behavior these past few days."

"I'm fine, really. I didn't want you worrying about me."

She slowly settled back into her chair. "You know, I've enjoyed the way you've been the last few days, I must admit. It brought back some of the happier times we had together."

"I've enjoyed it, too."

"You've been so much more relaxed and open toward me."

"Have I?"

She grinned. "Mm-hm."

When she looked at him like that, every thought he'd managed to gather fled his mind. He reached for her and she willingly allowed him to pull her over until they were both sprawled sideways across the bed.

"More relaxed, you say?" He took her hand and placed it on a part of his anatomy that was far from relaxed.

She chuckled. "I had no idea I had such an instantaneous effect on you."

"Then I must be one hell of an actor. I react to you every time I see you...in the shower...in my bed...over breakfast...while you're soaking up the sun...I have a great deal of difficulty keeping my hands off you.'' All the time he was talking, his hands were rapidly removing her clothes.

She followed his lead, until they were lying there with nothing between them but the sea air wafting through one of the portholes.

This time Marisa became more assertive, shifting so that she was over him, her hands framing his face. "Let me make love to you, all right?'' she whispered, placing feathery kisses over his face.

Max felt her breasts brush against him, her hair tickle his shoulder, then felt the movement of her hips, hands and hair touching, exploring and brushing against him. By the time her mouth had touched him intimately he was having trouble getting enough air in his lungs.

Enough! He couldn't take any more of this without exploding! He hauled her across him, lifting her so that she was sitting with her knees on either side of his thighs. He placed his hands at her waist and slowly positioned her until she took his hard length deep within her. She gave a quick sigh of delight just as he pulled her forward enough to taste one of the delectable breasts placed so conveniently before him.

He allowed her to control their pace, taking delight in her responses to what he continued to do with his mouth and hands. How he loved this woman! She was everything he could possibly want in a wife. Thank God he'd realized that sometime in his misty, forgotten past.

When he'd reached the end of his control he took over by once again holding her lightly between his hands and guiding her movements to meet his stronger, faster ones. She rode him well, her mouth seeking his as they were flung across the finish line in a burst of motion.

She collapsed across him, holding him tightly. He could feel her rapid heartbeat throbbing against his chest, hear her panting breaths trying to fill her lungs once more. The scent of her floral perfume wafted between and around them. Her taste was still on his lips. He slowly ran his tongue across them to enhance the moment.

When she raised her head what seemed to be a long time later, she was frowning slightly. "Max?"

"Hmm?"

"Maybe we shouldn't have been quite so energetic. Is your head all right?"

"Who cares? The rest of me is doing just fine, thank you."

"But I'm worried about you."

"The doctor said I'd have some residual pain and soreness. I'll be okay."

"No. I mean about your memory loss."

"Oh, that."

She slipped to his side and propped her head on her hand. "Yes, that." She poked him in the stomach lightly with her index finger. As though caught up in the experience of touching him, she ran her fingernail into the downy hair that grew on his chest and drew circles, watching as a path opened, then closed around the tip of her finger.

"Max."

"Mmm?"

"What do you remember about O'Donnell?"

"Not much," he admitted.

"Not that he's a traitor and may have been responsible for some of your men being killed?"

He forced himself not to physically react to her words as his mind raced at the implications of what she'd just said. His men? Killed? A traitor?

Whatever his occupation, it was dangerous. He knew that he worked out of Washington, D.C. A horrifying thought occurred to him. What if he was a gang lord? No! He wouldn't be. He couldn't be. Not and have such a strong negative reaction to the idea.

"Tell me about O'Donnell."

"Do you remember that I heard him planning to take care of somebody? He may be involved in the missing artifacts and other smuggling that's been going on."

"But we don't know?"

"No. You were going to get me out of the area first. I was going to continue to look for Timmy." She paused. "You remember Timmy?" He shook his head. "Timmy's my nephew. My sister's husband may have taken him."

"You were looking for him?" he asked, horrified at the thought that his wife would be doing something so dangerous.

"I was the only one she knew to ask," she said. Max heard the slight defensiveness in her tone and wondered if this is what they had argued about.

He wouldn't be at all surprised. All of it fitted. She had told him she was going to look for Timmy.

He had told her not to, but she had, anyway. He'd followed her, obviously in time to get her away from this O'Donnell character.

Well, he'd certainly picked an independent one, he'd give her that. Obviously, she believed in doing what had to be done regardless of the consequences.

He admired her for that...in a way. He'd just have to learn to handle her with a little more finesse. Or maybe he'd learned his lesson. It sounded as though he was a real workaholic. Probably didn't spend enough time at home.

Maybe he'd needed that crack on the head! At least it seemed to wake him up!

Eight

The pain! Oh, God, but the pain made him feel as though his head was shattering. He fought his way out of a deep sleep, trying to understand why he hurt so badly. What was wrong with him?

He forced himself to sit up on the side of the bed. He'd been working too hard, that's all. He'd been so worried about— There was something that he'd been so worried about. What was it?

Something wrong in the field, that was it! He was losing agents and didn't know why. His head was pounding so hard that he could scarcely think. Maybe if he could take something for it. He reached for the lamp beside his bed but couldn't find it. He was more tired than he thought.

He got up and eased around the bed. He'd catch

the hall light, which would give him enough illumination to find the kitchen. Every step was—

"Max? Is something wrong?"

He whirled around in surprise. There was a woman in his bedroom! Who in the hell—

A light came on, flooding the room with a brilliance that seemed to blind him.

"Max? What's the matter? Where **are** you going?"

That voice! He knew that voice. This wasn't the first time it had haunted him.

The room began to whirl around and around, shadows blending with the brilliant light...shadows and light...darker and darker...shadows and a slowly...dimming...light.

He felt himself falling and he sighed with relief. At last he was escaping from the pain.

"As I explained to you earlier, Marisa, head injuries can be very mysterious. I don't have any explanation for this latest development. I don't believe he reinjured himself when he fell. Luckily he was close enough to the bed that most of his weight fell across it. I can't explain why he has been unconscious for the past two days. I wish I could. The swelling around his temple has gone down; his pupils are back to normal. It's a mystery."

Max lay there quietly, his eyes still closed, and listened. He was aware of a clarity of thought that had often eluded him in the past. It was as though he was standing at a point and could look back and see forever, then look forward and see equally well.

He'd been injured. But he was all right now. He remembered being thrown off balance as he left the trawler. He remembered falling and pain exploding in his head.

He remembered—he flinched from the memory. He was with Marisa. Somehow he had been convinced that they were married. How could he have believed that? How could his mind have tricked him in such a way? Was there part of him that had secretly wished it to be so?

He heard the door close softly across the room. Slowly he opened his eyes. The first thing he saw was Marisa leaning against the door, her hands covering her face.

"Marisa?" he managed to say.

She jerked up her head and their eyes met. Hers were filled with tears. "Oh, Max! I thought you were dying."

She ran across the room and knelt beside the bed. "I couldn't bear losing you again. It was bad enough the first time. I couldn't go through it again!"

What had he done? These past few days had been a fantasy he had played out, a chance to pretend that he had a loving wife, to pretend that he was a married man. He refused to make allowances for the fact that he had lost his memory. He knew that her pretending had been done as protection for them. She had used the same cover they had used during their last assignment. They had played a married couple on vacation. It was a good one that worked for them.

Unfortunately he had been one of those fooled this time.

The question was, what to do now?

"Marisa, I'm sorry."

She took his hand and held it between both of hers. "Please don't apologize, Max. The doctor said these things happen sometimes. How does your head feel?"

He thought about that for a moment and realized that he no longer had a headache. "It feels fine," he said, smiling. "Are you okay?" he asked, touching her cheek with his finger.

She gave a teary chuckle. "Much more than okay, now that you're awake once again." She gave him a mock stern look. "And I don't care how insistent you become, there's going to be no more lovemaking until we're absolutely sure that the activity didn't cause you to relapse!"

That was something, anyway. How could he deal with his tumultuous emotions if he continued to make love to her? Never had he felt such a confusion. He felt as though he'd just awakened from a dream—a wonderful fantasy of a dream—only to find that it had actually happened.

Despite all of his intentions, he had managed to get involved with Marisa once more, only this time she had made it clear that she wanted to work on their relationship.

How could he admit to her that he hadn't a clue how to go about doing such a thing? He'd gotten one thing right. He was a workaholic. His work was what he did best; what he felt most comfortable doing. He didn't have a very good track record with relationships. All of the people who had meant something to him—his parents, his sister, even Johnny, had all died.

Was what he felt for Marisa love? He didn't have a clue. Was he ready to make a commitment to work on a relationship? Two weeks ago—even one week ago—he would have said no.

Now he wasn't sure what to do. He felt as though he'd just stepped off a cliff and was hanging in air with nothing to support him. None of his past decisions could help him now.

Marisa came to her feet. "Let me go tell Henry the good news. I'm sure he's going to want to check you once again."

Damn, but he was tired of being poked and prodded. He wanted to get back to work. He had a job to do. That was the important thing to remember. He had a job to do.

"When do we arrive in Monaco?"

"George thinks we should be there when we wake up in the morning." She gave him a teasing smile. "I thought you weren't in a hurry to get there."

He closed his eyes. What could he say to her that wouldn't seem out of character? Or at least out of character for the loving man he'd pretended to be?

Pretended? Was that what he had done? Or was that loving man actually a part of him, buried deep inside his psyche, wanting to surface?

"I'd feel better getting the situation with O'Donnell cleared up, that's all."

"So would I, especially if Troy is involved. I wish I could understand why he would take Timmy like that. It never made sense."

"To spite your sister, didn't you say?"

She glanced at him, then away. "I suppose." She patted his hand. "I'll go get Henry. You lie still and rest."

When she left the room Max slowly sat up. The dizziness he'd felt earlier was gone. He touched his temple lightly. It was a little sore, but not much.

He'd been in tough situations before. Now he was going to have to deal with this one.

"I can't thank you enough for all of your help, George," Max said the next morning as they prepared to leave the yacht.

"Henry did the work, Max. I'm just glad we spotted you when we did."

"Yes, it could cause a man to consider the possibility of miracles, couldn't it?"

They eventually took their leave of their genial host and climbed into the cruiser for the trip to shore. The harbor was filled with vessels of all sorts arriving and departing. Max sat beside Marisa and watched the activity with a keen eye.

"There's something different about you," she finally said to him.

He turned his head and looked at her. "You're probably missing my Technicolor face. It looks rather bland these days."

"It's not that, Max. You just seem more aloof, somehow."

"I've been thinking about what we're going to do once we get to shore."

"That's it! You're no longer treating our time together as a vacation. You're back to work now."

"I suppose that's true."

"I miss the man on vacation."

He gave her a half smile. "I'm not even sure he exists."

"I know. It was a real shock for me, too, but a very pleasant one. I suppose it was finding out that you *do* love me that made such a difference. Where there is love anything can happen, even miracles."

He thought about her remark for the rest of the ride. *Where there is love.* Is that what made the difference? He did have a sense of no longer being alone in the world.

He rather liked the idea now that he was becoming adjusted to it.

As soon as they reached the quay, the crew members assisted them off the cruiser and waved goodbye. Marisa looked toward the streets. "Now what?"

"I need to make a phone call. Let's find a phone."

They walked several blocks before they found a public telephone. Within minutes Max was waiting for a distant phone to be answered. When it was, he said, "This is Max."

"I have your transportation arranged."

"There's no need. I'm all right now."

"Meaning?"

"My memory is back. My headache is gone. A few days' rest was all I needed."

"You're the best judge of your condition."

"Yes. Has there been any update on O'Donnell?"

"He reported in on schedule. Gave us information that would make certain that any men we send out would be in the interior for the next few days."

"So there's a good chance there will be a delivery made along the coast soon."

"That's what I concluded."

"Do you have men covering him?"

"Nothing so conspicuous. He would recognize them. I'm counting on the fact that he doesn't know we're on to him."

"But he saw Marisa."

"Does he have any reason to believe she'd report him?"

"Not particularly. He's aware that she left the Agency soon after I was promoted."

"Which might lead him to suspect that there's no love lost between you."

Interesting choice of words, Max decided.

"I'm going to try to send Marisa back to the States. However, I don't have any authority to force her to go and she insists that she wants to stay."

"Is there a problem with that?"

"You know the policy. She no longer has security clearance."

"Under the circumstances, I would suggest we bend the rules. If it weren't for Marisa, you'd still be working blind regarding the leaks in our system.''

Max knew when he was licked.

"I'll call after I've made contact."

"You do that" was the dry response.

He hung up and turned to Marisa. "We need to rent a car and buy a map of the area."

"We? Does that mean you're no longer going to argue about the fact that I want to go with you?"

"Would it do any good?"

"No."

"Then I'll save my energy. Let's go."

They were within half a block of the car rental place when a black limousine silently drew up beside them. Out of habit long ingrained, Max grasped Marisa's arm and moved away from the car. But he was too late.

"Just get in the car and the lady won't get hurt," he heard as he was shoved into the back seat of the limousine by two men with handguns. Marisa stumbled in behind him. The automobile shot away from the curb and headed for open country.

Max cursed under his breath. He'd been behind a desk for too damned long. He should never have let this happen.

Marisa was already righting herself and peering around the car. The window between the driver and the back seat was up. They could not identify the driver.

"What do you suppose this is all about?" she asked in a low tone.

"I think O'Donnell has known where we were all along," he replied.

"Was he behind the explosion on the trawler?"

"I wouldn't be at all surprised."

"Then how does he know we survived?"

"He's one of the best in the business. He may have had contacts all along the coast watching for us. We weren't exactly inconspicuous this morning coming off that yacht."

"What are we going to do?"

"Wait until we see what we're confronted with."

Max watched for landmarks, tried to spot familiar terrain, but it was difficult since he hadn't been in Europe for several years.

He settled back and waited for the next scene to begin.

After more than two hours the limousine pulled between two stone pillars and followed a long, winding drive toward a weathered chateau. Nothing looked familiar.

As soon as the car stopped, the back door nearest Max opened. He stepped out, then turned and assisted Marisa. The man who had opened the door motioned for them to climb the steps to the front door. Before they reached the top, the door opened. A middle-aged woman in a domestic's uniform nodded and led them into a large room.

"M'sieur will be here shortly," she intoned, then turned and left.

Although the home itself was old, it had obviously been renovated and the furnishings were quietly luxurious. The paintings were the kind seldom seen outside of museums. When Max heard the door open behind him, he turned.

A man he'd never seen before walked into the room and strode to Marisa.

"Thank you, my dear. You did exactly as I suspected you would. Harry will be pleased."

Max heard her gasp the name "Troy!" So this was the man married to Marisa's sister.

In his late forties, he was slim with a debonair demeanor that Max assumed would be pleasing to most women.

"Do you know where Timmy is? Did you take him? I've been looking all over for you—"

"Yes, I know, my dear. And I had to lead you on quite a chase until you decided to get some help." He turned and walked over to Max. "I don't believe we've met, although I've certainly heard a great deal about you. My name is Troy Chasen and you must be the famous Max Moran."

Max gave him a straight look, then lifted his brow. "I'm not certain what I'm supposed to be famous for. Would you care to clarify that statement?"

"Ah, Harry didn't mention your modesty… another admirable virtue."

"Troy," Marisa said, joining them beside one of the Old Masters' paintings. "What is this all about?"

"It's really very simple, my dear, and really ingenious on my part, I must admit. Harry has been complaining about his employer's irritating habit of ruining many of our shipments of the past few years. He—or actually, we—decided to get rid of the troublesome fly in our ointment. The problem was how to coax him into our web. It was only a fortuitous accident that Harry discovered that my sister-in-law was Marisa Stevens, a former agent with whom he had worked. That's when I knew exactly what I needed to do to get our friend here to visit us."

Marisa gasped and Max looked at her. She'd turned ashen as she stared at Chasen in horror. "Oh, no, Troy!"

"That's right. I've always known your little secret, my dear, I just didn't realize who Max really was until recently. It was easy enough to check out the details, as well as the timing. Put that together with the various comments Eileen has made over the years and it was easy enough for me to draw an accurate conclusion."

"I haven't the foggiest idea what you're talking about, Chasen," Max said. "Just what in hell are you threatening her with?"

"Threatening? Why, nothing. What I counted on and what Marisa was predictable enough to do has delivered you into our hands, Max. Threatened with the loss of her son, Marisa immediately went to his father for help."

Nine

"Where is Timmy, Troy?" Marisa demanded.

Max stared at the two of them, trying to make sense out of a senseless remark. Was the man deranged? What was he talking about? Marisa had mentioned that Troy wasn't the father of Eileen's son—Marisa's nephew.

"He's safe, Marisa. For the moment."

"How could you have done this, Troy? He's just an innocent child. You were always so good with him. Why would you put us both through such horror?"

"Necessity, my dear. Nothing more or less. We decided that Timmy would be the perfect lure to get Max over here, away from his protected environment."

"But he doesn't know," she cried. "Don't you understand? He never knew!"

Max had once noted, quite objectively, that in periods of high stress, most particularly in life-threatening circumstances, time seemed to slow down, as though to give a person the opportunity to take in every action around him, analyze it and act in order to protect himself. This strange phenomenon had served him well at different times during his career. This time, he could think of nothing to protect him from the knowledge he'd just received.

The actual force of the blow when it finally struck him was so strong that he felt himself stagger for a moment. Both Marisa and Chasen were watching him intently. Marisa registered distress. Chasen registered detached amusement.

Anger surged through him as he began to put all the pieces together. Everything had been planned, right down to her phone call asking for help. Somehow they had known that he would run to her side.

No! That wasn't what Chasen was saying. They thought he knew about the boy. They thought the boy would be the lure to get him over there, the boy he'd never known existed.

"So now that you have me, what do you intend to do with me?"

"Ah, yes. Get to the bottom line, is it? Harry always said you never wasted time with extraneous details. He seems to know you well."

"Cut the crap, Chasen. What do you want with me?"

"I want you to get out of our affairs. My part of the bargain was to produce you. It's now up to Harry to dispose of you."

"Where's Harry?"

"Unavoidably detained, I'm afraid. Unfortunately, we weren't able to guess exactly where you might surface along the coast, so we were prepared for several eventualities. Therefore, his absence couldn't be helped. We do have a nice room where the two of you can spend your time waiting for him. He should be here by morning."

"I want to see Timmy," Marisa demanded.

"I'm afraid that's not possible. It wouldn't do the child any good to see you so upset, anyway. But don't worry, Eileen and I will be wonderful adoptive parents. He's already used to us, spends as much time with us as he does with you. Of course he'll be sad to hear that his mother was killed in an unfortunate accident while abroad, but he's young. He'll get over it."

Chasen nodded his head and two burly men stepped into the room. "These gentlemen will show you to your room."

Neither Max nor Marisa spoke as they followed one of the men up a winding staircase and down a long, well-lit hallway. Max glanced over his shoulder and wasn't surprised to see that the second man had followed them.

The first man opened a door and waved them through. As soon as they walked past him, he shut and locked the door.

Max immediately went over to the windows and

discovered that they were barred. In less than five minutes he'd checked to see if there was another way out.

There wasn't.

Only then did he turn and look at the white-faced woman who sat in a straight-backed chair by an empty fireplace.

"Care to fill me in on the missing pieces?" he asked in a low voice.

Marisa turned and looked at him, her eyes filled with agony. "I fully intended to tell you, Max. When I realized how you felt about me I knew I'd made a dreadful mistake by not contacting you when I first found out I was pregnant. But I didn't know. I just didn't know."

"When, exactly, did you intend to tell me? I have a son...five years old, didn't you say...and I have to hear about it from some slimeball who's nonchalantly plotting to have me killed, and you reassure me that you intended to tell me? When?"

"I started to tell you when we were working in Teresa's garden, but I couldn't figure out a way to explain, since I'd already called Timmy my nephew."

"Does he know who his father is?"

She shook her head.

"Then how the hell did you explain his birth? Even five-year-olds are rejecting the stork story and the cabbage leaf theory."

"Max, please, I—"

"Max, please? Please, what? Please don't be angry? Please understand? Is this where you're going to tell me about how wonderful love is? How you kept the news that I had a son from me out of love?"

She came out of her chair. "Yes! Yes, I did. The man I made love to the night in the cave, the man with whom I made that beautiful baby boy ceased to exist once we returned to Washington. You became cold and autocratic, not the warm and tender man I thought I'd gotten to know."

"Well, for your information, cold and autocratic men have just as much right to be told they're going to become fathers as warm and tender ones have!"

"I know that! I'm not trying to excuse what I did. There's no excuse."

"I'm glad we've found something we can agree on."

They stood facing each other like two boxers in a ring, their bodies tense, their anger palpable.

"I had no idea I was pregnant when I resigned. I'd been at my sister's almost two months before it occurred to me that something was wrong. At first I thought it was because I was so upset. I'd quit the profession I enjoyed, moved across the continent from the man I loved—"

"Cut the bull, Marisa."

"You can stand there and look me in the eye and tell me that I don't love you?"

"Maybe you do. I have no way of knowing whatever it is you feel or whatever you want to name it. Let's just say I don't want any part of this wondrous love you keep throwing around. It's too damned painful. You ripped my insides out, lady, when you threw the job in my face and walked away. I was brand-new in a position of authority and responsibility. You didn't give me a chance to explain before you started giving me hell for being a chauvinist. You blamed me for everything any man had ever done or said to you that caused you to feel oppressed, from your father on.''

"I was out of line," she murmured.

"No kidding." He spun away from her and strode across the room. He reached the window, glanced out, then spun to pace back toward her. "You gave me all kinds of grounds to fire you that day, but I didn't. I sat there and listened. I took it. Why? You wanna know why? Because I thought, believe it or not, that I would then get the same opportunity I was giving you to tell you what I thought about the situation, what I felt about your remarks, and what I felt about you. But you didn't give me that chance. Oh, no! You sailed out of there like a queen who'd effectively berated her serf. So I decided to give you a chance to simmer down. I thought by the next day we would both be calm enough that I could explain why I wanted you to work in Washington, why I thought we should spend some off-duty time together.''

"I felt like such a fool when I got home that night," she admitted. "I'd made a complete ass of myself.''

"If you're looking for an argument on that one, you won't get one from me.''

She turned away, slowly walked over to the chair

she'd recently left and sat down, resting her face in her hands. "Oh, Max. I've made such a mess of things!"

He hadn't moved. "I'll second that."

She glanced up at him, stung by his coldness. "Well, you don't walk on water, either, you know."

"I've never pretended I did. But I've always done my best to be straight with people. You've had almost six years to get over whatever was bugging you. Six years to get in touch with me, either by phone, letter, or personal visit. Six years, Marisa."

"I know that! You have no idea how many nights I lay in bed writing imaginary letters, making imaginary phone calls, visualizing myself visiting you with Timmy, introducing you to him..."

"What does he look like?"

The sudden conversational change caught her off guard. "What?"

"The question wasn't that difficult."

"Oh! Well, he's got blond hair. It's getting darker as he gets older. And his eyes are a sherry color, like yours."

Max turned away, so that she was staring at his back.

"He's about average height for his age, a little thin, a wiry build, I guess you'd say. Very active. He's—"

"Why didn't you tell me about him?" he said in a low voice, his back still to her.

"I didn't know how! How do you tell something

like that…'you probably don't remember me, but'…or, 'Surprise'…or, 'by the way, Max, how do you feel about children'…or—"

He turned and looked at her in disgust. "Never mind. I get the picture."

She began to sob. "Damn…I was…determined not to…cry. I haven't…cried since I…found out he was…mis…sing. I reminded my…self that I was…a…pro…fessional…and I was…going to…find him…no matter…what!"

"Even if it meant asking me to help you."

"Yes. I mean, no, I didn't think about you at first. It was only…it was when I saw Troy talking to Harry and I…heard what they were saying…and I knew that something was drastically wrong…and that Troy was mixed up in something much worse than I could have imagined and that Harry was a part of it…and you trusted Harry and—"

He walked over to her. "Okay, okay, settle down, all right? You're right. I trusted Harry as much as I trusted anybody. He would have been one of the last ones I suspected. You may have saved a lot of lives by warning me when you did."

"But you may lose yours because I did!"

"I've lived with that risk for years. It comes with the territory."

She glanced around the room in despair. "So what are we going to do?"

He glanced over at the massive bed. "Get some sleep."

"Are you serious?"

"I couldn't be more serious. We're going to

have to be ready when Harry gets here in the morning. That means we're going to have to be rested and alert. One point in our favor—according to Chasen, Harry intends to make our demise look like an accident. That will give us a little more opportunity to mess up his plans.''

"Do you think Timmy is here?"

"My honest guess? No, I don't. I think Chasen wanted you to believe he has Timmy, but it wouldn't surprise me to learn that once you were over here Timmy was returned to your sister."

"She would have let me know."

"How?"

"I never thought of that. I could call her and ask. Oh, if only I knew he was all right I could rest easier. I've been so scared to even let myself think about what could have happened to him."

"Well, since our kind host has not seen fit to place a telephone at our disposal, you can shelve that idea for now." He walked over to the bed and pulled the spread down. "Do you have a problem with sharing the bed?" he asked without looking at her.

"I, uh, no, of course not. I, uh—"

"I give you my word that I will not touch you."

"Oh."

He'd been removing his shirt as he spoke, but her last monosyllable caused him to pause and look over his shoulder. "I'll be damned if you don't sound disappointed!"

"It's not that. I just thought about those days on

the yacht when everything was so different between us.''

He kicked off his shoes and stepped out of his pants before replying. ''The reason for the way I behaved on board ship,'' he said crawling into bed without looking at her, ''is quite simple. I was suffering from amnesia. I heard the doctor refer to me as your husband so I thought we were married.''

She stared at him in astonishment. ''You mean, all that time you thought that I was—''

''I thought we'd taken a vacation as a sort of second honeymoon. It seemed logical and it fitted all the circumstances. And if you'll remember correctly, you certainly didn't fight me off.''

She slipped out of the summer dress she wore, kicked off her sandals and padded to the other side of the bed. Max already had reason to know that George's daughter had a very provocative sense of style with regard to her underwear. He closed his eyes when she crawled into bed beside him.

''Max?''

''What?''

''I've never had any desire to fight you off. Not ever.''

Why had she decided to give him that choice piece of news at that particular time?

He turned his back to her and pounded his pillow.

''Max?''

''What?''

''We could both be killed tomorrow.''

"I'd say the odds are definitely in favor of that, yes."

"Do we have to go to sleep angry with each other?"

"I don't care how you go to sleep. Just do it."

"Max?"

"What!"

"I never wanted to hurt you."

"Oh, wow, Marisa. That makes everything okay then, doesn't it?"

"I love you, Max."

He didn't say anything.

"I believe in love. With all my heart. I believe that love can create miracles. I've seen it happen. I've felt it happen."

"Good, then love us up a miracle tomorrow and maybe we'll live to tell this to our grandchildren."

They were both silent, thinking of the implications of that last remark.

"Max, just hold me for a little while, all right? If you have to, pretend you're married to me again. I just don't want to be alone."

He heard the plea in her voice and almost groaned out loud. The woman had the damnedest ability to twist him around her little finger. No one had ever had that ability before or since. He hated it. He really did.

Then he rolled over and gathered her into his arms. They lay there together for several hours, neither one speaking, wondering what tomorrow would bring.

Max felt her body snuggled close to his before

he surfaced from sleep. She felt so good to him, and she fitted the curl of his body as though made for him. His arm was wrapped around her, hugging her closely against him.

What a hell of a time to find out that he was a father. He hadn't been in this much danger in years. He'd grown rusty, that was obvious by the way they had been so easily picked up and brought to their present location. He was past his prime and he knew it.

Because he had always been on his own, he'd never worried much about an assignment. He knew that he could be killed at any time, but so what? Everybody had to die sometime. In the meantime, he was doing something he enjoyed.

For the first time in his life he felt a strong desire to live, at least until he could see his son. He had a son. Timmy. Was that for Timothy? He wondered why she had chosen that name. Not that he would have wanted her to use his name. Maximilian was a mouthful. He'd never used his full name. Few people knew what it was, or that it was a family name.

He tried to picture his son. Did Marisa carry pictures of him? Even if she did, she wouldn't have them now. All she'd managed to hang on to was her passport.

She stirred against him, causing an immediate reaction within him. Not that he intended to do anything about it, but at least he knew he wasn't dead yet. If he had his way, he'd get through the next few hours, then head back to the States.

He wanted to live. Perhaps his determination would even the odds they had to face in the next few hours.

"Max?" she murmured in a sleepy voice.

"Yes?" He unconsciously tightened his arm around her midriff.

"I'm glad I'm with you. I've missed you so much these past few years. Being with you on the yacht was the most wonderful time of my life. It really was like a honeymoon."

"I know. I've been lying here thinking about it. Is there a chance you could be pregnant? I didn't think to protect you either time."

"No. It's not the right time, Max."

There was a knock on the door. Max rolled out of bed in one smooth movement, grabbed his pants and slipped them on before he said, "Yes?"

"Mr. O'Donnell has asked that we bring you downstairs" was the response.

"Give us five minutes, all right?"

"We'll tell him."

He turned to Marisa. "Not much time. I'll let you have the bathroom first."

She slipped out of bed and hurried to the adjoining room. Within a couple of minutes she came out and began to dress while he went inside. He looked into the mirror and rubbed his jaw. He didn't have time to shave. He'd have to go as he was.

Marisa was dressed and waiting for him when he reentered the bedroom. A moment later they heard another tap on the door. She reached for his hand. "Here we go," she said, taking a deep breath and exhaling with a gusty sigh.

"We'll do just fine. We've always made a great team. There's no reason to think we won't make it today."

Ten

Max saw Harry O'Donnell as soon as they arrived at the top of the staircase. O'Donnell stood with his back to them, speaking in low tones to one of the men standing guard by the door. He turned as soon as he heard them on the stairs.

"Good morning, Max. I hope you slept well."

Max didn't respond. He continued down the stairs with Marisa beside him. He studied his adversary carefully for any signs of weakness, but Harry was good. He showed nothing.

When they reached the massive foyer, Harry nodded to Marisa. "We meet again. You shouldn't have run away from us in Barcelona, you know. We would have been most willing to answer your questions."

Marisa stared at him without speaking. Never

had Max been more proud of her. Her training served her well. Not by the tiniest movement did she show any sign of nervousness or apprehension.

"Not very talkative, are you, but then perhaps I wakened you too early. Sorry about that." He waved them into the salon where they had seen Troy the night before. "We're having coffee in here this morning."

Max squeezed Marisa's hand in reassurance and she looked at him with a serene smile. They were in this together, all the way.

"You've probably wondered why I've gone to so much trouble to have you visit me here in my home," Harry said, sitting in the wing chair across from the sofa where Max and Marisa had chosen to sit. A young girl in a maid's uniform came in bearing a large silver service. Harry motioned for her to place it on the table between the sofa and chairs.

How civilized we're being, Max thought to himself as he watched Marisa pour coffee in three cups and hand each man one of them. We're so very proper as this jerk gloats over us.

Harry didn't seem to be enjoying himself as much as he might have hoped. Obviously their lack of response was irritating him somewhat. Good. An emotional man was easier to deal with because he wasn't thinking as clearly.

"I have you to thank for my home and fine surroundings, Max."

"Do you?"

Harry nodded, pleased once again. "You see, it

was when you were promoted over me that I decided I'd had enough of playing the dedicated public servant. Or in our case, private servant. I deserved that promotion. Not you. I'd been with the Agency longer and accomplished a hell of a lot more than you ever did.''

''I had no control over their choice, Harry. No more than you did.''

Harry looked over at Marisa and smiled. ''I obviously wasn't the only disgruntled one. You left not long after his promotion. You can imagine my shock when I learned that Troy's sister-in-law was Marisa Stevens, *the* Marisa Stevens I'd known in the Agency. And when he mentioned that you had given birth to a son a little less than nine months after leaving, it was easy enough to guess what had happened. You tried to trap Max into marrying you, and it didn't work.'' Harry laughed. ''Even I knew his views on the subject of marriage. He's never bothered keeping them a secret.''

''What's the point of this conversation, Harry?''

Harry smiled. ''I'm just enjoying the various nuances of this unique situation. You've been getting in my way these past couple of years, Max. I had to take out a few men with whom I'd worked amicably and it irritated me. I won't mind getting rid of you.''

''Do you really think no one else knows about you, Harry?''

''Ah, but you don't have proof of anything. After your death, evidence linking you to certain... misadventures...will be discovered.''

Max laughed.

The muscles in Harry's face tightened. "I'm so glad that I afford you so much entertainment." O'Donnell came to his feet. "Your deaths will be reported as an unfortunate accident. A couple of tourists traveling too fast on the winding coastline roads. It's easy to miscalculate a curve and go over the edge. It happens all too frequently."

"A fine plan, except for one minor problem."

"Which is?"

"Getting us into the car in the first place."

Harry's smile widened. "Oh, that won't be a problem at all. You see, you'll both be unconscious when you're placed in the car."

"I see."

"We've covered every possible eventuality. Why, I'll be one of the most visible mourners at the funerals. Two fellow agents on vacation. I might even mention that you had stopped by to spend the night with me while touring the countryside."

"And the car?"

"Already rented in your name."

"Ingenious."

"I agree."

Marisa leaned forward. "Where is Troy?"

"Earning his keep. Your visit has been a trifle awkward due to the timing. We expected you to show up several days ago."

"I take it you have a shipment coming in."

O'Donnell smiled once again. "I haven't the foggiest idea what you're talking about. I'm a U.S.

agent, Max. You know that. Anything more would be a conflict of interest.''

''Try treason.''

O'Donnell chuckled. ''Even more dramatic, but hardly accurate.''

''We'll let a jury of your peers make that decision.''

''Don't you wish, Max. Don't you wish.''

The door opened behind them and Harry looked up. One of O'Donnell's men said, ''We've brought both cars around.''

''Good, good. We need to take care of this matter as soon as possible.'' He motioned for them to stand. ''Sorry to rush you like this.''

Max knew what they had to do, and he knew he could count on Marisa. Without looking at her he strode toward the door, knowing she was somewhere behind him. The man at the door turned just as Max's foot hit the door, slamming it, while his arm came around the man's throat. He hooked his foot around the man's ankle and pushed, placing him in a vise. With his other hand he reached inside the man's coat and removed the pistol hanging in his shoulder holster and then turned both the man and himself to face the room.

All of this happened within five seconds.

Marisa barreled into O'Donnell's chest, catching him off balance, and with a practiced grip on his arm and shoulder, threw him over her shoulder so that he landed on top of the table holding the silver service.

The clatter was immensely satisfying to Max, who watched with the pistol in his hand.

Marisa found O'Donnell's pistol and held it on him, standing with her legs spread, both arms gripping the handle of the pistol.

Max shoved the pistol he was holding into the side of the man he'd disarmed and said, "Get over against the wall."

Keeping his eye on the man, he walked over to the rope pull that signaled the help, and tugged it.

In less than a minute the maid opened the door and came in. Her eyes widened when she saw the two men being held at gunpoint. Max smiled at her. Her eyes got larger.

"I'm afraid we made a mess of that lovely service you brought in earlier. Would you mind asking the chef to prepare more coffee, and perhaps something to eat. We missed our evening meal and are a little hungry."

The young woman scurried out while Marisa began to laugh.

Harry seemed to have regained some of the breath that had been knocked out of him when Marisa had launched herself into his rib cage. He no longer lay gasping in the shattered remains of the coffee table, silver service and china. "You're insane, Max."

Max didn't bother to reply. He just waited.

Within minutes the door opened once again. This time the maid was accompanied by four men, one of whom was obviously the chef. The other three appeared to be kitchen and garden help.

The chef took in the scene before nodding to Max. "Doesn't look as though you've lost your touch, boss. I couldn't have done it better myself."

"I'm glad you approve," Max responded drily, as the kitchen help pulled out handcuffs for O'Donnell and his henchman. "It took you long enough to get here."

"Hey, you're the one who wanted to play it this way. We were ready to take him last night."

Harry stood, his hands locked in front of him, and glared around him. "Who the hell are these people?"

Max smiled. "Oh, just some of my former agents. My boss let me know yesterday that he'd called in some of my most effective, but unfortunately retired, men. None of them ever worked in your sector, so I knew you wouldn't recognize them."

He walked over to Harry. "Let me introduce you." He nodded toward the man by the door. "The tall, black-haired, bearded one is Quinn McNamara, lieutenant colonel, retired, of the United States Air Force." He nodded to the two men who had handcuffed the man at the door. "The red-haired gentleman with the unrepentent grin on his face is Tim Walker, who currently resides in Colorado, his sidekick is Steve Donovan who did some work for me at one time in addition to his duties as a television news reporter."

Glancing at the man who stood beside Marisa, he said, "This man is Joel Kramer, now best known for turning out thriller novels based on some of his less savory adventures.''

He looked at Harry for a long moment before he continued. ''I know my reputation in the department with regard to the subject of marriage. These men preferred home life to what you and I chose, Harry, but they were prevailed upon to help us set the trap.'' He turned back to Quinn. ''What's going on outside?''

The dark-haired man replied, ''All of his people have been rounded up. We're watching his business associate. We'll be in on the arrival of the shipment that's due tonight.''

''Thanks, guys, for pitching in like this. I wasn't certain if you'd be available when I mentioned your names to the boss earlier.''

''You think you're so damned smart!'' Harry snarled, standing between Marisa and Joel. ''You think you've managed to get off scot-free. Well, I'm not going alone, you son of a—'' With a flick of his wrist Harry pulled out a small pistol no larger than his palm and fired at Max, who was standing less than three feet away.

Max saw the movement and heard the explosion at the same time he felt the bullet hit his chest. There was no pain at first. He felt as though a hand had punched him hard, taking his breath away. He saw Joel grab Harry and wrest the gun away from him, saw Marisa run to him calling his name, heard the commotion behind him.

All he could think about as he felt his knees crumple beneath him was *I never did get to meet my son.*

Eleven

"Daddy, why did you leave me?"

"Mommy, where are you?"

"Daddy, when are you coming back to go fishing? I've been waiting to go with you. I'll never go with anyone else, Daddy. Just you."

"Amanda? Come here, sweetie. Come to Maxie. See, Mom? She can walk. Watch her walk to me, Mom."

"Leave me alone. You're not my family. I don't have a family. Go play with your own kids."

"Don't touch me. Just leave me alone. No, I don't want to go play with the others."

"I'm not wearing those stupid clothes. I don't care where you got them. I can buy my own stuff. Just leave me alone."

* * *

"I don't care what you think. I didn't take your dumb earrings. Why would I want them? How come I'm the one you always ask when something is missing?"

"I don't care what time it is. I'll come home whenever I feel like it. You're not my boss."

"Get out of my room. You have no right to go through my things. No right! Can't a person have a little privacy?"

"Don't play tough with me, Julio. I'm not impressed. You're nothing but a two-bit punk. I've had tougher guys than you for breakfast. Now get lost!"

"Listen. This is my place, you hear me? It's not much but I pay the rent for this room, so you get the hell out and leave me alone."

"Aw, Johnny, I can't go back to school. It's been too long, man. I've been out too long. Give me a break, Johnny."

"Hey, Johnny, just wanted to let you know. I got accepted at UCLA. Yeah, no kidding. So, what do you think? Will I ever fit the part of big man on campus?"

"Max, can you hear me? Max, this is Marisa. Oh, Max, please hang in there. I know it's tough. I know you're really hurting, but I need you...and Timmy needs you, too. I want you to get better so I can yell at you again. I want you to yell at me. I deserve it. I got you into this mess. Oh, Max, please don't give up!''

"Max? This is Joel. I really feel rotten about this. Guess I've been out of the business for too long. I never thought to look for a hidden weapon. Man, he was quick.

"Look, all the guys are here to see how you're doing. I'm going to go now so that they can see you. Hang in there, buddy. You can make it. You're the toughest one of the bunch!''

"As you can see, there was considerable damage done to the chest area. The bullet barely missed the heart. The lung was punctured but seems to be responding nicely now.

"He came through surgery, which was a miracle in itself. He'd lost a considerable amount of blood. As soon as he was stabilized they flew him from France to our private hospital.

"He'd recently received a severe blow to the head that had weakened him considerably. We think it's a miracle that he's still alive.''

"Where there is love, Max, miracles can happen.

"It was a miracle that he survived surgery.

"It was a miracle he's still alive.

"Love can work miracles, Max. You just have to believe in them.''

"Hang in there, buddy. You can make it. I know you can.''

"Timmy's waiting to meet you, Max. He really needs you in his life. So do I, love. So do I."

"Run along and play, Maxie. Mommy's got to get the baby down for her nap."

"Yes, you may feed your sister, but try not to make a mess."

"Here, Max. Hold still. We want to get a picture of the two of you together. Now, then. That's it."

"No school for the next three months? Won't that be fun? A chance to play every day. And when you go back to school in September, you'll be a big old second grader. It won't be long until you've grown up big and tall, as big as your daddy."

"Mommy loves you, darling."

"Hey, big man, your dad loves you."

"See, Amanda loves you, too."

"I love you, Max."

"I love you."

"Love creates miracles. You can make it."

The first time he opened his eyes, the bright lights blinded him. He closed his eyes and kept them closed for a long time. Or at least what seemed like a long time.

The second time he opened his eyes, the room was in shadow. He kept his eyes open and looked around the hospital room. He was alone. There was a rustling sound like water trickling, as well as a steady beep from somewhere close by.

He was alive and hooked up to all sorts of machines. He started to wonder what time it was, but fell asleep before the thought was completed.

The next time he opened his eyes, he saw Marisa, sitting beside the bed and holding his hand. He attempted to tighten his grip and discovered how weak he was. Even that small movement caught her attention and she glanced at his face.

"Hi," she said in a whisper. She tried to smile but her mouth quivered.

She looked like hell. She was pale, and there were dark smudges beneath her eyes. She had lost weight, so that her cheekbones were more prominent than before, which drew attention to her eyes.

He licked his lips in an effort to moisten them. "This is getting to be a habit, me laid up in some bed." His voice sounded rusty from disuse.

"How are you feeling?"

He tried to smile, but wasn't certain of his success. "Like I was shot."

"I'm so sorry," she whispered.

"It wasn't your fault."

"Oh, but it was. I was the one who got you involved in this mess."

"No. It was all part of my job. What happened after I went down?"

"I thought those friends of yours were going to rip Harry apart. The shots caused the men on the outside to come running. We must have had twenty people on that case."

He closed his eyes, thinking about his superior's decision to call in all the troops. So he hadn't completely relied on Max's reassurances that he could handle the situation. There were times when it felt good to be outguessed.

"Why don't you sleep now?" she whispered when he started to speak.

"I need to know what happened."

She stroked his hand. "Some of the men took charge of Harry while the rest were determined to get you to medical attention." She looked away, then back at him. "Even though Harry was thoroughly searched, he obviously had hidden a capsule of cyanide. They found him dead in his cell the next morning."

So it was over. Harry was gone, the smuggling ring that they had been after for so long appeared to be stopped.

"What about Troy?"

"Unfortunately, he got caught in the crossfire between our people and the men bringing the cargo in. He was killed instantly."

"How is your sister taking it?"

"It was a shock to her, of course, but she said that she felt a certain amount of relief. She had discovered some time ago that he wasn't the man she had thought he was when they married. They had not been getting along. She was afraid of him. He'd made it clear that he wouldn't consider a divorce."

"No wonder. He didn't want his financial situation to be scrutinized."

The soft whoosh of the door opening caused them to look up. A bright-eyed nurse came in. "Mr. Moran, you need to rest. The monitors are showing an increased pulse rate." She smiled at Marisa. "I'm sure you understand."

"Are you coming back?" he asked, trying to sound nonchalant.

"Yes" was all she said.

He smiled and was immediately asleep.

Marisa left the hospital, feeling a sense of hopefulness that she had not had since Max had been shot. She would never forget the horror of that moment, or the days and nights of wondering if he was going to make it.

She had no more reason to stay. In fact, she needed to return to Seattle and Timmy, although Eileen insisted that he was doing fine with her and that there was no reason to be concerned.

Max had been right. Timmy had been returned to Eileen the day after Marisa had left. He'd been full of excited tales about all the things he'd done with one of the men who worked in Troy's warehouse. He'd never understood what had happened.

Now, at last, Max knew of Timmy's existence. She wished he had learned about his son in another way, but there was no point worrying about that now.

When Max was recovered, they would talk about his meeting Timmy. Timmy was such an outgoing little guy that he'd probably take to Max with no problem.

The problem was how Max was going to respond to the little boy. She knew that Max had been alone most of his life. He'd never allowed anyone to get

close to him. Would having a son make a difference to him?

Only time would tell.

He felt as weak as a three-day-old baby and he
hated it. Everything irritated him—most especially,
the insistent cheerfulness of the nurses. When the
door opened again, he scowled.

"What a picture of cheerful recuperation you
make," Marisa said, coming in the door.

"I'm fed up with cheerfulness!"

"I see they have you up now." He was sitting
in a large overstuffed chair by the window.

"Not fast enough to suit me."

"My, we are in rare form today."

"Now don't you start on me. I've had it up to
here with bossy females telling me what to do."

She smiled and sat down in the straight-back
chair by the bed. "I know. You're used to being
the one giving the orders. Not much fun when
you're on the receiving end."

He crossed his arms and glared at her. When she
continued to smile, he relented. "What's that
you're wearing?"

She glanced down at the dress she'd bought the
day before. She'd been forced to buy a small ward-
robe since her belongings had been shipped from
Barcelona to Seattle. She started to explain, when
he said, "Not the dress. I'm talking about the perfume."

"Just something I picked up, why?"

"No reason. You're looking more rested these days. How are you feeling?"

"Much better, now that you're improving."

They stared at each other for a moment before Max dropped his gaze. "There's no reason for you to be hanging around here. Shouldn't you be with Timmy?"

"Yes. That's one of the things I came to tell you. I need to get back to Seattle. School is starting soon. I need to plan my classes."

"So you came to say goodbye."

"That's right. And to invite you to come visit us when you're feeling better."

"I don't think that's such a good idea."

"Why not?"

"You've got your own life. You and Timmy have done just fine without me. There's no reason for me to confuse him."

"Max?"

"What?"

"I've told Timmy that you're his father, that you were hurt and that I was staying here until I was certain you were out of danger."

"You did what? Why would you do such a thing? Especially now. You never bothered to tell him about me before, so why—"

"I didn't tell him before because I was a coward. I ran from a situation I didn't know how to handle. I hope I've matured a little since then. Besides, things are different now."

"What do you mean?"

She grinned. "I know how you feel about me."

"So?" he asked belligerently.

"Max," she said in a patient voice, "I love you very much. I understand that you don't have any reason to trust or believe in love, but I have enough trust for both of us. The most important thing is that you're alive. The rest can be worked out."

She stood and walked over to him. "They say that grouchiness is a sign of recovery. If that's the case you're doing great!" She leaned down and kissed him very lightly on the lips. "Take care of yourself. Call me when you can. I hope you'll consider coming to Seattle for a visit soon."

He watched her walk out of the room, out of his life, and he wanted to yell at her to leave him alone. He didn't need her in his life. He didn't need anyone in his life. He was used to being alone. He much preferred it.

The ache in his chest was due to his recent injury. He'd get over it and resume his life. Nothing had changed. Nothing at all.

Twelve

"**Y**ou wanted to see me?" Max asked, standing in front of his superior's desk.

"Sit down, Max" was the reply.

He would rather face a firing squad than the upcoming interview.

"How are you feeling?"

"I'm making it."

"You came back to work too soon."

"I'm all right."

"Didn't the doctors suggest you give yourself a couple of months to fully recover?"

"I was going crazy, sitting around my place doing nothing."

"Then I would suggest that this is a good time for you to take a vacation."

"I never take vacations, you know that."

"Perhaps it's time for you to consider developing new habits."

"I can't just walk away from my job, sir."

"Are you under the impression that you're indispensable?"

"Obviously not. You've gotten along without me for several weeks now."

"Galling, isn't it?"

"I don't know what you mean."

"You've made this job your life, Max. How long have you been with the Agency?"

"Almost twenty years."

"You could consider retirement, you know."

"And do what?"

"Develop some hobbies, perhaps? Get married? Have a family?"

"What has Marisa said to you?" he asked suspiciously.

Obi-wan gave him a beatific smile. "Ah, so you have someone already in mind."

"Absolutely not. No, sir, I don't. I mean, I'm willing to face up to my responsibilities. I've already set up a monthly income for her and the boy, and—"

"Are you saying you have a son, Max?"

"Didn't you know?"

"Despite my reputation, I am not omniscient" was the reply. "How old is your son?"

"Five."

"A delightful age. I take it that he's Marisa's child?"

"Yes."

"Well, then, it looks as though you've managed to get a head start on that family!"

"You don't understand…sir. I mean, I know nothing about this fathering business. I lost my parents when I was quite young. I haven't been in a family environment for years. I'm not husband material, that's all. As for being a father—"

"Obviously, you've given the matter considerable thought."

"I've thought of nothing else since I found out about the boy. If I thought I could be the father he needs, of course I'd do whatever was necessary. But I can't just—"

"Have you met the boy?"

"No, sir."

"Well, then. Your course is clear. Take some time off, go to Marisa—she's in Seattle, didn't you say?—and get acquainted with your offspring."

"But, sir—"

"That's a direct order, Max." The man behind the desk looked at his calendar. "Report to me again on November first."

"*November!* That's almost three months…sir."

"Goodbye, Max. Have a safe journey. Be sure to give Marisa my regards."

Who did he think he was, *God?* muttered Max to himself as he returned to his office. Nobody could force him to do anything. He could resign. That's what he'd do. Resign.

Yeah, he missed her. He couldn't deny that. Despite everything he could do, his thoughts continued to return to those days they had spent on the yacht, when he had felt young and free to love Marisa in every way possible.

He'd wake up in the middle of the night, dreaming of making love to her. Her response to his lovemaking haunted him.

He'd thought about asking her to move back to D.C. but had eventually discarded the idea. She had a full and satisfying life in Seattle. Besides, she'd never hinted that she would consider the possibility of such a move.

Max reached his office and opened the door. Two workmen were in there.

"What's going on?"

One of them looked around. "We're moving everything out of this room. We have orders to paint and recarpet."

His boss never left anything to chance. Max took a few of his personal belongings out of the desk and left the building.

When he landed at the Seattle-Tacoma airport, it was raining. He had decided against calling Marisa to tell her he was coming. He wasn't absolutely certain he was going to see her. He might charter a boat, sail through the San Juan Islands, do a little fishing.

He hated to fish.

So maybe he'd drop by her place for a limited visit. He knew the address by heart. It would be the polite thing to do, as long as he was this close.

He retrieved his luggage from the carousel and

walked outside. When a taxi pulled up, he got in and gave the driver Marisa's address.

Might as well get the visit behind him.

She probably wasn't home. It was Saturday. She was probably running errands or shopping. He'd leave a note to let her know he was in town.

By the time the taxi reached the Seattle suburb where Marisa lived, the rain had stopped, and in the thin, watery sunshine drops of water gleamed on every surface.

Max paid the driver, grabbed his bag and got out.

The house was Victorian, with gingerbread trim. He glanced around, studying the street that seemed filled with trees. In some ways it reminded him of the house in Southern California where he'd lived with his parents—large lawns fenced in, roses climbing fenceposts and porches.

A quiet place. A safe place for children.

He made himself pick up his bag and walk up to her porch. Without hesitating, he rang the doorbell. The front door was filled with a frosted-glass pane. He could see nothing inside.

He reached for the buzzer again. Before his finger came into contact with the surface, the door slowly swung open.

Max started to speak, then realized there was no one there.

"Hello," came a small voice.

Max glanced downward and saw a small boy peering up at him under a mop of wavy, light brown hair. The eyes were the same color as those he stared into each morning in the mirror.

He froze. He could feel his pulse rate jump and perspiration break out on his forehead.

"Hi," he managed to reply.

"What do you want?"

"I, uh— Is your mother at home?"

"Yes."

They both waited.

"May I speak to her?" Max finally asked.

"Just a minute," the little boy said, then closed the door in Max's face.

Max stood there, undecided. Should he wait or ring the doorbell again? Obviously Marisa had trained her son not to allow strangers into the house, which was good.

There was no doubt that he was a stranger.

He had turned away to look out at the street once more when he heard the door swing open. "I'm sorry about leaving you out on the—" she began to say. Then she saw who it was. "Max! Omigod! I can't believe it! You're here!" She launched herself into his arms.

He drew her tightly against him and kissed her the way he'd been dreaming about for weeks. She felt wonderful in his arms—warm and vital, and he could smell that wonderful scent she'd been wearing at the hospital.

When she finally pulled far enough away to take a deep breath, she hugged him fiercely to her. "Why didn't you tell me you were coming? Oh, this is wonderful! Come in, come in. I didn't mean for you to stand out here on the porch."

She took his hand and led him into the entryway.

He glanced around, seeing highly polished wood and gleaming brass, hardwood floors with bright scatter rugs and a stairway that led to the floor above.

"When did you get here? How long can you stay? Oh, where did Timmy go? I want you to meet him."

Max grinned. He was feeling better by the minute. "I just got off the plane and I've made no plans at all. I've been kicked out of my office and ordered not to return to work until the first of November."

"Oh, that's wonderful!"

"It's going to take a little getting used to."

She led him into a large room that seemed to have a multitude of windows covered with some kind of gauzy material that allowed the light to come through. "Have you eaten? Would you like some coffee?"

"Coffee sounds good."

"Then let's go into the kitchen. Timmy? Come here, sweetheart. There's somebody I want you to meet."

Why had he thought this was going to be so difficult? Max asked himself several hours later. They'd just finished a wonderful meal. He couldn't remember the last time he'd had a home-cooked meal.

He was having difficulty visualizing this same woman tossing a man almost twice her size over her shoulder. Watching her with Timmy caused him to ache with an incomprehensible emotion.

He found Timmy fascinating.

"More pie, Max?" she was asking, bringing him out of his reverie.

"Oh, no, thank you."

He watched Timmy industriously clean his plate and smiled at the recent memory of being introduced to his son.

Timmy had come back from where he'd been playing when she called him. Marisa had knelt beside him and said, "Do you remember when I called you and said I was visiting with your daddy in Washington, D.C.?"

He eyed Max speculatively, then nodded. This kid was no dummy. He knew something was up.

"Well, he's come to visit us."

Max didn't know what to do. He knew nothing about kids. He could scarcely recall his own childhood.

They looked at each other in complete silence.

Marisa chuckled. "Come on, guys. I've got homemade cookies." She ruffled Timmy's mop of hair. "How about a glass of milk?"

He nodded, but he didn't take his eyes off Max.

They'd spent most of the day that way, allowing Marisa to fill in the silences with light conversation. She acted as though a man met his son every day. As though it was no big deal.

Now that they were finishing dinner, Max realized that he'd begun to relax. There was something about the homey atmosphere and Marisa's nonchalance that soothed him.

"Why don't you guys go into the living room while I clear the table."

"Let me help," Max offered, preferring to do anything rather than make conversation with the little boy whose gaze never seemed to leave him.

"Oh, that's all right. It won't take a minute. Go ahead." She made a shooing gesture toward the living room where Timmy had already gone.

Max reluctantly followed.

He sat on the sofa and watched Timmy hook up a miniature train that had been hand carved.

"Where did you get your train?"

"My aunt Eileen gave it to me for my birthday."

"When is your birthday?"

"June twenty-seventh."

"You're five now?"

"Uh-huh."

End of conversation.

Max was way over his head and he knew it. He just didn't know where to go from here.

"My mom says you work to get rid of bad guys and that you're really brave."

"Does she?"

"Uh-huh. And she said a bad guy shooted you in the chest and that you was sick for a long time."

"That's true."

"Does it still hurt?"

"Not much."

"That's good." He began to pull his train along the blue-striped border of the large area rug. He made the first circuit in silence before he spoke again. "Are you really my daddy?"

Here it comes. "Yes, I am."

"How come I never saw you before?"

Good question. "Well, I guess it's because I work long hours and never took the time to come out to see you."

"Oh. Didn't you want to see me?"

Now how did he handle that one? "Yes. I wanted to see you very much." He recognized the truth in his words as he spoke them. From the moment he'd learned about Timmy he'd felt a yearning to see him. But he'd been afraid. He was still afraid, but he wasn't certain what was causing his fear.

"I wanted to see you, too," Timmy said with a nod and began the second circuit of his train around the room.

"You did?"

"Uh-huh. I didn't know where you lived or anything. I thought you might live somewhere close. But Mom said you lived a long way away and that someday we could go visit you, but she never said when."

"Timmy?" Marisa called from the other room. "Come on. It's time to get ready for bed, darling."

His son got a pained expression on his face so familiar to Max that he almost laughed out loud. He'd caught a glimpse of the same expression on his own face more than once.

There was no way that Marisa could have forgotten the father of her child. Not with so many reminders.

"I have to go to bed now," Timmy said with commendable resignation. "Will you be here tomorrow?"

"I might be," Max offered cautiously.

"Good," Timmy replied with satisfaction. "I'd like that."

"You would?"

"Uh-huh. If it isn't raining tomorrow, I can take you out to my backyard. I have this big tree house that my mom made for me. We sit up there sometimes and look out. Maybe you'd like to do that with me."

Max could scarcely swallow around the lump in his throat. He couldn't say anything, so he nodded.

"Timmy! Your bathwater's getting cold."

"See ya," Timmy said with a tiny smile on his face.

Once again Max couldn't say a thing.

"He told me you built him a tree house." He and Marisa were in the living room once again, while Timmy was sound asleep upstairs.

"Yes. I decided that every little boy deserved a tree house, even though Eileen is constantly worrying that he's going to fall out of it and break something."

"Weren't you afraid?"

"Terrified. But I also knew that I couldn't coddle him. He needed the space to grow without being smothered."

"You've done a wonderful job with him, Marisa."

"You have no idea how good it makes me feel to hear you say that. There were times when I was so scared and so uncertain of myself. I wanted to call you, to talk to you about him, to ask questions. There's so much I don't know."

"I don't, either. It's frightening to think about how much I don't know about children."

"The nice thing is that they're patient. They'll wait for you to learn." They were quiet for several moments before Marisa said, "I want to thank you for opening the account for Timmy. You didn't have to do that, you know."

"I would have done it sooner, if you'd told me about him."

"You're never going to forgive me for that, are you?"

"It's not that, exactly. I just feel that I'm starting out as a parent five years behind."

"You'll do fine, Max. I know you will. We can work out a schedule where he can come to visit you whenever you have the time for him. Just think of all the things you can show him, particularly when he gets older. He'll have the best of both of our worlds. It will work out, I know it will."

She was saying all the right things, answering questions that he'd thought about but hadn't known how to bring up. Now that she was making it easy for him, he could relax, knowing that things were working out.

Couldn't he?

"I don't think that's going to work, Marisa. I've been on my own too long. I wouldn't know how to look after a child."

Thirteen

Marisa heard his words with a sinking heart. He'd been unusually quiet all day, but she had put that down to his normal reticence and the strangeness of being in her home and seeing Timmy for the first time.

"I see" was all she could say.

"I want to do more with Timmy. It's just that I don't know how. I haven't a clue how to behave around him."

"You did just fine today."

"Because you were here."

"Well, once you get used to him, maybe—"

"The thing is, I don't want to ship him back and forth between us. I think he deserves two parents who live together and look after him together."

Marisa stiffened, wondering if she was understanding him correctly. This was Max, the man who blew up whenever any of his men decided to marry. Surely he couldn't be suggesting that—

"I think we should get married."

He was. He was actually suggesting marriage.

"Oh, Max." He looked so tortured, like a man facing the agonies of a dental chair. She wrapped her arms around his neck and kissed him. Never had she seen him any more tense than he was at the moment.

She teased him by running her tongue across his bottom lip. He groaned and gathered her close to him. "Oh, God, honey. I've missed you so damned much." He buried his face against her neck.

"Max. Marrying me would go against all of your principles."

"I don't care," he muttered in a muffled voice.

"We live on opposite coasts."

"Mm-hm." He began to nibble on her ear.

"We can't just— Mm, Max, that feels so good."

He finally drew away and looked at her. "I know there are things to work out between us. But we owe it to Timmy to try. We brought him into this world. He deserves the best the two of us can give him."

"Is that the reason you want to marry me?"

"I'm not going to lie to you. The thought of marriage sends cold chills down my spine. I've got almost two months before I go back to work. I thought we could use the time to get better acquainted. I'd like Timmy to get used to me and I need time to get used to him. Meanwhile—" He began to kiss her along her jawline.

"Meanwhile?" she managed to ask.

"Maybe you can help me learn to be around little boys."

"You'll do fine."

When his mouth found hers, she melted against him, eager for his touch. When he finally pulled away from her, she lay against his shoulder, her eyes closed.

"I need to leave."

"You can always stay here," she said with a dreamy smile.

"I don't think that's a good idea."

She opened her eyes slowly. "Why not?"

"I think it would be confusing for Timmy. He needs to adjust to the idea of having me around more often on a gradual basis."

She sighed. "I suppose you're right." She studied him for a moment. "Max?"

He lifted his brows in inquiry.

"Are you sure that you want this?"

"Honey, I'm not sure about anything at this point. My entire life has been turned upside down. All I know is my job and it's just been moved out of my reach for three months. I'm drifting out to sea without a rudder or a paddle. All I could think about on the flight out here was that for the first time in my life, I have a place to go and people to see. I find that really scary."

"But you're not afraid of anybody, Max. You faced dangerous men on a regular basis for years. What's so frightening now?"

"I'm out of my element. I have nothing to offer

you or Timmy. It surprises me that you haven't found someone else in all this time.''

"I never wanted anyone else, even when I knew I didn't have a chance with you.''

He kissed her again, slowly and with great thoroughness. ''I need to go.''

"If you insist on leaving, I want you to take my car.''

"But won't you need it?''

"Not before morning. Then we'll have to decide a few things. If you're on vacation, then I want you to enjoy yourself.''

He smiled, a slow, masculine smile that made her heart race.

"What I mean is,'' she hastened to add, ''you've told me that you've never taken a vacation before. So we need to plan some trips. Maybe travel over to Vancouver Island on the weekends when I can go with you. Perhaps during the weekdays you and Timmy can spend some time together, get acquainted.''

He nodded slowly. ''I suppose.''

She grinned. ''You might try a little more enthusiasm.''

Max shook his head. ''I'm really way over my head on this one.''

She gave him a quick kiss. ''I have faith in you. Tomorrow we'll find you a place to stay not far from here, maybe get a rental car. What do you think?''

"I think I'm glad I came here.''

She hugged him. ''So am I. I'm going to show

you that being a daddy and eventually a husband can be fun.''

"Did you like to play ball when you was a kid?'' Timmy asked around a mouthful of hamburger.

Max studied the earnest face across the table in the fast-food restaurant where he and Timmy were indulging themselves after spending a couple of hours at the zoo.

"Uh, yes. I guess maybe I did.''

"Can't you 'member?'' Timmy asked sympathetically.

"Well, that was a long time ago, I have to admit.''

With a wise nod, Timmy suggested, "Back when there was dinosaurs and monsters and things, right?''

Max choked on his drink. "Not quite *that* long ago.'' He wiped some ketchup from Timmy's chin and silently handed him his drink.

During the two weeks he'd been in Seattle, Max had spent part of each day with Timmy. Marisa had been right. He was beginning to understand the boy and that scared the hell out of him. Feeling vulnerable was not a condition he enjoyed. Having a five-year-old walking around with Max's heart firmly clasped in his small hand made him more than a little nervous.

He also realized that he had been getting in touch with his own childhood once again. This time he was remembering fewer of the painful memories and more of the pleasurable ones.

One day he'd bought a kite and Timmy had

helped him to put the wretched thing together. He'd been reminded of the many times his dad had patiently worked with him on similar projects. Suddenly his parents seemed to be very close and very real to him. Long-forgotten conversations were surfacing, and he was getting in touch with the young boy inside of him that had hidden away in fear and panic. Timmy was coaxing him out to play.

Max didn't know what he would have done without Marisa. She continued to be nonchalant about the whole process of getting to know Timmy, ignoring Max's awkwardness.

Max felt as though he'd been an emotional cripple for years, as though he'd packed his emotions away and was only now rediscovering them. He was scared, but for the first time in a long while Max felt truly alive.

Now he stared across the table, able to recognize by his expression that Timmy was about to ask another of his innumerable questions.

"Was you ever a soldier?"

"Of sorts, I suppose. I wore a uniform for a couple of years."

Timmy appeared to accept his response, for which Max was grateful. He never knew what to expect from the boy.

"I'm going to be a soldier when I get big," Timmy announced with an emphatic nod, "and kill lots of bad guys."

"Bloodthirsty little guy, aren't you?" Max muttered.

"Huh?"

"Nothing. Are you about through with your

hamburger?'' Max looked at the meat and bread, all that Timmy had wanted at a place that bragged about putting everything on a burger. Preoccupied by his unrelenting and eternal quest for knowledge, Timmy had managed to take only two bites.

Timmy studied his burger for a moment, then resolutely picked it up and took a giant bite. Max had visions of the child choking and frantically tried to recall the Heimlich maneuver in case he was called upon to save his son's life.

His son. He found himself staring at the mop of unruly hair, the big eyes, the turned-up nose with its faint scattering of freckles and felt a warmth in his chest that spread throughout him. He smiled.

''Have you ever killed anyone?'' Timmy asked after he swallowed.

Fortunately, Max had already finished his meal by that time or he might have needed some medical assistance himself. He forced himself not to show more than polite interest in the question.

''No one who readily comes to mind.''

''Oh.''

Damned if he didn't sound disappointed!

''My friend Davey said that his dad was in the army and fought in Nam.'' Timmy frowned. ''Do you know Nam?''

''I've heard it mentioned once or twice,'' Max replied drily.

''Davey says his dad kilt lots of people. Sometimes his dad still dreams about it.''

''Yeah, that can happen.''

''I don't think I'd like that.''

''No.''

In a sudden shift of mood, Timmy brightened. "Do you like to fish?"

Max eyed him warily. "Why do you ask?"

"Davey and his dad go fishing all the time."

Max saw the trap that yawned widely before him. He just didn't know what to do about it. "Do they?" he asked in as noncommittal a tone as possible.

"Uh-huh. Once they took me with them out on this big boat."

"Did you enjoy it?"

Timmy's eyes sparkled. "Oh, yes."

"Did you fish?"

"Nah. I just watched."

"Do you like to fish?"

Timmy shrugged in elaborate unconcern. "I dunno. Nobody ever teached me how."

Max knew he could let it go. He could distract Timmy in several ways, but he knew what his son was trying to tell him. Over the past weeks he had learned to recognize the nuances of Timmy's seemingly unrelated questions. Timmy wanted a father. He wanted someone about whom he could talk with his friends.

For years Timmy had listened and learned about fathers and what they did and who they were. He'd listened but he'd had nothing to share. Until now.

"Would you like me to teach you how to fish?"

Timmy's eyes grew big. "You know how?"

"My dad taught me when I was about your age."

"And you'd teach me?" he asked in wonderment.

Max could feel his heart racing, his pulse pounding, and he knew his forehead was damp. ''I'll teach you.''

Once again Max approached Marisa's front door. More than two months had passed since the first time, but he was just as nervous.

He rang the bell. When the door swung open he immediately looked down at the small boy standing there.

''Daddy!''

Max felt his breath catch in his throat. The eagerness with which Timmy greeted him continued to astound him. He wasn't sure whether he would ever be able to take for granted hearing his son call him by that name.

''Hello, Timmy. You're looking remarkably well groomed.''

Timmy eyed him suspiciously, then glanced down at his new shoes, pants, shirt and jacket before he asked, ''What does that mean?''

Max grinned and picked him up, hugging him. ''It means that I didn't expect you to stay so clean.''

Timmy draped his arm around Max's neck and nodded. ''Yeah. Mom said I was going to be in big trouble if I got dirty.''

''And what would that be?''

Timmy cocked his head, thinking. ''I pro'bly couldn't play in my tree house and stuff like that.''

''That's quite a threat. I'll have to remember it for future use.'' He walked into the living room and sat down in one of the overstuffed chairs. Timmy leaned contentedly against him.

"You're going to sleep with my mommy," Timmy announced.

Max wondered if he would ever get used to Timmy's candid comments. "Is that so?"

Timmy nodded. "Yes. My mom said so."

"Well, then it must be true."

Timmy smiled. "I'm glad. Mommies and daddies are s'posed to sleep together."

"Ah."

"But first you're going to take a trip."

"That's true."

"Over to Victoria."

"Uh-huh."

"Without me."

The conversation was suddenly making sense. "Well, yes, we are, but we won't be gone long. We'll scout around to see all the fun things we can do so that the next time we go you'll go with us and we can do all those fun things together."

"Really?"

"Really."

"You promise not to have any fun without me?"

"I wouldn't think of it."

Max glanced up at the sound of Marisa's laughter as she walked into the room. She, too, was dressed in festive attire. She wore a white lace dress over a soft pink material that somehow made her skin glow. He wasn't sure how she did that. All he knew was that he loved her so much that his chest ached with the feeling.

"I'm not certain I like the idea of your promising not to have fun while you're with me."

Max grinned. "Well, there's fun and then there's fun."

Timmy climbed down from Max's lap. "Wow, Mom! You look like the Christmas angel on our tree!"

"I couldn't have said it better myself, Timmy," Max said, standing. "I take it you're ready."

She nodded. "I know this is going to sound ridiculous, but I'm really nervous."

"Join the club."

"I mean, I'm not nervous about what we're doing, it's just knowing that all those people are there, watching."

"You're the one who insisted on letting everybody know."

She nodded. "I told you I'm being silly and I know it."

Timmy took her hand. "If you don't want to go away, you can come to the movies with Auntie Eileen and me," he offered in a soothing manner.

Max saw the mischief gleam in Marisa's eyes as they met his. Damn, but he loved her sense of humor. She was waiting for him to comment, but he refused.

"Thank you for the invitation, Timmy. I'll get over being nervous, I'm sure."

Max wished he could be so sure about himself, but he didn't say anything. He knew that he wasn't going to change his mind. He just wanted the whole thing behind him.

He leaned over and kissed Marisa softly on the lips. Timmy giggled.

"Isn't there some rule that the groom isn't suppose to kiss the bride before the wedding?" she murmured when he lifted his head.

"I believe the tradition is that the groom is not to *see* the bride," he replied. "The way I look at it, we shot tradition all to pieces when we planned to take our five-year-old son to the wedding. But I absolutely draw the line about company on the honeymoon." He took Timmy's hand, then reached for Marisa with the other one. "C'mon. We've got people waiting to see if I'm actually going to go through with this. I wouldn't want to disappoint anybody!"

As soon as they pulled up in front of the small church, Max knew that their invitations hadn't been ignored by anyone. Not only were Marisa's sisters, Eileen and Julie, there, but he also spotted Quinn and Jennifer McNamara, Steve and Jessica Donovan, Tim and Elisabeth Walker, and Joel and Melissa Kramer. None of those men were ever going to let him forget what a rough time he'd given them for getting married and leaving the Agency. Was it any wonder that each of them had come to witness him metaphorically eat his words?

During the ensuing greetings and congratulations, and especially during Timmy's introduction to everyone, Max knew that he wouldn't have wanted it any other way. Somehow it seemed fitting to have them witness his change of heart.

He remembered the scenes when these former agents had come to tell him they were leaving the

Agency and why. He remembered his cynicism and scorn at their utter conviction that what they were doing was right for them. Only now could he remember the patience and compassion he'd seen in their eyes at the time. He'd been puzzled then. Now he understood. Somehow he would have to find a way to apologize for his narrow vision. At long last, he was part of the group of men who were ready to admit to their vulnerability without fear of jeopardizing their strength.

The ceremony wasn't as painful as he had expected—nor was the informal reception and unmerciful teasing he received shortly thereafter. But he was more than ready to catch the small plane that flew them to Victoria at midafternoon.

When he closed the door to the honeymoon suite behind the courteous bellhop, Max felt as though the world had been locked out. For the first time in months, he and Marisa were finally alone.

She stood in the middle of the ornately decorated suite, glancing around. "The Canadians really know how to make you feel welcome, don't they?" she murmured, pointing to the bowl of fruit and a large arrangement of flowers.

Without commenting, Max walked over and slipped his arms around her waist. "Still nervous?" he asked in a low voice.

She gave a shaky laugh. "I'm not sure. I feel a little strange. I've never been married before."

"I have." She gave him a startled glance before he went on. "When I woke up on the yacht and heard you refer to me as your husband, I felt very married. As I recall, I complimented myself on my excellent taste.'' He brushed his lips across her cheeks. "I still do.''

He could feel the tenseness in her body slowly leaving her. She wound her arms around his neck and hugged him. "Oh, Max! Thank you for saying that. I've been having the most horrific thoughts about having trapped you in some way. I didn't sleep at all last night thinking about it.''

"I didn't sleep last night, either, but it wasn't because I was feeling trapped into anything.''

She glanced up at him. "No?''

He pulled her closer so that her body was molded against him. "Uh-uh. I kept thinking of what I intended to do as soon as I finally got you alone.''

She smiled up at him, her eyes shining.

"Come to think of it, how do couples ever get any privacy after their first child? It's a wonder there aren't more only children in this world!''

"Max?''

Why was she looking at him in such an amused way. "Yes?''

"You're already missing Timmy, aren't you?''

"Missing Timmy! Are you kidding? That kid can come up with questions faster than a Senate investigating committee, and every bit as penetrating. I feel as though I've been given a reprieve.'' He took her hand and drew her into the bedroom. "Of course I did think about how much he would have enjoyed the plane ride and the chance to see Puget Sound from the air. We'll have to go shopping tomorrow and maybe find him a souvenir for—'' Marisa placed her fingers across his lips.

"I miss him, too, you know. But we'll be home in a couple of days."

He took his time removing her dress and underdress, treating her as though she were a gift-wrapped package that he was savoring. When he lifted her to place her on the bed, he had only to remove her shoes and panty hose. "Do you have any idea how much I love you?" he whispered, stripping off his clothes and stretching out beside her.

"Care to show me?" she whispered, while her hands lovingly explored him.

"I intend to spend the rest of my life showing you, starting now."

* * * * *

Don't miss these next exciting titles
from Annette Broderick:
Callaway Country, Silhouette Single Title,
on sale May 2000
Maximum Marriage: Men on a Mission,
a special anniversary collection,
on Sale October 2000
And look for Annette's anniversary
Silhouette Desire, on sale November 2000!

Dear Reader,

I have always been fascinated by storms. Perhaps because they were so rare where I grew up, in relentlessly sunny Southern California. The interest remains to this day; I'll watch any documentary on hurricanes or tornadoes, and the Weather Channel is my default background noise on "busy work" days.

I suppose this story is a good example of the answer to the perennial question of "Where do you get your ideas?" In this case it's simple. Toss two strong, independent, yet lonely people into a pot. Add a child whose vulnerability and innocence must be protected. And then...well, then you stir up a hurricane.

Enjoy!

Justine Davis

UPON THE STORM
Justine Davis

To BaBa,
who has weathered her own storms
with style and courage and grace

One

___

He plants his footsteps in the sea,
And rides upon the storm.

—William Cowper

He'd had the dream again, so he wasn't surprised when he awoke to rain. The accompanying wind made the windows rattle. A ferocious wind, howling eerily in the darkness, like it had then. It was always the same, always the terror, the fear, the water, and the howling wind and rain. And then the sweetness, the unbearable, unbelievable sweetness...

He sat up, shaking his head sharply. You're not going through this again, Dalton, he told himself determinedly, and tossed back the covers. Ignoring the aching tightness of a body not as quick as his mind to abandon the lingering, all too familiar dream, he swung his feet to the floor.

He wondered what had happened to all that determination when he came out of his reverie to find himself standing in front of the bathroom mirror as it began to steam over. As usual, it had begun when his eyes, as they always did, strayed to the faint, white line of the scar that had marked his temple for the past three years.

With a sigh of disgust, he turned away from his rapidly fogging reflection. *All the people who figure I spend a lot of time looking in a mirror would never believe what happens when I do,* he thought dryly as he yanked open the shower door. He paused when he heard the pounding on the outside door and a familiar voice hollering through the wood panel.

"Trace! They're almost ready for you."

Right on time, as usual, he muttered silently, then leaned back to shout through the half-open bathroom door.

"I'm up, Roger. Give it a rest."

He showered and dressed, then sat on the edge of the bed to tug on his shoes. As he straightened up, his gaze slid to the shelf of books on the wall opposite him, unerringly going to the tall volume at the far end. He could just make out the lettering on the spine, not that he needed to. He knew every inch, every page, of that book far better than he wanted to.

It was incredible. The photographs in it did with

flair and drama what few had, conveying, in the flatness of two dimensions, the incredible power and unstoppable force of a hurricane. It would have sent a chill down his spine even if those amazing photos had been as close as he'd ever been to nature gone berserk.

The pages had brought it all back, the fear, the awe, the certainty of impending doom. That he'd gotten himself into that mess by virtue of his own unbelievable stupidity only made it worse. He should have been dead, he'd thought again as he looked at the pictures that caught the overwhelming, ferocious strength of wind and water. He would have been dead, if it hadn't been for—

And that had been the exact moment when the realization had struck. He'd been staring at a two-page spread, a shot of an unexpected doorway amid the sand, a doorway to a small cavelike hut dug back into the low, sandy bluff until it seemed part of the landscape rather than an independent, man-made structure. And the message had finally gotten through to the brain that had been busy reliving those hours of horror.

"My God."

He had closed the book with a slap, staring down at the cover. Christy Reno. There it was, in tiny print, almost overwhelmed by the power of the cover photograph. All the time he'd spent looking for her, and here she was, right in front of him. He'd opened the book to those pages again, staring at the tiny place that had once been the center of his world.

He had turned to the back of the jacket, then the inside flap, but there was no picture, and just the barest amount of information about the photographer. Not nearly enough.

He hadn't fully believed her. She'd told him, and he hadn't believed her. Nobody could be that reckless, to weather a hurricane of that size in such an exposed place, just for the sake of some photographs. "Just innate insanity," she'd said blithely, never telling him the destination of those photographs. He'd halfway believed her, though; there was no other reason for anyone to be there. Except maybe for an idiot whose own temper and ego had gotten him caught in the middle of it...

God, he had never expected her to disappear like that. He had tried to find her after the furor had died down, but she had vanished. No one seemed to know where she had gone. For the first time in his life he'd been furious at the celebrity he'd worked to achieve; if it hadn't been for the media crush at the Coast Guard Station, he never would have lost sight of her.

She had vanished so completely, and his dreams of that time were so real, so vivid, that he'd begun to wonder if he had dreamed *her,* as well, conjured her up out of the mists of his battered brain. What had happened had been crazy enough, unlikely enough...he wasn't sure it could be real anyway.

Then, after nearly a year, Roger had handed him the book. Hope had surged in him, until he called the publisher, who referred him to her editor, who regretfully but firmly said Ms. Reno refused to release any personal information. When he had pressed, for the first time since coming back using the weight his famous name carried, he'd gotten an answer that had felt like a kick in the stomach.

"I'm *so* sorry, Mr. Dalton, but I'm afraid that you are…specifically mentioned in her instructions. Should you happen to inquire, we are to tell you nothing."

He'd run the gamut of emotions from disbelief to shock to hurt to anger, finally settling into a wrenching sadness that had lasted a long, long time. His life had been turned upside down, his emotions battered, his very soul somehow changed, and the reason, the catalyst, the wise, gallant spirit that had brought it about, had vanished like mist under the morning sun. That she had done it intentionally made it all the more painful to his newly awakened and battered heart.

He had wondered if, in some way, on some unseen balance sheet somewhere, this was the payback for the time when, drunk on the success he'd achieved, he had fallen into the pit of the users and the used, never caring who he hurt, or what anyone thought. He'd gone from party to party, from drink to drink, from bed to bed, and decided jadedly that all three were overrated. It had been a bout of dissipation that gained him a reputation it had taken almost three years of the hardest work of his life to overcome.

"No wonder she doesn't want anything to do with you."

He had said it bitterly to his own reflection. And

in a final paroxysm of humble self-disgust, he'd told himself that he deserved everything he got. And everything he'd lost. And in the quiet darkness of the most chastening night of his life, he'd made a solemn vow to continue what she'd begun.

He'd kept that promise, he thought. Any resemblance between him and the cocky bastard who'd left the *Air West* set in a huff to go belting home to Corpus Christi because the big boys wouldn't play his way had been ground to dust beneath his determined feet. Sometimes it had felt as if he were at the bottom of Mount Everest, equipped with only a shovel and trying to bring it down, but whenever he felt like quitting, the image of a pair of wide gray eyes kept him going. That and the forlorn hope that somehow, some way, wherever she was, she might hear of the change and know....

"Christy."

He whispered it as he stared at the spine of the book. He'd never quit trying. He'd even considered hiring a private investigator, but the thought that her anger over that might ruin any slim chance he had held him back.

"There has to be a way," he muttered suddenly, fiercely. And he would find it. Somehow.

"Let's go, Trace! They're waiting."

He sighed as he got to his feet. He slid on his watch, noting as he did that he would have to hurry or he would be late for the call. There had been a time when he wouldn't have cared, but that was long past. He grabbed the familiar jacket that, as always, was handy, then stepped out into the rain.

* * *

Christy knew she had to go, but she hated the idea. Her unease grew as she changed from the puddle-jumper that had brought her from the small coastal town of Eureka to San Francisco to the big airliner that would carry her to L.A. If something happened to her, what would happen to Char? As wonderful as kindly Mrs. Turner was, she didn't want her daughter raised by a stranger. Not like—

Stop it, she snapped at herself. This was old, worn ground. She wasn't like that other woman. She loved her baby girl with all her heart. God, she would miss her, even for the short time of these meetings.

"Come on," Jerry Farrell, her agent, had cajoled. "You're getting a vacation in sunny—well, not at the moment but soon—Southern California. Land of sun and surf."

And Hollywood. The words echoed in her mind now as they had then. She smothered a qualm and continued her inner chastisement. Quit griping. You should be glad.

Glad? Three years ago she would have been ecstatic to have a small press with the reputation of Dragon Books courting her, instead of the other way around, to have the chance at working on all the ideas that had been floating around in her head since she had taken her first picture.

"It's time, Christy. And they're anxious to get going again," Jerry had coaxed, and she had felt herself yielding to the temptation of dreams fulfilled.

She really didn't mind the meetings themselves, the brainstorming sessions that resulted in the mapping out of the basic plan of the book. Meetings that were about to begin again after a lengthy hiatus. Three years ago they had ended abruptly with the chance to complete the work that had lain half-finished for months, after the very subject she had been trying to capture on film had risen to destroy most of that work. So she had left the luxurious offices and gone to Texas instead and changed her life forever....

Christy loosened her seat belt but left it fastened, a habit ever since there had been more than just herself to think about. Pain wrenched at her again. She'd never been parted from Char since she'd been born, and no matter how many times she told herself that she was coming back, the thoughts of a mother who hadn't returned refused to be quashed. She settled back in the seat and tried to relax. It didn't work.

With a sigh she sat up and reached into the pocket on the back of the seat in front of her for the ubiquitous airline magazine. She thumbed through it without really seeing it, trying to remember the days when she had looked forward to gallivanting off to some distant part of the globe.

Her fingers froze in the act of blindly turning a page. God, he was even here. It figured, she supposed. He'd made about every magazine on the racks this month. And his series was about a pilot, so why shouldn't he be in an airline magazine? The show, with its stories about the life of a charter pilot and the people who hired him for all the various reasons people did, had caught the imagination of the country, and added to the already romantic image of pilots.

Of course, the fact that the star was the most gorgeous, sexiest thing this side of the sun didn't hurt. But she didn't need glamour shots to remind her. Those chiseled, even features, that thick, sun-streaked hair, the leanly muscled body, those incredible eyes, were engraved in her memory with an accuracy and vividness that far surpassed any photograph.

She felt an echo of that old twinge of pain and resolutely smothered it. It wasn't her fault that she hadn't known, that she'd been in the wilds of Alaska when *Air West* had first swept the country. She'd watched the show once, afterward, and found it altogether too painful.

She stared at the picture, at the tall, lean figure in the battered leather jacket with the aviator sunglasses dangling from the chest pocket, flashing that dimpled grin as he leaned on the wing of the lovely, graceful jet. She read the caption, which quoted him as introducing the small craft as the real star of the show. The printed paragraph then went on to make a pointed but good-natured observation that the "old" Trace Dalton would never have shared his star billing with anyone, let alone an airplane.

She'd heard about how he'd changed; it was practically impossible not to, even when she tried to avoid hearing anything about him at all. It showed even in photographs; there was a new gentleness in the formerly arrogant set of his mouth, a new depth in those breathtaking eyes that, like the sea, changed color as the sky did. She slapped the magazine shut with a sharp movement, stuffing it back into the pocket with a vehemence that startled as well as irritated her.

She was only aware of how long she must have been staring at the picture when the announcement came over the intercom that they were on final approach to Los Angeles International Airport. Into the lion's den, she thought. It's a good thing the lion doesn't walk among the peons.

The rain had stopped by morning, and Christy was glad. Her enjoyment of heavy, torrential rains had been dimmed by the memories they conjured up. She tried to think of something else, but the only thing that came to mind was Char. God, she missed her already! That brief phone call last night hadn't been enough. The child's animated chatter had only made it worse.

Christy wondered yet again how she had managed to produce such a cheerful, serene child. All things considered, she had expected a rather stormy, turbulent temperament. She wondered grimly if Char's mellowness would stand the test when the time came that she began to ask about her father.

"I had no choice."

She repeated the words for the millionth time as she sat in a cab on the way to her meeting. She'd had no choice, and she damned well wasn't going to feel guilty about it. If he'd been anybody else, she would have taken the chance. But he wasn't anybody else, and the fact that she hadn't known that at the time only made it more impossible, more unbelievable.

Forcefully yanking her thoughts off that worn road, Christy savored the freshness in the air as she checked the address on the building in front of her. It was in the Wilshire District, a tall, modern structure of bronzed glass. Definitely high-rent territory, she mused. Then she saw Jerry and knew she was in the right place, although she still didn't know why he'd insisted on meeting here instead of his office. He saw her then, too, and hurried toward her.

She found herself smiling as she was greeted effusively. A far cry from when she was doing Alaska on forty-nine cents a day, she thought. Amazing what a few book sales will do. More than a few sales, she amended to herself proudly. The first book, the one she had practically had to finance herself, had more than paid her back. The whimsical character study of what she had labeled the ''Urban Coyote'' had struck a chord in a society whose booming growth put more and more people in direct contact with the clever creature they had seen only on film in old westerns. And those sales had been enough to interest the likes of Dragon Books.

''You look wonderful,'' Jerry said enthusiastically, and Christy grinned at him.

''You said no jeans and tennis shoes.''

She remembered his heartfelt plea on the phone before she'd left. She had laughed but agreed, despite her doubts that it would matter much what she wore. Christy Reno was not a great fan of her own looks and was generally unaware of the effect she had on people. Men and women alike were not immune to the gamine charm she exuded, although their reactions to it were quite different.

She thought her mouth too wide, her gray eyes too big for her small face, and her baby-fine, near-black hair too flyaway for any but the simplest style. She had long ago given up the desire for long, luxuriant locks and resigned herself to the short, tousled cut that suited her best.

And as for her shape, diligent exercise kept her trim and taut, but she would never, ever have the flat, boyish figure that was so in vogue these days. Even before Char, there had been no chance that Christy Reno, even at a distance, would be mistaken for anything but female.

She'd kept her promise to Jerry, and the suit she'd worn was far from jeans and tennis shoes; the pale blue color turned her eyes the color of the dawn sky, the long, clean lines of the fitted jacket made the most of her figure while maintaining a businesslike air, and the skirt was short enough to bare a womanly amount of shapely leg without being blatant. She was glad Jerry approved; she owed him a great deal.

Jerry Farrell was a thin, wiry man with nearly white-blond hair in a short brush cut that made him look decidedly younger than his forty-four years.

He was genial, kind and generous personally, and a coldhearted perfectionist about his work. He combined those qualities into a unique method of drawing that same perfection, sometimes painfully, out of the people he worked with. He would settle for nothing less than your best. Sometimes, Christy thought with wry amusement, the best he coaxed out of people surprised even them.

And his unwavering support and loyalty in the most trying time of her life, even when she had refused to discuss it with him, was something she would never forget.

Lost in her reverie, Christy had missed most of what he was saying at his usual, machine-gun pace.

"Whoa, Jerry! Slow down, will you? I'm not on L.A. double-time yet. And why are we here?"

"Sorry," he said, not slowing down a bit. "I'm just wound up over this new opportunity. I mean, Hurricane Productions! Appropriate, isn't it, after the last book? They're very good, with a good reputation, especially for a fairly new company. They've had great success with their other documentaries, and they want to do a book tie-in with this one. Come on, we don't want to be late—"

"Jerry, *what* documentary?" she asked patiently.

"I told you," he said, ushering her through the building's outer doors. "They want to do one on you."

Christy sensed the blood draining from her face and felt an odd tingling in her fingers that told her the shock was racing through her entire body. On me? she thought numbly, barely aware of Jerry guiding her to the elevator.

No. Her every instinct for survival, every ounce of her hard-won pride, rebelled at the thought. To parade her life, her past, her work, and, God help her, her mistakes before the world? To possibly bring herself to the attention of the one member of that world she had worked so hard to avoid? No.

"—fascinating that anyone would take the chances you have, the risks, and turn them into such magnificent pieces of work. They feel the public will be equally fascinated."

The elevator rose smoothly. Christy gripped the rail behind her back as if she expected it to fall the full fifteen stories of the building. "I can't," she whispered.

Jerry looked at her oddly. "But it's a wonderful chance. It seems that the head of Hurricane is quite a fan of your work. It was his idea." Jerry's brow furrowed for a moment. "He wants to see you alone first, but I'll be waiting."

Christy took a deep breath, fighting for control. Personal fame was something she didn't dare risk. "I am...a very private person, Jerry. I could never do something like this."

"At least listen to the proposal," he urged, clearly puzzled by her reaction to a plum most people would have jumped at. For his sake, she thought, she would listen. But nothing on earth could change her answer. The elevator doors slid open.

The heavy, carved-wood door was bare except

for the letters *HPI* just below eye level. If she hadn't known, she never would have guessed what kind of business was conducted behind that door; she appreciated the presence of subtlety in an unsubtle business.

The office was small but comfortable, with several plush chairs and a lovely antique table that apparently served as a receptionist's desk; it was empty now. Jerry gestured toward a door to the right.

"Go on in. He's waiting for you."

Christy looked at him for a long moment. This seemed very strange to her, and she could see Jerry wasn't happy with it, either. But the head of Hurricane Productions apparently got things his own way. She looked at the inner door, which was marked Private. Only then did she realize she had never asked the name of the man she was about to see. She looked back and was startled to see the outer door closing behind Jerry, clicking shut with a final sound.

Shrugging off a strange sense of foreboding, she reached for the inner door. Seconds later, she was wishing she had listened to her instinct.

"Oh, God," she whispered, staring at the man standing by the window across the room.

"Don't run. Please."

The husky plea froze her, and her chin came up at the word run. Then it dropped. She couldn't deny that running was exactly what she'd intended. And exactly what she'd been doing, for a long time.

Her mind was reeling. The only thing it could

seem to absorb was the fact that he was wearing
that jacket, the one in the picture on the plane, the
same one, she realized now, that he'd been wearing
that day. She could see the jagged scuff mark on
the right shoulder, could see the dark stains on the
battered leather. She wondered why he didn't buy
a new one. It wasn't as though he couldn't afford
it. She almost laughed at herself, seizing on the
most inane thing....

Even though he'd known, Trace was as stunned
as she was. The image he'd carried for so long, the
picture he'd told himself couldn't be true, was here
before him. And he'd been right. The vision wasn't
true; the reality was much more vivid. He'd
thought her beautiful then; he'd never guessed she
could look like this. That pale blue cloth caressed
her slender yet voluptuous figure, giving her gray
eyes a blue tinge that made them look like the first
touch of sunrise on the night sky....

Neither one of them said any more, each seeing
in the other's eyes the unraveling of the skeins of
memory, knowing that they had both battled to
bury the memories in some dark, cold place. And
that this was the moment to set them free...

Two

He'd never been so furious. Who the hell did Ringer think he was, anyway? Directors were a dime a dozen; it was *his* name, his face, that sold the show, and he'd damned well had enough of that arrogant little—

He swore sharply as the car skidded on a turn, then yanked the wheel around and jammed his foot once more on the accelerator. His scowl was as dark as the sky, his mood considerably darker.

They could just sit and stew, he thought with a grim pleasure, Roger had tried to placate him, to stop him, talking of the time lost, the shooting schedule, the crew, the network brass, none of which he gave a damn about, and he'd said so in one short, crude phrase.

Seeing he wasn't getting anywhere that way, the

man had tried to dissuade him by bringing up the approaching storm.

"I grew up in Corpus Christi," Trace had snapped. "Don't tell me about hurricanes. Besides, it's supposed to veer north, anyway. Just call and get me the damn ticket, Red."

He'd used the nickname intentionally, knowing Roger hated it. It had had the effect he wanted; the older man shut up.

So he was home, under threatening skies, pushing the rental car to the limit. He had his own expensive Italian sports car at the house, kept there for whenever he took a notion to drop in and play the hometown-boy-made-good, but he hadn't wanted to send for it. The last person he wanted to see was his self-righteous little brother.

Or his mother, with her constant sniveling about how hard her life had been. When his father had been alive, she'd railed at him for not making enough money. When he'd died—probably nagged to death, Trace thought bitterly—she'd complained that he'd left her in dire need, although she always seemed to have enough for a new dress, while Trace and Tony went without jackets through more than one wet winter.

When he'd pushed himself to the limit and then beyond, working every day after school until dark, trying to make enough money to quiet her wailing, he'd wound up in the hospital, and she had screamed at him for what it was costing. She'd worked herself into a frenzy of self-pity at having been left a poor widow at thirty-four, with never a thought for the son who had lost his father at sixteen, or his even younger brother.

He supposed she had wanted to convince him that she was special and deserved to be pampered. What she had accomplished was to convince him that she was spoiled, greedy and impossible to please, and he'd sworn the day he got out of the hospital that he would never try again. And if he looked upon the rest of womankind in much the same way, he didn't care.

He skidded to a halt in the nearly deserted marina parking lot and slammed the door as he got out, his anger still simmering, as it had been ever since he stormed off the set and told the world in general to go to hell.

Robert Ringer was a stiff-necked son of a snake, and Trace Dalton had had his fill of being ordered around like some bit actor. He was the star of this show, and if they'd forgotten that, it was time they remembered it.

He strode down the gangway to the dock, his anger growing at the fact that it seemed to be pitching under his feet. He ignored the intense swaying of the trees and the fact that the sound of the wind was occasionally punctuated by the crack of a small branch snapping under its force. He looked for one of the dock boys, ready to snap out an order to get his boat ready, but none was in sight.

"Afraid of a little swell and a few gusts of wind," he muttered scornfully, walking to the end slip that held the long, low, powerful speedboat. He'd bought it a few months ago, after the end of the first season. It had been a little foolish; the series had ended strong after its shaky start, but that was no guarantee it would continue that way. He hadn't cared; the need to show up everyone who'd told him he was a fool had been much greater than any caution he had felt. And the need to show Tony. Especially Tony.

He rolled back the canvas cover, a little perturbed at having to do it himself in this wind. What the hell do I pay these guys for, anyway? he grumbled as he stuffed the roll of blue canvas into the locker at the head of the slip. As if conjured up by his thoughts, an astonished young man in one of the marina's red shirts appeared.

"Mr. Dalton? It is you! What are you doing?"

"What does it look like?" he asked sarcastically.

"But the near-gale warnings have been up for hours, and they're talking about going straight to strong gale warnings right now! Even the Intracoastal is too rough. You can't go out now!"

Trace stared at him icily. "Don't tell me what I can't do. I've had a bellyful of it. It's my damned boat, and if I want to take it out, I will!"

"But the hurricane—"

Trace cut him off with a brief, harsh suggestion about what he could do with his hurricane. He'd heard on the radio that it wasn't due for hours yet, and even then, Corpus Christi would most likely get only the fringes. He would stick to the protected Intracoastal Waterway, the long stretch of water between the Texas coastline and Padre Island, and he would be back in plenty of time. And right now, tackling the storm-driven seas suited him just fine.

He cast off, letting the throaty roar of the motor drown out the boy's continuing protests. As soon as he was clear of the breakwater, he shoved the throttle forward, sending the sleek craft slicing through the rising swells. The rush of air whipped his hair fiercely, and the slam of the hull as it hit the water was strangely satisfying. Even the surrounding gloom, ominous in its rapidly darkening intensity, seemed to fit his agitation.

He went on and on, barely aware that the swells were growing, the wind sending foam from the waves in streaks. His agitation grew with the conditions, until it changed somehow from anger to a sort of reckless exhilaration. Somewhere in his head a little warning was trying to be heard, but he didn't want to listen.

Then an out-of-synch swell hit him, coming from a different direction than the others, and he came back to reality with a sharp thud. He realized that the waves, even here on the leeward side of the long, narrow strip of land that was Padre Island, were beginning to surge above him. And the warning that he'd ignored came crashing home; he would be fighting a dangerous following sea all the way back. He edged the throttle back, and when the next swell lifted him out of the trough, he looked around.

What he saw in the distance, on the Gulf side of that tiny strip of land, sent a chill rippling down his spine. Those waves had to be ten feet high, if not fifteen. Streaks of wind-whipped foam marked every surface he could see, spray was starting to kick up, and he could hear the howl of the wind on that side, ominously, and even more menacing than the wind that whipped him here.

He had no choice but to run for it, but the thought of taking the low, broad-beamed little craft back with that heavy swell behind him was not a pleasant one. Serves you right, he thought, swearing fervently at himself. You'll be lucky if you don't have to beach it to save your stupid neck.

He battled the surging water for what seemed like forever; if he made any headway, he couldn't tell. He had to slow to keep the bow of the boat from digging in as it slid down the slope of the waves; at best the stern would lift clear of the water and the prop would race. At worst...

He didn't want to think about the worst, but he knew with a grim certainty he was going to have to. Caught in a wider trough than he'd been seeing, he edged up the throttle just a little, only to have the propeller scream as a sideways swell lifted it clear. The vibration as it hit the surface again rattled his teeth and nearly wrenched the wheel from his hands, and when he heard an ominous crack from somewhere abaft of him, he knew his luck had run out; it was time to run for the beach. Any beach.

Just turning into the swells was a relief in itself. He cut the throttle back even more, dreading the sound of the racing prop when it was lifted clear of the water and the hideous shudder when it came

back down and bit deep. He slowed till he was
barely making any headway at all, just enough forward movement to be able to steer, all the while
aware that he was becoming rapidly exhausted.

Everything else seemed to fade away; his reckless flight and his reason for being here dwindled
into foolish insignificance. He was fighting for his
life now; he knew it in his soul, even **if** he refused
to acknowledge it in his mind.

He almost made it. He could see the beach, wind
whipped, wave torn and utterly beautiful. He was
so tired he even thought he saw someone there, a
slim figure in red, a bright splash of color in a
world gone wet and gray. Then a wave—one of
those crazy, rogue waves—appeared, some freak
combination of cross seas that surged above him
like a giant, seeking claw. It gripped the little boat
like a toy, and he hung suspended for one brief
second before it slammed him down in a crushing
blow.

He heard a tearing, splitting sound, and then he
was falling, or flying, he wasn't sure which, because he couldn't tell the sea from the sky. Then
the water closed over him, drawing him down with
frightening strength. He fought, hanging on desperately to the one gulp of air he'd managed to take
before he'd hit.

Just when he thought he couldn't last, he broke
the surface and sucked in a breath that was half
water. Coughing and gagging, he tried again and
got more air this time. He tried to smother his
panic. He'd been close enough to shore to see

whatever that was that looked like a person. He could make it...if he could just figure out which way "it" was.

He rode a swell up for a look; it wasn't as close as he'd hoped, but it wasn't impossible. At least, that was what he told himself. He could do it, with a little luck. Unless, of course, he'd run as completely out of that as had the boat he'd been so fond of. He thought of tossing up a prayer, but decided in a brief moment of grim self-knowledge that if there was a God, He probably wouldn't believe in any sudden changes of heart from someone like Trace Dalton.

And for a moment he thought he wouldn't need any help. He was, incredibly, drawing closer to the beach, which was now deserted, if indeed that slash of red hadn't been his imagination. He was exhausted, his arms and legs felt like lead weights, but he kept going, every stroke an agony of effort. Every time he found a swell to ride forward, the cost seemed to be searing minutes of being dragged down by the undertow. Still, he thought he could do it.

Then, just as he was trying to speed up his stroke to pick up another swell that might gain him a few more precious feet, he caught a glimpse of something out of place, something menacingly solid in the midst of the swirling water. He had only a split second to recognize it as a splintered, twisted mass of fiberglass and metal before it caught his temple, sending a blinding flash of light and a searing stab of pain through his head.

Nothing was working. He tried to send the message to his arms to keep stroking, to his legs to keep kicking, but something was wrong. The salt water stung his eyes, and he realized he was looking up at the surface, not the spray-clouded sky. With every feeble movement the ache in his chest increased.

Doggedly he kept trying and was rewarded with a stronger kick, but it cost him. The ache became a burning, piercing pain, he heard a roaring in his ears, and he knew he was down to seconds.

The part of his mind that was rebelling against the pain told him to let go, lured him with the promise of peace, sweet, painless peace. The grim, self-abasing part of that mind, newly awakened, told him nobody would miss him much. Tony, maybe, in memory of the days when they had been so close, and perhaps the fans, who didn't really know him...

The pain in his head faded to nothing beside the agony of his lungs, and he made one last desperate effort to overcome the sluggishness of his rattled brain. It took the last of his air, and in that moment he felt his hand break the surface. He tried to follow it up, but there was nothing left, and in the fraction of a second before he opened his mouth to end it, to let the sea have her victory, his only thought was what a damned stupid way to die.

It wasn't anything like he'd expected. He'd wondered, in the time after his father died. He'd thought it would be bright light, or pitch-black, not this weird, in-between fog. Even the first gulping intake of water had been different than he thought it—

Something hit him in the chest, hard. It hit him again, then grabbed him by the throat. So this was it, he thought from that gray, floating place he'd gone to. Funny, it didn't really hurt. He must be getting close to the end....

No sooner had he thought it than the pain struck. Searing, scalding pain, from his throat to the pit of his stomach. It ripped at him, a hundred times worse than that earlier agony. So the promise of peace had been a lie, too, he thought ironically, like everything else. He tried to curl in on the pain, ashamed of the tears that were stinging his eyes, thinking that he was proving himself a coward as well as an idiot; he couldn't even die with any kind of style.

The grip on his throat tightened, then moved, tilting his head back. Then, over the roaring in his ears, which had become strangely distant, a word.

"Breathe."

They talked to you? he thought in astonishment. It had been a low, strained voice. Odd. He would have expected calm. He wondered where he would wash up, when it was over. If he ever did.

"Breathe...damn it...! Help me!"

Again harsh, broken up by gasping breaths. Breaths? They had to breathe? The pain came again, worse this time, but surpassed by the shock of realization: The pain was air rushing into his lungs. Confused, he struggled to look for the source of the voice.

"Don't…fight…me."

Fight? He'd given that up, hadn't he?

"Just…float…and breathe."

A soft voice, husky between the gulping breaths. A nice voice. Soothing. Damn, it felt real, whatever it was. It felt like hands holding him, tugging at him. Lifting him. Then the pain again, clawing, tearing. Air. Where was he getting air? Or was this part of it? Had his mind just surrendered its grip on reality in these final minutes?

"That's it…easy…can you…kick?"

I'm supposed to help? This doesn't make sense. But is it supposed to? And why am I able to just float here and analyze this like it was a script? The pain again. It *was* air. Or did the water just seem like air, afterward?

"Come…on." The tugging was stronger, the roar that had faded somewhat was back, and he could hear the rush of the water again. "Kick…if you…can. Get there…faster."

Did he want to get there faster? If it would stop this burning, racking pain, he did. He tried vaguely to follow her instructions. Her? Where did that come from?

"That's it…. Again."

I can't figure this out. I'm just so tired….

"Again!"

Okay, don't get mad. I'll kick.

"Keep…going."

Why am I doing this? I'm tired. Isn't this supposed to be over? I wish that roaring sound would stop.

"Just...a little...more."

Just a little more? If it was almost over, why did it still hurt so much? It shouldn't hurt anymore. Or had everybody been wrong all these years? Did it just keep on hurting forever? Even now that he didn't have to float, or kick, it still hurt. It felt good to lie down, though.

Lie down? On what? He tried to concentrate; this was important, somehow. He could still hear the water, still feel its chill...but he could hear something else, too, closer than that annoying, howling roar. Someone gasping for breath...and someone else making a strange, gurgling sound. And there were hands again. Touching him. Rolling him over.

Pain ripped through him, making what had gone before seem like a mere twinge. Convulsion after convulsion gripped him, tearing, racking coughs, the brackish taste of seawater and the acid of bile burning his throat, his mouth. He was choking, trapped between gulping in cold, delicious air and ridding himself of the insidious, salty poison. Vaguely he heard the voice, felt the hands pounding on his back, then hard, small fists. He wished they would stop; they were making him keep coughing up that horrible stuff.

Why wouldn't it stop? He clenched his fingers, only vaguely aware of being able to move them again. They were digging into something wet and hard...and soft. Sand? He gulped in more air, able to take two panting breaths before the gagging began again.

At last the fists stopped, and he managed three

breaths before the next spasm, then two before the next, then four.

"Can you...try and walk? We've got to...get inside."

Walk? She's kidding, isn't she? I can't walk. So why is she making me get up? It *is* a she. I can tell. She's so small...and her hands are so smooth.

"Crawl, then. We've got to move."

Crawl. Was that part of it? A shoulder shoved him upward, a shoulder with surprising strength in its slenderness. A shoulder he seemed to know... Was that what had hit him before?

"Now!"

Water again. He could feel it, even though he couldn't seem to see anymore. It tugged at him, while those small, smooth hands pulled the other way. It didn't hurt nearly so much now. He could crawl, couldn't he, if that was what she wanted? He sent out the signals to his arms and legs, wondering if they still worked in the old way.

"That's it."

The voice was soft, coaxing, sweet. He would do anything for that voice. Were they moving? He thought so, but he couldn't see; something was still stinging his eyes. He kept trying.

"Almost there."

She'd said that before. Lies again. But hadn't that been just before he'd been able to stop kicking? Maybe it wasn't a lie. That voice wouldn't lie, would it? He tried again.

Then she was gone, and he heard an odd noise, but before he could wonder at it, she was back.

Poking at him, shoving him, urging him to his feet. He tried to tell her he couldn't walk, but then he was up, staggering. She could make him do anything with that sweet voice.

The roaring was muffled now, and he was suddenly warmer. The sound of the water had retreated. What gray light there had been was gone, but it didn't matter, his vision was so blurred anyway. He swayed, but that persistent shoulder braced him, and he felt those hands moving over him, tugging at him, at his clothes. Then more water, warmer, gentler, somehow. Then something soft and dry patting at him. He felt oddly distant, floating, as he had before, in the water.

Then he was lying down on something wonderfully soft, and with the soothing warmth of something over him. This was more like it, he thought, wondering what that odd touch was on his forehead. Was it almost over? Could he let go now? Slide into that beckoning darkness that he'd expected since he'd surrendered to the inevitable? If he asked her, would she tell him? He tried to form the words.

"Shh. It's all right now. Just rest."

So this was it. At last. He hadn't expected it to be so hard. He wished he could see, could see her, before... The hand that felt so cool and smooth on his forehead was the last thing he remembered.

Three

Christy sat in the single chair the small room held, watching the man in the bunk. Although wider than a single bed, it was barely long enough for him, even though it was more than six feet.

The bunk, the small table that served as a desk that was at its foot, the chair she sat in and the narrow counter and bank of cupboards along the opposite wall took up most of the space, leaving only a narrow path for walking down the center of the eight-by-ten-foot room. A small alcove with a hand pump for water and a fairly modern marine head were later additions, the sole concessions to modern convenience.

A golden glow came from a kerosene lantern on the desk; she had a light powered by batteries, but saved it for times when the lantern was too bulky or too dim. She preferred the softer light, anyway; now she watched it play over the hair of the man in the bunk. Almost dry now, it seemed blond and brown at the same time, but with a naturalness she knew was real. That it felt like thick silk she already knew from when it had brushed her fingers as she checked the wound on his temple.

Her brow furrowed at the thought. It was an ugly cut, a gash barely missing his eye. It probably needed stitches, but she had done the best she could with the butterfly bandages that had been in the first-aid kit. The salt water had probably been a blessing in disguise; the cut looked clean, and it hadn't bled much after she'd gotten him out of the water.

She hoped he didn't have a concussion. He'd been completely out of it, but then, he'd nearly drowned. She'd read that you should wake someone with a concussion every couple of hours to make sure they weren't in a coma, but she doubted if she could even get him to raise an eyelash; he was dead to the world. She didn't think he'd been totally unconscious before; he'd responded to her words, if sluggishly. A good sign, she hoped. If he was in a coma, she couldn't do anything about it, and knowing wasn't going to help any.

She wondered yet again what on earth he'd been doing out there. She was crazy enough, she freely admitted, but at least she was here for a reason. A reason that, while not necessarily sane, was as good as there could be for being in the middle of this chaos if you didn't have to be. And she was on dry—well, dry for now, anyway—land at least.

It had felt strange, undressing a total stranger and putting him in her bed, even if it was only hers temporarily. She had tried to think of him impersonally, as some helpless being she was now responsible for, but it had been difficult; he was very nicely put together. Everywhere.

She felt her cheeks heat at the memory of his naked body, at the long, lean lines of rangy muscle, the flat, ridged stomach, narrow hips and taut, tempting buttocks. She'd tried not to look any farther, but by the time she pulled the blanket over him, she'd seen all there was to see. And even cold and shivering, he was a beautiful sight.

Stop it, she ordered. He's hurt, whoever he is, and he needs help, that's all. She shifted in the chair. It wasn't the most comfortable thing, but she was tired, and her body ached from the day's exertions. Think how he must feel, she told herself, smothering a yawn.

She propped an elbow on an arm of the chair and rested her chin in her hand. It was lucky she had gone out for a last few shots while there was still a bit of light, she thought, or she never would have seen him. Her eyelids drooped. She'd planned on experimenting with some night shots with that high-speed film, but it certainly wasn't going to be tonight....

It was dark when she awoke, and the sound of the wind outside had increased, as had the sound of the waves; she should get some good shots tomorrow. Her eyes went to the bed. He hadn't moved, but the steady rise and fall of his chest told her that at least he was still breathing. She laid a gentle hand on his forehead.

Warm, but not hot, she thought gratefully. She moved to turn down the lantern to conserve kerosene, even though she had brought twice as much as she should need. As she had with food and water, an instinct she was grateful for now that it appeared she had company for the duration; there was no way for either of them to get out of here until the storm was over.

At a sudden memory, she went to the counter to pack away the camera she had put there hastily before taking her unscheduled swim. She kept all her gear in waterproof packing, more because of the dampness of the air and the spray that seemed to penetrate everywhere than any fear of being flooded. This little place had lasted through countless storms like this. She was sure it could handle one more.

She'd shifted the chair so that she could sit in it sideways, her back propped against the cupboards and her legs over the arm, a folded blanket serving as a cushion and a pillow. In that position she managed to sleep, although brokenly. She didn't mind. It gave her the chance to check on her patient whenever she woke. He slept on, unmoving; she hoped that didn't mean he wasn't going to wake up at all.

When she awoke to the gray light of day, she got out of the chair, moving a little stiffly until she was able to stretch cramped muscles. She glanced at the bunk. No change. Going to the cupboard, she pulled out the camera pack and took out the second camera, this one loaded with daylight film. She selected a couple of filters and tucked them into the pocket of the equipment vest she then slid on.

She was hesitant about leaving him, but she didn't know how much longer she was going to be able to venture outside. And if the course of this hurricane, whenever it finally decided to move, altered even slightly westward, it was going to get real interesting around here.

She dropped to her knees as soon as she rounded the corner of the hut, knowing better than to try walking in this gale. She squeezed her eyes shut against the spray, thankful that the sand seemed too wet to blow. The walk took longer today than ever, but she could only judge her progress by the sound of the roaring wind and the crashing waves.

Get interesting? She stared as she topped the bluff. It was time to run up the hurricane flags, red-and-black squares time. The wind was fierce, thick with spray, the water a mass of whipped foam. She'd begun this project in the Cayman Islands last year, and the height of that hurricane had looked only a little worse than this.

If it hadn't been for the rotten luck of that film-storage bag breaking open, wiping out all her work, she wouldn't be here now, she muttered once more.

And the man inside would probably be dead. She hadn't thought of that. Strange. What were the odds against her being in this particular place, under these ridiculous conditions, and just at the right moment? With a wondering shake of her head, she edged over the top and began to shoot.

She was damp and shivering when she got back to the little room. She wiped the equipment dry and tucked the finished roll of film away carefully before she pulled on dry socks and a sweater. She lit the lantern; the sheltered little room, with only the tiny window in the door, was chronically dim.

The chaos she'd seen on the windward side took her to the small weather-band radio that sat on the counter. She flipped it on, keeping the volume low. Either the storm had grown in both size and intensity, or it had changed course; if what she'd seen was Charlotte's "skirts," she didn't want anything to do with the rest of her.

Static crackled through the little speaker, but after a moment she had heard enough and flipped it off. A course change. Seventy-knot winds and building, and a lot closer than she had expected. Wonderful. Bring your flippers.

She picked up the notebook where she logged her shots, and, sitting down in the chair she'd left beside the bunk, she began to scribble rapidly from memory. She'd given up trying to wrestle with it outside, knowing it was useless. When she'd finished, she reached out and dropped it on the desk.

She glanced at her watch, calculating silently. He'd been out for nearly seventeen hours, and she was starting to seriously worry. She moved to sit on the edge of the bunk and reached out to press the back of her fingers to his forehead. At her first touch he stirred, murmuring something so low she couldn't hear, and relief flooded her.

His lips looked dry and cracked, and she rose and got a small cup of water and a spoon. Knowing the dangers of trying to make an unconscious person drink, she dipped the spoon in the water and ran it across his lower lip, letting only a few drops slide off. His mouth moved automatically, taking the moisture, and she did it again. He managed a few more drops this time. And then, when she moved to do it a third time, his eyes were open and trained on her.

Were they blue or green? She couldn't tell, then felt silly trying to decide such a thing when they were so full of confusion and apprehension. He swallowed heavily. His lips parted as if to speak, then shut again. He was watching her with an intensity that was, she supposed, understandable. Then, hesitantly, slowly, he lifted a hand, reaching out toward her. When his fingers met her arm, he pulled them back, startled, his eyes widening as he looked up at her.

"You're...real," he whispered, his voice harsh with the sound of a raw throat. She raised an eyebrow in puzzlement. "I...thought I was...that you..." He trailed off, looking disconcerted, and a bemused understanding suddenly dawned in Christy's mind.

"I'm real," she said softly. "And alive. And so are you."

He looked up at her in in disbelief, giving her

an idea of how close she had come to being too late.

She was close to being right; Trace couldn't quite believe he was really still alive. But as much if not more, he couldn't believe that she was real. He'd never seen such eyes, huge, misty gray, framed by a thick, dark fringe of lashes and made even larger by the tousled, gamine-cut bangs that gleamed sleekly in the golden light. Her mouth was full beneath a pert nose and, right now, soft with concern.

"You're all right," she said quietly.

It was the voice. Soft, husky, low and soothing. And it belonged to this lovely vision he still wasn't certain was real. But it couldn't have been her. His eyes traced the slender column of her neck, the fine features of her wide-eyed face. It couldn't have been her, not out there, not in that watery hell.... His eyes reached the delicate but determined thrust of her chin, and his conviction wavered.

"You..." he began, his voice rasping painfully. She leaned forward, setting aside the spoon and holding out the cup of water.

"Here." She slipped a hand behind his head and lifted gently. "This should help."

He had to believe she was real; that was smooth, warm flesh beneath his head. He took the water gratefully, and it soothed his raw throat. Then, as she was easing his head back down to the pillow, he spotted a slash of bright red against the far wall, a jacket hanging on a nail, and an image of a slim figure in red on the beach flashed through his mind. He tried again, although he knew the answer now.

"It was...you?"

"What was?" she asked, not sure what he meant.

"The voice...your voice...you pulled me out?"

"You helped." She smiled gently, realizing now that he had never seen her. He'd been worse off than she thought.

"Why?" he whispered, stunned.

She shrugged. "It seemed like the thing to do at the time."

"You...could have drowned." The thought of this beautiful creature out in that tumultuous sea, risking her life to drag him to safety, was too incredible for his slightly befuddled mind to cope with.

"And you *would* have drowned. But neither of us did." She changed the subject briskly. "How does your head feel?"

He blinked. He'd been aware of a dull ache above his right eye, but only now did he remember the twisted chunk of what had been his boat coming at him from out of the treacherous water. He lifted a hand automatically to touch the sore spot, but she grabbed his wrist.

"Uh-uh," she cautioned. "You probably should have had stitches, but I did the best I could. Better not mess with it." His hand dropped to his side, but his wrist felt her slender fingers as if they were still there. He flexed his fingers at the oddness of it. "I'm sorry I couldn't get you to a doctor," she went on, "but I'm afraid you're stuck here until this is over."

"I...wouldn't be anywhere..." He trailed off, but Christy knew what he meant. She shrugged again. "Where is...here?" he asked, looking around the tiny room.

"An old Weather Service lookout. They used it back in the 50s, before the first weather satellites went up."

"How did you get here?"

"Voluntarily," she said with a grin.

He sucked in a breath; God, she was beautiful! He felt a sudden staccato beat of his heart that startled him. He must still be feeling the effects of what had happened.

"I had to sign a waiver, though, promising not to holler for help no matter what and absolving them of all responsibility if I die from anything short of a giant squid attack."

His own brush with death was far too fresh for him to laugh. "Why?" he asked, astonished.

"To take pictures," she said simply.

Forgetting, he raised an eyebrow in disbelief, then winced. "Damn," he muttered.

"You really should have had stitches," she said, her brow furrowing with concern. "I'm afraid there'll be a scar."

"Better than dead," he said dryly. "Even for me."

She looked at him quizzically. "*Even* for you?"

He started to do it again, but caught himself in

time. "Yeah," he said, "my face being my fortune, and all that."

"Oh," she said, a little uncertainly. "What do you do?"

The eyebrow went up that time, and he grimaced. When the pain eased, he studied her for a long moment. "You don't...know me?" It sounded arrogant even as he said it, but he didn't know how else to ask. Or why all of a sudden he cared how he sounded.

Her eyebrow shot up this time. "Should I?"

"Boy, I must really look bad," he said, wondering why the flippant remark, the kind of thing he always said, sounded so hollow in his ears.

"You look fine, considering," she said, then realized what he'd meant. "You mean, I really should know you?"

"Er...most people do," he said, feeling oddly sheepish about it.

Christy studied him for a long moment, searching for something familiar. "I'm sorry," she said finally, honestly. "I don't. Most people? You're that well-known?"

It had been a long time since he'd had to introduce himself to anyone. "I'm Trace Dalton." He expected wonder; what he got was a blank look. "You been on another planet lately?" The words slipped out in his old, cocky manner, and he regretted them immediately, even before he saw the withdrawal in those beautiful gray eyes.

"Not exactly."

"I...I'm sorry." God, how long it had been

since he'd apologized to anyone? "It's just that..." He let out a sigh, exasperated, and not sure if it was at himself or at the way he was feeling. "I'm an actor."

"Oh." She sounded singularly unimpressed.

"I've...become kind of famous in the past year," he said stumblingly, irritated at how awkward he sounded. What was wrong with him? Did running into someone who didn't know him throw him that much? Or was it just her and the feeling he got that she wouldn't have acted any differently even if she *had* known who he was?

Her chin came up. "That explains it," she said evenly. "I spent the last year or so in Alaska. Pardon my ignorance."

Lord, he felt like a fool. He'd never been so disconcerted before, especially since he'd become the darling of the celebrity watchers of the world.

"I didn't mean to..." To what? Insult her? He supposed he had, making it sound as if she were some kind of idiot not to know who he was. Or maybe he hadn't meant to sound arrogant? He seemed to do that without even trying. Had he just never noticed it before?

She stood up and began to turn away. "Can you eat something?" I guess I can't starve him, even if he is a jerk, Christy mused dryly.

Great, he thought as the chill in her voice echoed in his ears. She saves your life, risking her own to do it, and within five minutes you've got her so mad she won't even look at you. "Look, you don't underst—"

He broke off as she turned back and met his look coolly. Go ahead, idiot, make it worse. Damn, those eyes were burning a hole in him! How could she make him feel so guilty without even saying a word? He took a breath. "I...think so. Thank you." That sounded safe enough. And he *was* hungry, surprisingly.

Without a word she took the three steps to the end of the counter and fiddled for a moment with the small propane stove there. An actor, Christy thought wryly. And an arrogant one at that. How can someone who's come so close to dying still be so cocky?

Only if it's second nature to him, she answered herself silently. Wonderful. Trapped in an eight-by-ten room with an eight-by-ten glossy who figured the whole world had heard of him by now. She heated up what was left of the stew she'd had yesterday. Darned if she was going to fix a whole new meal for him! A glimmer of a smile quirked one corner of her mouth; she wondered when Mr. Big Shot had last eaten leftovers.

"Can you do it," she asked when she came back with the bowl, "or do I need to feed you?"

Stung, a sharp retort leaped to his lips, but Trace bit it back. It was difficult; he hadn't had much practice lately. "I can do it," he said, with enough meekness to ease Christy's anger a little; she'd seen his effort at restraint. Maybe there's hope, she thought as he struggled to sit up.

She set the bowl down and reached for the blanket she'd used, to help prop him up. She turned around in time to see his eyes shift from himself, where the blanket on the bunk had slid down to just below his waist, to her, and she knew he had just realized he was naked beneath the covers. To her surprise, he flushed.

Trace was no less amazed than she was. Lord, he'd done scenes that showed more than this; what was he so uptight about? The fact that she had obviously undressed him? Or that she was so clearly unimpressed by any of it—his fame, his much-publicized face, even his vaunted, watchable backside, which, he would guess, she had seen all of? Among other things. Boy, he thought as he took the bowl she held out, I've heard of being cut down to size before, but if she takes one more slice, I'm going to disappear....

As it turned out, he couldn't do it alone, and he was frustrated and embarrassed by his weakness and the wobbliness of his hands. She fed him efficiently, silently, and he hated it. He wished she would say something, anything, to ease the strain. "It's good," he said once, tentatively; she made only a small sound that was carefully noncommittal. He gave up and finished in silence.

She set the empty bowl aside, then looked at him consideringly. "The bathroom's over there if you need it," she said, nodding toward the small, curtained alcove. "Can you make it, or shall I help?"

To his own disgust, he colored again. What the hell was the matter with him? "I'll make it," he grated out.

One delicately arched brow rose. "Fine," she

said shortly. "I'll turn my back if you're feeling modest. I draw the line at going outside."

He stared at her. She had to be kidding. She didn't really think he would ask her to do that, did she? But there wasn't a sign on her face that she wasn't dead serious. Anger stirred in him again.

"It's a little late to be worrying about my modesty, isn't it?"

The delicate chin came up. "Perhaps I'm worrying about mine."

There was ice in her tone, though her expression stayed even, and his color deepened. *He'd done it again*, he thought wearily. What was it going to take to stay out of trouble with her? She pointedly turned her back to him.

He looked at that slim figure, the straight, rigid back, the slender shoulders that hid such steely strength, the tight, curved bottom.... His body tightened.

Damn, what was she doing to him? How could she make him so angry one minute and the next have him imagining the delectable body beneath the bulky sweater and tight jeans?

His jaw tightened, and he threw back the blankets with a fierce motion. He sat up and swung his legs over the side rail of the bunk, finding out instantly that such hasty motion was unwise.

"Damn." He swore softly as pain shot through his already aching head, and his hands groped for support blindly. Then she was there, dropping down beside him, steadying him. The pain receded.

"So much for anybody's modesty," she said.

She felt a pang of guilt for being so short with him. He'd been through hell and was still hurting. Maybe it was just the pain talking. "Are you sure you don't want to wait a while longer?"

"I'm not sure I can," he said wryly, beyond embarrassment now. Without another word she slipped an arm around his back and pulled his arm over her shoulder. She stood, and, with her help, so did he. He was intensely aware of her hand on his bare skin and figured all he needed to complete his disgrace was to be unable to control his response to her when he was naked to her gaze and had nowhere to hide.

Desperately, confused by his uncharacteristic reaction, he shook his head sharply. It worked; swirling pain made his vision blur and he wobbled on his feet, but the pulsing beat receded.

It was awkward, and it exhausted him, but after a few minutes, gratefully alone in the small bathroom, he was a little steadier. She helped him back to the bunk and pulled the blankets over him without comment. He raised a hand to his aching head reflexively, pulling it back at the last second as he remembered her warning about letting it alone.

"Hurt?"

"No," he snapped, in the tone of a man who had been asked one stupid question too many.

"Too bad," she said coolly, forgetting her resolve to be more understanding. His jaw tightened in irritation that she could make him feel so contrite with just her tone.

"Of course it hurts. What do you expect?"

"I expect," she said with exaggerated casualness, "that you got just what you deserved. What were you doing out there, anyway?"

He let out a long sigh; it all seemed rather silly now. "I had...an argument with someone."

"Oh?"

"In L.A. On the set. With a director."

"And you came here to work it off by taking a boat out in a hurricane? Must have been a hell of an argument."

"It was," he said defensively. "He's an arrogant, domineering jackass, always ordering me around like I'm some kind of bit player or something."

"I thought that was what directors did," she said neutrally.

"You don't understand." He brushed off her comment. "He thinks he's the only director in the world, with the only good ideas. Try and make a suggestion, and he blows his stack." He was trying to stir up his anger again, but for some reason the spark wouldn't catch.

"Hmm," she murmured, deceptively casual. "Maybe you should trade, then."

"What?" He looked at her blankly.

"You direct and let him act."

"Him? He couldn't act his way out of a paper bag! That's the problem. He should let the actors act and stick to—"

He broke off suddenly as something in her expression registered. His words echoed in his ears, and he realized what he'd said. No wonder he couldn't stay mad, he thought sheepishly; he shouldn't have been mad in the first place.

"Oh, boy," he groaned softly. "I walked into that one, didn't I?"

"Hmm," she said again, leaving him to interpret her meaning as she turned to rustle around in the cupboard for a moment. Then she filled a glass with water and came back to sit on the edge of the bunk. "Here." She held out two aspirin. "This should help. Shall I hold the glass?"

"No," he said shortly, tightly. "I've been humiliated enough for one day, thank you." He took the pills without noticing her suddenly thoughtful expression. He got them down and dropped back on the pillow, closing his eyes.

Four

Christy watched him, seeing the moment when he slipped into sleep. Those last words had explained a lot. He was an actor, no doubt with a lot of pride, pride that was sorely battered right now. She should have realized, she thought.

She got up after a while, gathered her equipment and stepped out into the furor once more. It would soon be time to use the ring, she knew, thinking of the heavy steel ring set in deeply embedded concrete just outside the front door of the hut. She had some nylon mountain climbing rope, with a stainless-steel clasp to be fitted to the ring, the loose end to be tied around her waist, in case of an accident.

Or plain old zero visibility, she thought, peering through the rain. She didn't last very long this time, but she hoped she had gotten some good shots, especially the ones from the beach on the windward side. A beach that seemed considerably smaller than it had before, she thought uneasily as she scrambled back over the small bluff. Yes, the ring was definitely in order.

She slid the door shut after her as quietly as she could manage. It moved sideways on a raised track; the foot-high lip kept water out unless it reached record heights, and the sliding door eliminated the problems the traditional swing-out door would have with high winds. Very clever, those weather people, she mused as she shed her wet clothes gratefully and slid into the dry ones she always kept inside.

She hung the wet ones up on the rack in the alcove, then flipped on the small heater that kept the tiny room livably warm and almost dried the wet clothes in two days or so. She toweled her hair dry. Here, at least, the tousled, fringed cut was an advantage; it dried even in the damp air.

She padded quietly back into the room, stopping when a small, muffled sound caught her attention and she turned to look at the bunk.

He was asleep, on his side and curled slightly. And obviously dreaming. That small sound came again. Not a pleasant sound, or a pleasant dream, she guessed. She sat down on the edge of the bed and reached for his shoulder. His skin was smooth and warm, stretched taut over hard muscle, and it was a moment before her tingling fingers could move to shake him awake.

"Trace," she said, conscious of using his name for the first time. "Come on, wake up."

That sound again, then a startled jump and a short, strangled cry. His eyes shot open, and for a brief second terror glowed in them.

"It's all right," she said quickly. "It was just a dream."

Trace sat up, heart hammering in his chest. He closed his eyes, but the dream was still too fresh; he opened them again quickly. She was looking at him, an odd softness in her wide gray eyes.

"Sorry," he muttered.

"It was just a dream," she repeated softly. "Are you all right?"

He nodded slowly, gingerly. God, it had been so real.... He'd been back in the raging water, and she had been on the beach, watching. Only this time she had known who he was and decided he wasn't worth the risk.... He shuddered.

Without thinking about it, she reached down and took his hand. It tightened around hers, and she could almost feel the racing beat of his pulse through her fingers. It must have been an awful dream, she thought, and didn't have to use much imagination to guess what it had been about.

"It's all right," she soothed. "You're safe now." He looked up at her. They were blue, she thought. His eyes were a clear, glowing blue. Or were they? The thick, brown lashes lowered and veiled those amazing eyes before she could be sure.

"I...don't even know your name," he whispered.

"Christy."

"Christy. That's pretty." His fingers moved, picking at the blanket as if he were nervous. "I... Christy?"

"What?" The lashes lifted. No, they were green. Sea green.

"I'm...sorry."

"For anything in particular?"

"For being...an ass, mainly."

"Oh. That."

He winced. "Yeah, that. It seems to...come naturally."

"You said it, not me." The corners of her mouth were twitching with her effort not to smile, and he felt a spurt of hope.

"Could we...maybe...start over here?"

She looked at him thoughtfully. "As in, you just woke up?"

"Yeah. For the first time."

She grinned suddenly, and it was like sunshine in the little room. "I think we could manage that."

He was a little taken aback at the warmth that flooded him. He smiled back at her, but his tone was solemn. "In that case, thank you. For saving my life."

"You're welcome," she said softly, then wrinkled her nose; he felt his heart twist inside him and didn't know why. "Now," she added, "I don't want to hear any more about it."

"But—"

"You thanked me, I accepted, it's over. Deal?"

He couldn't resist that coaxing voice. "Deal,"

he agreed, and felt her fingers tighten around his. Damn, she was amazing. She had more strength and determination and courage than anyone he knew, most particularly including himself. Yet she looked so fragile.... She looked beautiful, he thought. He'd never before seen her out of the bulky sweater she always wore inside; he hadn't realized that her spun-steel strength didn't stop her from having some of the most tempting, luscious curves...

He was much too aware of her, and of the sudden thudding of his blood beneath her hand. He was searching for something to say, anything to take his mind off the surging response of his body. This was crazy, he thought yet again. He just didn't feel like this, ever. Then a sudden, shrieking gust of wind made them both jump.

"Sounds like it's getting worse," he said quickly, glad of the distraction.

"It is," she confirmed, telling him what she'd heard on the weather band that morning. "You ought to hear it out there. This place is pretty well soundproofed."

"And leak proof, I hope?" he said wryly. "I never even wanted to *play* submarine."

She laughed, pleasantly surprised by his sudden good humor. "This may be your first time, then. But this place has stood up to a force-five hurricane, so I think it'll stand up to ol' Charlotte here."

He gave her a lopsided grin, and she laughed again. When he smiled, she thought, you would never believe that the arrogant man she'd met earlier even existed. He looked at her curiously.

"Doesn't your family worry about you being out here?"

"Family," she said in an abruptly odd tone he didn't understand, "has never been a problem for me." She turned his question around without even trying to hide the switch. "What about you? Does your family know you're—"

"You mean do they know what incredibly stupid stunts I'm capable of?" he finished for her dryly. "Yes. If you mean will they care—" he shrugged "—not much."

She looked startled. "What?"

"Oh, Tony—my little brother—might care. We were pretty close once. My mother?" He laughed harshly. "Not a chance."

"You mean that, don't you?"

"If my mother had been the one on the beach yesterday," he said flatly, "I'd be dead, and she'd be complaining about how much the funeral was going to cost." He saw her lips tighten and sighed. "I didn't expect you to believe me. No one does."

"No," she said softly. "I looked like that because...I do believe you."

He looked at her eyes then, those huge gray eyes, gone dark now with compassion and something that resembled pain. And understanding. "You too?" he whispered. "Your mother...?"

"I don't know. She didn't stick around long enough for me to find out." A look of shock came into Christy's eyes; she never talked about her mother. Never! She scrambled to change the subject again. "What about your brother? You said you were close?"

He recognized what had been done, but he didn't push it. "Once. You know, the big brother, little brother stuff. He's eight years younger than me, and he followed me around like a puppy. He was only eight when our dad died.... It got worse then. He stuck to me like a burr. I didn't mind, I knew he was scared...."

He trailed off, but Christy heard the words "...and so was I," as clearly as if he'd spoken them. Sixteen, with a mother who didn't care and a little brother he had to be father and mother to...

"I hung on until he was thirteen, but I had to get out. He knew how close I was to cracking, so he...understood." Trace didn't know why it was happening; he never talked so much, especially about this, but it just seemed to keep coming. "I lit out for L.A. and rattled around for seven years before I became an 'overnight success.'" He chuckled ruefully. "I bussed tables, parked cars, washed cars and pumped gas into cars. And those were the good jobs. There were some others I'd just as soon forget about. And some people."

"Just do what I tell you, kid, I'll make you a star?"

He looked embarrassed. "Yeah. Now and then. I passed on it." He grinned crookedly. "With the guys, anyway." She wrinkled her nose at him, and he laughed, not sure why that little gesture had such an effect on him. "I only fell for it once with a...lady. Boy, did I feel stupid when I realized I was just the latest in a long line.''

"Everybody's entitled to one," she said lightly.

"Sure." He made a wry face. "Anyway, Tony came out to see me once, when he was eighteen. He didn't like it much. Then, when I got *Air West*—the series," he explained, reminded with a little shock how long it had been since he'd had to do so, "he came back. I tried to get him to stay. I could afford it then, but he wouldn't. Said he liked Corpus Christi. And he still didn't like L.A. much. But I kept pushing him. We had a major fight. The first serious one we'd ever had.''

He looked pained, as if something about that long-ago conflict with his brother had only now come clear. "What?" she prompted softly.

"He told me—yelled, actually—that it wasn't L.A. as much as it was me he didn't like." He swallowed tightly; his words had the constrained, awkward sound of words spoken for the first time. "He said that I'd changed, that I was a...a 'conceited, pompous jerk,' I think was the phrase. I thought he was just envious." His eyes closed, and his voice dropped to a near whisper. "But he was just telling the truth.''

After a moment, Christy asked quietly, "Have you seen him since?''

"Once. I came home to try to talk to him. He wants to be a vet, he's great with animals. He had the grades, and two of the local vets were willing to sponsor him when he got out of college. But he'd given up the idea, because he couldn't afford it. He was barely making it at the university, even with a scholarship. I thought if I offered to pay his way..." He let out a long breath. "He told me to go to hell. He'd pay his own way or not go at all."

Christy made a small sound, and he opened his eyes. "A charity case," she breathed, barely aware of speaking out loud.

Trace sat up a little, looking at her in shock. "That's exactly what he said. How did you know?"

"Because I know just how he feels," she said tightly, the echo of old hurts clear in her eyes.

"But he's my brother."

"It doesn't matter who it is."

"Who was it...for you?"

"A teacher."

He knew she didn't want to talk, but he pressed her anyway. He told himself it was for Tony, to help him understand, and he almost believed it. "What teacher?"

She sucked in a short, sharp breath and waited so long he thought she wasn't going to answer. Then, softly, painfully, she did. "He was a photography teacher. At the high school I went to for my junior and senior years. He...caught me looking at one of the blowups in the display case outside the room when I should have been in class. I thought he was going to turn me in. But he just asked what I thought of it."

Trace tried to picture her at sixteen. It wasn't hard; she didn't look much older than that now. "What did you say?"

A tiny smile curved her mouth. "I told him what it needed was a broken rail on that fence, or a nice piece of litter on the grass. It was too damned perfect to be real."

So young to have given up on perfection in life, he thought, just as he had been. He remembered the hollow feeling that surrender had brought. What had brought her to it so early? "And?"

"He laughed. Said he agreed. I was in his class the next semester. And all my last year. I didn't have a camera, but he loaned me one. He spent hours with me, after school in the darkroom. He pushed and pushed, and sometimes I hated him."

If she'd thought about it, she would have been just as shocked as before; she never spoke about this, either. The words were proof of that, choppy and hesitant. Trace did nothing that would interrupt the tentative flow.

"But he never gave up. He told me I could do what he'd always yearned to do, make people look at things a little differently, make them notice the world in a different way for a moment or two, even make them think...."

She was lost in it now, the words coming more easily, with soft reverence. "Nobody had ever made me feel like that. Like I was worth something. Nobody ever had faith in me before. It scared the hell out of me. But I didn't dare let him down. He made me enter some contests, even though I knew I wasn't good enough. But I won." Her voice rang with the wonder of it, even after all this time. "I got a scholarship. To a very good school that specialized in photographic arts. But it wasn't enough, and I told him I wasn't going."

"And he offered to help?" She nodded. "Let me guess," he said ruefully, "you told him to go to hell?"

She couldn't help smiling at his look. "Words to that effect." Then she looked at him intently, suddenly earnest. "Don't you see? When you don't have anything, any offer like that feels like... charity. I didn't have much pride, but I couldn't take his money."

He could just see her, young, bright, seeing a dream slip through her fingers. It hurt with a force that startled him. "What did you do?"

"I went to school. He found another way. It might work for you, too," she said eagerly. "He put the money in the bank, and I borrowed against it. Collateral, I guess. Anyway, I owe the bank, not him. I'm paying it back, and he's making interest on his money. I can stand that. Maybe your brother could, too."

Her desire to resolve the conflict between a man she barely knew and the brother she'd never met puzzled him. "Why does it matter so much to you?"

She lowered her eyes. "You were close once. You could be again. Should be. At least you have him...."

"And you, Christy?" Softer still, he asked, "Who do you have?" She didn't speak, but he read her answers in the suddenly tight line of her mouth.

Pain twisted in him again. "I'm sorry. I had no right to ask that."

"It doesn't matter anymore," she said softly, not realizing her eyes gave the lie to her words as she raised them to his. "But will you try again, with your brother?"

He didn't hesitate. Only because of her did he have this second chance; he couldn't refuse her. He nodded slowly. "I will. If I have to wrestle him down and pin him to get him to listen...like I used to. Although, these days, I'm not so sure I could win anymore."

The conversation was back on safe ground, and he worked at getting that look out of her eyes. Ignoring the nagging ache in his head and never even realizing how long it had been since he'd been the slightest bit concerned about somebody else, he told her the most ridiculous stories he could remember about his little brother's antics, then his own, until they were both laughing freely.

That's what I wanted to see, he thought with satisfaction, looking at the gray eyes alight with mirth. Now that's a face you wouldn't grow bored with, not in a million years! Before he could take that startling thought any farther, she had risen from her cross-legged position on the side of the bunk and gone to the cupboard to cheerfully ask him what he wanted for dinner.

"Backpacker Haute Cuisine," she intoned regally. "We have lasagna, chili and veal parmigiana." She spoke airily, tossing sealed foil packets

at him in rapid succession. "And chicken caccia-
tore, spaghetti—"

"Aack!" he yelled, throwing up his arms in de-
fense against the bombardment of freeze-dried
food. "Help!" He was laughing, ducking and bat-
ting away the flying packages, when a sobering
thought occurred to him. "I'm messing up your
rationing here, aren't I?"

"You're in luck. You just happen to be ma-
rooned with an overkill expert in the preparation
department. I always bring twice what I need. Water, propane, kerosene, food...we can eat like this
for weeks."

"Oh. Lasagna, then." He was relieved until
something she'd said came back to him. *When you
don't have anything*...When you remember how it
was not to have anything, wouldn't you have a ten-
dency to make sure you had plenty of everything
when you got to where you could? He had. But
even food? Had she been that badly off? That pain
again, knife-sharp and twisting.

How on earth, he wondered, could the human
race come up with two women who were so incredibly different? His mother, who'd never lifted
a finger in her life, who'd let two sons scramble up
whatever way they could, with any love or caring
coming from a father who was so often too weary
to give it...and Christy.

Christy, who had every reason to wail and rant
against the world as his mother always had, yet had
met it head-on, making her own way, asking for
and taking nothing from anyone, while somehow

hanging on to enough compassion to worry about a rift between two brothers she didn't even know. And who had the incredible courage to brave a hurricane for a stranger.

The food, when she handed the plate to him, smelled delicious. "It's probably not what you're used to, but it's not bad."

"I grew up on TV dinners, canned spaghetti, and peanut butter and jelly sandwiches," he said dryly. "This is big time."

She looked startled, then grinned. "I hope you still like *PB* and *J*, because that's lunch tomorrow."

"I can hardly wait."

The lasagna tasted nearly as good as it smelled and was a pleasant surprise. "Scrambled eggs for breakfast," she said brightly as she cleaned the dishes.

"You're good at this," he said with a smile.

"This? This is a picnic. No snow, and not even any bears to worry about."

"Bears?" he asked, startled.

"Bears."

He looked blank for a moment. "Oh. Alaska?"

"Um-hmm. Brown bears. Doing their last-minute shopping for the winter hibernation. Dodging them had its interesting moments."

"Er...I suppose you went there to take pictures, too?" She nodded. "Why?"

"Oh, just innate insanity, I suppose," she said cheerfully, "although I do manage to sell a couple here and there. How about some aspirin?"

His mouth twisted wryly. "Does it show?"

"Just a little. You've had that kind of glassy-eyed look since we ate."

"Hmm."

"Hurts, huh?"

"I'll take the aspirin."

Five

He awoke to dim, gray light coming through the small window and an empty room. He sat up, gratefully aware that the ache in his head seemed to be gone. He reached up tentatively, touching the bandaged spot. It was sore, but it was the normal soreness of a cut, not the throbbing ache of damage below the surface. She was a heck of a doctor, he mused. Although what she'd accomplished in healing that gash, she undid with what she did to his blood pressure.

He could hear the wind howling and the sound of water; whether it was rain or the sea he couldn't tell. She was out in this? Wasn't that carrying it a little far?

He stood up and was pleased to find himself steady on his feet. He made it to the alcove on his own and managed to figure out the marine head after a few minutes. He saw his clothes hanging over what looked like a small butane heater, but when he felt them they were still damp, so he resigned himself for a while longer to the sacrifice of his modesty. Such as it was, he thought. But he seemed to be a hell of a lot more aware of his nudity around her than anyone he could remember. He saw a towel that looked dry and reached for it.

In the act of wrapping it around his waist, a sudden memory surged up, not an image, but a feeling, of this same fluffy, dry softness patting at him, and he realized she must have dried him after she'd gotten his clothes off. And probably rinsed him, as well; there had been no itchy salt residue on his skin.

He felt color rising to his face even though he was standing there alone; the thought of her touching him so intimately while he just stood there in that odd gray fog made his blood start to pulse heavily, then settle somewhere below the pit of his stomach.

He knotted the towel hastily, striding across the room as if motion could erase what he'd begun to feel. He peered out the tiny window in the door and stood stock-still in shock. If the traditional picture of hell had consisted of water instead of fire, this would be it. Was that worth a couple of photographs? Why did she risk it?

If she didn't, a little voice answered inside his head, you wouldn't be standing here wondering about it. You'd be at the bottom of that cauldron out there.

He turned away from the grim scene. His eyes swept the tiny room, the radio, the stove and the various other items on the counter, to the kerosene lantern on the table at the foot of the bunk....

The bunk. The only place to lie down in this cramped space. He'd been here two nights now. Where the hell had she been sleeping?

He leaned back weakly against the door as the next obvious question came to him. Where was she—or he—going to sleep from now on? This weather could go on for days, until Charlotte made up her mind....

A little desperately, he flipped on the weather radio. Through the static came the grim news that the storm was picking up both wind and travel speed as she closed in on the Gulf Coast. The only question was her landfall: would she stay to the north, hitting them with only the admittedly destructive fringes of her whirling might? Or would she veer westward once more and vent her rage on them more directly?

He turned the radio off before the announcer could begin to speculate about what would happen if the high altitude winds that steered the storm pointed her west sooner, towards Corpus Christi and a small, vulnerable hut built into a sandy bluff. He tried to think of what Christy had told him, that this little place had withstood the biggest storms thrown at it, but all he could think of was that she hadn't said anything about it being occupied at the time....

He had to do something; he couldn't just wait, worrying. He thought about going out to look for her, but he knew her well enough already to guess that she wouldn't appreciate it. *Besides, Trace, old pal, you'd probably do something stupid and get yourself into trouble again. And she might really decide you aren't worth saving this time.*

His stomach growled unexpectedly. Well, that he could handle, he thought. The least he could do was fix breakfast. Just because he hadn't cooked a thing for a year...

He had just gathered everything when the door slid open and the roar of the world outside invaded the little sanctuary. Christy scrambled in and quickly shut the door behind her. She shook herself, reminding Trace of a long-legged foal after a roll in damp grass. Then she saw him and stopped dead.

"You're up," she said unnecessarily, an odd note in her low voice.

God, Christy thought as she looked at him. Until now she'd been able to make herself think of him as someone helpless, injured, to be treated with the same impersonal distance as a nurse treated a patient. But there was nothing helpless looking about the man who stood there now. Her eyes trailed over him, over the wide, strong shoulders, the sleek, muscled expanse of his chest, with no concealing hair to mask any slackness; there was none.

She couldn't stop herself. Her eyes moved down

over the ridged tightness of his belly to where a
path of golden-brown hair began at his naval and
trailed downward, glinting softly in the dim light
before it disappeared below the edge of the stark-
white towel that rode low on his narrow hips.

Somehow that white towel, so precariously knotted on his right side, seemed more provocatively
sexy than if he'd been naked. Especially when her
memory was all too able to provide the missing
details. With a convulsive little movement she
turned away, tugging off her slicker and setting her
gear down on the table.

"Ready for breakfast? Or is it brunch?" Trace
asked, wondering why she was looking at him so
oddly; Lord knew she'd seen more than this.

She didn't dare look at him again. "I think it's
brunch. It's nearly noon," she said, fussing a little
unnecessarily with the waterproof pants she wore
over her jeans. Despite their protection, she was
still soaked from the knees down, and she shivered
a little as she gathered up dry clothes and started
for the bathroom to change.

She couldn't resist another peek as she went by,
and he caught her glance. "Like the outfit?" he
asked, trying to make light of the awkwardness he
felt at the unknown look in her wide gray eyes.
When she threw him a flashing, teasing grin, it took
his breath away.

"I didn't think there was anything wrong with
the other one," she quipped, then disappeared behind the curtain.

He gaped after her, forgetting the food in front

of him. That incredible wave of heat swept him once more, and he put a hand on the counter to steady himself. Damn, what was wrong? This just didn't happen to him! Women openly drooled over him, and he stayed coolly uninvolved. Even, he'd been told, in bed. There it had its advantages in a mechanical competence and a controlled endurance that usually managed to satisfy his partner while leaving him unmoved, feeling no more than a thankful release of pressure. He didn't care enough to feel anything more, and doubted that he ever would, or could. Or even wanted to.

So what the hell was this? The circumstances? The woman? Both? He heard her rustling around, heard the curtain being drawn back, and bit his lip fiercely. *Easy, Dalton. A towel isn't going to be much cover if you keep thinking about things like that.*

He busied himself with the food, and by the time they sat down to eat he was back in hand. She sat cross-legged on the bed again while he took the chair, resting his feet on the edge of the bunk. He was surprised; the eggs tasted good.

"You look startled," she teased at his look.

"I am," he said dryly. "You would be, too, if you'd ever tasted my so-called cooking."

"Then I'll let you savor it and not tell you how hard it is to ruin this stuff."

"Thanks a lot," he complained, but he was grinning.

He protested when she began to get ready to go

out again, but she was quietly adamant. "It's what I'm here for."

"But it's crazy out there. Haven't you got enough?"

"Maybe. But I won't know until I get into the darkroom and by then it will be too late to make up what I might have missed. I've been through that once. I don't want to go through it again." She smiled crookedly. "I think a third hurricane might be tempting fate just a tad too much."

He paced the floor practically all afternoon. She'd explained about the rope and the ring, and that had reassured him a little, but he still didn't like the idea. "What good will that do if you get hurt?"

"It's better than a trail of bread crumbs," she'd said with a grin that did nothing to ease his mood. He'd wanted to go with her, but she'd refused.

"You'd look pretty silly running around out there in a towel," she'd told him, hiding the fact that the last thing he looked in that damned towel was silly. Breathtaking, tempting and incredibly sexy, yes, but never silly.

He'd been so worried that it irritated him a little when she came back looking flushed and exhilarated. She tugged off the wet gear and ran a hand through her tousled, damp hair.

"I got it!" she exclaimed. "The greatest shot! It was a killer wave, a rogue, like the one..." She trailed off, eyeing him as she realized what she'd been about to say.

"I get the idea," he said, unable to stay angry in the face of her enthusiasm.

They turned on the weather radio while they ate, and the news was double-edged. Charlotte had stalled just off the coast. While it meant she was only close enough to pelt them with rain and buffet them with her fierce winds and driven seas, it also meant she was gathering strength and would be all the more ferocious if she at last struck.

Christy got up and turned off the radio, cocking her head to listen to the wind. "I wouldn't want to be stuck in that when she really starts to blow."

"We *are* stuck," Trace said wryly.

"I mean like the Coast Guard and the guys who have to evacuate people. They must have told me a dozen times that I was on my own, that they wouldn't be able to get to me if it got real bad...." She turned to look at him. "Will they be looking for you?"

He winced. "Don't remind me. That's one of the things I never thought of when I pulled this brilliant stunt."

"So someone knew you were going out."

"One of the guys at the marina. I suppose he must have told somebody. He tried to talk me out of it...and I bit his head off," he ended with a sigh.

Typical, he thought. It had never occurred to him to think about those who might have to bail him out of his self-inflicted predicament. That there might be people risking their lives to look for him even now, people whose job it was, was bad enough; that it had been Christy who had risked hers was nearly unbearable.

"I wish we could let them know," Christy murmured.

Trace let out a long breath. "Me too. But I guess I'll just have to hope they're too busy to spend much time looking for one stray idiot."

Christy studied him for a moment. "You're being pretty hard on yourself, aren't you?"

"Maybe it's about time," he said grimly. He meant it; he wasn't at all happy with what he saw when he looked at what he'd become. Somewhere along the line he'd lost that eager kid with something to prove and become a cold, uncaring indifferent...

He felt a chill as the words formed in his mind. The same words he had always used to describe his mother. God, he'd become just like her. He looked up to see a pair of wide eyes soft with understanding.

"It's hard, isn't it? Looking at yourself and not liking what you see?"

"You don't miss much, do you?" he said uncomfortably.

"I've been there," she said softly.

His eyes widened. "You? Why?"

Christy's eyes dropped; unlike many people, she wasn't her own favorite topic of conversation. Especially this particular subject.

"Christy?"

She looked up. She knew that look in his eyes; she'd seen it in her own mirror many times. He was wrestling with something she'd fought early in her life, earlier than most, she supposed. That feeling, that doubting of your own self-worth, was not something she would wish on anyone.

"I...spent a lot of time wondering what was wrong with me. Why everyone I thought...cared about me left."

"Left?" She let out a shuddering sigh, and what he saw then in her eyes made him speak hastily. "Don't, Christy. I'm sorry. I didn't mean to make you talk about...something that still hurts."

"It does," she said, shaking her head. "It's crazy, but it still does." She laughed, but it was humorless. "I thought I'd left it behind, and then it sneaks up on me like this."

"I'm sorry," he said remorsefully. "I shouldn't have—"

"C'mon," she said, her laugh steadier now, "you're blaming yourself for enough right now. Don't take this on, too."

He looked at her in wonder. Whatever it was, it was clearly painful, and it was just as clear that she was not going to let it control her. After a mother who whined at a change in the weather, and a long trail of glittering women who wailed at a broken fingernail, he felt as if he had found something pure and clean and good for the first time in his life. "You really are something, Christy."

She gave a harsh little sigh. "You know where that came from? My name?" He looked puzzled. "It's where they found me. On a doorstep. Christy Way, in Reno, Nevada. Wrapped up in a blanket.

The house belonged to a doctor. I went back when I was sixteen. I thought he might have known her. My mother, I mean. I wanted to ask her why she didn't…want me.''

"Oh, God," Trace whispered, his voice harsh, his throat so tight he could barely get the words out. He wanted to reach for her, to hold her, but he was afraid she would pull away. He knew from the short, choppy little bursts of words that she had not told this story often.

"I was adopted when I was still a baby. I remember them, a little. But she died when I was five. He didn't…want me anymore, afterward. He sent me back." She made a small jerky movement that could have been a shrug. "I bounced around a lot after that. Foster homes. I was lucky. None of them were too bad.''

Lucky? Trace's mind was reeling. Lucky because the foster homes she'd lived in weren't "too bad"? He was filled with a sudden shame that he had ever dwelt on his own misfortunes; his childhood took on an entirely different look when compared to the bleakness of hers. *Family has never been a problem for me,* she's said.

"God, Christy, I'm sorry."

It was a shrug this time. "Ancient history. It doesn't usually bother me. I worked it all out a long time ago.''

"Worked it out?"

"That it wasn't really my fault. That it wasn't…something about me that made them leave." She looked up then, studying him seriously. "For a long time, I felt like you do now. But you can change it. It's never too late."

Trace didn't know if he could speak. The horror she had sketched out with those flat, emotionless words had moved him beyond the ability to respond. He swallowed heavily. "I—it's different. None of what happened to you was your fault. Not like—"

"Was it?" she cut in quickly. "Was it really your fault? Didn't it all stem from the way your mother treated you?"

That's no excuse, he thought in a sudden flash of self-loathing. My God, he was just like her, whining, blaming...

"It doesn't matter anyway," Christy was saying. "Why, I mean. As long as you know. As long as you change it."

"I'm...not sure I can...."

"You've already started," she said, going on when he looked at her in surprise. "You are *not*," she said firmly, "the same man who left that dock three days ago."

He opened his mouth to speak, then shut it again. She was right. He'd known it, felt it, from the moment he'd awakened to see her looking at him, to feel her cool, slender fingers on his forehead.

"You just have to keep going," she said softly.

"Yeah," he said, his voice low and tight. He was so full of emotions he hadn't felt, hadn't allowed himself to feel, for years that he felt as if his chest was about to burst. He closed his eyes, letting his head loll back on his shoulders.

Christy studied him for a moment, reading the turmoil in his face. She wished she could help, could find some magic words to ease his way, but she knew all too well that what he was going through was a solitary battle.

She couldn't seem to stop her eyes from moving, and they swept over him, down the long, leanly muscled, powerful legs, across the sleekly bare chest with its flat, male nipples, then once more to the intriguing path of golden-brown hair that led her gaze irresistibly down to the length of white fabric. She could see the edge of the towel, below the knot on his far hip, where the cloth fell open along his muscular thigh, and she could picture the flesh bared by the gap. In her mind's eye she could see perfectly what the thick, white cloth hid, how the golden hair kept going until it widened into a thicket of curls....

She bit her lip, ordering her rebellious imagination to knock it off. He was a celebrity, she reminded herself somewhat fiercely. *He probably had a legion of faithful fans of the female persuasion,* she said to herself scathingly.

Funny, she had almost forgotten that. She found it hard to think of him that way, especially since he had dropped the arrogant, self-centered facade. *But there was no reason to be having such...racy thoughts about him,* she told herself.

It was just the situation, she thought. Stranded here, in such close quarters, she wouldn't be human if she didn't have this kind of reaction to a man like him. At least she supposed so; she'd never had this kind of reaction to a man before. The height of naïveté, that's you, Christy my girl, she said to herself ruefully.

A gust of wind howled outside, and they both glanced a little warily at the door. "I should have brought a tape player or something," Christy said uneasily. "All I brought are books, and they aren't much good at drowning out noise."

"Easy on the word 'drown,' okay?" Trace said with a wry grimace. Christy looked startled, then grinned back, glad he could joke about it. "Maybe you should read aloud," he suggested when another gust whistled eerily.

She wrinkled her nose at him. "Maybe you should. You're the actor, after all."

"I'd rather listen to you," he said seriously. "You've got a great voice."

"What?" she asked, startled.

"A great voice." He lowered his eyes, picking idly at the edge of the towel. "It was the only reason I...didn't give up in the water. I was afraid if I didn't do what you said...I wouldn't get to hear it anymore. That you'd get mad and go away."

His eyes closed again, and she saw gooseflesh rise on his arms. God, he had come so close! "But you never quit," she said softly.

"I did. But then you were there."

"You held on long enough." She grimaced at the memory. "I heard you go by the first time, even over the wind. I couldn't figure out why you were—" She broke off when he gave a harsh little chuckle, but went on when he didn't open his eyes or speak. "I was just coming back from the other side when I saw you again. I didn't hear the engine, so I don't know why I even looked. But I saw that wave...."

"I never did."

"It was terrible. It just picked up the boat and crushed it. If you hadn't been thrown clear..."

"I would have gone down with it," he said grimly, plucking at the towel again. "Almost did anyway. It was a piece of it that clipped me on the head."

"I'm sorry. It looked like a nice boat."

"I'm not. Not really. I only bought it when Tony wouldn't let me help him." He sighed ruefully. "I guess I thought if I couldn't impress him with how big I'd made it, I could impress everyone else." The harsh chuckle again. "At least it's insured. I can use the money for Tony now, if he'll take it like you said."

Just the change evident in those few words gave Christy hope. He just might make it, she thought, if it doesn't all go down the drain when he goes back. That he actually lived amid the glitter and lights she'd only read about seemed impossible to—

She sucked in a breath as he lifted his head to look at her intently with those incredible eyes, looking now as green as spring grass and reflecting the golden light of the lantern. A sudden vision of what he must look like on screen struck her, and it didn't seem at all impossible anymore.

He looked as if he were about to speak when the

wind picked up speed, and they glanced simultaneously at the door again.

"Maybe reading aloud isn't such a bad idea," she joked.

"Where are your books? I'll get one."

"I'll do it," she said hastily; she'd had about all she could take of him running around in that damned towel. She scrambled off the bed, grabbed her backpack and pulled out the first book that came to hand. She didn't glance at it until she sat back down; when she saw it was a volume of poetry, she looked at him doubtfully.

"Just pick one," he said quietly, seeing the title and her look.

Coloring a little, she opened it, then looked at him again. "Wouldn't you rather—"

"—listen to you. Please."

With a sigh, she looked down at the page the book had naturally fallen open to: Blake's "The Tyger." It was one of her favorites, but she felt suddenly very shy. As if sensing her hesitation, Trace turned slightly away from her, closing his eyes and lounging back in the chair. With surprise she realized that made it easier, and she marveled at the sensitivity of this man she had first thought so arrogant.

By the second verse she was into the rhythm of the words that she loved, her shyness vanished. Blake's words, his perfect description of that fierce, feral beast, seemed to so fit the storm that raged around them that as she read, the darkness outside seemed indeed his "forests of the night."

The last words seemed to echo for a moment before Trace, his voice slightly husky, said simply, "Thank you."

She blushed, absurdly pleased by his quiet words. She flipped through the pages, reading whatever caught her eye; he listened without speaking, a slight smile curving his mouth.

Then they sat in silence for a while, listening to the wind that seemed somehow more distant now, farther removed from the warm, lantern-lit cocoon they were in.

Trace reflexively lifted a hand to probe at his temple.

"Still hurt?"

"A little. But it's a lot better."

"Maybe you should take some aspirin and get some sleep."

And there it was, he thought. He sat up. "Christy? Where have you been sleeping?"

"You're sitting in it," she said lightly. "I thought about the counter, but I figured I'd probably fall off."

"You've been sleeping in this chair?" He shifted again.

"It's not too bad, turned sideways. It works."

"Not anymore," he said firmly, nodding toward the bunk. "You're staying right there."

Her chin came up at his tone. "Oh?"

"I'll use the chair."

Christy pointedly let her eyes scan his six-foot length. "Don't be silly."

"Look—"

"It doesn't make sense, Trace. You're too tall for that little chair."

"Damn it!" he burst out. "It's bad enough you had to save me from my own stupidity without—"

"I'm trying to save you from your own stubbornness."

"I'm using the damned chair!"

Christy opened her mouth, a retort on her lips, but shut it again with the words unspoken. He was really bothered by this, she thought. Was this truly a new Trace Dalton, or just the real one, hidden for so long beneath the arrogant facade?

He lowered his eyes and let out a long sigh. "I'm sorry. I didn't mean to snap at you."

"All right," she said slowly, eyeing him carefully. "Is this where I'm supposed to give the 'We're adults, not teenagers, we should be able to handle sharing a bunk' speech?"

His head shot up. "I—" he dropped his gaze again. "I didn't mean that."

"I know. But it does seem to be the logical solution."

Logical. Right. The thought of sharing that too-narrow bunk with her, of having her so close yet so untouchable, was torture; he knew the reality would be hell.

"I'm not sure I'm that adult," he muttered, so low that Christy couldn't be sure of what she'd heard.

"What?"

"Nothing."

Christy gave an exasperated sigh. "What's

wrong? Are you afraid I'm after your famous body?''

I'm afraid you're not. For a horrified second he thought he'd spoken the words out loud. But she was just waiting, looking at him levelly, so he knew he hadn't. "I...no."

"Fine, then." She scooted toward the edge of the bed as if all were decided. Trace rolled his eyes heavenward.

"Did you ever stop to think I might be after yours?''

She stared at him in astonishment. "Why? I mean, you must have lots of beautiful women after you. Why on earth would you want me?'' As if the truth of her rhetorical question was self-evident, she slid off the bunk and disappeared into the bathroom alcove.

Trace gaped at the still-swinging curtains. She didn't know. She honestly didn't know. As impossible as it seemed, she didn't know how beautiful she was, how those misty gray eyes pierced his very soul, didn't know the effect of those luscious curves and long legs, didn't realize the shivers that low, husky voice sent down a man's spine....

The curtains slid back, and his breath caught in his throat. She was wearing a demure nightshirt that covered her from her collarbone to just above her knees, from shoulder to wrist. There was no reason for his heart to start that hammering beat. Except that the nightshirt was made out of a gray satin cloth that turned her eyes to molten silver and, without revealing anything, managed to sinuously suggest every curve and hollow of her slender body. It shifted in rippling waves with every step, enticing him with the change of shimmering light and shadow.

"Damn." He ordered his surging body to calm down.

She walked past him without a word, going to the lantern that was making a hissing sound that indicated it was nearly out of fuel for the day. She didn't speak, merely paused with her hand on the knob that would douse the wick, looking at him. He knew what she meant; it was decision time.

"Damn," he repeated, and hurled himself up out of the chair and strode angrily across the room. He jerked the curtains of the alcove shut with an abrupt motion, then yanked the towel off and flung it over the rack. It wasn't doing much to disguise his aroused state anyway.

He seriously considered cranking about a gallon of cold water over his too-active body, but another thought made him turn to look at the rack that held his clothes. She had told him that she'd rinsed the salt water from everything as best she could, although she wasn't sure of how successful she'd been with the jacket. He lifted the now stiff leather garment and reached for the dark blue briefs he'd been wearing that day.

Good, he thought grimly, they were still damp and most definitely cold. He yanked them on, shuddering a little as the chilly cloth enclosed his heated flesh.

"Damn," he said a third time. *But at the rate*

you're going, he told himself caustically, *they'll be dry from sheer body heat in about thirty seconds. You'd better move fast.*

Hours later he lay awake staring at the darkness, knowing he'd underestimated this particular hell. That it was completely one-sided only made it worse; he could hear her quiet, even breathing as she slept peacefully beside him.

She had casually suggested he take the side against the wall so she wouldn't wake him when she got up to go out in the morning. He didn't know which irritated him more, that she was taking this so placidly, or that she was planning on going back into that chaos again, so he gritted his teeth and said nothing about either, just slid over on the narrow bunk.

It had seemed like forever before he had finally quieted his begging body and gone to sleep. His peace didn't last, for soon he was slipping into a deliciously erotic dream in which she had come to him, her silken skin soft and smooth against his, her—

That was when he had awakened to find the dream was real. Apparently seeking his warmth in her sleep, she had snuggled next to him in the dark. He could feel the spun silk of her hair beneath his cheek and her long legs, smoother than the satin of the nightshirt that had ridden up to let his press against them. His arm had gone around her, drawing her into the curve of his body, and he could feel the tempting, soft weight of her breasts above his forearm, so close that he had to curl his hand into a fist to keep from moving it to caress those beckoning curves.

It didn't help. As if he'd actually done it, he could feel the soft warmth of her breast rounding into his hand. As if he'd done what his fingers had wanted, he could feel the soft peak hardening beneath his touch. He smothered a groan.

His flesh rose to the feel of her taut, rounded bottom tucked into the bend of his hips. He was hot and hard and aching, and he didn't understand it. He'd never felt like this, so completely out of control.

Moving with agonizing slowness, he began to inch away, his body screaming a silent protest, his brain ordering it to go on; having her know would be too much for him to bear. He froze once when she murmured something, but she didn't awaken, and he pulled free and rolled away, drawing himself into an aching, throbbing curl.

Nobody would believe it, he thought with painful irony. All the celebrity columnists who loved him for the grist he provided for their gossip mills, all those back in L.A. who knew about his various peccadilloes with this month's—or even this week's—flame, would probably laugh their heads off at the thought of him lying there in the dark, sweating, aching for the silver-eyed waif beside him, who wanted nothing to do with him. It was a long, long time before he slept again.

Six

Christy clung stubbornly to the last vestiges of
sleep, snuggling into the warmth. She could hear
the wind howling, but she was too warm and comfortable to care. It felt so good just to lie here,
pressed to his broad back....

She came awake in shocked surprise, her cheeks
flaming. She was indeed pressed to Trace's backside from shoulder to knee, one hand resting on the
smooth, warm skin of his muscled side, her legs
intimately entwined with his.

God, she thought, inching away, *please don't let
him wake up!* He was curled up facing the wall—
Probably trying to stay away from you, she thought
grimly—and it took her a few moments to disen-
tangle herself.

She had a hard time concentrating on her work

that day. Focus, she ordered her mind and her fingers, staring through the lens at the grayness: gray sky, gray water, gray clouds. The lack of color didn't matter; her memories had enough vividness to color everything. Damn, she couldn't take much more of this. Why didn't this storm *do* something?

Although he said nothing, he was so edgy when she went back for lunch that she felt a sudden fear that he had been awake after all, that he knew. The thought made her eat hastily, in a hurry to get away again. That evening he was worse. Pacing, snapping at her, until the old, arrogant Trace would have been a relief. Studying him from beneath lowered lashes, Christy saw dark circles beneath eyes that, tonight, looked blue and cloudy.

"Are you…all right?"

"Fine," he snarled. "Just fine."

Damn it, he thought later as he slid reluctantly into the bunk, he was not going to let her do this to him again. He'd spent nights with some of the most glamorous women in Hollywood, beautiful, admired…

And as substantial as cotton candy, he interrupted himself glumly. And not one of them had ever made him feel the way she did. His jaw tightened.

Christy stood with her hand on the lantern, looking at him a little warily.

"What's wrong?" he grated.

"Nothing," she said and turned down the wick. She walked over and sat down on the edge of the bunk, not moving.

"Are you just going to sit there all night?"

"Maybe. I'm not used to sleeping with a grizzly bear."

"Who *are* you used to sleeping with?" He didn't want to hear the answer, but he couldn't stop the harsh words.

Her temper snapped. "No one! And I'm beginning to remember why I prefer it that way!"

No one, Trace thought, startled at the strength of the relief that filled him. She plopped down angrily and tugged the blankets up over her shoulders with a sharp, short motion. "Christy," he began softly.

"Good night!"

His arm lifted, his hand reached for her, pulling back at the last second. Leave it, he told himself. It was better this way. If she were mad at him, it would be easier. He couldn't take another night like last night; it had to be easier.

It wasn't.

He'd been pacing all day, it seemed, first angrily, then worriedly. She'd been gone again when he awoke after lying sleepless until early morning. She didn't show up at midday. He swore viciously; she was obviously still mad at him.

His angry mood evaporated when the sounds from outside began to penetrate. He didn't need the radio to tell him that Charlotte had made up her mind, but he flipped it on anyway. The static was so bad now that he could only pick up a few words here and there, but the combination of "landfall" and "Matagorda" told him all he needed, and more than he wanted to know. Charlotte was about to strike, a bare fifty miles away. And Christy was out in it and didn't know.

He continued his pacing, stopping only to peer out the small window. Water. Nothing but water. Damn, anything could happen out there.

That was enough. He couldn't just sit there anymore. He would drag her back physically if that was what he had to do. He went to the alcove and grabbed his jeans; they were dry at last, but stiff, and he had to tug to get them on. Then his shirt and the equally stiff jacket, and he was moving again.

He almost forgot to slide the door closed behind him as he looked around in stunned shock. It was worse than he'd thought. Much worse.

He fastened the latch, then knelt down to look for the rope. It took him a moment to find it, and when he did, his heart went cold. It was pulled tight, cutting into the ground until a thin layer of the wet sand covered it. Enough to tell him that it had been that way for a while, taut with the weight pulling it from the other end. Christy.

That he had to crawl to follow the rope didn't matter; once he was five yards from the hut he couldn't see anything anyway, and once clear of the lee side of the bluff, it was impossible to walk against the wind. He felt as if he was back in that gray fog, unable to tell up from down, sky from sea.

The sea. He could hear it now, could feel the

thundering vibrations as it pounded the shore, but he still couldn't see it. He followed the rope.

Then he *could* see it, looking unworldly amid the grayness. It was stark white, an unbroken mass of churning, wind-whipped foam, and the spray that rose above it was nearly as thick as the water itself. He followed the rope.

It couldn't be this long, he thought numbly as he traced the path of that taut cord. There wasn't a rope in the world this long. It was a trick, some sick practical joke, and he would be following this damned rope forever. He really had died; the nights with Christy had been his purgatory, and now this was his hell. He followed the rope.

He was practically on top of it when he felt the edge of the bluff begin to give way beneath him. He scrambled back and tried to peer through the driving rain. The blue nylon line disappeared over that crumbling edge, and his heart began to hammer in his chest.

He flattened himself and inched forward, fighting the urge to hurry. He might send the rest of that precarious bank of sand sliding downward, and until he knew...

He knew. He could barely see her; she was half buried under the crushing weight of wet sand. He threw caution to the raging winds and scrambled down the slope.

She was alive. She moved her head when she heard him, looking at him with wide, dark, dazed eyes. He could see now why she couldn't get free; the very rope that had led him to her was pulled so tight across her body that she couldn't free her hands to dig herself out.

"Fell...it crumbled..." she mumbled, so vaguely he wasn't sure she even knew he was there.

"Are you hurt?" He had to know before he tried to move her. After a moment she shook her head. He freed her arms, but the weight of the sand was too much, he couldn't pull her out. He began to dig furiously, clawing at the sand like an enraged animal, tossing it heedlessly, cursing the wind that pulled at them mercilessly. He slid his hands under her arms once more, and this time he freed her from the deadly grip.

He cradled her against him, feeling her trembling. "It's all right, love, it's all over," he crooned over her bent head, pressing his lips to her wet, sandy hair.

He was suddenly aware that seawater was swirling around them, and he moved to pick her up. In that moment, as he looked at the relentless approach of the surging waves, he realized the true horror she had faced. Trapped, helpless, and watching her executioner close in on her.

"Oh, God, Christy!" He crushed her to him in a fierce embrace. "God," he repeated numbly, "how long...?"

"I don't...couple of hours, I think," she whispered, her voice thin and barely audible.

A couple of hours. Hours of knowing exactly how you were going to die, of having to watch it happen, slowly.... He shuddered, then scrambled to his feet; she was a featherweight in his arms.

"Can you stand? Just for a second? I can't pull us up the bluff without both hands. Just hang on to my shoulders."

"I...think I can walk," she said, then made a liar out of herself by collapsing the moment he let go of her.

"Come on, baby, just put your arms around me. That's it." He lifted her easily, and when she had tightened her grip on him, he began to haul on the rope. His hands were raw from the wet, sandy rope by the time he crested the bluff, but he never even slowed down. Christy shifted as if to slip down, but he wouldn't let her. Hand over hand he followed that wonderful rope back, coiling it as he went, thinking he would have it bronzed someday.

The journey seemed endless, but at last they were at the hut. He set her down only long enough to untie the rope from her waist and unlatch the door. Then he carried her inside and across the room to the alcove. He gave her no chance to protest, just took off the waterproof gear and tossed it aside.

She let him pull off the equipment vest; he was a little more careful with it, but still set it aside quickly. He reached for the top button of her shirt, tugging it through the sodden cloth. She was shivering, fueling his haste.

It was harder to tug off the clammy, wet jeans. He had to tug fiercely to get them free of her long legs, but finally she was standing in brief, blue lace panties and a matching blue bra. He ruthlessly ignored the part of his mind that was registering how incredibly lovely she was, the part that was taking in the beautiful curve of her waist, its tininess emphasizing her slenderness just as the gentle curve of her hips emphasized her womanliness, the part that was seeing the lush rise of her breasts above the lace.

She made an embarrassed sound of protest when he reached for her again, but he hushed her. "I owe you this, remember?" He unfastened the bra, steeling himself not to notice how the ripe fullness of her breasts spilled free. He slipped the other scrap of lace down her long, lovely legs.

Judging from the past two nights, he thought that her nudity would have ripped away what little control he had left. To his surprise, although his body surged at the sight before him, nothing took precedence over his concern for her.

He washed her gently, then patted her dry, as she had him. He picked up the soft, warm sweater she usually wore inside and tugged it over her head, breathing a little easier when its length and bulk hid her from his eyes. Without a word he lifted her once more and carried her to the bunk, tucking her into it with exquisite care.

He found a can of soup and heated it quickly. After pouring it into a heavy mug, he gave it to her, sitting on the edge of the bed until she drank it. She was regaining some color, and the dazed look was fading as the shock receded. He took the cup, refilled it, and gave it to her again before he finally went to pull off his own wet clothes.

His briefs were damp, but drier than any of the towels right now. He hung his clothes back on the rack, resigning himself to another couple of days without them. He was almost getting used to parading around in front of her nearly naked, except for the difficulty of hiding his reaction to her.

He poured the last of the soup into a cup for himself, then sat beside her again. She'd finished half of the second mug and was now just cupping her hand around it, savoring the warmth. She watched the steam rise from it, following the swirling pattern until, as if driven to it, she spoke.

"I slipped. The sand gave...I rolled down the slope...until the rope caught. It came down on top of me. I thought if I just waited...that you would come. Then...I saw the water...." She shuddered. "If you hadn't come then..."

With one swift motion he took the cup from her and set it aside, then pulled her into his arms. "Shh," he said, holding her. "It's all right. I did." And the thought of what he would have found if he'd waited another ten minutes seared him to his soul; he held her tighter.

She raised her eyes to his. "Thank you," she whispered.

"You're welcome."

"You saved—"

"Uh-uh," he interrupted. "You thanked me, I accepted, and that's the end of it, remember? That's how it works."

She smiled, a small, shaky smile; it was a thousand-watt grin to him. But it faded as a howling gust of wind reverberated outside. "She's moving in, isn't she?"

He didn't lie to her. "Yes. From what I could hear, the worst should hit us tomorrow." He studied her, wondering if she could deal with this after what she'd been through.

"And?" she prodded softly.

Yes, she could, he realized. She could handle just about anything. "It's going to hit a lot closer than we thought. Matagorda Island, they said."

Her eyes widened, and her mouth tightened, but she only nodded. He got up then, going to pick up the book and pull the chair close to the bunk. "I'll return the favor, if you like." Christy nodded quickly.

He thumbed through the pages, looking for something to read for, as his father used to say, the sound, not the sense. He paused, smiled, then sat back and began to read.

Christy had studied the poem in school and read it since, but never had she heard "The Rubaiyat of Omar Khayyam" like this. His trained voice made the words sing, and the unusual names rolled liltingly off his tongue. She savored the sounds, wondering how in the world someone who could make words sound like this could possibly think her voice was worth listening to.

She was so rapt, so caught up in the lively, ringing rhythm, that she immediately caught the barely perceptible break in his voice as, near the end, a verse struck home. It was the barest change in tone, the slightest of wry notes, but as the sense of the words came to her, she understood.

"Indeed the Idols I have loved so long
Have done my credit in this World much wrong:
Have drowned my Glory in a shallow Cup,
And sold my Reputation for a Song."

He regained the lilting beat immediately, so quickly that if she hadn't known, she might have thought she had imagined the change. She waited for a moment after he had finished, then repeated his simple words.

"Thank you."

He started to shrug, then stopped. "My pleasure."

"It…may take more than a song to buy it back," she said softly, "but you can do it if you really want to."

He didn't pretend not to understand. "I never really cared about it before. But I do now."

The lantern hissed suddenly, and he got up. She made a tiny, choked sound, and his head shot up to look at her. She was staring at the golden light, her fingers tightening around the blankets. It came to him then: after what she'd been through, the last thing she wanted was darkness.

"I'll refill it," he said quietly, "and lower it a bit."

"Yes…please," she said, her voice tight, far-away, her eyes following him.

He trimmed the wick so there was just enough light to illuminate the corners of the small room, then walked back and turned the chair sideways; she looked at him quizzically.

"Just rest. I'll be fine here."

"But I—" She stopped abruptly, and he saw a flash of embarrassment coloring her cheeks in the second before she lowered her head. He sat down on the edge of the bunk.

"What?"

"I…nothing." She plucked at a thread on the blanket.

"Christy, talk to me. Please?"

She lifted her head then, and he saw in the huge gray eyes what it cost her pride to say the words. "Would you…hold me? Just for a while?"

His stomach knotted, and with a convulsive movement he swung his legs up and stretched out beside her, holding out his arms. She came to him instantly, and he settled her against him in a comfortable embrace, resting his cheek just above where he was stroking her hair with one hand. He felt her gradually relax, and when at last she slipped into sleep, he felt as if he'd been given some wondrous prize.

He was so full of tumultuous emotions that he couldn't begin to sort them out; he was having difficulty just breathing. Was it just because it was her, this good and brave and noble person in his arms, was it because she was so special that he felt so special that she allowed him this? Or was it knowing that she trusted him, in spite of the fact that she'd had little reason in her life to trust anyone, that made him feel so...so honored? It seemed a corny word to use, but he knew it was the right one. Again he lay awake long into the night, but this time it was to savor the feel of her in his arms.

He had breakfast ready when she woke and she thanked him rather solemnly; he knew it was for more than just the food and nodded in understanding.

She never even mentioned going out again, for which Trace was thankful; he'd been ready to hogtie her if she even suggested it. Instead she got out the gear she'd had with her the day before and began to try to clean it up. The rolls of film she'd taken seemed undamaged, and she tucked them away in the bag with the others without a word. Trace grimaced at the thought of what might be on those rolls.

They avoided mentioning what they both knew, that Charlotte had struck with full intensity. No longer were they being whipped with her lesser winds, pelted with the fringes of rain, they were under siege from the full force of her might. Christy spread the gear out on the table silently.

She began to strip down the camera and the lenses, to try to undo some of the damage. It was a job, she said, that would have to be done again by a professional, but anything she could do now would only make it easier.

She even let him help, although he was reduced

to brushing some pieces he couldn't even name with a fine camel's hair brush. He worked carefully, keeping up a continuous stream of questions about each piece she handed him, hoping to keep her mind occupied. When at last she had packed everything away again, she straightened up to look at him with a glint of amusement in her eyes.

"You can stop now. I'm fine."

"Er...stop?"

"The questions. I appreciate it, but really, I'm all right now, you don't have to keep me talking." He shrugged sheepishly, and her voice went warm and soft. "I...it happened. It was horrible. I will never forget it. But I'm not going to let it haunt every day of my life."

He looked at her in awe. "You have more guts than anybody I've ever known."

"Me?" She laughed. "Not me. Guts is getting up in front of a television camera and...er—" she glanced at the blue briefs he wore "—baring all to the world, so to speak."

He laughed. "I've bared more than this, on occasion."

Oh, help, Christy thought. Bared more? Exactly what was left to be bared was etched in her mind as if with acid.

"And quit changing the subject, anyway," he interrupted her thoughts, for which she silently thanked him. "Just take the compliment, will you?"

"If you fix dinner," she shot back.

"It's hopeless," he groaned in mock despair.

They both fixed dinner, treating themselves to beef burgundy and even dessert, a foil package grandly labeled Apple Cobbler. Trace looked at it doubtfully, Christy with optimism, and the final result fell somewhere in between; it looked terrible, but tasted exactly like the name.

"I'm not sure I want to know how they did that," Trace said as they cleaned up.

"Ignorance *is* bliss sometimes," Christy agreed with blithe unconcern.

She asked him to read again that night, wanting to hear his voice send the words flying again. It was a book of short stories this time, by a famous author of westerns, and she found herself smiling at the drawl that crept into his voice as he read. She wondered if it was real, if he'd had to work to lose it after he'd left Texas for the bright lights.

It seemed only natural that she would slip into his arms again after they turned out the light. She had promised she would be all right in the dark now that the initial horror had faded, but he couldn't quite brace himself to turn his back to her. And he wasn't sure he wanted to, not even to save himself. Last night had been easier; she'd been shaken, frightened, and he'd used that to bludgeon his raging senses into submission. Tonight she was all too vitally well and alive, and he gritted his teeth as she snuggled down and rested her head on his shoulder.

Christy knew she was treading on dangerous ground; she was enjoying this far too much. She was enjoying the feel of his shoulder beneath her cheek, the feel of hard muscle under sleek skin where her hand had—naturally, it seemed—come to rest on his chest. She wondered if he could feel the pounding of her heart; she was amazed that he couldn't hear it.

Not that it matters, she told herself sternly. *He's probably used to women going into a dither whenever he's around. You're a fool, Christy, my girl, and if you had an ounce of brains you'd get yourself back to your side of this stupid bunk and stay there.* When this was over, they would go their separate ways, Hurricane Charlotte no more than an unusual memory. She scolded herself, gave herself orders and then at last gave up, deciding to enjoy the moment and handle the rest later.

They awoke to a shrieking howl that seemed too loud, too uncanny, to be mere wind. They sat up abruptly, both looking warily at the door. It came again, even louder, then again, and they both swallowed heavily.

Trace got up and lit the lantern, then scrambled back to the bunk; somehow things seemed less eerie in the golden light. But it didn't lessen the sound, that screaming, piercing sound. The door rattled in its track, and Christy could almost feel the wind through the walls. It rose to a shriek, and the flicker of the lantern's flame made her heart leap in fear.

Just when they thought it could get no worse, a violent blast struck, howling at an ear-splitting pitch, shaking everything, and there was the sound of shattering glass as the tiny window gave way, sending shards flying. They stared in horror as water sprayed through the opening, neither of them voicing the ominous question, Was it rain, or the ocean?

They slid down to huddle beneath the blankets. It was an ancient, primeval response, a heading for cover no matter how useless, how hopeless. It went on and on, until Christy wanted to scream. Only the knowledge that the sound would be sucked up by the raging wind stopped her; she wondered if even Trace would hear her.

They were clinging to each other, knowing they had no options, no place to go. Hearts pounding, breath coming in quick pants, they waited. And listened to the world gone berserk, fully expecting each breath to be their last.

"Oh, my God," Christy whispered. Trace could barely hear her, but her look froze him. He followed her gaze in time to see a crack appear in the concrete above them. It was small at first, but then grew, rapidly, jaggedly, until in a sudden burst of speed, it raced for the far wall above the door.

Instinctively Trace moved, levering himself over her, protecting her body with his own, expecting at any moment to feel the collapsing ceiling crashing down on him. After a moment he risked a glance. Sand was slipping through, slowly but enough to drift into small piles on the floor. Yet still the roof held. It might hold long enough, it might...

He turned back, meaning to reassure her. She was looking at him, her eyes wide with apprehension—and something else he couldn't name. It was

that which made him abruptly aware of the feel of
her beneath him, of the softness and warmth of her.
He tried to resist, but drawn by a force as unstoppable as the storm raging outside, his mouth came
down on hers.

He'd thought about kissing her. Often. In his
mind, it had always been a slow, lingering kiss,
with all the time in the world to savor it. But now,
when it happened, it was a match held to tinder,
and the flames roared up instantly.

Her lips were warm and sweet beneath his, and
they parted for the urgent probing of his tongue.
She met him, her tongue teasing, touching, tasting
his, as fiercely as he did hers, and searing heat spiraled through him.

His body surged to aching fullness so swiftly it
made his head spin. He felt her hands tangle in his
hair and press his head to her, crushing his mouth
even harder on hers. He drove his tongue deeper
into that honeyed warmth, demanding, and she answered him with a soft, low moan of pleasure that
he somehow heard amid the tumult.

They became creatures of the storm, desperate to
drive back the impending doom. The roar faded
next to the pounding of blood in their ears, and the
world narrowed to the two of them and the sudden
certainty that nothing mattered except how they
could make each other feel. Together they could
throw that grim dirge back in the face of the fierce
storm, and no matter what the end, the victory
would be theirs.

Christy clutched at him as he nibbled down the

delicate line of her jaw, tiny sounds coming from low in her throat. She could feel him, rigid and pulsing against her belly, and she knew he was the answer to that hollow, unbearable ache that was building inside her. He could make it stop. He had to make it stop—she couldn't bear any more. She wanted him, hot and hard and completely; he would fill her, drive the need out of her with his own body.

Trace had become a driven thing, a creature he didn't even recognize. He didn't know why she had the power to do this to him, didn't know how she had already made him feel a hundredfold more than he'd ever felt, even in the supposedly climactic moments with other women. He was beyond caring. He hadn't known he could be so hot, so hard, so desperate, could ache so badly, need so much, burn so fiercely.

His hand slid down to cup her breast, a shudder rippling through him as her flesh swelled into his palm just as he'd known it would. His fingers reached for the crest and found it taut and ready, as if waiting eagerly for his touch. He groaned hoarsely. As if the demon of the storm had gotten into him, he was seized with an uncontrollable need to have her naked beneath him. He clawed at the shirt, then the panties.

She helped him, wriggling feverishly, but before he could lower himself to her again, she was pulling at his briefs, and he knew she had the same need to feel him naked against her; his entire body clenched at the thought.

He lowered his head to her, capturing a taut nipple and flicking it with his tongue. She moaned, and again somehow he heard it; it fired his already seething blood. He took the other nipple, tugging, teasing. She arched her back, thrusting herself upward to him, never guessing at the blazing need that convulsive movement caused in him. He suckled her flesh, first one peak, then the other, until she was gasping.

He couldn't wait. Her every move was driving him mad with the heat of his own response. He moved to settle between her thighs. She opened for him, eagerly, and he knew if he didn't plunge into her waiting warmth he was going to burst, to fly apart in a hundred quivering, helpless pieces.

Christy felt the first, probing touch of his swollen shaft and wanted to cry out, to beg him to hurry. Her breasts were still tingling from his caress, her nipples still wet and hard from his mouth, but they were nothing compared to the need that drove her now, the need to have that hot maleness inside her. Please, she begged silently, oh, please...

Trace thrust into her fiercely, urgently. He felt her go rigid with shock and tried to wait for her body to adjust. He saw the look of surprise, of wonder, in her eyes, but he had no time to think about it now. He had to move. Her slick, wet heat was scalding him, searing him to the core.

He drove forward once more, with more force than he'd intended, but before he could wonder if he'd hurt her, she was rising to meet him. Again she rose with him, their bodies moving together so powerfully that it took their breath away. They drove at each other, clawing, straining, each taking as much as being taken. Christy's head was thrashing on the pillow with every thrust, every muscle in her body seeming to ripple in time with the slamming collision of flesh against flesh.

Trace was gasping, groaning, as she took him in deeper and deeper. God, she was so sweet, so small, so tight, she was killing him! Her hands slid down his back to grasp his hips, then moved to clutch at the flexing muscles of his buttocks, pulling him into her. He couldn't hold back when she touched him like that! He thrust again, harder, and she bucked wildly beneath him, driving him hard and deep, his name torn from her on a sharp cry as every muscle went rigid.

And then he felt it, the rippling, stroking caress of her hot, coaxing flesh around the sheathed length of him, drawing him up so far inside her that he thought she would hold him forever. It set off a chain of explosions inside him that went on and on, sending signals of unbelievable pleasure along already singing nerves, flowing outward in a rushing wave, then returning to him as if from her, as if the signals had jumped the gap between their bodies as easily as they moved within them. He arched his back, forcing himself hard into her slick, hot depths. He wanted to climb inside her and never come out; she was sweet and safe and home.

Through a golden haze of pleasure Christy saw him, saw him throw back his head, the cords of his neck standing out as he cried out her name in a

shout of agonized pleasure. Then he collapsed atop
her, panting, spent, and she couldn't tell if the in-
voluntary, shuddering convulsions were his or hers.

She held him close, little ripples of heat and
pleasure still racing along nerves she couldn't believe weren't singed to ashes. She'd never known,
wouldn't have believed, it was possible to feel so
much, to soar so high. Her breath was coming in
rapid gasps, in counterpoint to his harsh pants. She
loved the feel of him, his weight pressing down on
her, his arms wrapped around her shoulders as if
he were afraid she would somehow slip away. She
felt safe, protected, utterly content for the first time
in her life.

Trace tried to move, to relieve her of his weight,
but he couldn't seem to find the strength. He was
drained, floating on a warm, soothing sea, needing
and wanting nothing more out of life than to stay
in this wondrous place forever.

The chaos outside continued as fiercely as before, but they were drifting in the warm, gentle aftermath, and nothing could touch them. The roar
seemed muffled, distant, and had nothing to do
with them.

At last he slid off her, keeping his arms tightly
around her so that she turned with him. He held
her close, and she pressed herself to him, both of
them clinging to the warmth, to the safety. It was
new and precious and special, and they hugged the
sweetness of it tightly, loath to surrender it. And
somehow, amid the furor, the magic held for them,
and, amazingly, they slept.

Seven

Christy choked off the sweet, stinging memories before they could batter her with the knowledge of how quickly things had changed after that. She hadn't realized she'd sat down, hadn't even realized the couch had been there, but she came out of her reverie to find herself sitting. Trembling.

He hadn't moved. He was still standing by the window, and his eyes were wide and troubled and full of the mists of memory. Blue, she thought. Deeply, searingly blue, drawing on the color of the royal-blue shirt he wore. Under the jacket. That blessed leather jacket. He must have had it cleaned, treated somehow, to make it wearable again. And again she wondered inanely why he'd bothered.

Hurricane Productions, she thought numbly. God, she should have guessed. Instead she had walked in like a lamb to the slaughter, no warning, no chance for escape. More than anything in her life she wanted to run—and she couldn't move.

But he could. He left the window and took three long strides toward her. She cringed despite herself. He stopped.

"You...hate me that much?" His voice was low and harsh.

Her eyes shot upward. Hate him? How on earth could he think that? "I don't...hate you."

"Then why?" It burst from him with all the force of three years of trying to bury it. He closed his eyes against the pain. "God, Christy, why?"

Her heart was racing, fluttering like some wild, caged thing, frantic to escape. Did he know? She would have expected anger, perhaps worry that she would try to stake some kind of claim on him, but never would she have expected the agony in those incredible eyes. His jaw was rigid with tension, and his pain was reflected in every chiseled plane of his face. And, actor or not, she couldn't doubt the pain was real; she could feel it radiating from him as she had once felt the heat of his body. She flushed at the memory.

"Why?" she managed, stalling. He didn't know, did he? "Why did you think...I hated you?"

"What was I supposed to think? One minute you were there, then you were gone. I—" He paused to swallow heavily. "I tried to find you, when I finally got free of that...circus. No one knew where you'd gone."

He raised a hand to touch the scar at his temple,

a movement that had become automatic. Running a fingertip over the tiny pucker of flesh at his eyebrow was sometimes the only thing that convinced him he hadn't dreamed it all. He dropped down wearily in a chair across from her, not daring to come any closer, sensing how close she was to running.

"I went back to the Ranger Station," he said flatly, dully, as if the words were being dragged from him over what feeble resistance he had left. "I talked to the guy who'd been there the day you got there, the guy who picked us up. He said he didn't know where you'd gone, or even where you'd come from. He'd asked, he said. And for more than that."

Christy lowered her eyes. She remembered the young ranger who worked at the Padre Island National Seashore. He'd been very nice, very helpful, and very concerned about what she intended to do. He'd also asked her to change her mind and let him take her out to dinner instead. She'd been flattered—he was a very nice-looking young man—but she had, as always, declined.

Trace went on, in that dull, weary voice. "I made him dig out the waiver you signed, but it only had your agent's name and address. I called. He wouldn't tell me anything."

"He...didn't know. Where I was, I mean. I...went away for a while."

He gave a harsh chuckle. He leaned forward, resting his elbows on his knees. "I wish I could have. When I realized you...weren't going to come to me, I wanted to go away. Far away. I couldn't understand. The only thing that made sense was... that you hated me. For what happened that last night.''

"Oh, God." He'd given her the most beautiful night of her life, taught her more in those hot, swirling moments about life, about love, about herself, than she had ever thought to know. And he thought she hated him for it.

"Then I thought maybe you just...didn't believe I'd really changed. That when we got back, and you found out who I'd been, what I'd been, that you didn't want anything to do with me. I thought..." He bit his lip, then took a deep breath. "I was afraid you thought I'd just used you, used the...the situation, to get you into bed with me." He studied his hands where they had locked together, knuckles white with strain. "It would have been...typical. For the old me. The one you must have found out about when we got back."

Christy opened her mouth, but she couldn't speak. He sounded so humble, so full of that self-directed disgust she'd seen in the hut. He was ripping her apart inside.

"But I kept trying. I called anyone and everyone I could think of. Finally I went to Reno."

She stared at him in shock. "You...what?"

"I went to Reno. I started with the police, then the hospital, then the juvenile court." His mouth twisted wryly. "It was ironic, really. For the first time I was determined not to play the big celebrity game, to leave all that behind, and I ended up doing it more than ever. I signed more autographs and posed for more pictures... But I didn't care, not if it meant...they'd help me find you.''

''My God,'' she breathed.

''I talked to your doctor, the one who found you. You said you'd gone back there. I hoped he might have known from where. I thought I could go there and look. But he didn't know.'' He looked up at her. ''The Sawyers have two more foster kids now,'' he said, ''but they still remember you.''

Christy's eyes widened. ''You...saw them?''

He nodded. ''They said you were only with them for two years, but you were why they continued with the foster parent program.''

''I...they were good to me.''

''I know. I could tell by the way they talked about you.'' His throat tightened at the memories of what they'd told him of a young Christy, fighting to overcome her shaky start in life, proud yet frightened, and determined to make something of herself on her own.

''But they wouldn't tell me any more. They got...protective, I guess.'' His mouth twisted again. ''They knew about me, all right.'' He sighed. ''I think I liked them all the more for it.'' She'd had few enough people to watch out for her in her life.

''They're...very special.''

''Yes. And so is John Donovan,'' he added softly.

Christy's heart turned over. God, how long had

he spent tracing the threads of her scattered, confused life? And why?

"Do you know one of your pictures is still in that display case?" He saw her shiver under the onslaught of emotion that swept her. He remembered that afternoon so clearly. Although he'd tried to keep a low profile, he'd wound up causing a near riot in the halls of the school when one of the more observant students took a second, then a third, look at the man in the battered leather jacket talking to Mr. Donovan outside the photo room.

It had taken nearly an hour of signing his name on everything from paper towels to book covers, and a picture taken by every member of the Photography II class, before he'd been able to sit down and talk to the man who had been her mentor. He'd smiled through it all, determined that this new leaf would stay turned.

"He told me how he'd found you, how you took to the camera like a 'duck to water,' he said. How you never thought you were good enough, and he had to send your first contest entry in without you knowing about it."

Christy blinked at the sudden stinging behind her eyelids. "I was furious."

"So he said. 'And that,' he said, 'is something to see.' I told him I knew that."

She was huddled on the couch now, arms wrapped around herself as if trying to keep herself from flying apart.

"But when I asked him if he knew where you were now, he clammed up. Told me he didn't much care for what he'd heard about me, and he wasn't saying anything unless he knew you wanted him to." He laughed, that short, harsh, painful chuckle again. "I've never been so…stymied. My reputation got them to see me in the first place, then it made them refuse to tell me anything. Hoist with my own petard…"

Christy was stunned. She never would have guessed he would go to such lengths to find her. And she never would have guessed she would receive so much protective help from the people who had been havens in her stormy life.

"Trace," she whispered, but no other words came. After a moment he went on, in the tone of one unburdening a tortured soul.

"So I came home. I went back to work. And I started to climb out of the hole I'd dug for myself. 'You just have to keep going,' you said, remember? Sometimes that was the only thing that kept me from quitting. I'd look around at all the people I'd made hate me, at all the bad feelings I'd brought on myself, and I wanted to give up. But then I'd think of you and feel so damned ashamed of even considering quitting, when you never had, with ten times the reason…"

"I…" Again, no more words came; he looked up and saw the eyes he'd dreamed of for so long, wide, dark and misty gray.

"Then I saw the book." His voice had dropped to a mere whisper of sound, taut and strained. "It was like…reliving it, all over again. I was up all night, just staring at it. I saw the listing of the

Alaska book. I couldn't believe it. It had been right out there, all that time, and I never knew.''

He shook his head slowly, as if in pain. ''All I could think of was how many people, probably even some I knew, had your name sitting on their bookshelves, and I never knew. It wasn't until the next morning that I realized I was holding another chance. I thought...I hoped that maybe...you'd heard. I knew the papers were blaring my... conversion, I guess they called it, all over. I hoped you had. That you knew why. That you knew I...meant what I'd promised you.''

He stared down at the plush, blue-smoke carpeting. ''I meant it all. My work, my attitude...even Tony.'' He glanced at her. ''He's in school now. You were right. He...took my help, that way.''

Christy tried to speak, to acknowledge him, but her throat was too tight.

Trace took a shuddering breath. ''I called Dragon Books. They told me...what you said. That's when I knew...that I'd been right in the beginning. That you...hated me.''

''I don't...hate you,'' she repeated, forcing the words out past the choking, aching lump in her throat. She hadn't hated him, even when she'd given those instructions. Even though she'd known then...

''Then why?'' he asked again, huskily. ''Why did you run?''

She stared at him, torn. The changes she'd seen in that photograph on the plane—a thousand years ago—were even more evident in person. He was no less compellingly handsome, but there was a new gentleness about him and a strangely older, wiser look in those dramatic eyes.

Had she done that to him? Was she the reason for that sad, almost haunted look in his eyes? It didn't seem possible, but then, neither did all he'd done. She was confused, still dazed by the shock of seeing him, but she couldn't shake the feeling that she owed him this, at least.

"I...that morning...when they came for us..." She stopped. Although the memories of those days with him often rose unstoppably to batter her, she had usually managed to avoid thinking of that last morning. They had been startled awake by, of all things, someone shouting her name through the battered door of the hut.

For all her fury, Charlotte had not lasted once she'd finally struck. After teasing them for days with the outer fringes of her might, she had swept through in haste, as if eager to expend herself on the land that would be her undoing. Fifteen hours after she had finally set her course she was gone, and they had been roused to a brilliant, sunny September day that had been nearly as big a shock as the unexpected voice shouting through the sliding door that was, judging from the pounding going on, jammed shut. From that moment, things had happened so fast that she'd had no time to think.

Only a quickly spoken warning from Trace had saved her from slicing her feet to ribbons; she'd forgotten about the shattered window.

She had called out to reassure the young ranger

as she scrambled into her clothes, tautly aware of Trace close behind her, and of the awkwardness she was feeling at their mutual nakedness as the world began to close in on them. He had grabbed his own clothes, and she was even more aware of all the things they hadn't said.

"I...when I saw how he looked at you...I think I began to realize," she said slowly. Dan Rogers's expression of relief at finding her safe had changed to one of shock the moment he had seen Trace standing behind her. "My God," the young ranger had gasped. "We thought you were dead! We've been finding pieces of your boat...the reporters have been all over us, asking when we were going to find your body."

"Realize what?" Trace asked, his voice low and gentle, as if he was afraid anything above a whisper would break the spell and she would slip into silence again.

"Just...how famous you really were. When I saw that newspaper, on the Coast Guard boat... then I really knew."

He remembered it, that glaring headline, "Charlotte Strikes," with his own name and the fact that he was missing in letters only slightly smaller beneath it.

"People died, towns were washed away, but you were bigger news...almost bigger than Charlotte herself."

"It shouldn't be that way," he said tightly. "I didn't *want* it that way."

"I know. But that's what I realized. That

whether you wanted it or not didn't matter.... You *were* big news. You were someone the whole world really did know, enough so that they didn't even have to explain who you were. Just your name was enough." A sadly rueful expression came over her face. "And I didn't have the slightest idea who you were."

"Christy, don't—"

"But even if I hadn't figured it out then, I would have when we got to the dock."

"God, I'm sorry about that." He'd sensed a change in her before, but the tension that had shot through her when she spotted the mass of hovering, circling reporters on the Coast Guard dock had been almost visible. The flashes had begun to snap from the moment the boat had come into sight and had never stopped. "If I'd known...hell, I should have known. The damned vultures follow me everywhere."

"It's their job," she said quietly. "You're what people want to know about."

He sighed. "I suppose it wasn't their fault. I'd never minded before. Egged them on, in fact. Played their silly game for all it was worth. They had no way of knowing I was...changing the rules."

"You...handled it like it was nothing. But I guess it was, for you."

"What're a few reporters, after a hurricane?" She looked away. "Did they scare you? Is that why you...left?"

"Partly. That's…a different world, Trace. Not mine. Yours. You belong in that world."

Not to me. The words echoed in his head as if she'd spoken them. Was that what she was thinking? "I know it was crazy for a while, but…later? Why did you stay away?"

She smiled tightly. "You don't exactly just pick up the phone and call the biggest superstar in America."

"I'm not the—" He cut off his sharp words, then began again. "I made sure you would have gotten through."

She raised her eyes to his. "You don't even realize, do you? You live with it all the time… narrowing your life down to who's on some list or something. To only the people you decide you have time for."

He winced; she was hitting awfully close to the reality of his life. "Did you really think I wouldn't have time for you? You, of all people?"

She dropped her gaze. "No. I knew you would find time. If nothing else, out of…gratitude or something."

"Gratitude?" He fairly shouted the word. "I thought we settled all that."

"I know. But I still thought it, at first."

"At first?"

She nodded wearily. "Then I realized that we…were even on that score. After that day I fell and you came for me."

"But you still didn't contact me."

She let out a long, slow breath. "I'd…never really paid attention to all those gossip rags, or even to the legitimate ones. But all of a sudden it seemed like they were everywhere. And you were always the top story. Along with everything you've ever done."

Or everyone, he thought, flinching. "I told you, I...hadn't been an angel," he said tightly.

"It wasn't that. I'd seen the change you went through, and I knew that whatever had happened before, you were going to try. But I—" Her voice caught in her throat, and it was a moment before she could go on. "It was better this way, don't you see? I understood, and you didn't have to...be kind."

He stared at her. "Kind?"

She tightened her grip on her elbows, trying to stop the little quivers that were shaking her as she nodded. "If I just...went away and didn't bother you, you wouldn't have to be kind about it. About just walking away, I mean, after..."

"Is that what you thought?" He sat up, suddenly rigid in the chair. "That I wanted to just walk away?"

"Didn't you? I mean, I know it...didn't mean that much, that it just happened, because we were scared. And I understood," she repeated.

"Understood what?" His voice was deadly quiet.

"That you didn't...couldn't really want me. Not back in your world."

"So I get lumped with all the rest of them, is

that it? All the ones who left? Because no one else ever wanted you, I didn't, either?''

She stared at him, bewildered by the anger in his tone as well as by his words. ''Why would you? You could have anyone. The most beautiful women in the world. Why would you want me?''

In that moment he saw the abandoned little girl, certain that there must be something inherently wrong with her that made it impossible for anyone to truly care about her. He wanted to pull her into his arms and hold her until that little girl was only a distant memory. But he didn't dare, not yet; he couldn't risk losing her again, not after he'd waited so long.

''Why would I want you?'' he asked softly. ''How about because you're the bravest, most compassionate, most gallant person I've ever known? Not to mention the quickest, brightest, sassiest wildcat—'' he said the words caressingly ''—in the world.''

Christy shook her head in disbelief. ''But I'm not!''

''Hush,'' he said shortly, but not angrily. ''The most beautiful women in the world, you said? Maybe some people see them that way. Maybe I did, once. And I can't deny that I've been with my share. But there's not a one of them who can hold a candle to you. And not one of them who I want the way I want you.''

''But you can't!'' she burst out. ''You don't... even know where I came from, or who—''

''I know you,'' he cut in relentlessly. ''Who

your parents were, or why they couldn't stay with you, doesn't matter. You do."

Desperate, she fell back on the old, tired argument she had used so unsuccessfully on herself when she would awaken in the middle of the night so filled with longing it nearly smothered her. "It was just…the circumstances," she whispered.

She gave a start at the sharp, harsh sound that broke from him. "God, Christy! Don't you think I haven't told myself that a thousand times? That it was the situation, the storm, the thought that we might die in the next minute, that made it so incredible? Don't you think I haven't called myself a hundred kinds of fool for waking up in a cold sweat, wanting you so badly it hurt? It *hurt*, Christy."

He shook his head at the memory. "I used to laugh at guys who told me about feeling that way. I was lucky, I thought. Nobody would ever get to me that way. I'd always be in control. And it worked, in ways I never expected. It seems to attract some women. Especially the ones like you talked about, the ones who take it as a challenge, as a chance to prove how irresistible they are."

His eyes fastened on her like a man looking at his last chance at the life preserver before he sank out of sight. "And then there you were. Clean and honest and good, like they could never be. And without the slightest idea of how beautiful you were, what you could do to a man with just a look from your silver eyes…"

After a moment he went on hoarsely. "That's

why it wouldn't work, telling myself it was only the time and the place. You had me climbing the walls long before that night.''

''I...did?'' Christy stared at him, her eyes wide with turmoil. ''I...didn't know.''

He let out a strained, wry laugh. ''That's what I mean. There's not one of those women you keep talking about who wouldn't know, down to the last flicker of an eyelash, exactly what effect she had on a man. And you do more with a look, with the way that chin of yours comes up when you're mad, than they can do with all their...charms. And you don't even know it.''

''I thought...it was just me,'' she murmured, almost to herself.

''Just you?''

She colored, but made herself go on. ''Who was climbing the walls.'' It was Trace's turn to stare. ''I kept telling myself that it would be over soon, that you would go back to your world, to—'' she glanced at him ''—all the women who were probably waiting for you. But you were there, running around in that damned towel... I told myself I was a fool, that somebody like you wouldn't even look twice at me, that back in your world, you were used to women with...experience.''

''Experience?'' He was looking at her so oddly that the thought that he might have misunderstood made her cheeks flame once more.

''I didn't mean...you weren't...'' She swallowed and tried again. ''I mean, I wasn't a virgin.''

"Weren't you?" he said softly, still with that odd look.

"No!" she exclaimed, embarrassment making her hug herself even tighter. "There was somebody else, once. When I was seventeen. I thought he could make me feel...wanted, I guess. Like...you did. But I just felt...used."

Trace could barely speak, he hurt for her so. No one, in all that time, until him. He'd guessed there had been only a few when she had registered the surprise and wonder on her face as he'd entered her, but he had never suspected this. He felt humbled in a way he'd never known before this gray-eyed sprite had come into his life. "And you think that means you weren't...a virgin?"

She looked at him blankly. "Doesn't it?"

"Physically, maybe. Emotionally?" He shook his head. "I think we both were."

He saw her absorb the idea, could almost see her turning it over in her mind. "Both?"

He saw her doubt and couldn't blame her for it. "I know. I ran around a hell of a lot back then. But I never...felt anything. It didn't mean anything. I just didn't know it then. I didn't know it could be any other way for me. Until you." He lowered his eyes. "And now that I know...the other isn't good enough anymore." He gave her a tight, embarrassed little laugh. "Not that it matters. I gave up after I humiliated myself a time or two. My body knows I don't want anyone else."

She shuddered under the impact of that admission, that baring of heart, soul and battered ego.

How very, very far he had come.... God, she had put him through hell. But she had never thought, never dreamed, that he could feel that way. Not about her. And to admit it so openly, so honestly... That old, arrogant facade had hidden more courage than she'd ever thought of having. She knew she couldn't match it.

"I don't...I can't..."

She shuddered again, and he could see that she was teetering on the edge of mental exhaustion. He was feeling it himself, that drugged, numbed sense of a mind forced to deal with too much in too short a time. He stood up.

"Christy, please...can we get out of here? You need a...break from this, and so do I. We can get something to eat and unwind. Will you? We can talk it all out, soon, but let's just let it rest for a while."

He held a hand out to her. Numbly, barely aware of what she was doing, she took it.

Eight

She looked at the interior of the new, luxurious but surprisingly unobtrusive silver car curiously.

"I dumped the Ferrari," he said briefly, noting her look. "It didn't feel right anymore."

"I know."

She'd heard that he had donated the expensive car for a raffle, a raffle that had brought in thousands of dollars to a local charity. It had been the first in a long chain of events that had made the headlines everywhere.

He flushed. He hadn't meant to sound as if he was blowing his own horn. He pulled the driver's door shut sharply.

She was puzzled when they pulled in behind a large gray building and he got out to lead her toward what was obviously a back door. It had begun to rain again, and they were nearly running when it dawned on her. Of course. Trace Dalton couldn't go in the front door. He would cause a riot.

"Christy, don't," he pleaded, feeling her sudden stiffness. "I just don't want us to be disturbed, that's all."

That was unlikely, she thought as she took the chair he held for her. They had the room to themselves, a small, private banquet room that was clearly meant to seat at least a dozen people. And she had no doubt that it would stay that way; she didn't need the obsequiousness of the owner, who had personally met them in the kitchen and led the way, to tell her that. This further proof that the rich and famous were definitely different did nothing to abate her growing unease.

She sat silently, tracing the elaborate pattern on the silverware with a nervous finger, not even hearing Trace's orders to the awed waiter. She wasn't even sure what meal he had ordered. Was it lunch? Or dinner? Anything seemed possible; she felt as if she had relived years in that office.

"Hurricane Productions," she murmured.

"It seemed like a good name," he said softly, seeming to suddenly find the silverware pattern fascinating himself. "I wanted it to be special. I wanted to do...something real, I guess. Something different. Because *I* was different."

He paused, as if he half expected her to deny it. She said nothing, just continued to outline the intricate curves on the knife's handle.

"Christy?"

The slender finger stopped its circling. Slowly, reluctantly, her head came up. He looked into eyes wide with mingled doubt, pain and confusion.

"I'm sorry, Christy. Maybe I was wrong to trick you into this." His hand went to the scar again. "But I had to know what went wrong. It was... killing me. But I never meant to hurt you." He brushed tousled, rain-dampened hair back from his forehead, letting out a weary sigh. "If you want to go, I'll take you back."

Surprise overtook the other emotions in her eyes. "You'd do that? After all this?"

"Nothing's worth that look in your eyes."

She studied him for a moment. "What about the look in yours?" she asked softly.

Those eyes widened, searching her face. Before he could speak, the flustered waiter arrived to set plates before them with all the reverence of one making an offering at a shrine. And the warmth that had glowed briefly in her eyes was gone.

It was the longest meal of his life. He barely tasted what little food he ate, and he picked at the rest idly. At last he gave up. He stared at his plate. "I went to a backpacking store once, a couple of years ago." His voice was low. "I got some of that freeze-dried food. Apple cobbler, as a matter of fact. It tasted the same."

He didn't expect her to answer; she'd said almost nothing through the entire meal. Nothing since the moment when that light had died in her eyes. He knew why, knew that she was thinking once again of the world he lived in, thinking she'd been right, that there was no place for her in it. He didn't know how to convince her, to make her believe—

"You went to a store?"

His head shot up. "Yes. I couldn't explain what I wanted, or why, to somebody else when I wasn't sure myself."

"Must have been great for business."

There it was again, that stiffness, that cool withdrawal. He carefully set down the fork he'd been toying with. "Do you want me to quit?"

Her brow furrowed. "What?"

"Quit. Hang it up. Walk away."

She stared. "From what?"

"From this damned world of mine you're so sure you don't belong in."

"Quit acting?" She was astonished. "Why on earth…?"

"If that's what it takes to convince you, that's what I'll do."

"Convince me?"

"To give us a chance." His eyes were fastened on her face with an intensity that was almost tangible and added to Christy's stunned confusion. "That's what it is, isn't it? Why you don't believe how I feel about you? If I was a…a car salesman, you'd believe me, wouldn't you?"

"Believe you?"

He took a deep breath and reached across the table to take her hands in his. With the look of a diver on the highest platform, he braced himself for the plunge.

"I love you, Christy Reno." Her eyes widened

with shock, but he gave her no chance to protest. "I've spent three years trying to change it, but I can't. And if you get up and walk out on me right now, it still won't change it. No matter what you do, where you go, you'll carry that with you, even if you decide never to see me again."

"Trace, no..." It was barely a whisper; he ignored it.

"I'm not going to be one of those people who drift in and out of your life. I'm here for good. It's up to you to decide how."

Her face was pale and her eyes shadowed as she stared at him. Slowly, as if in a daze, she shook her head.

"I mean it, Christy. It won't make a bit of difference to how I feel if you leave right now. Oh, I'll hurt, but I've lived with that for three years. And I still love you." He gave a short, harsh laugh. "I don't seem to have any choice. But I've done it alone this long, I guess I can keep on doing it, if you make me. I hope to God you won't." He tightened his grip on her hands. "And if quitting is what it takes..."

He shrugged, as if he'd been talking about changing his hairstyle. Christy's look of shock turned to disbelief, and in that moment he saw the wary, distrustful child who had been deserted too many times. She thought he was bluffing. He got abruptly to his feet.

Christy stumbled a little as he grabbed her arm and pulled her toward the door. He paused to let her regain her balance, but neither of them spoke nor slowed again as he led her somewhat ungently toward the car.

"Where are we going?" she ventured to ask after he had driven several miles in grim silence.

"To show you I meant what I said."

His tone didn't invite further questions, and she subsided into silence. It was easy enough to do; her mind was whirling. He loved her? She shook her head in inward denial. He couldn't. Not Trace Dalton.

But he'd looked for her. He hadn't forgotten, not in three years. Even though he said he'd tried. She stole a sideways glance at him; his face was drawn, his jaw set, as he stared out at the rainy pavement. Could it be true? Lord knows she hadn't been able to forget him. She never would forget him, even without the daily reminder she had....

Her heart plummeted. Even if it was true, even if he did love her, that love would never survive what she'd kept from him. No matter what he thought he felt, it wouldn't sustain the blow of that complication. But God, it had been wonderful to believe, just for a moment...

He pulled into an underground parking garage. Without a word he got out, walked around the car and opened her door. She followed him meekly, sensing he was not in a mood to be trifled with, wondering what on earth he was doing. Her curiosity escalated when she saw the name of a well-known agent on the office door he held open for her. She saw the surprise that registered on the face of the receptionist, the surprise of seeing an unexpected guest.

"Is he alone, Sheila?"

"Why, yes, but—" Her eyes flickered doubtfully to an inner office door.

"It's important," he said brusquely and, still gripping Christy's wrist, headed for the door.

A pair of bushy, salt-and-pepper eyebrows shot up on the balding forehead of the man in the big leather chair. He spoke quickly into the telephone he'd been holding, then replaced it in the cradle as he stood up.

"Trace! I wasn't expecting to see you again so soon." He held out a hand as he smiled jovially; Trace shook it rather stoically. Concern showed suddenly in light brown eyes masked by thick glasses. "Nothing wrong with the contract, is there?"

"No. Yes."

The older man blinked. "I see." He glanced at Christy. "And I suppose this lovely creature is responsible for this uncharacteristic state of confusion?"

"Christy Reno, George Boyce."

The introduction was brief to the point of rudeness, and the bushy brows shot up another notch. It had been a long time since George had seen this Trace Dalton. He'd forgotten how much of a change there had been. He nodded at the young woman who seemed to be trying to back away. She was blushing, a rather charming touch that George found himself believing despite years spent in a

town full of women who could turn both blushes
and tears on and off at will.

"So what is—or isn't—wrong with the contract?"

"Nothing. But cancel it."

The eyebrows reached their zenith. "What?"

"You heard me. Cancel. I quit."

"But you've been fighting the network for
months for the okay! You can't quit this picture
now!"

"I'm not quitting the picture, George."

The round face regained its smile. "If that was
a joke, it was a rotten—"

"I'm quitting, period."

George Boyce stared. "What?"

"You heard me," Trace repeated grimly. "I'm
quitting. Everything."

"The producers aren't going to like this,"
George warned, bewildered. "They count on your
outside appearances to help sell the series—"

"Everything, George."

The little man went pale. "You can't mean...?"

Trace was answering George, but his eyes were
fastened on Christy's shocked face. "When shooting resumes after the hiatus, it will be without me.
I am officially retired."

The astounded look on George Boyce's face told
her that none of this had been planned. If he had
known about this, the portly man facing her should
be the actor, for it was an award-winning perfor-
mance.

"Put the word out, George. No interviews, no questions."

"But, Trace," he gasped, "why?"

"It's personal. And for once it's going to stay that way. I'm sorry to spring it on you like this, but I had no choice."

Christy's eyes narrowed at his choice of words. Her shock was giving way to anger, the anger of someone being backed into a corner. He was bluffing. He had to be. Nobody loved anybody enough to do this. He just couldn't take no for an answer. He was trying to make her give in and using this to do it. Her chin came up.

Trace saw it, welcomed it; any sign of emotion was better than that cold silence. "Still don't trust me, do you?" he said softly. He turned to George. "Announce it this afternoon. Call the studio first. And keep them off my back." His tone softened for a moment. "I know it'll be rough, George. I'll make it worth it. This year's percentage again, maybe?"

"You really mean it." The eyes behind the glasses blinked in final comprehension.

"I mean it."

Christy had to believe him now. She sat staring at the flickering screen of the television, staring at the picture of Trace that glowed behind the newscaster's shoulder. And listening to the voice delivering the news that had stunned the entertainment industry.

"—citing only personal reasons for the startling

move. Producers of Dalton's popular series, *Air West*, expressed shock at the news and hope that something can be worked out with the star."

They cut to a clip of a harried studio executive, who unctuously expressed his sympathy and understanding about Trace's changed mental state since his "terrible experience" three years ago, but somehow all Christy could see were the fading dollar signs in his eyes.

Christy sat back in the overstuffed chair and tried to control the emotions ricocheting around inside her. She never should have come here, she thought; she needed time to absorb all this alone. But Trace had been emphatic, and she had been so numb, that she had acceded to his stubborn insistence that he wasn't letting her out of his sight. She could have her own room, she didn't even have to speak to him if she didn't want to, but she was staying under his roof.

And so now, her bags already tucked away upstairs in the airy blue-and-white room overlooking the beach, she sat in his living room, all too aware of his eyes burning into her from across the expanse of white tiled floor.

She sensed him move toward her and turned her head to stare out the huge floor-to-ceiling windows at the ocean. She wondered why he'd bought this house; she would have thought he'd had quite enough salt water to last him a lifetime.

"Now what, Christy?"

She turned back to find he had knelt beside her chair and was staring up at her intently. Her gaze flicked to the television screen, then back to those incredible eyes, turquoise in the fading light, shadowed slightly by the thick fringe of lashes. He read her expression easily.

"I knew you wouldn't believe it wasn't a setup, not unless you saw it like that." He jerked his head in the direction of the screen.

"Why?" Her voice still sounded dazed. "You can't quit—"

"I just did."

"But—"

"You still don't get it, do you?" He reached for her hands. "None of it means anything anymore, Christy. It's only been a way to get through the past three years. It lost its glow the day you made me wake up and take a good long look at myself and what I'd become."

"But you changed—"

"And it's a battle, every day. It would be so easy to slide back into it. There's always somebody to kowtow to me, to pile on the flattery, to pump me up into believing my own publicity. And I've been afraid for three years that the day would come when your memory might not be strong enough to help me fight it. Sometimes you seemed so far away...."

She wondered if he knew how much aching longing he had let into his voice, just as she wondered if he knew how much that tone tore her apart. Here, now, in this moment, she could almost believe...

"But you're a star—"

"To hell with that! If that's what's keeping you from giving us a chance, then it's not worth a damn to me!"

She stared at him, unable to doubt that he meant what he said despite her mind's insistence that it was impossible. He tightened his fingers around hers.

"I love you, Christy. Please don't run from me. I've kept the promise I made you, just give me a chance to prove it to you."

His words were coming in choppy bursts, as if he'd had them stored up for a long time, never sure he would ever have the chance to say them. He loved her, Christy thought dazedly. Or he thought he did. But so had the others....

"Don't lump me in with them," he said quickly, reading her thoughts as easily as if she'd spoken them. "I'm not one of them. I'm not going to disappear on you. Please, Christy, give me a chance."

She couldn't convince him. She could see the fierce determination in his eyes, and she sighed inwardly. She owed him this, she supposed, after all he'd gone through to find her. He would soon realize that it wouldn't work. All she had to do was give it time. He would see that he'd been wrong, and then she could at last put him out of her mind. She'd long ago given up trying to put him out of her heart.

"Give me a month, Christy. Just a month. You were going to be here two weeks anyway, what's two more? Then—" He lowered his eyes, but not before she saw him blink rapidly. "Then I'll get out of your life—if that's what you want."

It will be what you want by then, she thought, her eyes on his bent head, her fingers itching to reach for the tousled silk of his hair. *I can't live in your world, nor can I live with myself if you give it up for me. You think now your work doesn't matter, but you'll come to hate me for coming between you and what you want to do, should do.*

"Christy?" He didn't look up.

"All right."

She saw him suck in a breath, and his head shot up, his eyes wide with shock. "You…mean it?"

"I mean it. One month. You'll know by then."

"So will you," he said firmly, so unwavering that for a split second she almost believed he could do it, just by sheer force of will. But then that last little bit of reality, that final bit of ammunition with which she could have ended things here and now, came back to her, and she felt a harsh pang at the futility of his gallant effort.

Perhaps she should tell him now. Bring it all to a halt, make it easy for him to send her packing. No, she couldn't. She could solve this on her own, and he need never know. If she told him, he would probably always wonder, always think she would be waiting in the wings with some kind of claim or demand. She would let him learn how impossible it was, and then she would quietly depart, without a scene. She could give him that, at least. And she resolutely refused to admit that there was anything else to her decision to stay.

* * *

The morning dawned bright and crystal clear. The living room was full of golden light, blending well with the bright colors of the comfortable furniture, giving it an open, airy feel that was emphasized by the huge windows that opened to the expanse of the sparkling Pacific Ocean.

Christy paused at the bottom of the stairs, a little disconcerted at how at home she felt here. Had she chosen the furnishings herself, she could not have found anything she thought more suited to the house. More suited to herself. The realization disturbed her.

She had called Mrs. Turner—collect, of course—to let her know she would be here longer than expected. By that time it had been too late to speak to Char, and for once she was almost glad; she wasn't at all sure she could handle the strain of pretending all was well just yet.

Drawn by the calming view of the glistening water, she crossed the room, her bare feet sinking into the thickness of the large, colorful throw rugs that were scattered cheerfully around the gleaming white tile floor.

She was back in her beloved jeans and a big, white silk shirt, worn strictly for comfort. She had no idea how slenderly fragile the loose folds of the lustrous fabric made her look, nor how the jeans lovingly molded every inch of her long legs and the taut curve of her derriere.

She quietly slid open the door leading to the deck. She hadn't seen Trace since last night, when he'd gruffly told her to go to bed, she looked exhausted. She couldn't deny it, but he had looked just as bad, and she thought perhaps he was still sleeping.

Not that she had slept much last night. It had been hours before her weary mind had stopped spinning, and when she had at last slipped into sleep, her subconscious had stubbornly refused to let her forget that he was right down the hall.

She took a deep breath of the salt-tanged air, leaning over the railing to peer up and down the beach. In the aftermath of the rain, it was virtually empty.

"Good morning."

She spun around, startled. He was sitting at a round table in one corner of the deck, shaded by a jauntily tilted, brightly colored umbrella. He was clad only in a faded pair of navy sweatpants and a pale blue T-shirt that seemed painted across his broad chest. To Christy it was infinitely sexier than any designer outfit could ever be.

He looked as if his night had resembled hers; shadows darkened his eyes, and his face was drawn and rough with the stubble of his beard. His hair was windblown and tangled, and she wondered if he had gone to bed at all.

"I— It's a beautiful morning." She looked out at the beach again nervously.

"Sit down. I'll fix breakfast."

"You don't have to."

"I know. An omelet okay?"

"I— Fine. Thank you."

She felt uncomfortable with this studied politeness, but he seemed unaware of it as he went inside. She turned her gaze back to the steady, calming roll of the surf and tried to empty her mind and enjoy the loveliness of the morning.

"Hey, Dalton! What the hell's going on? Your phone's out, and there's this stupid rumor on the news—"

Christy stared at the man who had come bounding up the steps; it was hard not to. He was huge, six-four at least, and the image of the perfect Nordic blond. He was impossibly tan, and his eyes were impossibly blue, and if she hadn't been looking at him in person, she never would have believed he was real.

He was staring at her the same way, although why he should doubt her reality was beyond Christy. Yet he was looking at her as if she had just disembarked from the 7:00 a.m. UFO.

"Who the hell are you, and what are you doing here?"

"I might ask you the same," Christy said mildly. She'd stopped being impressed by sheer bulk when she'd managed to toss the school bully over her shoulder at twelve, after one crack too many about her lack of parents.

The platinum blond eyebrows shot up, and a glint of admiration flickered in the blue eyes. He looked her up and down with a new interest, this one blatantly and purely male. "I must say, when he decides to break a rule, he does it with style. And with excellent taste."

"A rule?" She focused on the one thing she didn't chalk up to typical male bluster.

"He's never brought a woman here." Christy felt her stomach knot oddly, but she held the man's gaze steadily. "Until now," he said softly, a glimmer of realization joining the admiration in his eyes. "It's you, isn't it?" he murmured softly. "This is your house."

Nine

Christy raised an eyebrow at him. Whoever this Norse god come to life was, he wasn't making much sense. "Me?"

"You're the one. This is your house."

Nuts. Beautiful, but nuts. Christy shook her head sadly. The Viking grinned as if he'd read her mind. "I'm Eric Petersen." He held out a massive hand. "I live two houses down."

Christy took his hand, or rather, let his engulf hers. "With an *'EN,'* I presume," she said dryly.

"Of course," he agreed. "What took you so long?"

"Have they released you prematurely, or are you just out on a pass?"

"Huh?"

"From the asylum," Christy said gravely.

The blond giant roared. There was no other description for it. He laughed furiously. "Oh," he choked out, "I think he was right. You're worth the wait."

He truly was crazy, Christy told herself. She was so fascinated by the sight of this rollicking mountain of manhood that she nearly jumped when Trace spoke from the door.

"If you came for breakfast, Petersen, forget it. I've only got two dozen eggs."

"I'm wounded to the quick!" Eric exclaimed dramatically. "I only came by to check on you, since there's this ridiculous rumor going around—"

"It's not a rumor."

The blond was startled into silence. His eyes went from Trace to Christy, then back. "You really quit?" he asked after a moment, his voice solemn now.

Trace nodded. The big man shifted uneasily, aware of the sudden current of tension. Trace set down the plates he was carrying as if oblivious to it. Eric spoke quickly, lightly. "Puts a whole new meaning on 'I knew him when,' doesn't it?"

"Shut up," Trace said pleasantly, "or you won't get the coffee you really came over here for." He went back inside.

"Did you?" Christy asked.

It was Eric's turn to look bemused. "Did I what?"

"Did you know him when?"

He laughed. "No. I met him about a month after

he moved into this place, a couple of years ago. Found him sitting in the surf, drunk to the gills and soaking wet. I didn't even know who he was then. I just figured I'd better pull him out before he drowned.'' He shook his head. ''He just kept saying I wasn't the right one, to go away.''

Christy's heart twisted, and she made a tight little sound of pain. Eric's crystal-blue eyes held her gaze.

''I didn't understand until later. He told me. It all came tumbling out like he'd had it bottled up for so long he couldn't stop it. I think it was because I was a stranger.''

''Who talks too much. Get the hell out of here, Eric.'' Trace was white-faced, staring at his friend.

''Er...yeah. See ya.'' The blond giant beat a hasty retreat that left Christy smiling inwardly at the thought of him being intimidated by anyone or anything, while outwardly she watched Trace with concern.

She ate her omelet in studied silence, aware that Trace was only picking at his. At last she laid down her fork. ''Don't be angry with him. He sounds like a good friend.''

''He is. Usually.'' He stabbed at an errant mushroom.

''I'm sorry he told me, if you didn't want me to know.''

His fork clattered as he dropped it on the plate. His head came up, his eyes searching her face. ''There's nothing I don't want you to know. I just don't want your pity." He laughed sourly. "And believe me, I was pretty pitiful then."

"Eric didn't seem to think so. There's a world of difference between pity and compassion, Trace. It took me a long time to learn that." His eyes widened. "I don't want *your* pity, either," she added softly.

He let out a long breath, and Christy relaxed a little. After a moment she risked the question Eric's words had made her both want to ask and yet dread. "Why did you buy this house?"

"I got tired of living in a hotel."

"A hotel?" She didn't know what she'd expected, but that wasn't it. "Is that where you lived? Before, I mean?"

She didn't have to specify before what; he knew what she meant. "No. I had a penthouse, a condo, chrome and glass, the whole celebrity bit. Fancy, modern and as cold as ice. I never spent a night in it after I got back."

"Why?"

He didn't look away, although she sensed he wanted to. "Because it only reminded me of what I'd turned into. I was afraid that if—" He broke off, and he did look away this time. "It sounds crazy, but I was afraid if I spent just one night in that place, it would get me back, and I'd go right back to being the jackass I'd become."

His voice was low and strained, and although he hadn't really given her the answer she'd wanted, why *this* house, she didn't force it. "Tell me about Eric," she said, feeling it was safe to ask now.

"You won't believe it. I didn't."

"He looks like he's a football player, so I suppose he's a ballet dancer?"

He laughed. "Not that kind of you won't believe it. He's a pilot. A private one. Flies a Lear jet for some corporate bigwig who owns that house he stays in."

"Nice boss. He—" She stopped. "A pilot?"

"Um-hmm. Convenient, huh? I did more than a little brain picking over the past two years. He should have gotten paid as a technical adviser."

Christy was stunned, but not by the fact that he had so conveniently found an invaluable resource. It was that he so easily, so naturally, spoke of his work, the work that had been his life, in the past tense. "Trace, you can't quit."

"We settled this last night."

"But—"

"No. It's my decision, Christy." He reached across the table for her hand. "You gave me a month. I want it without this hanging over us. Just let this month happen, love. No what if's, no you can't's. Just you and me. Please?"

Whatever backbone she'd ever had seemed to disappear when he looked at her like that, seemed to melt away at that pleading tone in his voice. "All right."

"Good. No more talk about it, then. Or anything else that will get in the way. Promise?"

Anything else that will get in the way. It was all she could do to keep from crying, but she managed a nod. His eyes, nearly as blue as Eric's, lit up with a joy that made it hard to remember what she'd been upset about in the first place.

She didn't know precisely when she'd lost track of the original plan. It could have been the day Trace had packed up a ridiculously huge picnic lunch and driven them to a remote, lovely spot up the coast and plied her with champagne and fresh, sweet grapes. Or it could have been the day when, by pulling God knew what strings, he arranged to have an exclusive gallery that was showing an incredible collection of photographs opened on its "dark" day just for them, to peruse at their leisure and in complete privacy. Or the weekend they drove to the mountains, to a cabin set in thick pines that filled the brisk, clean air with their scent and fueled the lovely fire at night. Or when Eric had taken them on a soaring flight over the night-lit city.

Or it could just as easily have been the simple moment on the beach, when he turned to look over his shoulder at her and she caught the pure exultation that lit his eyes.

She didn't know and was no longer sure she cared. Her nightly collect calls home, and the plaintive voice of a daughter who'd had quite enough of Mommy being gone, reminded her of the impossibility of it all. But by morning she seemed to have forgotten the lesson. And the plan.

And she knew the maelstrom over his sudden retirement and disappearance from the Hollywood scene was still going strong, even though he never mentioned it. And, keeping her promise with difficulty, neither did she. If he was having regrets or second thoughts, he never let them show.

On the evening when she had completed the last of her meetings with the publishers, she left the building to find a limousine that had to be at least twenty feet long waiting.

"I don't believe you," she gasped as she climbed in to find him elegantly attired in a dark blue tux.

"Good," he said simply, "because this is fantasy night, my lady. Cinderella time." He tapped on the glass behind the driver. "Off, pumpkin," he said grandly, and Christy giggled in spite of herself.

He meant what he'd said. From the austere building that housed Dragon Books, they drove to a small and very expensive boutique, where he picked out a flowing gown of pristine white shot with glittering silver threads. She protested, but he grandiosely waved her words aside.

"Not tonight, Ms. Reno. You can yell at me tomorrow."

And in the end he won. She took one look in the mirror after she had slipped on the dress and was stunned into silence. She exited the fitting room still a little in awe. "I didn't know it would look like this," she breathed.

"I did."

His eyes went over her hungrily, seeing how the delicate fabric clung lovingly to her curves, yet made her look ethereal and about as substantial as a cloud. Her eyes were wide and as silver as the glistening threads that caught the light and sent it flying.

Christy saw his look in the mirror, and her breath caught in her throat. In all this time, she hadn't seen that look. He'd never even hinted that he wanted any more from her than the easy companionship of these past weeks.

She had wondered, or perhaps feared, that it was because he knew it wouldn't be the same. That without the heightening of their senses by the storm and the danger it would be routine, ordinary. He'd told her he didn't believe it, but she'd seen none of the heat of those words in his actions since.

She had wondered, then blushed at her own thoughts as she battled her newly reawakened body. Was she alone in this? Perhaps he just didn't want that—or her—anymore, she told herself. And almost believed it, until that moment when she found his eyes on her heatedly. Only then did she realize that what she'd been seeing was a fire that had been carefully banked and tamped down, not one that had gone out.

She decided to test her theory during the rest of that fantasy evening, as he'd called it. When he held the door open for her at the elegant, exclusive restaurant, she purposely brushed against him. He backed away quickly, yet so smoothly she couldn't be sure it was intentional.

As they slid into the velvet-upholstered, high-backed and very private booth at the back of the dimly lit room, she bent so that her breasts brushed lightly over his arm. This time she was sure; he stiffened, and she saw a muscle jump in his suddenly tight jaw.

Well, Christy, my girl, now that you know, what are you going to do about it? She ran a finger around the rim of her fluted champagne glass, unaware of what her caress of that small circle was doing to the man beside her. *He's obviously waiting for you to make the first move,* she told herself. *Probably afraid you'll take off running again if he does.*

Did she want to run now? Did she even have the strength to deny herself these last, precious weeks with him? Wasn't it enough that she would have to go soon? Would it be wiser now, before she got in any deeper? She nearly laughed; she was already in far over her head.

"No frowning, not tonight." His voice was soft and warm and flowed over her like golden honey.

No, not tonight. Tonight was a fantasy, the fantasy she'd dreamed of and been denied for three long years. He was here, with her, looking exactly as her memory had painted him so vividly every day of those years. She would live it, every minute of it, for soon it would be all she would have. She lifted her eyes to his and smiled, a slow, lazy curving of her full lips that made him suck in a quick breath and look at her sharply.

She barely tasted what she was sure was a delicious meal, and she had no need of the champagne to feel intoxicated. By conscious decision she had let down the walls, dropped her considerable guard and rather recklessly dared the chips to fall where they might.

Trace wasn't quite sure what to make of this transformation; he'd been walking on eggshells around her for so long, and this new, exhilarated, carefree woman was someone he didn't know how to handle.

When, after the meal, she asked him to dance with her, he thought she was kidding. The band was playing a slow, dreamy ballad; the thought of holding her so close sent ripples of heat through him. God, he didn't dare; he couldn't.

What he couldn't do was look into those wide, sparkling gray eyes and say no. Feeling more like a man going to his doom than a man looking forward to dancing with a beautiful woman, he got up and held out his hand to her.

Something short-circuited in his brain in the instant when she came to him openly, eagerly, nestling into his arms as if that was where she'd always longed to be. He forgot his plan, forgot that he was going to move slowly, never pressing her for more than she was ready to give. He forgot everything except that he was holding her, and that he was never, ever going to lose her again.

His arms tightened around her, and he held her close, for the moment unable to stop or care about his body's surging response to her, or the fact that she had to know it. It was magic, this night, and just for a moment he could pretend that the evening's end would be other than it must be.

The fantasy held for them; no one recognized

him until they were ready to leave. A final stop, a final glass of champagne on a hilltop overlooking the Pacific, and a final dance to music only they could hear, and at last, reluctantly, they began to race the sunrise home.

Trace came back to reality with a thud when the limousine pulled away, its discreet driver clutching an exorbitant tip to assure his silence about the identity of his passengers. The fantasy was over, and the only thing waiting for him now was a cold and lonely bed. He shuddered, but hid it in the quick movement of shedding his jacket.

He tried to chide himself out of it, telling himself that at least she was there, with him, even if he had to maintain his distance. Nothing could be worse than the hell of three years of not knowing where she was at all. This was enough. It had to be enough. Smothering a sigh, he turned to face her, ready for that agonizingly platonic walk up the stairs.

He stopped dead; she wore that soft, enigmatic smile again, and without realizing why, it staggered him. Without a word she took his arm and started up the stairs. He gritted his teeth when they stopped at the door of her room, wishing he could run for it. He couldn't take many more of these chaste little hugs good-night.

She leaned toward him, and he pulled back defensively, knowing he had stretched his control to the limit tonight. Her smile never wavered as she looked up at him from beneath lowered lashes.

"It's a fantasy, remember? I think it deserves at least a good-night kiss."

He froze, staring at her. Her cheeks were flushed, her eyes lustrous and her lips parted in silent invitation. His own lips trembled at the memory of hers beneath them.

"Christy," he whispered raggedly.

"Don't give up," she said softly. "The night's not over yet."

Her hands slid over his shoulders to lock behind his neck, and he groaned low in his throat. "Don't," he said shakily. "I can't—oh, Lord," he gasped as she pulled him toward her, amazing strength in those slender arms.

"Don't think," she whispered. "It's fantasy. Just feel."

He stared down into those huge gray eyes and was lost. He lowered his head, meaning only to brush her lips with his before he fled down the hall in desperation. But the moment his mouth met hers, the instant his lips tasted her soft, sweet warmth, fire leaped through him, bringing nerves so long battered into submission raging back to life.

His hands moved to cup her face, to tilt her head back for his kiss, to press her harder against his mouth. Some last remnant of sanity clamored a warning to go slow, but his body was screaming for the relief it had been denied.

Christy's senses leaped into awareness, as if they had been waiting for this moment, as if all those thoughts of him, all those dreams, all the sleepless nights, had built up the pressure inside her until it burst into heat and flame in the first moment she knew he was going to kiss her.

The last of her doubts were left behind in the dust as her heart took off and soared. Any lingering thoughts that it had been merely circumstances that had made their first encounter so incredible were singed to ashes in the first fiery response of her body to the feel of his mouth on hers.

Trace felt the tender, delicate probing of her tongue on his lips, felt the searing response of his body, felt it clench fiercely, and knew if he didn't stop now he wouldn't be able to. With a gasping breath he tore his mouth away, feeling every muscle in his body go rigidly taut in protest. She was looking up at him, that smile on her lips, her eyes dark and smoky....

"Don't look at me like that." His voice shook.

"Why?" She knew perfectly well what he meant; she'd made no effort to keep her feelings from showing in her eyes.

His hands went to her shoulders as if he needed her support to stand. "Because I can't take this!" He swallowed heavily, closing his eyes as he let his head loll back. "I've run through enough cold water to fill the damned ocean. Hell, I've tried the ocean, too. It's not cold enough, either, even at three in the morning. You don't know what hell it's been, leaving you here every damned night!"

"Don't I?" she whispered. His head snapped upright, his eyes searched her face. "You're not the only one who remembers. I—" Her voice caught.

"I just thought you didn't want to...touch me anymore."

"Didn't want—Lord, Christy, I didn't dare touch you!" He broke off and pulled her close. His hands slid down her back, pressing her hard against his hips, a shiver going through him as she came in contact with his urgently inflamed flesh. "That's what just looking at you does to me," he said hoarsely, "and has since the first time I saw you. I never dreamed you would think—"

She made a small little sound, and he felt the movement of her head against his chest. *Of course, you idiot,* he told himself bitingly, *of course she didn't know.* She wasn't one of those worldly, jaded women who had filled his world for so long, who could calculate down to the last iota a man's reaction to them. Nobody had ever truly wanted her in her life, and he expected her to read his mind?

"I'm sorry. I thought you knew, that it was... obvious."

"I...wasn't sure. Until tonight."

"I promised myself I wouldn't push, that I'd give you time." He laughed wryly. "We didn't exactly get a chance to know each other under normal circumstances. I knew the minute I touched you, kissed you, I'd want more. Much, much more."

She tilted her head back to look at him, seeing concern battling with passion in his eyes. She felt the first quiverings of apprehension; he'd shown no sign of changing his mind, no indication that he'd seen it couldn't possibly work. Indeed, that was a knowledge she'd had a hard time hanging on to herself these past two weeks.

She should tell him, she thought. He was trying so hard, never knowing it was futile. Never knowing that their time together was almost over. The words died unspoken when his mouth came down on hers again, sending ripples of wildfire racing through her. It was selfish, it was wrong, but she couldn't deny herself this; she wanted him with a fierceness that vanquished all else.

She clutched at him, her hands sliding down to his chest, her fingers curling, reaching for the heat radiating from him beneath his shirt. She heard him make a low, husky sound, and his tongue plunged forward, probing the depths of her mouth with hot eagerness. The brush of his tongue over hers sent a spurt of blazing heat through her, and she moaned against his lips.

His mouth was both gentle and fierce, cajoling and demanding, and she responded to the combination ardently, eagerly. When he drew back his tongue she felt bereft and followed with her own. His low groan when she slipped into his mouth fired her, and she pressed forward urgently.

He responded quickly, his arms tightening around her, his mouth suddenly fervent and undeniable. He was sapping her strength with every coaxing movement of his lips, every stroking caress of his tongue. Her muscles were turning to jelly, her bones to some molten, flowing liquid, and she began to sag against him.

He felt her sudden weakness and pulled his mouth away for a gasping breath. "Christy?"

She looked up at him, dazed, able to think only that he was the most beautiful thing she'd ever seen. She reached up with a hand that was trembling and traced his mouth with a slender finger. She saw his eyes close for a moment as if he were in pain. When he spoke, she knew he *was* in pain; his harsh whisper echoed with it.

"Help me, Christy. I can't do it alone."

Help? she thought, perplexed. Then she felt his hands shake, as if he wanted to let go of her but couldn't. She thought she understood then, and moved the hand that had been caressing his mouth to the black tie at his throat. She gave it a tug with fingers made unsteady by the thought of taking off more than his tie; the knot came loose easily.

"What are you doing?" It was a groan, breaking from him as he grabbed her hands and held them still.

"You said to help," she said uncertainly.

"Oh, Lord, Christy, I meant help me stop!"

"Why?"

She said it so simply, so innocently, that it took away what little breath he had left. "Because I know what's going to happen if you don't," he choked out.

"Not here, I hope." She glanced around at the shadowed hallway as if that were the only problem.

"That," he grated, "is entirely possible." And he knew it was; the way he felt right now, he could easily take her right here and now, in this narrow hall, on this cold tile floor. "Christy, please."

"It's my fantasy, isn't it? Shouldn't I get to decide how it ends?" She freed one hand and reached for one of the studs fastening his classic pleated tuxedo shirt. She unfastened it and moved to the next with both hands, aware of his eyes watching her every move.

"Christy." He caught her hands once more, and she could see the rapid rise and fall of his chest, could feel the tension radiating from him. He lifted her chin with a gentle but unyielding finger. "Are you sure? I don't want this if you're not. It means too much. You mean too much to me to force this before you're ready."

Stop it! she cried silently. *Stop making me think, stop being so kind, so gentle, so...so loving!* She didn't want reality intruding on this, not now, not when she needed him so desperately. She barely got the words past the choking tightness in her throat. "It's not like it's the first time."

"Yes, it is," he insisted fiercely. "You—we weren't thinking then. I don't think we had a choice. You do now."

"Then I've made it." She undid another stud. "Let me have my fantasy, Trace."

Something disturbed him about her words, but then she parted the edges of his shirt and leaned forward to press her lips against his bare chest, and all rational thought fled. His body came to sudden, full hardness in one wild, surging flood, warning him that this time it would not be denied.

Like a striking hawk his mouth came down on hers, but it was as if the white-hot talons dug deep into his own vitals. She met his fierceness with her own, taking his lips, his tongue, as he took hers, each wanting to devour the other.

He shuddered as she slid her hands beneath his open shirt; the feel of her hands on his naked chest snapped the last fragile thread of misgiving. Without breaking that fiery kiss, he swept her up into his arms, heedless of the small silver bag she dropped or the silver high-heeled sandal that slipped from her small, arched foot at his first step.

She felt like a featherweight in his arms as he strode down the hall, kicking open the door to his room rather than release her to turn the knob. He carried her through; the slam as he kicked it shut again echoed in their ears.

Christy jerked reflexively at the sound, her head lifting. Her eyes widened; only now did she realize where she was. She had seen this room only once, briefly, when he had shown her the house for the first time. It was huge, airy, made bright and open by huge windows and a large skylight; now it was awash in the silver glow of the moon's last light.

He set her down beside the big bed that sat beneath the skylight, turned so that the first sight on awakening would be the rolling expanse of the Pacific. She staggered slightly as her one heel-clad foot threw her off balance; his arm was there immediately to brace her as she kicked the shoe off.

Steady now, she found herself facing the next stud on his shirt, the gap above it giving her a tantalizing glimpse of muscled chest. She lifted her hands, meaning to undo that fastening, but the sleek, hot skin was much too tempting, and her fingers slid under the parted cloth.

She felt him tense, heard his rapid intake of breath. He let it out in a long sigh as her hands stroked over his chest, only to take it in on a gasp when her seeking fingers found the flat discs of his nipples. She raked her nails gently across that suddenly taut flesh and heard him groan low in his throat.

She moved quickly then, her fingers hurrying to unfasten the last of the studs, her hands lifting to smooth the shirt back off his shoulders. He twisted to free his arms from the sleeves, and she watched the ripple of his muscles with eyes that had turned to molten silver. When he dropped the shirt carelessly on the bed she leaned forward, bracing her hands on either side of his chest as she pressed her lips to his heated skin.

With another groan he moved them, his hands going to the zipper of the Cinderella dress. It drifted down to rest in a froth of silver and white at her feet, revealing a lustrous teddy of silver silk. It shimmered in the moonlight as she breathed, her breasts rising with each breath.

Trace shivered with the sudden burst of sensation that ripped through him. He was remembering another time, another place, when she had been clad in shimmering silver. He had taken her in a frenzy then, no less fierce or turbulent than the storm that had raged outside. He felt that same need now, the need to bury himself in the fire he'd dreamed of for so long, the fire he'd feared was gone from his life forever.

Shuddering, he grasped her shoulders and held her away from him. "Slow down, love,' he said thickly. "We've got a long time to make up for."

"Then we should get started." Her voice was low and husky, and it sent impossible rushes of ice and fire rippling up and down his spine.

"I've waited three years for this. I want to go slow. Very, very slow."

At his words, a qualm tried to work its way through the heat pooling deep and low inside her, but Christy banished it without a thought. Tonight was her fantasy, the dream she would live on for the rest of her life. She clung to it so fiercely that she was able to ignore the twinge that went through her when he took a small foil packet out of the nightstand, to protect her as he hadn't been able to on their night of hell and heaven.

"All right," she whispered. "Slow…"

Ten

Trace's hands clenched into fists as her hands went to the thin straps of the teddy. He wanted to reach for her almost as badly as he wanted her to continue; the sight of her undressing for him with that innocent, open sexiness roused him to a fever pitch he'd never known before.

When she slipped the silver straps off her slender shoulders, the teddy slid downward, only the outward thrust of her nipples keeping it from falling completely. When he looked at the bared curves, when his eyes fastened on the tight little peaks that kept their tenuous hold on the sheer silk, he felt a surge of boiling, swelling heat that told him he was frighteningly near to being out of control.

He nearly laughed, grimacing inwardly at the memory of the Hollywood sex symbol who had

nearly become a sexless symbol. The body that
rose to the mere thought of this gray-eyed waif,
that drove him to erotic dreams of her that made
him feel he had all the control of an adolescent
who'd just discovered why men and women were
different, had pointedly and repeatedly refused to
cooperate for anyone else. He'd wisely given up
the attempt before the rumor mill got hold of it,
knowing he wouldn't get away for long with "just
tired, I guess," for an excuse.

And now here he was, ready to explode like a
green kid at just the sight of her. Desperately he
tried to marshal the last remnants of his splintering
control. "Christy," he said raggedly, then could
say no more.

She looked up at him, saw his eyes on her hotly,
still vividly green, and it was as if he had touched
her, caressed her with eager hands. It took her
breath away, filling her with the urgent need to
have those hands on her, touching her as he had in
her dreams. She gave a little shake of her shoulders
that sent the teddy slithering to the floor to mingle
with the silver-and-white foam of her dress.

Trace made a torn, choking sound, and she saw
his knuckles go white as he clenched his hands into
hard, merciless fists. With a slow graceful movement, she slipped off the matching silver satin panties. She stood naked before him, for the first time
in her life experiencing the feminine pride of knowing she had the power to do this. At the same time
she felt incredibly shy, and the color rose in her
cheeks as his eyes, hot and dark now, drank in
every sweet curve and shadowed hollow.

He reached for her, but then he stopped and let

his arms drop to his sides, his hands cramping into fists once more.

"Christy," he choked out. "Lord, I don't dare touch you." He closed his eyes, and she saw a shiver ripple through him. "I'm hanging on by a thread just looking at you."

"Then maybe I'd better finish what I started," she whispered. She saw every muscle in his belly ripple and then go rigid at the first touch of her hands on his waistband. She heard the low whistle as his breath left him in a rush when she tugged at the zipper. Her cheeks were flaming even hotter at her own new-found boldness, but suddenly nothing in the world was as important to her as seeing that beautiful, sculpted body again.

Her fingers couldn't help but brush the bulging swell of him as they moved downward, and for the briefest second she thought she felt his hips move convulsively toward her. She heard a low, strangled sound; then every muscle in his body tensed, and the motion stopped.

Trace knew he was in deep trouble the moment she moved again. Her slender hands slid both the tuxedo pants and his briefs off with slow care, but the freeing of his achingly erect flesh did nothing to ease the painful heaviness that was weakening his knees. Not when Christy was caressing him, his legs, hips, lingering in the hollow at the top near his buttocks before she knelt to take off his shoes.

He'd had women undress him before, but he'd always viewed it with detached amusement, especially when it was so clear in their eyes that their main motivation was to see if the celebrated Trace Dalton body lived up to its billing. There was nothing detached about him now; he was totally, seethingly involved, and only the fear that he would go off like a rocket the instant she touched him kept him from begging her to change the direction of her gentle stroking.

Christy lingered a moment near the floor, trying to regain what little composure she could before facing him again. She had nearly cried out in stunned surprise when that potent male flesh had sprung free from all restraint. She'd never really seen him in the urgent haste of the storm, and now that she had, she couldn't quite believe it. Had he really been inside her, like that?

A sudden, vivid memory flashed through her fevered mind, a memory of a wonderful, swelling fullness, driving away that hollow ache, vanquishing all fears. Yes, she thought, oh, yes, he had been there, had filled her until there was no room for fear or pain or doubt....

They lay down on the bed together. Subtlety was gone now, reduced to a drifting pile of ash in the inferno kindling between them and joined by the cinders that were all that was left of his wish to go slowly. Flames leaped along singing nerves, shimmering, hot and golden, and the firestorm that ignited rivaled Charlotte's intensity.

Trace's hands slid down her slender shoulders, seeking, searching, until his fingers curved reflexively to cup the firm swell of her breasts. He heard her gasp as his thumbs flicked her nipples, nipples already hardened in anticipation. He couldn't wait another second; he had to have that tight little peak in his mouth. He lowered his head to her, another spurt of unbearable heat searing him at the way the moonlight fell in a tantalizing strip across her breasts, as if drawing him to the nipples that seemed oddly darker in the silver light.

Christy felt three years of longing rage to the surface with the first touch of his mouth on her breast. He tugged the nipple to taut hardness, then suckled so deeply that she cried out, arching toward him. The thick lashes lifted, and she wondered how his eyes could look so green in the silver light. When he paused as he looked at her, she nearly cried out in protest as the wonderful, fiery sensation ebbed. She twisted in his arms, her body begging silently for him to put his mouth on her again. A low sound of pleasure came from him before he spoke thickly.

"What is it, love?" His hand slid to her other breast, his fingers catching and teasing the nipple. "Do you want me here, too?" She twisted again, moaning. "Tell me, Christy," he urged, needing to hear it, to be sure she wanted it as much as he did.

"Yes, please," she gasped, beyond embarrassment as her back arched, offering the neglected breast to him.

Hot, piercing pleasure stabbed through Trace at that shy, innocent offering, and his body clenched fiercely. Once more he knew he was holding on by only a precarious thread of control that was slipping by the second. When he took that eager peak between his lips, circling and teasing it with his hot, wet tongue, she cried out his name so sweetly that he felt it all the way down to that throbbing, pulsing part of him that was so swollen and hard he didn't dare move for fear of shattering into a thousand pieces.

And then it was Christy who moved, her hands clutching at his shoulders as she twisted away, as if the pleasure had become too much to bear.

"Please," she gasped out, "I want..."

"Anything," he whispered hoarsely. "Just tell me."

"I want... Can I...touch you?"

He shuddered, closing his eyes against the strength of the need that ripped through him, the need to have her do just that. Followed by the certain knowledge of what would happen if she did.

"I'm sorry." Her voice was shaken, and she began to pull her hands from his waist. "I shouldn't have—"

"Christy, no." Somehow he found the power of speech and grabbed at her hands. "It's just that... it's been a long time, and I—" He stopped as he met her eyes and saw the hurt there. Without another word he dragged her hands down his body, clenching his jaw as he spread them over himself.

Christy's doubts melted away at the astonishing feel of him in her hands. He was hot and hard and satin-smooth, and she could feel every hammer beat of his heart beneath her fingers. Tentatively she flexed those fingers and nearly jumped when he groaned raggedly and his hips jerked, pushing that thick, throbbing length between her palms.

"Trace?" she whispered, all her wonder and innocence ringing in the single word.

He muttered something low and garbled and wild; then he shuddered violently as his hips moved again, plunging his eager flesh against her slender hands. And again, until she quickly learned and made the movements herself, adding the stroking pressure of gentle fingers to the convulsive bucking of his hips.

Suddenly he clenched his teeth to bite back a growling, guttural cry, and she heard a hissed "stop" as his body went rigid. She didn't want to stop; she loved the feel of him, the vital, pulsing heat of him, and all that she was learning from his response to her touch. And she slowly drew caressing, circling fingers up the hot length of him once again.

The harsh, guttural cry he'd stopped escaped now, spiraling pleasure mixed with a pain and despair she didn't understand. Then she felt the boiling, pulsing explosion begin for him, felt the last convulsive jerk of his hips, and knew why he'd wanted her to stop.

His body arched up with the tautness of a bowstring. She couldn't be sorry or embarrassed; she was too full of wonder and pleasure that he had trusted her with these most intimate, vulnerable moments, and more than a little stunned at the fierceness of his response.

When he fell back limply at last, it was a moment before she realized something was wrong, that he had pulled away from her and was muttering something in that tone of remorse she'd heard before.

"—didn't mean to…I'm so sorry, Christy."

She reached for him, but he pulled away again. He wouldn't look at her; her heart quailed, and her racing blood slowed in fear as she began to think she had done something horrible in her naïveté. Yet he was carefully gentle when he began to wipe her hands with his discarded shirt.

"Trace?" Her brow was furrowed in bewilderment.

He sighed, a sound rife with disgust as he began to clean himself up. "Great," he muttered. "I dream about this night for three years, and when you're finally, really here, I go off like a firecracker with the world's shortest fuse."

"Is that— I mean, I—" She took a breath and tried again. "Did I do something wrong?"

He froze, then met her eyes at last, only then seeing her doubt and uncertainty. "Oh, Lord, Christy," he groaned, "I'm sorry. You drive me so crazy that sometimes I forget how innocent you are."

She flushed, and she couldn't have said if it was because of his remark about her innocence or his admission that she drove him crazy. He saw it and, discarding the shirt, pulled her into his arms.

"I didn't mean for that to happen," he murmured against her hair. "I...just couldn't wait, not with you touching me like that, not when I've waited so long to feel your hands on me."

"You...have?"

"I've thought about it, dreamed about it, wished it, prayed for it.... Hell, I would have sold my soul for it, if the devil had ever been around to take it."

Pleasure flooded her suddenly, unexpectedly. "You wanted me that badly?"

"So badly I couldn't hold back any better than a schoolboy with a hormone problem," he said dismally. He hugged her closer. "I'm sorry, Christy."

"No. Don't be. I...it makes me feel...special. That you let me—" She broke off, floundering in her embarrassment.

"Didn't do much for you, though, did I?"

"You'll never know how much," she said softly, doing a great deal to soothe his slightly bruised ego. Then she wriggled in his arms and looked at him with a glint in her silver eyes that was suddenly, unexpectedly mischievous. "And I'm getting the distinct impression that you're not quite through yet, anyway."

She couldn't help her delight; she might be naïve, but she had passed basic biology in school and knew that this was not the norm. And no matter how she looked at it, whether he had just been without a woman for too long or he truly wanted her so much, she came out the winner.

Trace had felt it moments ago, that tingling return of desire, startling him with both its speed and intensity. No matter how hard the logical part of his mind tried to chalk it up to long months of celibacy, his heart knew better. But he could keep his promise now; he could go slow and sweet and long, until she—

"God," he said suddenly, as her hands found and stroked him with unerring certainty, "you learn fast!"

Christy smiled, a secret, feminine smile as old as time as she savored the feel of him pulsing to new life beneath her touch. "Teach me more," she whispered.

And he did, although not in the way she had asked. Instead of showing her how to please him, he seemed unstoppably intent on showing her that he knew exactly how to please her. His hands stroked and caressed every trembling inch of her, seeking out and finding sensitive spots she hadn't known existed, sending currents of heat racing through her from so many places that she thought she would explode when they all merged together in that boiling, white-hot pool deep inside her.

She couldn't think as his strong, supple fingers made erotic centers out of the most unlikely places: the arch of her foot, the back of her knee, the inside of her elbow. She couldn't breathe when those same fingers found the hotter, secret places, and that hot, swirling pool inside her began to churn under the pressure of a growing, aching heaviness.

He stroked and caressed her breasts until she was moaning, arching her back to thrust them into his hands, begging him with every bit of silent pleading she could manage to move his fingers that last critical inch and touch her throbbing, begging nipples.

"No," he said quickly when she began to close her eyes again. "Look at me, love. I want to see your eyes."

She hesitated, but then the moonlight was gleaming in wide gray eyes. The moment her gaze met his again his fingers moved, catching and rolling her nipples, tugging gently. A gasp rose from her, and her head rolled back as she lifted herself convulsively, but Trace saw the flare of pleasure, of passion, in her eyes, saw the wonder and the awe.

He knew then that there had been no one since that night, no one who had touched her like this, made her feel like this. It was a heady feeling, and it strengthened his determination to make this a flight she would never forget.

He teased and tormented those deep rose crests until she was moaning again, her slender body twisting when his hand slid down over her flat stomach to tangle in the dark curls below, to knead and caress the soft mound. She didn't even realize that she had parted her legs for him, that she had tilted her hips to give him access; she only knew that if he stopped she was going to die.

Through the haze of need and pleasure she heard him ask her something, although she couldn't comprehend the words. But whatever it was he wanted of her, there could be only one answer, and she gave it to him.

"Yes," she breathed. "Oh, yes."

His fingers moved gently, probing, parting her flesh with exquisite care, pausing only when he had to fight down a shudder of his own when he encountered the slick, wet readiness of her. The knowledge that she responded to him so completely, that she was so ready, was almost his undoing. Unexpectedly, he was thankful now that things had happened this way, that his body had been unable to resist the long dreamed of touch of her hands; he knew he would never have been able to hold out long enough to do what he wanted to.

He felt her startled jump, her gasp and sudden intake of breath as his fingers moved, and knew he had reached his goal. He carefully, relentlessly began to message that tender spot, that pulsing center, savoring the tiny little cries that rose from her. He felt the heat radiating from her and ordered his mind not to think of what it would be like to sink mindlessly into it, not to remember how tight and hot and sweet she was.

Christy knew the odd little sounds she heard were coming from her, but she couldn't stop them, couldn't even seem to care. All she knew was that her body had come alive under his hands, and he was drawing her up to some high, dancing place and that she would burst if he didn't take her all the way.

She felt the first, beginning ripples, and her every muscle tensed as she reached for it, lifting her hips, pressing that throbbing core that had become the center of her world harder against his hand. She cried out his name as her fingers dug into his shoulders, and...

He stopped. Slowly, that teasing, coaxing hand withdrew, and with a low whimper she lifted heavy lids to look at him. Her heart was thudding, her blood still pounding hot in her ears, and she looked at him in bewilderment.

"Trace?"

He smiled, a lazy, satisfied smile, and in the eyes still glowing green in the silver light was a look she'd never seen. "Easy, love," he murmured.

"But...why...?"

"Because it's time to start all over." His voice was as thick as honey and twice as sweet. "This time like this."

He bent over her and pressed hot, feverish kisses over her brow, her lowered eyelids, the tip of her nose. "My hands were just learning the way," he breathed against her ear.

She gasped, knowing he intended to follow the same long, passionate path with his mouth and knowing she could never stand it. "Trace, no, I can't—"

"Yes, you can, love. This is the first time we

never had, Christy. This is the way it should have been.''

His mouth moved over her, along every path his hands had taken. By the time his lips closed over her nipple, drawing it deep into the hot cavern of his mouth, she was writhing, one soft little cry of his name barely dying away before the next one began.

Trace felt the pulse pounding in his ears, felt the throbbing, demanding ache rising from his swollen manhood, and ignored it all. Nothing was more important, and, to his amazement, nothing was giving him more pleasure, than watching her fall apart in his hands and under his mouth.

He felt her tense when he pressed soft kisses across the tender flesh of her inner thighs, heard her suck in her breath when his breath parted the dark curls at their juncture. ''Please, Christy. Trust me.''

She shivered, a protest forming on her lips, but a vision of him lying open to her, masking nothing of his unbridled response to her touch, flashed through her mind. He hadn't wanted her to touch him because he had known what would happen, she realized suddenly. But when he knew how much she wanted it, he had held nothing back from her. Could she do any less?

And then she realized her aching, throbbing body had made her decision for her; her thighs had opened for his gently probing kiss. At the first touch of his mouth, his tongue, she arched in shocked surprise. He stopped.

''Christy, did I hurt you?''

''No,'' she gasped. ''I...I just didn't know...''

A smile curved his lips, and a low, pleased masculine laugh rumbled deep in his chest. "You've only just begun to find out, love," he promised, and bent his head to her again.

Christy shuddered again and cried out, her body engulfed in a blazing inferno like nothing she'd ever felt before. She cried out again and again, not knowing what she was saying, only knowing that the tension, the building, swelling heat and fire within her had to have some outlet or they would erupt, taking her with them in a fiery explosion that would leave nothing of her behind.

Her vision blurred at the edges, and all she could see was Trace's bent head and her own hands entangled in his silky hair. She didn't remember moving her hands, didn't remember reaching to push his head away because she couldn't bear any more of this all-consuming fire, then clamping her fingers in his hair to hold him to her because her heart had shifted to that pulsing spot beneath his mouth, and if he left her it would cease to beat.

Pleasure, hot and bright and shimmering, rose from that hot, boiling turbulence he'd begun in her, and she arched upward fiercely, heedless of the wantonness of her position as she lifted her hips to make it easier for his probing, stroking tongue.

"That's it," he murmured thickly against her flesh, trying desperately to ignore his body's demands for one final moment. "Open for me, love."

"Trace...oh, Trace!"

She knew she had screamed it, but as the explosion began for her, she couldn't stop herself. She barely heard the low growl that ripped from him at that passionate cry, only knew that he had moved suddenly, quickly, leaving her stranded once more on the edge of the pinnacle. No, her mind screamed, she couldn't take it again, she couldn't.

And then he was there, hot and hard and demanding, groaning low and harsh when his aching shaft brushed her slick, hot flesh. *Yes,* her mind screamed. "Yes! Now, please, all of you, right now!"

With a low, guttural exclamation he thrust forward hard and fast, and Christy cried out again. Oh, Lord, it was too much, he was too big, too full, too hard, she couldn't take him, she couldn't hold him....

The molten, liquid heat broke free then, flooding her with a searing, consuming tide of pulsing, throbbing pleasure that shook her to her soul. She cried out his name, her hands clutching at him, her nails digging, clawing at his back as she bucked wildly, her body clenching around the swollen male flesh that stretched it so sweetly.

In that moment she felt him let slip his own control, felt the sudden rippling of the muscles beneath her fingers, felt the shudders that swept him and heard the sound of her name ripped from deep inside him. He slammed into her in a final, convulsive thrust, a fierce, triumphant sound erupting from him as he threw his head back and arched himself against her, his body quivering with the explosive violence of pouring himself into her sweet, hot depths.

Christy awoke to the golden light of morning streaming in through the skylight, turning Trace to a gleaming, perfectly sculpted image before her sleepy eyes. Still naked, he was sitting sideways on the bed beside her, cross-legged, his eyes unusually bright and an expression on his face that told her he'd been watching her sleep for some time.

In the moment when she forced her eyes fully open she saw him make a quick, furtive swipe at his eyes with the back of his hand. It was then that she realized the unusual shimmer in his eyes was the sheen of tears, and her throat tightened. She reached for him, wondering what was wrong.

He took her hand in his, lifted it and pressed a warm kiss against her palm, but made no move to come closer to her. Instead his eyes moved over her, drinking in the sight of her slender body bathed in the pure morning light.

"I wasn't sure about buying this house until I saw this room," he said quietly, unexpectedly, his voice thick and husky. "But then I knew. I knew you would look just like this in the morning, just like I knew how you could look painted silver by the moon."

Christy's eyes widened, the last remnants of sleep effectively banished. "You...bought it because of that?"

"I bought it for you."

You're the one. This is your house. Eric's words leaped into her mind unbidden, taking her breath away. After all this time...

"Even when I thought I'd never find you, never see you again, I wanted this place. I tried to fix it up the way I imagined you would like it. It made me feel better, somehow."

Christy sat up slowly. "You...imagined very well."

"You like it?"

"You know I do."

"I mean really like it? Enough to…live in it?"

She tensed. She saw him swallow, and he plucked at the fabric of the comforter he had pulled over them last night. A fine sheen of sweat was on his forehead, and she realized that, incredibly, he was nervous. Instinctively, automatically, she turned her hand in his and curled her fingers around his reassuringly. He looked up at the unexpected gesture.

"I can't let you go again, Christy. It would kill me this time. It damned near did last time."

"Trace—"

"If you don't like this place we can go somewhere else. I won't be making the kind of money I was, but I haven't spent much lately, it's all been invested. We'll do fine. I—"

"Trace!" She cut off the tumbling flow of words. "What are you talking about?"

He took a long, deep breath. "Marry me. Please?"

Christy paled; she had never expected this. "I—" She broke off, shaking her head.

"Don't, Christy! We can do it, we can work it all out! It was my work, wasn't it? The hassle, the reporters, the whole celebrity bit? That's gone now, or it will be as soon as the fuss dies down. And I don't regret it. Really. I found out I enjoyed what I was doing behind the scenes at Hurricane as much as I did acting. More, a lot of the time."

"But—"

"And you know how I feel about the rest. I don't care what or who or why about your parents,

Christy. It doesn't matter a damn to me, only you do. I love you.''

He saw her doubt and tightened his grip on her hand until it was almost painful, willing her to hear him and believe.

"Don't Christy. I won't let you lump me in with all those others, the ones who left you. You left me, remember? I'll never leave you. Damn it, I love you! You've got to believe that! Don't ask how or why. I can't answer that. It just happened. All you have to do is believe me.''

She shivered, her hand shaking in his, her eyes wide and dark as she stared at him.

"And that's the hardest thing in the world for you to do, isn't it, love?''

Christy saw the shimmer in his eyes again, but he didn't wipe at them this time. His jaw tightened, and he blinked rapidly, but he made no effort to hide what he was feeling. His brutal openness made her shiver again in the face of his emotional courage.

"You...love me?'' Her voice was tiny, as fragile as a newborn bird teetering on the brink of the nest. Would she take the chance and soar, or plummet back into that dark, safe shell she'd built around herself? Trace held his breath and prayed.

"Me?'' she repeated in wonder. He'd said it before, but he knew she was only now thinking of it as anything other than just words.

"I love you,'' he repeated. "I know there are things we need to work out, but there's nothing—'' He saw doubt flare again in her eyes and repeated the word fiercely ''—*nothing* we can't handle, if we do it together. Marry me, Christy. I'm not worth a damn without you. I—''

A loud, reverberating thump cut him off. They both jumped, turning to stare in the direction of the stairs.

Eleven

The thump that had cut him off was repeated, then came yet again, followed by a voice booming up the stairs. "Hey, lazybones, what the hell's going on around here? I heard some crazy— Oof!" Another thump, louder, more solid, with an accompanying vibration they felt all the way from the hallway. "Uh-oh." A moment of silence, and Trace groaned and rolled his eyes.

"Tony," he muttered. "I forgot he was coming."

"Er," the voice called awkwardly, "I guess I'll be downstairs." The thumps, clearly going in the opposite direction this time, began again and then faded away.

Trace turned back to find a furiously blushing

Christy scrambling out of the bed. "Christy, wait—"

"You'd better go see your brother."

"I will, when you come down with me."

"I have to dress, brush my hair—"

He strode over to a closet door and grabbed the thick blue velour robe that had been hanging there. He came back and wrapped it around her, then ran his fingers through the fine silk of her hair, tousling it thoroughly.

"There. Dressed and wearing my favorite hairstyle."

Her blush deepened. "I can't go down like this!"

"Why? Tony knows you're here. He's crazy to meet you. He said he can't wait to thank you."

Christy shifted uncomfortably. "I just gave you the idea. You provided the money."

"He didn't mean that," Trace said quietly. "He said he wanted to thank you for giving him his brother back."

Trace reached out to belt the robe around her, then to roll up the sleeves. The garment that fit him swam on her, trailing over her hands and baring a great deal of silken skin at the neck; and he stepped back and eyed it critically. "Maybe you'd better wear something else."

"I might suggest the same to you," she said in self-defense, running her eye with no small amount of pleasure over his naked body.

"It's only my brother," he said with a wicked

grin. "He's seen it all before. Doesn't have the slightest effect on him."

"Fine." She unbelted the robe and let it slide to the floor. "Then we go as a set."

His grin faded as he looked at her, standing in a stream of sunlight coming through the skylight, the glow pouring over her slender, naked body like transparent, liquid gold. His body surged instantly in response, and Christy couldn't stop her eyes from sliding down to the thatch of sandy curls that surrounded suddenly aroused male flesh.

"You, on the other hand," he said huskily, "have one hell of an effect on me."

Involuntarily she took a step toward him. The ridged muscles of his belly tightened in anticipation, and his arms came up to reach for her. Then a noise from downstairs brought them back to earth, both of them still gasping from the speed with which the wildfire had caught.

"You'd better get dressed," he said tightly, turning to reach for a pair of jeans that hung over the back of a chair.

"Yes," she said, not moving, her eyes fastened hungrily on the taut curve of his buttocks, the curve that still bore marks from her eager fingers.

"Christy," he said warningly, and her eyes flew to his face. "If you think I'm going to be able to get into a pair of jeans with you standing there like my wildest dream come true, looking at me like...like that, you're crazy. The zipper'll never stand it. Go get dressed."

Cheeks flaming once more, Christy scooped up

the robe and wrapped it around her before she scampered down the hall.

When she came out clad simply in white jeans and a red T-shirt, he was waiting, leaning against the table across from her door. A little flustered at finding he'd waited for her, she hastily finished tucking in the T-shirt she'd just pulled on. A gleam of silver behind him caught her eye, and she saw her purse and the shoe she had dropped last night.

"Thank you for picking these up," she said, wondering if she was ever going to stop blushing.

"I didn't." She stopped, glancing from the floor to the table, then back to his face. "I would guess Tony did. That's probably what he tripped over."

"Oh!" No, she was never going to stop blushing.

"Don't feel bad. That's probably the only thing that kept him from walking right in on us."

"Does he usually…walk right in?"

"He's never had a reason not to in this house."

She bit her lip; there was no missing his meaning.

"It can work, Christy, if you give it a chance. Don't let old hurts get in the way."

"There are…things you don't know—"

"There are things you don't know, too. They don't matter. I won't let them. We can do it, Christy. Keep thinking that." He took her arm and led her toward the stairs.

After an hour downstairs with Tony Dalton, she almost began to believe it. Trace's younger brother was as tall as he was and had the same quick grin, but there the resemblance ended. Where Trace's hair was that odd combination of brown and blond, Tony was all brown, with brows and lashes that were slightly darker. The leanness that gave the older Dalton his easy grace was an almost gangly lankiness in the younger one; Tony looked almost thin next to Trace's muscular solidness. And his eyes were a soft, cinnamon brown, unlike the volatile blue to green of his brother's.

But whatever the differences in appearance between the two, there was no mistaking the closeness between them, and no mistaking the warmth with which Tony Dalton embraced her the moment she came downstairs, not even waiting for his brother to speak, and indeed thanking her for returning to him the brother he loved.

"Wouldn't you like an introduction before you hug her to death?" Trace asked mildly, eyeing his brother with a raised eyebrow.

"Why? She wouldn't be here if she was anybody other than Christy."

That open, straightforward admission made the tiny bit of hope glowing inside her expand another notch. Trace had carefully laid out the fuel over the past two weeks, and last night had been the match to the tinder. The fire had caught and blazed, but instead of burning itself out in the cool light of morning, that tiny ember of hope had glowed on stubbornly.

Could they do it? Could they really beat the odds? Of course, he didn't really know what he was dealing with, but he was so very determined.... Determined enough to stand the blow she had yet to deliver?

She sat back and listened to the two brothers talk, encouraging them because she loved to hear the stories they told about each other. Their "remember whens" became a rousing game of "I can top that," and soon all three were roaring with laughter.

Even Christy, at Tony's quiet urging, managed to dig up a few funny stories, including one about a brown bear who had majestically patrolled his Alaskan territory wearing a very unmajestic cooking pot on one foot.

"He'd raided a camp, and the pot got stuck when he tried to get the food out. He got it off after a couple of days. A good thing, too. He could have starved, because he sure couldn't sneak up on anything with that thing clanking at every step."

That got Tony started on a few animal stories of his own, and it warmed Christy more than she would have believed possible to know that she'd had some small part in enabling this young man Trace loved so much to do what he had obviously been born to do.

Trace was positive Tony had planned it when, as he came back into the room with the lunch they'd all thrown together, his little brother turned to Christy and asked airily, "So, when are you two getting married?"

Christy nearly jumped a foot, and Trace froze in the doorway, scarcely daring to breathe as he waited to see what she would say.

"I...we..." She stammered to a halt, then grabbed for one of the sandwiches on the tray Tony had just set down. "We're talking about it."

Trace nearly dropped the glasses he was holding as he sagged against the doorjamb. She hadn't said no. She'd had the perfect chance to deny it, to say they were just friends, or any of the other banalities people used, and she hadn't done it. She had left that door open, and hope flared in his heart even as it weakened his knees.

When he could move he rejoined them, his eyes flashing a look at his brother that held both anger for his tactless question and gratitude for his timing. Tony gave him an angelic smile that said he'd known exactly what he was doing.

When Trace decided to pay him back by asking about what was apparently an active and healthy love life, Tony looked uncomfortable for the first time.

"I've been thinking," he said, "maybe it's time I settled down, you know, quit playing the field so much."

"You? The terror of Corpus Christi's female population?"

"Look who's talking! You used to cut a swathe or two amongst the local ladies, as I recall."

"The operative phrase there is 'used to.'" Trace's eyes flicked to Christy, and the warmth in them called up an echoing warmth inside her that was unlike anything she'd ever known. Not the heat of passion, but a soft, enveloping warmth, the warmth of a budding, growing security in his love, and the sense of family that had somehow expanded to include her, a feeling she had never known.

"Well, maybe you've got the right idea," Tony said, shifting in his seat as an unexpected flush rose in his face.

"Oh?" Trace raised a skeptical eyebrow. "Is this the same guy who just last summer was saying he was going to party his brains out at least until he was thirty?"

"That was before."

"Before what?"

Tony sighed, then looked up at his brother. "How do you feel about being an uncle, big brother?"

Trace's glass crashed down on the coffee table, ice and soda sloshing over the sides. "What?"

"Heather's pregnant."

"Heather? Which month was she?"

"The last three."

Trace stared at his little brother, feeling suddenly old and weary. No, not his little brother anymore. Without thinking first, he asked, "Are you sure it's yours?"

He heard Christy make a little sound, but he was more astonished by Tony's reaction; he got the distinct impression that his brother was about to flatten him. After a moment it passed, and the younger man sat back in his chair.

"She's not like that. And we were going to get married anyway. I love her. Don't judge everybody by that bimbo who tried to nail you, Trace."

Trace let out a breath. "You're right. I'm sorry. I'm just a little...wary, I guess."

Tony saw Christy watching them, her eyes huge and troubled. "It was a long time ago," he explained kindly. "Some little sl—schemer tried to foist her kid off as Trace's. Luckily he had the smarts to demand a blood test, so she backed down. Still made a big splash in the headlines, though."

Trace shifted uncomfortably at the unpleasant memory, but froze when he caught a glimpse of Christy's suddenly ashen face. "It wasn't mine," he said quickly. "I'd only been with her once and never saw her again. Until she showed up with a six-month-old kid and this story."

"Coincidentally right after *Air West* took off," Tony said dryly.

"I knew it wasn't mine," Trace repeated, a little anxious at her continued pallor. "I mean, it was only once, and longer ago than it would have had to have been, I think."

"You...think?" They were the first words she'd spoken, and the tight, strained tone of her voice did nothing to ease Trace's growing concern.

"Well, yeah." He flushed. "I didn't...keep track." He didn't understand why she was so upset. She knew he'd been a hellion in those days, he'd told her that, and she'd said it didn't matter, not now. "It wasn't my kid, Christy. Honest it wasn't. And it was years ago."

"I believe you."

"Then what's wrong?"

"I...don't feel too well. I think I'd like to lie down for a while."

Trace scrambled to his feet, then knelt beside her apprehensively. "What is it? Do you need a doctor?"

"No. Just some rest. And quiet."

Trace helped her upstairs, worried because she moved so stiffly, so rigidly, and because this had come on so quickly. And more worried when she insisted on using the room she'd stayed in until last night.

"It's...darker. I'll rest easier."

"Do you think you'll feel better later?" he asked as she stretched out on the bed. She knew he was thinking of the plans Tony had made to take them, along with Eric, out to dinner. "Just go along without me. Give the boys a night out. Maybe you can talk Tony out of becoming a family man, a fate worse than death, I'm sure."

Trace's brow furrowed. What was that supposed to mean? He reached over to touch her forehead, wondering if she was more ill than she'd let on. She twisted away from him, and he drew back, stung. "Christy?"

"I'm sorry. Just go, please. I'd feel worse if you stayed home because of me. I'll be fine by tomorrow."

Reluctantly he agreed, but an hour into the evening he knew he'd made a big mistake. He liked Eric a great deal, and he loved his brother, but there was only one place he wanted to be right now. He made it through another hour before they took pity on him and laughingly called it a night.

"Besides," Eric said with a laugh, "going out with you is too hard on my ego. All those women panting after you, and now that you've quit it's even worse. They all want to know what tragedy has befallen you and kiss it and make it better. Of course, I wouldn't mind it so much if I had a woman like Christy to go home to."

"Not a chance." Trace laughed. "She's one of a kind."

"Just my luck," Eric sighed dramatically. "Of course, I'd settle for any of those little sweeties over there gaping at you if they'd look at me the way Christy looks at you."

"What do you mean?" Trace looked startled.

"Give me a break, Dalton. She looks at you like you're an oasis and she's been in the desert for months."

"Or," Tony said blithely, "to be exact, big brother, she looks at you exactly the same way you look at her."

Trace rolled his eyes heavenward at their ribbing, but his grin spoiled the image, and they all laughed as they piled into Eric's car.

"So tell me, my friend," Eric said, nodding toward a trio of particularly blatant giggling females who had followed them outside and now stood staring, stopping just short of pointing at them, "when are you going to put them all out of their misery and take yourself off the market?"

"As soon as I can get her to say yes," Trace

answered bluntly, wishing he had driven; he would have risked the speeding ticket.

"Good for you," Eric cheered. "She's quite a woman, my friend."

"That," Trace said briefly, "is an understatement."

The house was dark when they arrived, and Trace felt his stomach knot anxiously. Had it been more than just a minor, temporary indisposition? Was she truly ill? He nearly dropped the keys in his haste, the feeling of guilt for leaving her that he'd been harboring all evening ballooning to monstrous proportions now.

Finally Eric grabbed the keys from him and opened the door, looking at him with an expression of tolerant amusement. Trace saw it and growled at him, "Just wait, ol' buddy. Your turn's coming someday, and I'm going to laugh my head off."

"Sure." The laugh of a securely single male echoed in the entry hall, and Trace scowled as he left Eric and Tony there to go upstairs.

He stopped quietly outside her door, listening. There was no sound, so he eased the door open gently, hoping he wouldn't wake her if she was still sleeping. He stood staring for a moment even after his eyes had adjusted to the darkness. The room was empty. What the...?

A smile crossed his face as the answer came to him. He left the blue-and-white room and walked quickly but quietly down the hall to their room. His smile became a grin when he realized how naturally he thought of it that way, as theirs. After last night it would never be anything else in his mind.

The drapes were still open, and the moon hovered over the skylight, flooding the room once more with that ethereal light. His body tightened at the memory of it bathing her slender, naked form as she lay, at long, long last, in his bed. That she had come here to wait for him made his heart leap in his chest; she was going to give them a chance.

The bed was empty. The room was empty. He flipped on the light, staring in disbelief. Where the hell was she? If she'd been downstairs Eric or Tony would have called him. His stomach knotted again, and apprehension made his stride unsteady as he whirled and headed for the stairs.

Something terrible had been wrong with her. She'd gotten worse, maybe had to call for help, or, worse yet, tried to go herself. And he, damn him, had been out on the town, leaving her here alone and hurting. There had to be a note downstairs somewhere, telling him what had happened.

There was nothing. He checked the kitchen, the entry table and the breakfast bar, where most of the paper clutter of his life wound up. The moment he explained, Eric and Tony dug into the search, with equally negative results. Tony checked the answering machine while Trace called his service. No messages.

"The paramedics?" Eric asked tentatively.

Trace closed his eyes in pain. "Maybe. God, maybe." He tried to dial, but Tony took the phone from his unsteady hand and made the call himself.

"They haven't been here," he said as he hung up, "but they gave me the numbers for all the nearest hospitals and clinics. I'll start calling."

"But how the hell would she have gotten there?" Trace was pacing now, neither knowing nor caring that his every thought, his every fear, was written clearly on his face.

"Your car was here, wasn't it?" Eric gestured toward the garage, and Trace ran to pull open the interior door. The silver coupe, bought for little reason other than that the color reminded him of her eyes, sat in its usual spot.

"Damn," Trace muttered. It wouldn't have helped, but it would have been a place to start.

"What exactly did she say was wrong?" Eric asked.

"Nothing much. Just that she didn't feel too well and wanted to lie down."

"No headache, nausea, anything?"

"No. Just tired." Trace flushed. "We...didn't get much sleep last night."

"Oh?"

"I...we...sort of had a reunion."

Eric stared at him. Realization, along with surprise, dawned in his clear blue eyes. "You mean she's been here all this time and last night was... the first time? Even though you'd been...together before?"

Trace's color deepened. "It's a long story, but...yes."

"Could that be what—no, you said she was fine this morning, that it came on suddenly."

"Yes." Trace didn't even bother to react to what Eric had begun to ask; he was too worried.

"Nothing," Tony said as he joined them. "She didn't go to any of the local places. Does she know anybody else here, someone she might call?"

"Other than the people at the publishers, just heragent—" Trace snapped his fingers. "Wait a minute, there was a letter here...."

He whirled and ran back to the blue and white tiled bar that separated the kitchen from the living area. He shoved aside the stack of messages he'd ignored, all from people demanding to know if the rumor they'd heard was true, and picked up the pile of papers beside it. He pulled out the file folder on HPI's next project and set it aside, along with the note from Jack Morris advising him that the backers had agreed to let him direct it. On top of it he put the copy of the press release he'd approved announcing his retirement from acting and from *Air West,* then thumbed through the rest of the stack.

It wasn't there. He knew it had been; he'd seen it this afternoon when he'd been getting the glasses out. "Damn, I know it was here, along with some other stuff of hers. It was the letter from her agent acknowledging that he'd gotten the copies of the final contract for her next book. It had his number on it. And now none of it's here."

Trace searched the pile again, unaware of the speculative look his brother suddenly wore. Or of his quiet disappearance up the stairs.

When Tony came back he spoke quietly to Eric for a moment, watching his brother as he prowled the living room looking for some sign. The big blond's face became an impassive mask as he nodded, then walked to the phone. Tony crossed the room.

"Trace."

"There has to be something. Damn, if she was that sick, there would be some sign." Trace turned haunted eyes on his brother.

"I don't think she was sick," Tony said gently.

"What?"

"Sit down, Trace."

"But—"

"Sit down."

Trace sat; he'd never seen that look in his little brother's eyes before. He watched as the boy he'd practically raised until he was thirteen looked at him with an expression that was weary and loving and infinitely sad all at once.

"She's gone, Trace."

Trace stared at him as if he'd spoken in Greek. "Of course she is, that's what this is—"

"All her things are gone."

Trace went from pale to ashen in the space of a breath. "What?"

"Her bags are gone. The closet's empty, except for a dress. Silver and white. And the shoes I tripped on this morning."

Trace shook his head in an agonized combination of denial and pain, and his brother thought irrelevantly of a proud, beautiful horse he'd had to watch being put down for one of his classes; the animal had been wounded beyond saving. Perhaps not so irrelevant, Tony thought, his own heart contorting in the face of his brother's pain.

And then Eric was there, his big body crouching beside a stunned Trace as he sat numbly on the couch, in the spot where Christy had sat mere hours ago. "A cab picked her up an hour after we left," he said softly. "It took her to LAX."

Tony thought he'd never seen anything as tortured as his brother's eyes the day he had come to him in Corpus Christi and solemnly apologized for the past few years of his life. He knew now that that had been the mere tip of the iceberg. Looking into those eyes now was like looking into the depths of hell.

Trace didn't move, he just sat there, staring, looking like a man trying to stave off the knowledge that he was mortally wounded, as if not seeing the knife would make the mutilation disappear.

"No," Trace whispered brokenly. "Not again."

"Trace," Eric began, feeling helpless in the face of something that his great strength and greater heart could do nothing about. He put a hand on Trace's arm.

"No!" Trace recoiled, and something wild and savage came into those anguished eyes. He leaped to his feet and without another word he ran for the door to the outside deck.

"Trace!" Eric yelled as he started after him, coming out onto the deck in time to see Trace throw himself over the railing, stagger as he hit the sand and then take off running. Eric began to follow, but Tony grabbed his arm to hold him back.

"Let him go, Eric. We can't help him now."

"But what if he goes and does something stupid, like walk into the damned ocean?"

"He won't. He came too close to that once."

"I know." Eric met Tony's troubled gaze. "That's why I'm afraid of it. He might be thinking it's as close as he'll ever be to her."

Tony paled, then nodded. "You're right. Let's go." They started for the stairs down to the beach. "Damn it," Tony swore softly. "I *liked* her. And I could have sworn she loved him!"

"She does," Eric said flatly. "I don't know what this is all about, but I do know that girl loves your brother."

"Then where the hell is she? Why is she doing this to him?"

"I wish I knew."

The two men, so different in appearance and yet alike in their anxiety over the man they were following, made their way down the beach, following a single, lonely set of footprints, each wondering what on earth had driven a wide-eyed, tousle-haired woman to cast the man she loved into hell.

Twelve

Christy set down her glass of milk and picked up the lists again. She set aside the one that enumerated the items of clothing and gear she already owned that she would need to take and concentrated on the roster of things she would have to get before she left. For the last time. No more jaunts halfway around the world, she told herself. If this book did as well as the rest, or even if it didn't, it was the last one. Her daughter needed a mother, not a world traveler.

She could live on what her investments brought in, thanks to the fact that the house was paid for. She'd bought the little remodeled Victorian mainly because of its huge backyard for Char to play in. She had also liked the cozy, homey feel of it, and the rich wood floors that complemented the few but quality pieces of furniture she had. It was full of deep, rich colors, and if it seemed a little heavy in comparison to a light, airy and open beach house, she made herself ignore it.

Quickly she rerouted her thoughts before they could slide into that old, familiar quagmire. She'd survived alone before, and she could do it again. If her own foolish lapse, her moment of believing in fairy tales, made it that much harder for her, then it was her own stupid fault. She set down the second list and picked up the third, the dates and itinerary for the trip to Australia she didn't want to take.

Dragon's people had insisted. There was a voracious market in the United States these days for all things Australian, and they wanted to cash in on it. Christy had dug in her heels, but in the end they had won; she couldn't help wondering if it had been because her mind—and heart—had been elsewhere during the negotiations. She could have persuaded them to accept something else, something closer, something that wouldn't require her to be gone so long. Char was only just now beginning to get over her absence of two weeks; how would the little girl deal with an absence of months?

She should take her along. She couldn't bear to be parted from her for so long, especially now. But Mrs. Turner had declared herself much too old to go gallivanting around the world to some "barely civilized place full of kangaroos and the like," and no matter how Christy tried to convince her of the truth, the woman wouldn't budge.

Only her innate sense of integrity, and the fact that she had given her word, stopped her from canceling out of the project entirely. That and a deeply buried, unstated need to get away, to leave the travesty of shattered hopes and useless dreams far behind.

She should have known. She'd been right from the start. There was no room in Trace Dalton's life for Char, and so there was no room for her. He'd said he loved her, they'd talked of marriage and a life together, but never once had he mentioned children. And that afternoon in his living room she'd found out why: he wanted no part of them.

Stop it, she ordered herself sternly. *You've gone over it a million times. You did what you had to do to protect Char.* Blood tests. Headlines. Those weren't for her baby, that innocent little girl who had welcomed her home with such joy that it had almost wiped away the pain that clawed at her. Almost.

She dragged her attention back to the schedule in her hand. They had covered it all, she thought as she spread out the map of the huge island country. The coastal cities, Sydney, Melbourne, Brisbane, Adelaide and Perth.

Then inland. Alice Springs, of course, and the world-famous Ayer's Rock, The Great Victoria Desert and more of the infamous Outback than she cared to think about. Ordinarily she would have jumped at the chance to see this audacious country, its genial, adventurous people and the odd set of animals indigenous to its shores. But now, when her precious little moppet was dearer to her than ever, it was tearing her apart to think of leaving. She'd done enough leaving lately....

Stop it! Just stop it, damn it!

Carefully she smoothed out the sheet of paper she had unknowingly crumpled in her fist and reached for the pocket calendar she'd bought to transfer times and dates and places into. She had just picked up her pen when there was the slam of a door and the clatter of feet from the back of the house.

"Mommy! Jimmy's here, an' Peaches. C'n I go out 'n' play?"

Christy smiled down at the eager little face, reaching out to straighten a lopsided ponytail of sandy-brown hair. "If you stay in the backyard. No leaving, not even to Jimmy's house, unless you ask first. Okay?"

"'kay. C'n we have cookies later?" The little girl eyed the plate that sat on the counter.

Christy laughed, giving the ponytail a tug. "I suppose."

"Jimmy 'n' Peaches, too?"

"Are you going to give that big one on top to Peaches?" Christy asked with a grin, knowing the child had had her eye on that particular chocolate chip cookie since it had come out of the oven this morning. The bright little face scrunched up as she considered that.

"Okay. Peaches needs it more, cuz she's just a puppy and has to grow lots."

Christy laughed, a little loudly, but she was trying to hide the sudden tightness of her throat; Lord, she loved this precious, sweet child.

She watched the little girl trot eagerly out the back door, then got up to open the drapes so she could keep an eye on the backyard. She could see Jimmy, his hand entwined in the fur of his wriggling puppy, a golden retriever that had to be the most patient, gentle animal Christy had ever seen. She had no qualms about them playing with the dog; if Peaches could put up with Jimmy's five-year-old rambunctiousness, she could tolerate anything Char could dish out.

And she trusted Jimmy, as well; bigger than Char, he exhibited a gentlemanly conduct toward the little girl that would have been amusing if Christy hadn't been so grateful for it. The boy lived next door and, for now at least, was a wonderful, convenient playmate. And she didn't mind in the slightest if Char had more than once come in grass stained and muddy; Lord knows she'd been a tomboy through and through herself, even at Char's tender age of two.

Actually, two and a half, Christy realized with a little shiver of shock. Time was slipping away from her, and her baby was growing up so fast. It seemed as if she'd matured frighteningly even during the two weeks Christy had been gone; it hadn't been her tiny baby who had looked at her with those too-familiar eyes and solemnly asked, "What's wrong, Mommy? You been cryin'."

The memory of those tiny hands reaching to wipe away her tears, of the tears shed by that pre-

cious child for no other reason than that her
mommy was crying and that made her sad, had the
power to bring the sting of tears back to Christy's
eyes.

God, she'd thought she was done with crying.
She'd done nothing but weep late into the night,
every day of the three weeks since she'd left that
house on the beach. That lovely, airy, beautiful
house where she had felt so at home, so safe, so
secure. The house that had been bought and fur-
nished for her. *Oh, God, Trace, why couldn't you—*

Stop it! She slammed her fist against the table,
but the pain wasn't enough, and the tears began to
slide down her cheeks once more. She, who had
never cried in all the cold years of her childhood,
had cried enough in the past three weeks to make
up for all that abstinence.

She'd thought nothing could be worse than the
days after the hurricane when she had made the
painful decision to stay away, only to find she had
a much more painful decision to make weeks later.
She'd been sadly, pitifully wrong. Nothing in her
harsh, barren life had ever prepared her to live with
the wrenching, tearing pain she felt now.

Every time she dropped her guard he was there,
blazing bright and clear in her mind. From the moment when she had first seen him, wet, hurt and
shivering, to the sweet moment when she had
looked at his beautiful, naked body above hers for
the last time, he was there, and she couldn't fight
him off. She cradled her head in her hands, heed-

less of the tears dripping through her fingers onto the map spread out before her.

"Running to Australia this time?"

Christy froze. The voice, so familiar and yet so strange, had come from behind her, near the door she always left unlocked in this quiet little town. Every muscle in her body stiffened, braced too late for a blow that had already fallen.

"Don't bother."

Every syllable was crusted with the ice that had replaced the gentle warmth she'd grown so wonderfully used to. With an effort she set down the pen she'd been clutching, marveling with an odd detachment that her hand trembled only slightly. Slowly, suppressing a shudder, she turned around.

He was leaning in the doorway, one shoulder against the jamb, his legs crossed casually at the ankles, his hands in his pockets as if he'd stopped in to cheerfully pass the time of day. Any semblance of normalcy ended there, though; he looked gaunt and haggard, new lines in his chiseled face making him look older than his years, and the bulk of his sweater couldn't hide the fact that he'd lost weight. She would still have thought him beautiful, but his eyes chilled her to her soul; they were cold, solid ice, and utterly unforgiving.

He glanced at the map he'd obviously seen. "Tears, Christy? Something go wrong with your travel plans?"

The words were harsh, cutting, and she smothered a gasp; a cruel glint had appeared in his eyes, the eyes that had been able to set fire to her with a glance. She'd seen them angry, laughing, loving—oh, God, how loving—but never had she seen them cruel.

"How…why…?" she stammered.

"How? Eric still has a lot of friends in the airline industry. It only took him a couple of calls to find out where you'd flown to. I'm surprised you didn't use a phony name." She blinked. "No, I see you didn't think of that. Odd, you're such a clever little bitch."

He said it flatly, without inflection, not even with anger. Christy paled, her hands clenching, nails digging into her palms. She tried to move, but her muscles only quivered. As if he read her intent, he crossed the room in three long strides, slamming his hands down on the table, staring at her with a glacial coldness that made her shiver once more.

"Why? I've asked myself that more times than I can count. Why should I give a damn about a bitch who plays with people's hearts like they were cheap little trinkets?"

Christy drew back, frightened by the icy control in his voice more than she ever would have been by anger.

"Funny," he said, in the uninvolved tone of a scientist whose specimen had just done something unexpected, "I never would have expected cowardice from you."

"You don't understand—"

"You're damned right I don't," he snapped, emotion breaking through for the first time. He realized it even as she did, and he straightened abruptly, folding his arms across his chest. "You want to know why I'm here?" His voice was cold again, a wind straight off arctic ice. "You owe me two weeks. I'll trade them for one simple answer. Why?"

It took all of Christy's wavering will not let her eyes flick to the backyard. She could hear Jimmy's voice and Peaches's occasional bark, and breathed a silent prayer that they were so engrossed they would stay there.

"Why, Christy?"

"I...realized it wouldn't work."

"So you ran? Without a word?" His lip curled into an unpleasant snarl. "Maybe I was wrong about you all the way. I never would have thought you didn't have the guts to tell me face-to-face. I never would have pegged you for a coward."

Christy cringed as his words reached that raw, open wound inside her and tore at it with steel-hard claws. "I...had no choice but—"

He cut across her words as if she hadn't spoken at all. "At least a note. 'It's been fun, Trace, now go to hell.' But your specialty is twisting the knife, isn't it? The dress was a nice touch." He laughed, short and harsh. "You know what I did with that dress? I slept with it for a pillow, because it smelled like you, that damned gardenia stuff."

That he said it in that plain, flat tone, as if it meant nothing to him, gouged Christy deeper and more painfully than if he had wept. "I...never meant to hurt you."

"So," he said with a contempt he didn't bother to hide, "you're a liar as well as a coward."

Something inside Christy snapped. She leaped to her feet, the chair teetering, then falling behind her as she squared herself, her chin coming up. Something flickered in those frigid eyes across from her, then was gone.

"Damn you," she spat out. "Who the hell do you think you are, coming into my house and calling me names when you don't have the slightest idea what you're talking about?"

She kicked the chair with a violent movement, sending it sliding across the polished wood floor; neither of them even glanced at it.

"I don't care what you think. I never meant to hurt you. I told you there were things you didn't know about me, things that would change your mind, but you wouldn't listen. Well, why don't you just accept that this is one of them, that you're right, that I'm a bitch and a coward and a liar, and get the hell out of here?"

Again something flickered in the depths of those incredible eyes; again it disappeared before she could name it. "I will," he said coolly, "as soon as I'm sure you don't plan on showing up again in three years for another one-night stand."

Christy went white, and her voice shook. "You bastard!"

Then she realized what she'd said, and her face changed from flushed to a bloodless pallor. Suddenly the very shape of her skull was visible, jutting beneath delicate skin drawn far too tight, and the man across from her was struck with the horrible knowledge that he was seeing a living death, that she could look no worse had she died before his eyes. For the first time his self-control wavered, and when she swayed he took a step toward her.

"Get out."

She had stiffened at his first movement, her chin coming up once more as she spoke tightly, through gritted teeth. If she had been looking at him, she would have seen the grudging admiration that flashed in his eyes once more, this time long enough to be recognized. And with it, for the briefest of moments, was doubt.

"Christy—"

"Get out. You don't want me or what I am. Do yourself a favor, go find some woman who can give you what you want—" her voice caught "—not what you don't want."

"What the hell does that mean?" The flat tone wavered. "Am I supposed to believe you care what I do or don't want?"

Once more, despite her trembling, her chin came up. She made no effort to hide the tears brimming in her eyes, and she met his brutal gaze unflinchingly. "I care. More than you know. More than you'll ever believe. Enough to do what I have to." She lowered her eyes then, blinking back the wetness. "You wouldn't be happy with me, Trace. Can't you leave it at that and go?"

He was staring at her as if she were an actor who'd read the wrong lines, as if someone had taken the expected scene and turned it sideways.

For the first time a hint of torture crept into his voice. "Why, Christy?"

Christy looked away, knowing the words were rising to her lips and that she wouldn't be able to stop them. "Because I love you," she murmured helplessly, but so low she was thankfully sure he couldn't have heard her with her head turned from him. Steadying her resolve, she raised her head and looked at him coldly. "Because I'm everything you said I was. Get out. Now."

The ice was back in place, intact and solid. "Oh, I will. But I have something to do first."

With a movement so swift that Christy's numbed reflexes were helpless to avoid it, he rounded the table and grabbed her shoulders. She bit back a cry as his fingers dug into her flesh; it escaped when one strong hand tangled in the fine silk of her hair, then tightened as he pulled her head back.

Suddenly his mouth came down on hers. Her lips were crushed against her teeth, and his tongue forced its way into her mouth savagely. His second hand joined the other, holding her immobilized as his fingers twisted in her hair. It was a harsh kiss, almost desperate, and Christy knew instinctively that she was receiving only a tiny portion of what he'd gone through in the days since she'd left. Her heart ached for him, and she surrendered to his need.

And in that moment the kiss changed. The pressure eased, and the fierce jabbing of his tongue became a softer, gentler probing. He made a small sound deep in his throat, and Christy couldn't stop herself from meeting his intimate caress with her own tongue. Stroking honeyed sweetness over hot velvet, her tongue teased, danced, and the fire leaped to life between them with undeniable force and speed.

Christy felt herself sway against him and was helpless to stop it. He was sapping her strength, turning her bones to hot, flowing liquid, as only he had the power to do. His hands released her hair and slid forward to cup her face with a gentleness that was startling after his earlier urgency.

His hands slid down over her shoulders, down her back, resting on the trim curve of her hips, then pulling her against him. Her gasp as she felt the urgent pressure of his aroused body was swallowed up by his mouth on hers, tasting, coaxing. As if of their own volition, her hands crept around his neck, her slender fingers tangling in the thickness of the hair at his nape, her thumbs caressing the sensitive flesh below his ears. She felt him shudder, heard him groan.

Then all she felt was the sudden iron grip of his hands on her tender flesh and the rush of movement as he shoved her away from him. He stood staring at her, his chest rising rapidly with his panting breaths.

"Damn you," he spat out, wiping his mouth as if the lingering taste of her was repugnant. Then he whirled on his heel and was gone.

Christy sagged weakly against the table, her knuckles gleaming white as she gripped the edge tightly in her effort to stay upright. She heard the cheerful squeal of Char's voice mingling with excited yelps as the children and their companion headed toward the house for the promised cookies. She knew she should feel grateful that they hadn't come in moments earlier, but all she seemed to have room for was that helpless, relentless agony that made the pain she'd lived with for the past three weeks seem mild.

God, how she'd hurt him! How could she possibly live with herself, with what she'd done to him? She shuddered, hating herself for even thinking of her own pain when his was so much worse. Was anything worth that, worth the frozen shell that had looked at her through those beautiful eyes?

She turned at the noisy clatter that came from the back door, saw the innocent, shining face of her daughter, and knew she had no choice. She had to live with what she'd done, even if she had to carry that guilt for the rest of her life alone. Char needed her, and she would be there. She had to be there. She might be a bitch and a coward and a liar, as Trace had called her, but in this one thing she could do as her heart demanded, she could do better than the unknown woman who had borne her and left her abandoned.

And if she did it with a heart that was shriveled and dead inside her, she had no one to blame but herself.

He sat in the rental car for a long time, staring at the little Victorian house. It was small but charming, painted a cheerful blue and white, with a cared-for front lawn and what looked like a small jungle behind it. But as he looked closer he saw that there was a plan, paths amid the riotous growth, little cavelike hollows to hide in, and a large, grassy area in the center. It was a far cry from the formal, landscaped garden his mother had favored, and a lot more inviting. A controlled wildness, he thought. Like Christy.

He smothered the pang of loss as well as the spurt of anger that rose in him at the thought of her. He wasn't quite through with Ms. Reno just yet. He got out of the car.

He was surprised to find the door still unlocked. In fact, he acknowledged coldly, he was surprised that she was still here, that she hadn't run again after his visit yesterday. *But you haven't found her yet, Dalton,* he told himself grimly. *The house may be empty.* He turned the knob quietly and slipped inside.

He nearly walked past her before he saw her. She was curled up on a wide window seat below the expanse of glass that faced the small, secluded street. Had she been awake she couldn't have missed seeing him, but she was sound asleep, her head pillowed on her slender hands. She looked sweet and innocent and utterly beautiful, except for the dark smudges that shadowed her eyes. He quashed a twinge of pity; he'd worn some dark circles himself in the past three weeks.

She was wearing the same clothes she'd had on yesterday, and he wondered if she'd been to bed at all. The thick bulk of her white cable-knit sweater and the snug jeans that hugged her long legs and slender hips made her look fragile and sensuous at the same time, but it was her feet that drew his attention. Those tiny, beautifully arched feet, bare below the delicate ankles, where he had pressed soft kisses and delighted in her shocked surprise at the unexpected sensitivity of that graceful arch.

She stirred then, making a small, troubled sound in her sleep. He couldn't stop himself from going to her, from sitting on the edge of the seat and reaching out to smooth a strand of the silken hair back from her cheek. She murmured something, a tiny breath of sound that coalesced into his name; his heart jumped, quivered, then raced as if to try to make up for the missed beat.

Slowly the wide gray eyes opened, and she looked up at him sleepily. A soft smile curved her lips, and that glow he'd treasured so much came into her eyes, turning them a bright burnished silver. It was a look reserved only for him, in the moments before she reached for him, as if she needed the feel of him beneath her fingers to believe he was real. And she did reach; her hand lifted, fingers outstretched.

And as quickly as if a switch had been flipped, it was gone and memory surged in to take its place. He saw a fleeting instant of pain and longing, and then the stiffness took over, and the lovely eyes became shadowed and unreadable. She sat up.

"Why did you come back?"

He took a breath, swallowed and tried to speak. No words would come; the loss of that look of joyous greeting seemed somehow worse than anything else, as if all the pain had been condensed into that single moment.

Christy didn't even try to hide the tremor of weariness that rippled through her, or the flat, dead sound of her voice. "Haven't you been hurt enough? Did you have to come back for more?"

"I came back," he said tightly, "for what I didn't get yesterday. The answer to my question."

"I told you why I—"

"I heard you. That's why none of this makes any sense."

Bewilderment broke through the unfeeling mask she'd carefully put on, but only for a moment; then the weariness closed in again. "I don't know how to make it any clearer. I told you I left because I knew it wouldn't work."

"And when I asked you again, Christy? What did you say then?"

She paled, her eyes suddenly alive and searching his face. He sat back, sure now that he'd been right.

"I know I wasn't supposed to hear it. And I didn't, at least not consciously, then. But last night, it came to me." He shook his head slowly. "And I was right, wasn't I?"

"All right! Yes, I said it!"

"God, Christy...never once, when we were together, did you ever tell me you loved me. I didn't care, I figured you'd get around to it, when you were sure." He let out a harsh, pained chuckle. "Then, when I ask you why you walked out of my life, you say 'Because I love you.' Damn it, Christy! If you meant it—''

''I meant it.'' She couldn't deny him that, not along with everything else, but she was getting edgy. She'd heard a sound from upstairs, and Char was due up any minute. ''Now will you go?''

With a sigh of weary exasperation he ran a hand through his already tousled hair. ''Are you crazy, or am I? None of this makes any sense at all.''

''Maybe it's not supposed to. Just leave it, Trace.'' Another sound from above, and she tensed involuntarily. Trace must have heard it.

He had. A look realization crossed his face, followed closely by one of bitter self-contempt. ''I'm sorry. I should have realized. Somehow the real reason never occurred to me. Pardon my overblown ego. I'm sure you'd rather not introduce us, so I'll leave before he comes down.''

Thirteen

Christy stared at him, nonplussed. After a long moment his meaning penetrated; he thought she had a man upstairs.

"Trace, no!"

She leaped up, took a step toward him, then stopped. Wasn't it better this way? Wouldn't it accomplish exactly what she'd set out to do? He already thought her a bitch, a liar and a coward, so what did it matter if he added cheat to that list? Or tramp, or whatever it was he was thinking?

It mattered. She didn't know why, but it mattered. He had stopped at her cry, but when she said no more he turned to go; the defeated slump of his straight shoulders was almost more than she could bear. She'd never felt so torn, never been so close to breaking down and telling him everything and praying he would understand. But she'd given up believing in useless dreams....

In the moment when his hand reached for the doorknob the decision was taken out of her hands by the scurry of small feet and a cheerful little voice.

"Mommy, Mrs. Turner's gonna make waffles! C'n I have—"

The little girl stopped, suddenly aware of a stranger's presence, and attached herself to Christy's leg. She peered around to study Trace for a moment, then shifted her bright-eyed gaze to her mother's white face. Sensing the tension she didn't understand, the sandy-haired little girl stepped in front of her mother in a protective gesture that would have been comical had it not been for the utter seriousness on her innocent face.

"Are you why my mommy's been cryin'?" she asked, her chin jutting upward defiantly.

My God, Trace thought, stunned, his eyes on that tiny chin, *she looks just like Christy.* Then his gaze lifted to the huge, blue-green eyes that were fastened on him somewhat threateningly. He paled, and his legs suddenly lost strength. He staggered two steps to a chair and sat down weakly.

"It's all right, baby. Go help Mrs. Turner and stay there till I come, okay?" When the child hesitated, Christy bent and pressed a kiss atop her head. "Scoot, sweetie." She watched the bouncing ponytail disappear through the kitchen door, then turned back to Trace, her face expressionless.

"Now will you go?"

He stared at her, his hands clamped around the chair cushion on either side of his knees, as if he couldn't sit upright without support. Inanely all he could think of was that here was the explanation for that death's head look when she'd inadvertently used the word bastard.

"My God," he whispered, "why didn't you tell me?"

"I told you there were things you didn't know. Wouldn't want to know. So go on, Trace. Go find someone you can be happy with."

Anger spurted suddenly. "Just like that?" he asked coldly. "I'd say you have some explaining to do!"

Her chin came up, the original for a small, brave little copy. "There's nothing you'd care to know, I'm sure."

"Oh, no? So I'm supposed to leave, just walk out and forget what I just saw?"

Only the rigidness of her hands clenched into fists betrayed her tension. "Just what is it you think you saw?"

He couldn't believe this, any of it. His head was reeling, and he was having trouble breathing past the tightness in his chest. "Why, Christy?" The words broke from him involuntarily. "Why didn't you tell me?" She shrugged, as if it hardly mattered, and anger spurted again. It gave him strength, and he got up suddenly. "Damn it, Christy, you were pregnant, you had my child, and you didn't even bother to tell me?"

Surprise flitted across her face. "You...believe she's yours?"

He stared back blankly. "What?"

She was unable to keep the sharpness out of her voice. "No blood tests? It was only once, after all.

And years ago. Anything could have happened since.''

As she spoke, his blank expression changed to one of shock, then one of agonized realization as he recognized the source of her words. "Oh, my God," he whispered, sinking back into the chair.

"Don't worry, you're safe. I won't have her subjected to that kind of a circus.''

He laughed, a hoarse, broken mockery of a laugh. "It would hardly be necessary.''

"What?" It was her turn to look blank.

His head came up. "I may be the stupidest idiot on the face of the earth, but I'm not blind. She's mine, all right.''

"I don't understand—''

"God, Christy, all I have to do is look at her, at those eyes...hell, it's like looking into a mirror. You've got to see that.''

"I do. Every time I look at her." Christy closed her eyes. "I didn't expect you to see it.''

"You really do think I'm a—" He stopped, his face taut with strain. "What do you think I am, Christy? So horrible that you couldn't come to me? Couldn't tell me?''

"I didn't think you'd believe me.''

"Why?''

She felt suddenly, unutterbly weary, and she sank back down on the window seat she'd vacated. "By the time I found out I was pregnant, I...knew who—or rather what—you were. Knew that you had a line of ladies that ran from here to anywhere you wanted to go. I knew you wouldn't believe it, and that I couldn't blame you for that." She laughed acidly. "I even guessed it might have happened before, being who you were."

She took a breath, aware of Trace's stunned eyes fastened on her. "Why should you believe me? I wasn't a virgin—" Her voice caught, and he knew that she was, as he was, remembering what he'd said about that.

"Did you ever stop to think that I might just believe you because...you're you?"

Her eyes went wide with puzzlement. "Why? You knew the truth about me, what I was, where I came from... Why should you believe I wouldn't lie to keep my baby from going through what I did? You're rich, why shouldn't you think I was feathering my own nest?"

Trace winced; he *would* have thought that— once. Yet he knew instinctively that, had she come to him, he would have believed her. Even then, before the undeniable proof he'd been presented with this morning. But even if he hadn't.... "Did you really think I would have let you go through that alone?" he asked tightly. "Even if I hadn't believed the baby was mine, I—"

"Don't you see?" she cried out, cutting him off. "That's exactly what I was afraid of! That you wouldn't believe, but you would help me anyway! I was a charity case most of my life, and I'd be damned before I would let my baby grow up that way! Maybe I didn't have a mother to teach me how to be one, but I try my best, damn it, and if nothing else, that child knows she's loved! It may not sound like much, but it's more than I ever had." She rubbed at her eyes tiredly. "I don't expect you to understand. But I couldn't come begging."

Trace's expression changed then, not a lessening of pain but rather a change from one kind to another. "I think I understand. I wish—never mind. Just tell me...why didn't you tell me this time? God, Christy, you could have told me a hundred times!"

"I...couldn't." She sighed heavily. "I knew that you love—that you thought you loved me." Trace drew in a breath, but she hurried on before he could speak. "I thought you would realize after a while that you didn't, not really, that it was just..."

"Lust?" Trace supplied tightly.

"Something like that. Or just storm-induced insanity. I thought you'd change your mind, realize you'd made a mistake, and that would be it. You'd never need to know."

"Never need to know? That I had a child?"

Christy winced at his bitter tone. "I was afraid that if I told you, you'd feel...obligated. Like you had to marry me, or support us, or something."

Trace closed his eyes as he let out a long, weary sigh. When he opened his eyes again, it was to look at her sadly. "You never believed it, did you? You've never been able to believe that anyone truly loves you. For all your courage and spirit, that's the one thing you just can't put behind you, isn't it?"

"I did believe it. With you. When you asked me to marry you that morning, for the first time I thought it might work. I thought you really meant what you said, that there wasn't anything we couldn't handle. And I wanted it so badly...."

"You did?" He looked doubtful, and she knew once more how much she had hurt him.

"Yes," she said softly. "I tried to tell myself I only stayed with you so you could see it was impossible. I never admitted to myself that that was only part of the reason."

"And the rest?"

"I wanted to be with you. To steal that time with you, so I would have something to...hold on to when I got so cold I wanted to cry." Christy wiped at her eyes, fighting to hold back a tide she knew she would never be able to stop if it began. "And then there you were, holding out the brass ring."

"But you didn't take it," he said, his voice husky with remembered pain. "Even then, you didn't tell me. God, Christy, you knew how I felt—"

"I found out." Her voice echoed with a bitterness she couldn't conceal. "You and your brother made it quite clear how you felt about children and their scheming mothers."

He went white. Her words echoed in his head, words about not giving him what he didn't want. Anger at her unfair assumption warred with guilt at the truth of it, from her viewpoint at least, and the battle showed clearly in his face. It was the intense hurt in her eyes that tipped the scales.

"She wasn't you, Christy. She was a...a groupie, a hanger-on. I was drunk. I know it's no excuse, but back then I didn't give a damn. And later I found out she'd tried the same thing before. I never would have thought that of you. I'd never even mention the two of you in the same breath."

"Are you saying you would have believed me?" She was watching him carefully.

He answered just as carefully, knowing she would detect any hedging. "Yes. I would have. We only had a few days together, but they were the kind of days that force you to learn more about someone than you learn in months under normal circumstances. I can't doubt that, because of what I learned about myself."

She kept her eyes on him steadily, and he dug deep for the feelings, the words, that would convince her. "Maybe I didn't know all the little things, your favorite color or what kind of car you drove, but I knew you were good and clean and honest and brave, and all the things that are the most important. Yes, I would have believed you."

Christy blinked against the sting of tears. "I wish—"

"You couldn't," he said quietly. "I see that now. Being who you are, with how you grew up, what happened to you, you couldn't. But I wish it, too. God, Christy, to go through that all by yourself! Was it...really bad?"

She stiffened, and Trace winced. She was still so skittish, like a fawn in a clearing, ready to leap away at the slightest sign of danger. He rubbed tiredly at the back of his neck, at muscles stiff with strain. "Oh, Christy, we've been at cross-purposes so many times...."

He sucked in a long breath, then lifted his eyes to hers. "I tried to hate you for leaving, but I couldn't." He saw her look, and his mouth twisted wryly. "I know, I gave a hell of an imitation, didn't I? Maybe I'm a better actor than I thought." He shrugged. "And now that I know why, and why you never came to me the first time... You've got to believe me. I never mentioned children because I just never thought of it. I didn't dare let myself think about a baby. God, our baby..." His voice echoed with a longing that shook her. "All I could think of was keeping you there, not scaring you off before you were sure of me, of how I felt, until you believed that I loved you. There wasn't room for anything else."

He sagged against the back of the chair, eyes closed, suddenly lacking the strength to even move. "Tell me what to do, Christy," he said hollowly. "I can't fight anymore. It's your call."

Christy looked at him, at the worn, bleak expression on his face, softened only by the ridiculously thick sweep of his lowered lashes. She knew she was trembling; she couldn't seem to stop it. Nor could she find the words to express all the confused emotions that were welling up inside her. Minutes passed in silence, and Trace's face seemed to go grayer before her eyes. At last he struggled up in the chair and then unsteadily to his feet.

"Okay, Christy. You win. I'm gone. I won't bother you again. You or—" His eyes flickered to the door through which the daughter he'd never known, would never know, had gone.

"Char," Christy whispered.

Trace winced, beyond caring about hiding his anguish. "Char," he breathed, every ounce of his pain in that one soft syllable spoken for the first and last time. "I hope her life is...less stormy than her namesake." He turned away from her.

His hand was on the knob once more when

Christy finally found the words. "That's the wrong door."

Trace stared at the door, then at her, thinking there was something wrong with his befuddled brain. Christy gestured toward the kitchen. "Your daughter's in there."

Trace stared, swaying a little. "Christy...?"

"I love you, Trace." She saw a muscle in his jaw jump. "Oh, I know it's too late for me, but... not for you and Char. She's a wonderful little girl, Trace. She deserves to know that she has a...wonderful father."

Tentatively, she held out a hand. After a long moment of searching her face, of staring into the depths of her troubled gray eyes, he reached out and enclosed her fingers in his.

Trace couldn't tear his eyes away from the tiny form in the bed. Snuggled into a soft, turquoise comforter up to the sassy little chin that was the image of her mother's, the child slept peacefully, her sandy hair a tousled halo around her sweet face. His daughter. The words still echoed in his head, sending little shivers down his spine.

After her initial reservations, Char had decided she liked this big man who had eyes just like hers. When he had shyly told her that he didn't know much about children and would she please teach him, she had been considerably taken with the idea of teaching a grown-up. She had plunged into the task enthusiastically, and if there were moments when the big man seemed to do more looking at her than paying attention, or when he would reach to touch her tentatively, gently, she wrote it off as the oddities of adulthood.

Trace had watched while Christy put the little girl to bed, Char protesting despite her yawns that she was not ready for this extremely interesting day to end. He'd felt numbly tired himself, emotionally battered, yet warmed beyond belief by that bright, innocent presence.

"She's beautiful," he said softly.

"Yes."

"When was she born?"

"June twenty-second."

He looked at her then, his eyes wide as the significance of the date registered.

Christy's mouth twisted wryly. "I know. Nine months to the day."

Trace swallowed, then looked back at the sleeping child. The reality was still tentative, the wonder of it still growing. "I wish—" He stopped, shaking his head. "I'm sorry you were alone. Was it… hard?"

Christy hesitated, then sighed. If anyone had a right, he did. "Long. I'd had enough the day before, but she was determined to come on the twenty-second. She was born at three in the morning."

He bit his lip; the thought of her pain made him shudder. One hand tightening over the other, he sucked in a short breath. "What…was she like? Then?"

He sounded so wistful that Christy felt tears sting her eyes. She reached toward the small bookcase next to the child-size table he was sitting on and drew out a large book. Gently she handed it to him.

If her talent with a camera was obvious in her books, her love of both photography and her daughter was clear in this album of pictures. Trace lingered over every page, from the first red-faced portrait to the first tottering steps, to the sunlight shot that took his breath away, so clear was the resemblance to her mother in the delicate bones of her face and that sassy nose and chin, and to him in the sandy hair and eyes turned to blue-green fire in the golden light.

Christy saw him blink rapidly, saw the hasty swipe of the back of his hand at his damp eyes. Emotion welled up inside her so strongly that she had to move; she dropped down to her knees on the floor before him. "I'm so sorry, Trace. I never thought...you would care so much. I had no right to keep her from you."

He lifted his eyes from the book to see tears streaming silently down her cheeks. He reached out and gently brushed them away. "I...can't say it doesn't matter, because it does. I missed so much. But I understand."

They sat in silence for a long time, watching their daughter sleep. Gradually Christy relaxed, propping her back against the side of Char's bed. Surreptitiously she studied Trace, trying desperately to store up memories against the time when he would leave. And wishing she could halt the certain knowledge that it was her fault, that she had destroyed her chance at making the dream come true because she had so completely underestimated him.

"I like your house," he said suddenly. "Especially the backyard."

Christy smiled. "I always wanted one like that, that you could play in and let your imagination run wild. I always had to do it in my head. I wanted Char to have it for real."

Trace smiled back, then looked once more at the little girl who had so quickly wormed her way into his heart. "Do you suppose she'll mind trading it for the Pacific Ocean?"

"No!" Christy came up on her knees in a violent motion, her eyes suddenly wild. "Please, Trace! I know you must hate me, but please, no!"

Trace stared at her, stunned. "Christy—"

"You've got the money to do it, you could win, I know it wouldn't take much to prove I—I'm not fit, but please, Trace, please don't take her away from me!"

"Take her—God, Christy!" He went down on his knees beside her, pulling her into his arms fiercely. He pressed her head to his chest, holding her so tightly that his arms ached as he soothed her. "Christy, she's beautiful, she's quick, she's bright, but most of all she's happy. How can you think you're not fit?" He chuckled ruefully. "I'm just worried that I won't be a fit father for her."

He felt her shiver, heard her gulp for air between the sobs that had overtaken her. He gripped her shoulders and held her back from him. "Christy, look at me." Slowly her tear-stained face came up. "When I said that about trading houses, I meant all of us."

Her eyes, shimmering with tears, widened. "You...what?"

His eyes flicked to the bed, then back to her. "I

think it's past time you made an honest man out of me, don't you?''

Christy paled, and her voice was a breathless whisper. "You can't mean... You still...want me?''

He pulled her close again. "Oh, Christy, I've got my work cut out for me, haven't I? So many years to make up for, for all the time nobody cared about you. But I'll do it, even if it takes the rest of my life to convince you how much I love you.''

He held her until the shivers stopped, until she was quiet in his arms. Then Christy made a small sound, and he leaned back to look at her. To his amazement, she was smiling through her tears.

"I was just thinking," she explained between sniffs, "that I'd be a fool to tell you if you ever succeed."

It took him a moment, but he got there, and a wide grin broke across his face. "Does that mean yes?''

"If you're—"

"Hush. I'm sure. Surer than I ever thought I could be. You wanted me before you ever knew who I was, Christy. Do you realize what that means? I was never sure if anybody wanted me for me, or for what and who I was. You said you love me, didn't you? Marry me Christy. I want...my family.''

Somewhere in her muffled, choked words, he heard a repeated "yes," and he pressed his lips to her hair.

"We'll make it, love, I promise."

"Yes," she murmured against his chest.

"Soon?''

"Yes."

He chuckled. "I seem to be on a hot streak. Maybe I should ask for tomorrow."

"Yes."

He backed her up again and looked at her. "You mean it?"

"If you want." Her brow furrowed. "But I have to leave next month."

"Australia?"

She nodded, biting her lip. "I didn't want to leave Char, but I promised—"

"Don't."

"Don't...what?"

"Leave her." He shrugged. "Think I can get her to like me in a month?"

"She likes you already."

He grinned, and her heart turned over. "Then you've got a built-in baby-sitter, don't you? But I don't come cheap. I want a wedding ring first, lady."

All of them. Together. A family. Christy nearly broke down again. "Oh, Trace. I don't know what to say."

"How about 'I love you'?"

"I love you. I love you, I love you, I love you."

"That'll do, for starters." He tilted her head back and kissed her, long and hard and deep, and full of the pent-up longing of the last lonely days. They were both breathless when he at last raised his head. "Just how upset is my daughter going to be when she finds me in bed with you in the morning?" he asked thickly.

"If you plan on being there from now on, I guess she'd better get used to it." Christy clung to him.

"Good. Because I plan on being there forever. Starting now." He lifted her in his arms and proceeded to make good on that promise. And all the others.

*   *   *   *   *

Don't miss *A Whole Lot of Love*
by Justine Davis,
Silhouette Desire #1281,
also on sale in March 2000!